BULLSEYE: SEAL

BY
CAROL ERICSON

Our policy is to use papers that are natural, renewable and recyclable products and made from wood grown in sustainable forests. The logging and manufacturing processes conform to the legal environmental regulations of the country of origin.

Printed and bound in Spain
by CPI, Barcelona

MILLS & BOON

First Published in Great Britain 2017
By Mills & Boon, an imprint of HarperCollins*Publishers*
1 London Bridge Street, London, SE1 9GF

© 2017 Carol Ericson

ISBN: 978-0-263-92915-7

46-0917

"I'm going with you, Josh."

"You're going to stay in the room with the door locked. I don't want you anywhere near this situation."

"You just said it wasn't going to be dangerous," Gina insisted.

"I didn't say that." He cupped her face with one hand. "Let me face the danger. You've faced enough—all your life."

She blinked her eyes to dispel the tears gathering there. Nobody, not her mother, not Ricky, not the DEA, CIA or the FBI, had ever once acknowledged the fear and danger she'd lived with her whole life.

She thought it had come to an end that day at her father's compound, but she couldn't have been more wrong. Only now she had Josh Elliott to protect her, and if he thought she needed to stay in the room for this encounter, she'd do it.

She nodded and sniffed. "All right. I'll wait in the room, but you'd better be careful."

"This is what I do."

Was it? Then what had he been doing at her father's compound the day the men in her life had been killed?

Carol Ericson is a bestselling, award-winning author of more than forty books. She has an eerie fascination for true-crime stories, a love of film noir and a weakness for reality TV, all of which fuel her imagination to create her own tales of murder, mayhem and mystery. To find out more about Carol and her current projects, please visit her website at www.carolericson.com, "where romance flirts with danger."

To Jeff B., my favorite marine and consultant

Prologue

The boy tottered close to the edge of the shimmering pool, and Josh Elliott held his breath. A woman, her long, dark hair falling over one shoulder, swooped in and plucked up the toddler, lifting him over her head. The boy's face broke into a smile, his little body wriggling with joy in his mother's grasp.

Safe in his mother's arms—or he would be once she got the hell out of there.

Josh puffed out of the side of his mouth to dislodge a bug crawling on his face. He'd become part of the dense foliage on the hillside in this southeast corner of Colombia, not far from the Amazon. If this mission took any longer, the plants would grow right over and through him.

The woman dipped next to a chaise longue to grab a towel and tucked it around her child's body. She gave a curt nod to the men gathered at the other end of the pool, and then headed for the house via the sliding glass doors. Josh released a long breath.

A voice crackled in his ear seconds later. "Go time, boys."

Josh swept his M91 away from the retreating figure

of the mother and her child and zeroed in on his intended target—her husband.

Ricky Rojas folded his arms, his expensive jacket tightening across his shoulders, as he cocked his head in the direction of the three men seated at the table. What Josh wouldn't give to hear their conversation right now—their plots, their plans—but his SEAL team's assignment didn't include capture and interrogation.

It only included death.

These men had already killed and would kill again. In the crack of two seconds, his team would be responsible for bringing down a high-ranking member of a vicious terrorist cell and the mastermind of a brutal drug cartel...and a few of his associates.

And the father of that child.

Josh swallowed. The kid would get over it, especially after he learned what a scumbag his old man had been. The wife? That might be another story.

A muscle ticked in Josh's jaw. They'd been told to keep the woman out of the range of fire. More senior people than he had made the determination that Gina Rojas had nothing to do with the Los Santos drug cartel.

If they believed the daughter of Hector De Santos, the kingpin of Los Santos, and the wife of Ricky Rojas was an innocent bystander while her father and husband traded arms and passage to the United States for terrorists in exchange for drugs, who was he to question their common sense?

A pretty face could still buy wiggle room out of anything—and Gina Rojas had a pretty face and a body that could bring a grown man to his knees.

Once the kills were accomplished, the CIA would be descending on the De Santos compound to search for leads and evidence, but he and his teammates would be long gone, swallowed up into the Amazon.

A maid scurried from the palatial house to deliver a tray of drinks to the men on the patio. When she disappeared inside, the crackling in his ear resumed.

"All clear. And five, four, three, two…"

At the conclusion of the countdown, Josh dropped his target, and all the other men fell with him courtesy of the other navy SEAL snipers positioned in trees and dug into the hillsides ringing the compound.

The maid rushed from the house and threw her hands in the air. She must've been screaming because several other servants joined her on the patio.

Josh shifted his scope to encompass Gina Rojas emerging from the house, without her son, thank God. While the domestic staff flailed and scurried about or dashed off for parts unknown, Gina stood still like a statue amid a battering sea. She put her arm around the hysterical maid and surveyed the carnage, her head held high, her gaze sweeping the hillside.

"Josh. Josh, you on the move?"

"Copy that."

He lowered his sniper rifle from the intriguing sight of Gina Rojas's unflinching demeanor and began to break down his weapon.

Either this hit was no surprise to Gina…or she didn't give a damn.

Chapter One

Thirteen months later.

RJ raised a chubby hand before spinning around and grabbing his new friend by the arm to drag him to the slide.

Gina sniffed as she waved to her son's back.

"It's better than having him cling to your leg, isn't it?" Denise Reynolds, the owner of Sunny Days Day-care, winked.

Gina rubbed the back of her hand across her nose. "Much better, but did he have to get over that stage so quickly?"

"RJ's an outgoing boy. He makes friends quickly, very adaptable."

"He's had to be." Gina hoisted her purse onto her shoulder and shrugged. "There's been a lot of upheaval in his young life."

"I saw from your application that you're relatively new to Miami." Denise bit her lip. "And I'm sorry about his father, your husband. That he's deceased, I mean."

"Yes, just over a year ago." Gina sniffed again for good measure. "We're still…adjusting."

"Well, I think Sunny Days is just the place for him

to adjust. One month and he already has a best friend, who started just a few days after he did."

"He already talks about Diego nonstop. His mother introduced herself to me right away. The boys already had one playdate and we'll be arranging another for them in the next few days." Gina's cell phone buzzed in her pocket, and her heart skipped a beat.

"Everything okay?" Denise tilted her head to one side, her perky blond ponytail swinging behind her.

"Just a pesky client." Gina patted the pocket of her light jacket. "Thanks for everything, Denise."

Gina whipped out her phone as she walked back to her car. She couldn't go into cardiac arrest every time someone sent her a text. Wedging her hip against the cinder block barrier between the daycare's parking lot and the walkway to the center, she swiped her fingertip across her phone's display.

Then her heart skipped two beats as she read the familiar words. Where are the drugs? Where are the weapons, *paloma*?

The same two questions, along with the endearment, texted to her every day for almost a week now, from the same unknown number. She'd responded to the text in several different ways already.

Wrong number.

Wrong person.

I'm calling the police.

It didn't seem to matter what she texted back. The same two questions came back at her each day as if on autopilot—with the same endearment. Only Ricky had called her *paloma*...when things were good, but that was impossible. Wasn't it?

She *could* call the police. She snorted and dropped her cell phone in her pocket as she opened her car door. Then she'd have to go through the whole process of explaining who she was and watch the officers' faces change from expressions of concern to scowls of suspicion. They might even call in her old pals at the Drug Enforcement Administration, and they could start grilling her again.

She'd take a pass. In the meantime, she'd continue to ignore the texts. The person texting her wouldn't try to make contact...would he? And that person couldn't be Ricky. Ricky was dead...wasn't he?

Glancing over her shoulder, she pulled out of the daycare's parking lot and checked her rearview mirror as she joined the stream of traffic. She had nothing to tell anyone who made contact with her, at least not about any drugs or weapons.

On her way to the realty office, she turned up the music to drown out her own thoughts and the memories of that day at her father's compound in Colombia. The CIA agents who'd swarmed the place after the carnage had interrogated everyone on the property, including her, for several hours.

They'd tossed the place, looking for money, drugs, arms—and they didn't find one single thing. As far as she knew, not even her father's computers had revealed any information about his thriving drug business.

The US and Colombian governments had seized all her father's assets—but they hadn't found everything. Then the CIA turned her over to the DEA and the fun started all over again. She had no desire to repeat that experience.

She wheeled into the parking lot of the realty office and dragged her bag from the passenger seat as she exited the car. She'd just passed her licensing exam but didn't have any listings of her own yet. She had to start from the bottom and work her way up, but she'd never been afraid of hard work.

The real estate business may not be her calling, but she'd had to find some gainful employment after she'd lost her business—the restaurant-bar she'd developed and run with Ricky before...before.

She slammed the car door. She'd tried bartending since that's what she knew, but that hadn't been her calling either, not if she couldn't run the place, and she didn't like leaving RJ with her mother so many nights of the week.

Gina yanked open the door of the office and waved to Lori, who was on the phone. Lori wiggled her fingers in the air in response.

A stack of binders piled on her desk greeted Gina and she plopped down in front of them with a sigh. Faith, the Realtor she was shadowing, had left a yellow sticky note on the binder at the top of the pile asking her to remove the old listings.

Gina flipped open the binder and perused each page, checking the house against a roster for those listings no longer on the market. For each lucky house that had sold, she slid the flyer from beneath the plastic sheath, making a neat pile on the corner of the desk.

Lori ended her call and slumped in her chair. "Clients from hell right there, but they're looking high-end, art deco in South Beach, and I'm going to do my best to find the perfect place for them. Can you do me a favor?"

"If it involves white binders, I'll pass." Gina heaved the first completed binder off the desk and dropped it to the floor.

"It involves meeting a client at a town house. It's empty. Owners already moved out, and it's an easy show. I'll cut you in on a portion of the commission if this person buys it."

"Is this buyer one of your clients?"

"No. The sellers are my clients. This person is a walk-in. Just called this morning." Lori jiggled a set of keys over her desk. "Easy show."

Gina wrinkled her nose at the rest of the binders. "Sure. Give me the details."

Fifteen minutes later, Gina was sitting behind the wheel of her car with a file folder on the seat beside her, cruising to South Beach. She enjoyed this aspect of the job more than sitting at a desk reviewing Florida property laws and regulations.

As she flew past the strip malls and heavily residential areas, she could understand why Lori wanted to spend her time selling in South Beach instead of this area, but Gina found the relative serenity of the southern end of Dade County preferable to the hubbub in South Beach where she and RJ had landed with Mom after the debacle in Colombia.

Debacle—was that what you called the deaths of your father and husband at the hands of some unknown snipers?

The Spanish-style building came into view on her right, the beige stucco, arched entrances and red-tiled roof a copy of several other residences on the street.

This was a town house, not a condo, so it had a door open to the outside and two palm trees graced either side of the entrance.

Her heels clicked on the tiled walkway to the front door, and a palm frond tickled her cheek as she inserted the key into the lockbox. Pushing the door open, she left it wide, surveying the small foyer before taking a small step down to the living room.

She glanced at the flyers in her hand and left a stack on the kitchen counter. She should probably familiarize herself with the place before the potential buyer showed up, starting with the kitchen.

All the appliances cooperated as she flipped switches and turned handles. The kitchen didn't boast the most high-tech gadgetry she'd ever seen, but everything worked and had a neat functionality. She could get used to a place like this.

She had to get out of Mom's condo—and all it represented.

She poked her head into the laundry room off the kitchen, noting the side door to a small patio, and then backtracked to the living room. The gas fireplace checked out, as did the blinds shuttering the arched front window. The sun filtered into the room, as she pulled them back. A set of sliding glass doors to the right led to a small patio, a stucco wall enclosing it.

Finishing up with the half bathroom, she headed up the staircase to investigate the two bedrooms and two bathrooms. The master had a nice walk-in closet, and she mentally filled the racks with her shoes and layered the baskets with her sweaters.

She closed the closet door behind her with a firm

click. She was here for the buyer, not herself, even if that buyer *was* late.

She glided into the second room, trying not to imagine RJ's toys stacked in colorful bins against the wall.

A sound from downstairs had her pausing at the window that looked out onto a small patio in the back. She cocked her head, and then heard the shuffling noise again.

She walked to the bedroom door and called out, "Hello? I'm upstairs. I'll be right down. Take a flyer."

Facing herself in the mirrored closet door, she straightened her jacket and smoothed her hands over her dark pencil skirt. For good measure, she rolled open the closet door and peered at the empty rods and shelves. The place looked mint.

As she slid the door back into place, a bang had her jerking and literally clutching the pearls at her neck. What was the buyer doing down there?

She raised her eyes to her reflection and swallowed as the hair on the back of her neck quivered. Why hadn't the client answered her?

She'd taken a safety class as part of getting her Realtor's license and knew the dangers of women flying solo while showing open houses. But this was no open house. Lori had made an appointment with this person, had gotten identifying information from him over the phone.

Sweeping her tongue across her lips, she backed away from the mirror. She strode to the bedroom door, calling out, "Hello? Are you still here?"

She jogged down the stairs, her muscles tense, her senses on high alert. When she reached the bottom step, she tripped to a stop.

The blinds across the window that she'd just opened now shuttered out the sunlight. Her gaze darted to the front door, now closed.

A clicking noise from the laundry room acted like a cattle prod and she lunged for the purse she'd foolishly left on the kitchen counter. Strapping the purse across her body, she ripped open the side pocket and grabbed her .22, the cool metal of the gun in her hand giving her courage.

She flicked off the safety and rounded the corner of the counter into the kitchen, holding her weapon in front of her. Not a great start to her career as a Realtor, but she'd do what had to be done to protect herself. That much she'd learned from Hector De Santos.

The door from the laundry room to the back of the building stood ajar and Gina crept toward it, locked and loaded.

Her heart pounded as the laundry room door suddenly swung open and a large man filled the frame of the doorway.

She raised her gun and took aim at his head. "Who the hell are you and what are you doing here?"

Chapter Two

Josh didn't trust Gina Rojas as far as he could toss her, but even *he* didn't expect her to hold him at gunpoint this early in their relationship.

"Whoa, there." He raised his hands, his own weapon heavy in the pocket of his jacket. "I'm just here to look at the town house."

She narrowed her dark eyes, her nostrils flaring as if sniffing out his lie. "Why are you sneaking around?"

"Sneaking?" He spread his hands in front of him. "Just thought I'd check out the laundry room and this back door."

"And the blinds?" She didn't seem to be buying any of this since her deadly little .22 was still pointing at his face.

Blinds? "Yeah, the blinds."

"Why'd you close them?"

His pulse ticked up even higher and it had nothing to do with Gina's weapon leveled at him. Someone *had* been here before he'd arrived, had closed the blinds and the front door—and then escaped out the back when he showed up.

"Testing them out." He cleared his throat. "Look, I'm sorry I gave you a scare. I'm really just here to look at the town house if you want to show it to me."

"What's your name?"

Wasn't her arm getting tired hoisting that gun?

She would be expecting the name of the person who'd made the appointment to see the place—and he couldn't give her that.

"I'm Josh Edwards. Is this an open house? I've been looking in this area for a while, saw the for-sale sign, saw the car in the driveway and the open door. I figured I could take a peek." He lifted his shoulders and twisted his lips into what he hoped was a passable grin. "I guess that wasn't such a good idea."

Gina's grip on her gun relaxed. "I'm expecting someone else at any minute."

"Understood. Can you show me around until they get here...without pointing the gun at me?"

Gina lowered her weapon and it dangled at her side, but she shook her cell phone at him in its place. "That other buyer is going to be here soon, and my office knows where I am and when to expect me."

"Good." He dropped his hands. "You can never be too careful."

Especially if you were involved with drug dealers and terrorists. Was that why Gina was so jumpy? And was this buyer she was expecting the one who closed the blinds and hightailed it out the back door when he heard him at the front door? Why would anyone do that, unless the intruder planned to steal Gina's purse, which she'd left out on the counter?

Or unless that buyer had a different motive altogether.

"Let's start over." He edged away from the laundry room and into the kitchen just in case she changed her mind and decided to take a shot at him. About a foot away from her, he extended his hand. "Josh Edwards, and I'm interested in the town house."

She tucked her gun into the purse hanging sideways across her body and took his hand. "Gina De Santos, Four Points Realty, and I'll be happy to show it to you."

De Santos? She'd ditched Ricky's name already?

She strode ahead of him into the living room. "Let's open up those blinds again and get some light in here, since it really is a good feature of the place."

While she tugged on the cords of the blinds, his gaze lingered on her backside, round and full beneath her slim skirt. She hadn't lost anything in the looks department in the past year.

He turned toward the sliding door to the patio. "This is nice. Should get lots of sun."

She joined him, smelling like some tropical hothouse flower. "Yes, but there's enough room out here for a table, a few chairs and an umbrella in case the sun gets too hot. The wall is tall enough to restrict a small dog... or children. Do you and your wife have children?"

"Me? No."

She raised her dark, sculpted brows at him.

Had he come off too strong? He'd decided long ago never to bring kids into this world. Look at her own son.

They returned to the kitchen where she pointed out a few features that held no interest for him at all.

"The laundry room—" she jerked a thumb over her shoulder "—you've already explored. Do you want to go out that back door, or did you see enough?"

He hadn't seen enough. He hadn't seen the person who'd been in the house closing the blinds.

"I'm good."

"You'll love the upstairs. For a single guy like you? Roomy master suite with a second room for an office or gym." Her gaze traveled up and down his body as she brushed past him.

The look she gave him made him hard in all the right places but he'd better rein in his galloping lust or she might pull that gun out on him again. Why'd she think he was a single guy? He'd said no to the kids, but he hadn't denied the wife. Probably had something to do with the look in his own eyes when she waltzed past him.

He followed her up the stairs, pinning his gaze to her swaying hair instead of her swaying derriere. If he could remember that she was most likely complicit in her father's deeds that would be enough to splash cold water on him. How could she not have known what was going on in that compound?

"Here's the master." She stepped aside and gestured him into the room.

He wandered around and poked his head in the closet, which he couldn't imagine filling in a million years. "Impressive."

While she was still talking about east-facing windows and views, he blew past her into the next room, anxious to make his initial report, anxious to get away from Gina De Santos and the way she stirred his blood.

"This room is smaller, has the mirrored closet doors. Could work as a gym." Again, that appraising inventory of his body that made him want to flex every muscle he had. "Or an office. What is it you do?"

"Software development. I work at home."

"This would be perfect for you."

They completed the tour of the town house and returned to the kitchen where she shoved a flyer at him. "What do you think?"

"I like…everything about it." He tore his gaze away from her liquid brown eyes and squinted at the flyer. "Might be out of my price range, though. Do you have a card?"

"Of course." She flattened her purse against her body as she unzipped the top, and he could see the outline of her gun in the outside pocket.

That purse was specifically designed for a weapon. The lady was serious about her self-defense. But why?

"Here you go." She snapped a gold-embossed card on top of the flyer. "Office number and cell."

He skimmed a finger across the glossy flyer. "This isn't your listing? It says Lori Villanueva is the listing agent."

"I'm helping her out. She was busy today."

Did that mean the intruder hadn't expected Gina to be here? Maybe it was just a thief looking for a quick prize, but then he'd missed the purse on the counter.

"Your original client never showed up."

She gave a little jerk to her shoulders. "Happens all the time."

"Then I'm glad I stopped by, so you didn't have to waste your time."

"I am, too, and I apologize for drawing down on you."

"Perfectly understandable and advisable...for a woman in your position."

She lifted her chin. "My position?"

"A Realtor working on your own. Can't be too careful these days."

"My feelings exactly." She scooped up the rest of the flyers and tapped their edges on the granite. "Call me...if you're interested in the town house."

"Will do." He left her to lock up the place and slid into the front seat of his rental.

He was interested all right—just not in the town house.

Josh pulled out his phone and texted a message to Ariel, his contact person on this assignment. He knew better than to question why he was reporting to a nameless, faceless woman instead of his superiors in the navy.

He'd been pulled off a deployment in Afghanistan and sent to Colombia with a short stop in the United States. His commander had briefed him there and the assignment dictated he return to the United States and make contact with Gina Rojas—De Santos. Done.

Ariel's response instructed him to compile a report on his first meeting…and to pursue the relationship to find out what Ricky Rojas's widow knew.

Easier said than done. He didn't have the savvy of that smooth SOB Slade Gallagher or the aw-shucks cowboy twang of his other teammate Austin Foley.

But he'd definitely seen a spark of interest in Gina's dark eyes when she'd assessed him. He'd had to capitalize on that, since he wasn't ready to tell her he'd been the navy SEAL sniper who'd killed her husband, even if he had been sent to Miami to protect her.

He looked up as Gina exited the town house and swiveled her head in his direction.

Lifting a hand, he pulled away from the curb. He didn't want her to think he was waiting for her or stalking her. She was jumpy enough. He'd have to put that in his report, too.

He made his way back to his hotel in the much more crowded area of South Beach. Whichever government agency was sponsoring this little reconnaissance mission had some deep pockets. Or maybe they'd just put him up in this swanky hotel because of its proximity to Gina's mother's place, who must still be living high on the hog courtesy of her former husband's drug money— not that the DEA could prove it or find it.

Back in his hotel room, Josh flipped open his laptop and wrote up a report on his initial meeting with Gina

De Santos. He left out the part about the sparks that had flown between them, although Ariel would probably tell him to use that to his advantage.

He hit Send on the email with its attachment and pushed away from the desk. He wandered to the window with its view of several pastel art deco buildings. At least that's something he'd gotten out of his previous relationship—a little culture thrown in with all the cheating.

Snorting, he turned his back on the art deco and flipped on the TV. He'd already figured out the hotel carried the channel with the UFC fight. He'd take the UFC over art deco any day—maybe that's why his ex cheated on him.

He reclined on the bed, placing his laptop beside him. Wouldn't want to miss an urgent message from Ariel.

He had no idea why the navy was sending a navy SEAL stateside to keep tabs on a dead drug dealer's daughter, but he'd figured it was the same reason why they'd sent two of his sniper unit team members on similar assignments in the past few months—Vlad.

Had their old nemesis really been the man behind the drugs-for-arms deal involving De Santos's cartel, Los Santos?

If that were the case, Josh would be only too happy to thwart Vlad's plans.

The fight proved to be too one-sided to hold his interest, and he clicked through the remote to find something else. As he settled back against the stack of pillows to watch an old comedy, his laptop dinged, indicating a new message.

He dragged the computer onto his lap and double-clicked the email.

Ariel's message left nothing unclear. *Get close to the subject to exploit or protect.*

It didn't sound like Ariel and her bunch, whoever

that was, believed Gina was as innocent as the CIA agents did a year ago. Exploit? If Gina had intel about her father's old operation, he'd be expected to get that from her. Protect? If she did have that intel she could be in danger from her father's old associates...or others.

Did Gina think she could play with fire and not get burned?

He dipped his hand in his front pocket and flicked the corner of the card he'd pulled out. Gina's office number and her cell number. Maybe he could offer to buy her a drink for showing him the town house...or demand she buy him one for pulling a gun on him.

Get close to the subject? He had no problem with that order—no problem at all.

GINA PEEKED INTO RJ's room one last time. The soft breathing and tousled, dark hair on the pillow drew her in like a magnet and she tiptoed across the carpet and crouched beside his bed.

She kissed her fingertips and then pressed them against his temple, whispering, "Sleep tight, baby boy."

"He won't even know you're gone. You know what a heavy sleeper he is."

"Shh." Gina sprang to her feet and shooed her mother from the doorway of RJ's room. "Even a heavy sleeper is going to wake up with all your yammering."

Mom placed one hand on her curvy hip and shook her other finger in Gina's face. "You're nervous, aren't you? You haven't been on a date since Ricky's death, and you're scared. Do you want a few tips?"

"From you?" Gina raised her eyebrows. "No, thanks."

"The first tip—" her mother breezed past her and picked up her oversize wineglass "—you should have your date pick you up at home, like a gentleman."

"Meeting him at the bar was my idea. I barely know the guy. I don't want him to know where I live." Gina leaned toward the large gilt-edged mirror above the fireplace and drew her pinky finger along the edge of her lower lip to fix her smudged lipstick.

Mom clicked her tongue. "You have to open up and trust a little, or you'll never get anywhere."

"Like I trusted Ricky?"

"Ricky was such a handsome boy, so charming although a little weak around the chin."

Gina rolled her eyes. "Maybe *you* should've married him."

"Don't be silly. I draw the line at men in their twenties. Now, give me a hot thirtysomething…"

"Mom." Gina made a cross with her two index fingers. "Way too much information."

Her mother, a vibrant and attractive fortysomething, smiled and took a sip of wine. "How about a glass of vino to get rid of those jitters?"

"I don't have jitters. I'm meeting a possible client for a drink." She grabbed her concealed-carry handbag with the special compartment for her .22 and hitched it over her shoulder.

"Oh, now he's a possible client? I thought this was purely social. Possible clients can see you at the office or arrange for a day of looking at houses."

"I'm looking at him as a possible client because I need to start building a business. I can't be Faith's gofer forever."

Mom leaned against the center island in the kitchen, cupping her wineglass with two hands. "Are you sure the real estate business is for you? I don't see much passion for it."

"It'll grow on me. I have to do something. I can't just

tend bar. It's a dead end." Gina slipped into her high-heeled sandals, feeling a spark of excitement for the first time in a while.

"Get your own place going again. You did such a good job with that little Tex-Mex bar you had in Austin." Mom held up her hands. "I know you don't have the money, but I do. I could be your first investor."

"I can't do that, Mom. I can't take your money."

"Don't be ridiculous, Gina. Don't be proud. I earned that money."

"It's dirty money." Gina flung open the front door and slammed it behind her. She caught her breath and waited outside to make sure she hadn't woken up RJ.

Her mother called through the door. "He's still sleeping. Get a move on."

Gina blew out a breath and crossed the hall to the elevator. Mom knew her too well. She'd been right about the nerves, too.

Josh Edwards's call hadn't surprised her too much. She'd felt the pull between them, had noticed the way he'd assessed her but wasn't sure he'd act on it. She wasn't sure she *wanted* him to act on it. Her trepidation had more to do with the fact that she didn't trust her instincts anymore rather than the fact that she hadn't dated since Ricky's assassination.

Maybe if she just pretended this was a work function, she wouldn't fall under Josh's spell. She'd keep her guard up and her .22 close.

The elevator landed in the lobby, and she crossed the marble tiles to the front door, waving at Enrique, the security guard at the desk.

Stepping into the night air of Miami, she inhaled the slightly sweet and spicy scent carried on a light breeze. She noticed this smell only here in South

Beach—a combination of the perfumes and colognes of the women and men out for a night on the town and the savory odors from the restaurants lining the sidewalks and the occasional food truck hawking authentic Cuban food.

The bar she'd picked for her date with Josh got a good crowd on weeknights, but didn't command the standing room–only business of some other, more popular clubs. Cicero's would do for a quick drink and some informal chatter—that's all she could commit to right now.

She made a left turn at the corner and crossed the street. Squaring her shoulders and hugging her purse to her chest, she stepped into the bar and did a quick survey of the room.

Josh, sitting at a corner table facing the doorway, raised his hand.

Gina wove between the high cocktail tables until she reached the corner of the bar. As she approached, Josh stood up and grabbed her chair, holding it out for her.

Ricky had always done that, too—didn't mean a damned thing.

"Thank you." She scooted the chair closer to the table, hanging her purse over the back, gun compartment on the outside. "Have you been waiting long?"

"I got here about fifteen minutes early. You're right on time." He tapped the glass in front of him. "I just got some water, but I hope we see that waitress again. It's busy for a weeknight."

Gina turned an appraising eye on the scene—attractive waitresses, a good number of bartenders hustling up drinks and sharp busboys cleaning up tables as fast as customers vacated them. "Management's on the ball here. We won't wait long."

The waitress appeared at their table seconds later, as if she'd heard Gina's assessment. "Ready to order now?"

"I'd like a mojito, please. The house rum is fine."

"Sounds way too exotic for me. I'll have a beer, please. What do you have on tap?"

The waitress reeled off a list of beers from memory, and Josh selected an IPA.

Gina folded her hands on the table. "Have you given any more thought to that town house?"

"I might want to see a few more." Josh quirked an eyebrow at her. "Do you have any more to show me?"

"I can show you whatever you like." She bit her bottom lip. Did that sound like a come-on? She had to admit that Josh looked fine tonight—his short, almost black hair slicked back and a sexy scruff on his jaw.

She cleared her throat. "I mean, I can show you condos outside our own office's listings. Just tell me what you like."

His dark eyes glittered as they seemed to drill into her.

"I mean, tell me what you'd like to see…in a condo." She grabbed a menu tucked against the wall and skimmed the appetizers without seeing a thing.

Josh's intensity was off the charts up close and personal like this, face-to-face over a small table. With that stare burning a hole in her, anything she said sounded like a double entendre.

"I like that area. Maybe I'll make a list for you." Josh tapped the edge of the menu. "Do you want to order some food?"

"Not really." She blinked at the menu in her hands and then held it out to him. "Do you?"

"No, thanks."

The waitress saved her from any more inane conversation by delivering their drinks.

Gina poked at the mint leaves with her skinny green straw. "Where do you live now?"

"I'm new to Miami. I'm staying in a hotel not far from here." He took a sip from his beer, watching her over the rim of his mug.

Why did it seem as if they were having a conversation as a subtext to the words they were speaking? Every word from their lips felt loaded with meaning. Was it just this crazy attraction between them? She'd felt crazy attractions before—they never ended well.

If he could afford to stay in a hotel in South Beach long-term, he could afford a nice little town house just about anywhere in Miami.

She sucked up some of her drink and the cool mint tingled against her tongue. "Staying in a hotel must get...tiresome."

"There are certain advantages. I don't have to clean up after myself, or cook." He winked.

She studied his face. The wink didn't match the man. It was almost as if Josh was pretending to be someone he wasn't, or maybe she'd gone from not trusting her instincts to analyzing every word and every facial tick.

"How about you? I assumed you picked this bar because it was close to where you lived. Are you in South Beach?"

"We're temporarily staying with my mother, who has a condo here."

"We?" He casually curled a hand around his beer mug, but his knuckles appeared white.

She dragged her gaze away from his hand gripping the glass and met his dark eyes. Maybe he thought she was ready to spring a husband on him. Would a child be worse?

"My son and I. I have an almost three-year-old."

"That's great. Pictures?"

"Really? I don't want to bore you." Was this an act? Feign interest in the kid to get to the mom? Was this something men did? The last time she'd dated she didn't have a child, so this was new ground for her.

"Family pictures don't bore me."

Her fingers traced over the weapon stashed in her purse as she reached for her cell phone. Cupping it in her hand, she tapped her phone until she found a few current pictures of RJ.

"Here he is." She held the phone sideways in the middle of the table, so they could both see it. She had no intention of handing her phone over to him.

"Cute little guy."

She swept her finger to the next photo. "Here he is with his newfound friend from daycare."

Josh squinted at the picture. "They look like buds."

She pulled the phone back. "My son just started going to that daycare, so I'm happy he made such a fast friend."

The waitress dipped next to their table with two more drinks.

Josh glanced up. "We didn't order another round."

"I know." She slapped down a cocktail napkin and placed the second mojito on top of it. "A friend of yours at the bar ordered one for you."

Gina twisted her head to the left, her gaze tripping over the patrons at the bar. "I don't see anyone I know. Did she give her name?"

"*He* and no." The waitress shrugged and spun around to return to the bar.

Josh downed the rest of his first beer and pulled the second one toward him. "You have generous friends."

"Are you sure it's not one of your friends? I don't

see any of my friends at the bar, not that I have many here in Miami."

"I don't have any." He clinked his glass with hers. "Maybe it was a mistake. Should we drink up before he realizes it?"

One side of her mouth turned up in a smile, but she didn't feel like smiling. That was too weird. Who would be buying her drinks?

"Can you excuse me for a minute? I'm going to use the men's room." Josh shoved back from the table. "I'll swing by the bar to see if I recognize anyone."

"Maybe once this person sees you up close, he'll realize he made a mistake."

"You'd better take a sip of that drink before he can take it back."

As Josh walked toward the restrooms to the left of the bar, Gina picked up the second mojito and sniffed it.

A black scrawl on the cocktail napkin caught her eye and she dragged the napkin toward her with her index finger.

The words jumped out at her.

Dump this guy. You're still married. Meet me behind the bar down the block from Joanna's place, paloma. R.

Chapter Three

As he washed his hands, Josh leaned into the mirror and practiced winking. He was pretty sure that was a move his slick buddy Slade would've tried, but Gina had looked at him like she was staring into the face of Ted Bundy.

Maybe whoever sent that second round of drinks over noticed how badly he was tanking with Gina and was trying to help him out? That was a strange move for someone to make. If a friend of hers was at the bar, why not come by and introduce himself?

Maybe the guy was there right now and having better luck with Gina than he was. Could she be any more uptight? Maybe Ariel and her bunch had sent the wrong SEAL out here to do the job.

He yanked a couple of paper towels from the dispenser, dried his hands and tossed them into the trash before shoving out of the men's room. He held the door as two men came barreling through.

When he walked past the bar, nobody stopped him to claim responsibility for the drinks. He approached the table and sat down. Gina greeted him with a tight smile, her purse clutched in her lap, the second mojito untouched.

"Everything okay?"

"No, actually." She folded over the corner of the damp napkin beneath her empty glass. "I just got a call from my mom, and my son isn't feeling well. He woke up, and he's asking for me. I'm sorry. I'm going to have to leave now."

He watched her lips as they formed the lie.

"That's too bad. I hope it's nothing serious."

"Just a stomachache, but he needs his mom."

"Of course."

"I can leave some cash for my drink."

"I've got this one." He stood up as she shot up from her chair. "Can I walk you back to your mother's place?"

"No, thanks. It's not far and it's still crowded outside. I'll be fine." She stuffed a white napkin into her purse. "W-we could try this again…if you want, later."

"Sure. I'll make my list of requirements first—so we'll have something to talk about next time."

The zinger seemed to go over her head. "Fine, yes. Call me." She pivoted toward the front door and practically leaped over the tables to get there.

As soon as she disappeared, Josh tossed some bills on the table and set Gina's full glass on top of them, since her second mojito seemed to be missing its cocktail napkin.

He'd seen a back door to the bar by the restrooms and made a beeline to that hallway. He slipped through the door and jogged toward the alley that led to the street. He flattened himself against the stucco wall and peered around the corner.

As he expected, Gina had already passed the alley. Her white jeans stood out in the crowd. *She* stood out in the crowd.

He joined the stream of people on the sidewalk, edging toward the curb, keeping cover. She glanced over her shoulder once or twice, but each time he stepped off the curb into the gutter and out of her view.

She turned and crossed the street, and he jaywalked to get out of her line of sight. He edged around the corner and spotted her several feet ahead of him.

Maybe she'd been telling the truth about her son. Her pale face and wide eyes when he'd returned to the table screamed *scared rabbit*, but maybe that's how she looked when her son was sick. Hell, what did he know about having kids?

Her mother's pastel-colored condo loomed down the block, and he'd have to end his sleuthing once Gina went inside. He'd probably never find out the truth about why she ditched the date early. It was probably that wink of his.

Then she passed the front entrance to the condo and his heart rate picked up. She wasn't going home to check on her sick child?

With one final twist of her head, Gina ducked into what looked like a bar almost a block down from her mother's condo. *Hello.* Maybe she wanted to pick up some ginger ale for the kid's stomach.

He didn't plan to blow his cover now by barging into the bar after her, so he cut down a small side street after the condo and headed to the alley running behind the buildings, including that bar.

He strode down the alley toward the back of the establishment, hoping it had a rear entrance. As he reached a Dumpster, a vision in white jeans and a red top stepped into the alley from beneath the black-and-gold awning of the bar's back door. A yellow light spilled over Gina's form beneath the awning.

Josh jerked back and ducked behind the Dumpster. Luckily, the light bulb that had been screwed in above the Dumpster lay in shards at his feet. Even if Gina glanced this way, he'd be nothing more than a shadow in the night.

And glance, she did. Her head turned from side to side as she rested a hand on the purse pressed against the front of her body.

Josh crouched and waited. She waited. They both waited for something…or more likely someone.

A slight movement across the alley caught Josh's attention and he melted against the wall, watching beneath half-shuttered lids.

A man emerged from the darkness, creeping like a jungle cat in his all-black clothing, his focus pinned on Gina, still in the doorway of the bar.

Josh's muscles tensed and his finger twitched as if it were on a trigger. He remedied that by slipping his hand in his jacket pocket and gripping the gun nestled there.

Through narrowed eyes, Josh followed the man's silent approach toward Gina. Could she see him coming at her through the blackness of the alley? The only light past the condo building was shining right on Gina. Where were the other lights from the other businesses? Josh nudged a piece of broken bulb with the toe of his shoe. Was this light broken by design?

A thrill of adrenaline percolated through his veins, and he hunched forward.

Gina's head jerked back. She'd spotted him—the predator.

She threw out one hand and her voice carried in the enclosed space of the alley. "Where is he?"

The man's voice came back, too low-pitched for Josh to hear a response.

"Where?" Gina tossed her long hair over one shoulder, giving a good impression of a woman in charge—but Josh picked up the tremor in the single word.

Once again, Josh missed the guy's response, but he pointed to the end of the alley.

Did Gina know this man? Would she go off with him? Josh couldn't allow that without knowing the identity of the man first. Somewhere in his job description for this assignment he'd read the word *protect*.

Gina shuffled forward without much enthusiasm, or at least not enough for her companion, who took her arm.

Wrong move, buddy. She shook him off and stepped back. "He can come here."

"He can't."

This time Josh heard him loud and clear.

"That's the only way." Gina shifted her stance toward the door, but the man was beside her in a second, his hand on her shoulder.

She twisted away from him and that's all Josh had to see.

He stepped out from behind the Dumpster and startled a cat who'd been crouching and watching, too. The cat yowled in protest at being outed from his hiding place, and two white ovals in the night turned toward Josh.

Josh took one step forward and that was enough for Gina's pal. He shoved Gina against the door where she stumbled and went to her knees.

"Hey!" Josh took off, but the man was anticipating his move.

He spun around and sprinted down the alley.

Josh ran up to Gina. "Are you all right?"

"What are you doing here?"

"I'm going after him."

"No!" She grabbed the sleeve of his jacket, but he slipped away and chased after the man who'd reached the end of the alley and a cross street.

Josh pumped his legs to catch up, but a white sedan squealed to a stop and the man jumped into the back seat. Josh sprinted to the end of the alley and tried to get the license plate of the car, but it had already woven into traffic and all he could see was a white blur sandwiched between two other cars and a bus.

Josh spit out an expletive and dived back into the alley. When he reached Gina, she'd pulled herself up and was brushing dirt from her white jeans.

"What the hell are you doing here? Did you follow me?"

"It's a good thing I did." He jerked his thumb over his shoulder. "What was that all about? Did you know that guy?"

She backed up against the door, pinning her shoulders against it. "Are you some kind of creepy stalker? Was it you who closed the blinds and the door of the condo yesterday? I should've shot you when I had the chance." She patted her purse. "And I still might."

"Me?" He jabbed an index finger into his chest. "What about that guy? Was he, or was he not trying to get you to go somewhere with him."

She blinked and brushed some hair from her eyes. "I suppose so, but he was trying to take me to someone I know…knew."

"Don't you think that's suspicious? Why didn't the person just come to you?"

"That's what I was telling him when you appeared out of the shadows like some kind of night crawler."

"Thanks for that visual." He dragged his fingers through his hair. "And you weren't *telling* him that. You'd already told him and it didn't look like he was taking no for an answer, and then when I showed up like a *night crawler*, the dude pushed you and I'm the creep?"

"I didn't say he wasn't a creep, too."

Josh closed his eyes for a second and took a deep breath. "Are you going to tell me what that was all about?"

"Why should I?" She jutted her chin forward in a manner that told him she was ready for a long siege.

"Oh, I don't know, because we were on a date and you lied to me to get away and meet some creep in an alley. I figure you owe me an explanation. I even bought the drinks."

She sagged against the door, her once-proud shoulders slumped forward. "He said he could take me to my husband."

Josh's mouth dropped open. If she really thought Ricky Rojas was alive and well and living in Miami, he had some really bad news for her.

GINA FLINCHED AT Josh's expression of shock. If they did have any chance at a normal, dating kind of relationship, she'd have to open up to him about her life at some point. She just didn't expect it to be in a dark alley with her hands stinging from a fall and this suspicion between them.

Josh cleared his throat. "You're married?"

"I—I don't know." She rubbed at a smudge of dirt on the thigh of her jeans. "It's a long story."

Josh reached across her and opened the metal door

of the bar. "Let's have another drink and you can tell me all about it."

She poked her head into the bright hallway that led to the noise and conviviality of the bar, and it all seemed so normal. She'd never told anyone her story and it bubbled and hissed inside her like some malignant concoction. She might not want to tell Josh Edwards the whole sordid tale but eking out a little at a time just might ease the pressure.

"Why the hell not?" She swept past him into the bar and the door slammed behind him as he followed her.

They couldn't find a table, but two stools beckoned at the end of the curved mahogany bar and they claimed them.

Josh rapped his knuckles against the wood. "Beer, please, whatever's on draft. Do you want one of those minty things again?"

"I'll have what he's having." She planted her elbows on the bar, hooking her feet around the legs of the stool.

Josh didn't waste any time. He spun around on his stool, bumping her knees with his, and leaned toward her. "Let's start with the basics. Are you married or not?"

"I was married to RJ's father, but I thought he died over a year ago."

Josh's dark brows collided over his nose. "You *thought* he died?"

"Yes, but the scene was kind of chaotic at the time, and I never actually saw his dead body. I mean, I saw his body, but for all I know he could've been faking it. I was *told* he'd died."

"Why would someone tell you that if it weren't true?"

"There are reasons, and I can't get into those."

The bartender placed their beers in front of them

and Josh absently clinked his mug against hers. "What makes you think he's alive now? Just because that violent individual in the alley told you so?"

"That's not all. There have been a couple of other signs...messages."

"From him?"

Her hand jerked at Josh's harsh tone, and the beer sloshed over the side of the glass and ran down her hand. She plucked a cocktail napkin from the artfully arranged stack and dabbed her knuckles.

"A couple of texts using a...nickname that nobody else would know."

Josh leaned back and took a gulp of beer. "Why would your husband text you? Why not call you or better yet, walk up to your mother's place and knock on the door?"

She flicked the beer mug with her fingernail. How much should she reveal to this man she'd just met yesterday? Telling him the whole truth, that her husband and father had been involved in the drug trade and both had been killed at the same time in a planned assassination—would make anyone run for the exit.

That's not something you just blurted out on a first date.

"It's complicated, Josh. He wouldn't be in a position to just come to me freely."

"Sounds...dangerous."

"It is." She twisted her hair around one hand and then dropped it as the strands abraded the scrapes on her palm. "That's why I don't want to drag you into it from your safe and sane world of software development."

"Yeah, safe and sane." His lips quirked. "Sounds pretty far-fetched to me. Would you really go off with a stranger in search of your husband? Or did you know that man in the alley?"

"Never saw him before in my life."

Josh shook his head. "I can't believe a savvy woman like you, a cautious woman like you, one who carries a .22 in her handbag on a date…"

She touched the purse hanging over her knee.

"Yeah, I know you have it in there. Anyway, can't believe someone like you would traipse off with a stranger promising to take you to your dead husband."

"I…" She pressed two fingers against her lips. She knew she'd been taking a risk meeting that man in the alley, but she had to know if Ricky was alive. "You're right, but he offered a compelling lure."

"That's exactly what it sounds like to me—a lure. That man in the alley wants something from you and figured the best way to get you to go with him was the story about your dead husband."

Hunching forward, she grabbed his wrist. "But what if it isn't a story? What if RJ's father is alive? I have to know."

"Forget about it, Gina. He's dead."

She flung his arm away from her. "You don't know that. You don't know anything. I'm sorry I told you."

"Why, because you don't want to hear the truth?"

"It's a possibility. Don't you understand that? I have to know for sure, for RJ's sake."

"He's dead, Gina."

"Stop saying that. How can you be so sure after hearing just a portion of the whole story?"

"I *am* sure."

"Why?"

"Because I was there when your father and husband were shot and killed."

Chapter Four

Ice water raced through her veins. She gulped against the sensation of drowning, but the air never seemed to make it to her lungs. She sputtered and gasped.

The stranger across from her squeezed her knee. "Do you need some water?"

"Water?" She gurgled. Why would she need water when the stuff threatened to overwhelm her?

"Gina, are you okay? I'm sorry. I didn't mean to spring it on you like this."

"Spring what?" She pressed her hands to her face, her skin cool and clammy beneath her touch. "Who are you? What do you want from me? Have you been the one sending those texts?"

His lying eyes widened. "Texts? Someone's been sending you texts?"

She tried to hop off the stool but forgot her feet were hooked around its legs, and she fell forward instead. His arms curled around her, breaking her fall as she landed against his chest.

"I've given you a shock." He gently lifted her from the stool and set her on wobbly legs. "A table opened up in the corner. Let's grab it."

She didn't want to grab anything with this man, but

she couldn't seem to form a coherent thought, never mind launch some kind of offensive against him.

She allowed him to lead her to the table and she plopped down in the chair.

He placed her mug of beer in front of her. "Have a drink."

Wrapping her hands around the heavy glass, she raised it to her lips and gulped down half the mug. Then she wiped the foam from her mouth with the back of her hand.

"Are you going to tell me who you are or am I going to whip that weapon out of my purse for encouragement?"

He had the nerve to smile, if that's what that twist of his lips meant.

"I'm glad to see you're coming around. You had me worried there for a minute."

"Stop stalling, Josh Edwards, or whoever you are."

"Josh Elliott—only a partial lie."

She ignored the hand he held out to her. "That doesn't tell me a thing. *What* are you and why are you stalking me and how do you know about my father and my husband and how they died?"

"I'm a United States navy SEAL." He pulled out a wallet and snapped an ID card on the table between them.

Pressing her lips into a line, she poked it with her finger as if it could bite her. It looked official, but she knew all too well anything could be faked or forged. "And?"

"We assisted the CIA in Colombia when they took down the controlling members of the Los Santos drug cartel and the two terrorists they were meeting."

She flinched, nearly biting her tongue. "Terrorists?"

"The two men your father was meeting with that day—known terrorists."

The ice in her veins turned to molten lava as rage coursed through her system. "My father was meeting with terrorists in his home, while I was there? While RJ was there?"

"Afraid so." He cocked his head at her.

He didn't believe she didn't know.

"How did you assist the CIA? I didn't see any military there that day."

He blinked once, his spiky black lashes falling over dark eyes filled with secrets. "That's classified information. Let's just say we were there for protection."

"Not mine."

"Did the CIA...rough you up?" His jaw tightened.

"Did they pull out my fingernails under a bright bulb? Not quite, but it was no picnic, and the DEA was even worse."

"I'm sure it was...traumatic to lose your father and husband in that manner."

She flicked her fingers. "That was then. This is now. What are you doing here?"

"I'm here to protect you."

She snorted. "From what?"

"From that man in the alley who pretended he was going to take you to your dead husband." He steepled his blunt fingers. "From whomever is sending you text messages."

The worry she'd been experiencing ever since she'd received that first text washed over her once again, and she clutched her stomach. The sudden pain in her gut could be from mixing mojitos and beer, but she didn't think so.

"Ricky really isn't alive?"

"No way."

She took a slow sip of beer this time and licked the nutty taste from her lips as she considered this latest piece of news. Would this navy SEAL have any reason to lie to her…about this?

"I still don't understand. Why am I in danger all of a sudden?"

Folding his arms on the table, he lifted his chin. "Why don't you tell me what was in those texts?"

She dug her cell phone from her purse and skimmed through her messages. She stopped at the first one she'd received and read it aloud. "'Where are the drugs? Where are the weapons, *paloma*?'"

"*Paloma?* Dove."

"I-it was Ricky's nickname for me. *Nobody* knew about that name. That's why I believed that man tonight when he said Ricky was alive."

"I wouldn't put much stock in that. Ricky could've told anyone about it. Drugs and weapons? What do you know about drugs and weapons?"

She jerked back, putting more space between her and Josh's intense gaze. He might be here to protect her, but he didn't trust her.

She didn't trust him either.

"I don't know anything about drugs or weapons. I had nothing to do with my father's business and didn't even know his business until shortly before I was married."

"Once you knew his business and your husband's was drugs, why would you choose to put your son in danger by bringing him to that house?"

Gina crossed her arms, digging her fingernails into

her biceps through the material of her silk blouse. She locked eyes with Josh, but this time the passion that kindled between them was anger, not sexual attraction.

She let a long breath out between her teeth that turned into a hiss. "It's complicated."

"And the other texts?" He sank back in his chair and sipped his beer.

"Same exact words, except the last message I received in the bar when you were in the restroom." She pulled a crumpled napkin from her purse and flattened in out on the table in front of him.

"Clever. He must've been the one who bought us the drinks."

She dropped the phone on top of the cocktail napkin. "My father was a drug dealer. I don't know anything about weapons."

"Do you want me to tell you?"

"Why wouldn't I?"

"I'm not sure you want to know the truth."

"Bring it."

"Your father, and the Los Santos cartel, had started dealing with terrorists out of Afghanistan. In exchange for the product from their poppy fields, he was going to supply them with weapons…and passage into the US."

Now she did feel sick.

She bent forward, leaning her forehead against the sticky table, her hair falling around her face. "I can't believe he'd do something like that."

And then she remembered what he'd done to her and she *could* believe it.

"Gina? Are you all right?"

Balancing her chin on the table, she peered at him

through the curtain of her hair. "Not really. I thought this was all behind me."

"Can you think of any reason why your father's associates would be contacting you?"

"Is that who you think it is?" She blew the hair out of her face, as she raised her head.

"That's a good possibility."

"Could it be the Feds?" She splayed her hands on the table, wiggling her fingers. "Maybe they're trying to trap me?"

"I think I would've been told, since essentially I'm reporting to the Feds."

"The FBI? DEA? You're working with them?"

"What did you say before?" He rubbed his knuckles across the stubble on his jaw. "It's complicated."

"But what you're telling me is that if it was some federal agency trying to trap me, they wouldn't have sent you out here to protect me from that agency."

"Exactly." He placed his hands over her restless fingers. "I'm going to ask you a couple of questions. Can you try not to go off on me? I'm just asking."

Her gaze shifted to his broad hands covering hers. God, his touch felt good—warm, secure. She nodded. "I won't go off on you."

"Is there any reason why these people would think you know something about your father's business? Did he give you any information? Leave anything to you?"

"There wasn't much left." She slipped her hands from beneath his. Unless you counted the bank account on Isla Perdida. The same type of account her father had set up for her mother when they split, the one Mom had been using ever since to fund her lifestyle. Blood money.

"They seized all his assets...and mine."

"I'm sorry about that." He drummed his fingers against his glass. "They must think you know something. They wouldn't contact you, otherwise."

"They're sadly mistaken. Do you think I'm in danger from them?"

"You could be." Sounding casual, Josh lifted his shoulders, but they were stiff, indicating anything but casual.

"Great." She pushed away the mug of beer. "What was your original assignment? Get close to the grieving widow? Why the pretended interest in the property? Why not just approach me?"

His gaze floated over her left shoulder and she wondered if he'd heard her. Then his attention snapped back to her face. "I thought it might be better to get to know you in a nonthreatening way first. I did shock you with all these revelations, didn't I?"

"Partly because I thought you were a mild-mannered programmer." Although there'd been nothing to suggest Josh Edwards/Elliott was mild mannered in any way, shape or form—her gaze skimmed over the powerful muscles on display beneath his shirt—especially form.

"My instructions were to get close to you." He cleared his throat. "This is a new type of assignment for me, so I wasn't sure about the best approach."

His lips twisted into a half smile, and her gaze lingered on his strong jaw imagining for a second what it would feel like to get close to Josh Elliott. Then she flipped her hair over her shoulder and said, "Honesty?"

"What?" The hand holding his beer mug jerked, and the amber liquid sloshed into small waves.

"I said you could've tried honesty in approaching me."

He curled his hands around the heavy, beveled glass and stared into its depths. "You really would've been open to a navy SEAL on a secret assignment appearing on your doorstep?"

"It's not like you were personally responsible for the deaths of my father and husband." She rolled her shoulders. "Besides, I accepted you when you did tell me the truth, didn't I? I mean, we're sitting here sharing a beer."

He held up one finger. "Ah, that's because I saved you in the alley, and you were still shaken up. I'm not sure you would've been so…accepting otherwise."

She screwed up her mouth and didn't bother refuting him. The man in the alley *had* shaken her up and she hadn't appreciated Josh's intervention at the time. Now that she knew Ricky really was dead, she was grateful for his protection. This might be a new type of assignment for him, but he'd caught on quickly.

Digging her elbow into the table, she buried her chin in one palm. "How exactly did the Navy SEALs fit into the raid on my father's place?"

"I can't talk about that."

"Okay, top secret." She tapped her fingertips against her cheekbone. "What now?"

"Keep your eyes and ears open, and be careful. I'll be here to look out for you until we can figure out why your father's associates are trying to contact you."

"If they tell me anything, I'll be sure to pass it along to you."

His dark eyes narrowed. "Tell you anything? Why and how would they have the opportunity to tell you anything?"

As she studied his glittering eyes, a chill touched her spine. In that instant she had an odd sense that she was staring into Ricky's eyes again. Josh's expression contained that same single-minded ferocity that Ricky had, but surely, Josh had a passion for good and justice, not evil and greed.

"I mean, if they text me again or, God forbid, call me since they seem to have my cell phone number."

Josh leveled a finger at her. "You're not going to run off and meet anyone again, are you?"

"No. I just thought…" She glanced down and studied her fingernails as she trailed off.

"Ricky's dead, Gina."

"I know." A single tear puddled in her right eye. Ricky had died a long time ago.

Josh slouched back in his chair and downed the rest of his beer. "Are you ready?"

She tapped her phone to wake it up, and the numbers of the clock glowed in the dark bar. "My mom's going to think I had one hot date."

"If you want her to think that, you need to take a couple of deep breaths. Your face looks—" he touched a finger to her cheek "—tight."

His fingertip seemed to scorch her, to brand her. She sucked in a breath, and then shook her head. He was right. The events of the evening had taken their toll on her. The fear still had her senses buzzing.

"With any luck, my mother will be sound asleep and not lying in wait to ask nosy questions."

"Did your mother have any contact with your father after the divorce?"

"Divorce?" She dropped her phone into her purse. "Your sources aren't very well-informed. My mother and father never divorced, but they had very little contact after the separation."

"Did they separate after she discovered his business, or did she know his line of work before they married?"

"Top secret." Her lips formed a thin line, and she dragged her finger across the seam. If Josh, and the US government, didn't know the details of her parents' lives, she sure wasn't going to inform them.

She still had to protect her mom.

Clasping her purse to her body, she pushed up from the chair. "I'm ready to go."

Josh hopped up beside her and placed his hand at the small of her back to guide her out of the still-crowded bar. They spilled onto the sidewalk, joining the rest of the late-night revelers, stragglers from spring breaks across the country and snowbirds escaping the last ravages of winter in the Northeast.

A few steps later, and a popping noise had the press of people scattering and yelping in confusion.

Gina tripped over a crack in the sidewalk and stumbled off the curb. The cars in the street honked, as people surged into the road from the sidewalk to escape the firecrackers.

As Gina stood on her tiptoes to find Josh, she noticed from the corner of her eye a car peel away from the curb where it had been illegally parked. She turned toward the white sedan, and the back door flew open. A man lurched into the street and made a beeline for her.

Taking a step backward, Gina bumped into someone who wouldn't budge. She put a hand out. "Excuse me."

"Stop pushing, lady. Somebody's gonna get hurt."

"Yeah, me." She twisted her head back around, and the man from the car was an arm's length away.

Gina shifted sideways, but the man anticipated the move.

His fat fingers clamped around her upper arm and

he almost lifted her from her feet as he dragged her toward the sedan.

She dug her heels into the asphalt. She was no match for him, but Josh was.

"Josh! Josh!"

As they got to the open door of the car, Gina grabbed onto the door frame. The big man peeled her fingers from the metal and twisted them back. She screamed amid another flurry of pops.

It was the driver of the car who'd been tossing firecrackers out the window.

Her abductor gave her a hard push from behind, and she fell face forward across the leather seats.

The man from the front seat growled, "Welcome back, Mrs. Rojas."

Chapter Five

The firecrackers were some sort of diversion. Josh craned his neck just in time to see Gina carried into the street by a sea of people.

He swallowed hard and plowed his way through the panicked pedestrians, losing sight of Gina in the process. A big white sedan, the same one that had carried away her assailant in the alley, blocked his view of the rest of the street and when he saw a large man at the open door, Josh's heart slammed against his chest.

He pushed a few people out of his way, and then jumped on the trunk of the car, sliding to the other side.

The big man was stuffing Gina into the back seat of the car.

Josh drew back his fist and landed it against the side of the man's head. The man stumbled back and Josh shouted, "Get out of the car, Gina!"

Encouraged by a pair of legs in white denim that appeared in the doorway, Josh went at the big man again who was quickly regaining his composure and reaching into his pocket.

This bunch didn't want a dead body in the street any more than he did, but the big guy would probably make an exception for him. Josh charged the man, which felt like running into a brick wall. He grabbed the man's arm, twisting it behind his formidable bulk in one fluid movement.

The guy grunted and Josh continued to apply pressure until the man dropped to his knees. The driver began to get out of the car, but the whoop of sirens stopped him in his tracks.

Josh kicked the man's fat gut before leaping over his body and making his way back to the sidewalk. The whole attack took seconds, and the cops were rolling in for crowd control.

The squeal of tires told him the men in the sedan weren't going to stick around to answer questions about why they were tossing firecrackers onto a crowded sidewalk.

Josh's gaze swept up and down the street. Had Gina run to her mother's building? He squinted toward the purple awning, hoping to see her waiting there for him.

When someone wrapped an arm around him from behind, he spun around, fist clenched.

Gina held up one hand. "It's just me."

Warm relief rushed through his body and he pulled her into his arms. It's what he'd been wanting to do all night anyway.

"Are you all right? That big guy wasn't the same one from the alley."

"No, but I think the driver was the same guy."

He rubbed his hands up and down her arms. "Did he hurt you?"

"Just my fingers." She shook out her hand. "They really want me to go with them, don't they?"

"They sure do. They were behind the firecrackers. They wanted to create a panic and separate us."

"It worked. I nearly got trampled in the street. Before they drove off, I tried to get a license plate but there was no plate on the car."

"They'd never allow themselves to be traced through something like a license plate. Even if the car had one, it would've been stolen." He squeezed her shoulders before releasing her. "But good thinking."

"Maybe I should've just gone with them."

"What?" That was *not* good thinking. "Are you crazy?"

"Maybe they'd just tell me what they want and I could tell them I didn't have it, and they'd leave me alone." She chewed on her bottom lip.

"You know that's ridiculous, don't you? You already know what they want. They texted that to you—drugs and weapons. And you already told them you don't know anything. Do you think they believe you?"

"I don't know." She tucked her fingertips into the front pockets of her jeans, crossing one leg over the other where she stood. "I didn't recognize those two to-night, but some of these guys have to be past associates of my father. Maybe I can reason with a couple of them."

"You don't follow the news much, do you?"

"What do you mean?"

"Does it look like the drug cartels are big fans of reasoning with anyone?"

"But my father…"

Josh sliced his hand through the air to stop her. "Your father was a vicious killer getting ready to deal with terrorists."

Her face blanched and her eyes glimmered like dark pools.

Anger bubbled in his blood. Didn't Gina realize by

now that the company you kept could get you killed? How could she have ever married a man like Ricky Rojas, a member of her father's cartel?

Look what had happened to his own mother.

A shaft of pain pierced his temple and he massaged it with two fingers. "Let's get you home."

She shuffled her feet like a zombie as he walked her to the entrance of her mother's building. He hadn't meant to hurt her, but maybe someone should've shocked her out of her naïveté long ago.

Or was it something other than naïveté?

Ariel, his contact for the assignment, had indicated that not only was he supposed to protect Gina De Santos but find out if she knew anything. Maybe she did know something. Maybe that's why she wanted to meet with her father's associates. He'd have to keep an eye on her.

As he glanced down at her wavy dark hair dancing around her shoulders and the curve of her hips in those tight jeans, he had a thoroughly primal male response. He wouldn't have any problem keeping an eye on Gina.

She turned at the doorway of the building. "Do you want me to call you when I hear something, or what?"

"Is this place secure?" He tipped his chin toward the pink art deco building with its purple-striped awning.

De Santos must've laid quite a settlement on his ex. That's probably why they didn't do the split legally.

"It's a safe building, and my mom has additional security, cameras. I'll be fine here."

"Touch base with me tomorrow if anything happens. Are you going to work?"

"Of course."

Her quick glance encompassed the luxury condo. "I

have to make a living and support my son, even if I'm not sure realty is my thing."

He took her hand and smoothed the pad of his thumb over her knuckles. Guilt had been nibbling at the edges of his conscience ever since he snapped at her. He didn't know her story, didn't know what demons had pushed her into the arms of a drug dealer.

"Be careful and please don't meet with these people. They don't love you like I'm sure your father did, for all his faults."

An explosive little sob burst from her lips and she stabbed the buttons of the security keypad for the door. With one foot inside the ornate lobby, she twisted her head over her left shoulder. "I'll keep you posted, SEAL."

Josh watched her through the glass as she sauntered to the elevator. She flicked her fingers over her shoulder, and a flash of heat claimed his chest. He hadn't been as subtle in his…admiration as he thought if she knew he was watching her like a boy with his nose pressed against the candy case.

Josh blew out a breath and turned on his heel, diving back into the press of people still hopping from bar to club to bar. As he floated through and among the crowd, he felt as if he inhabited his own private island apart from the rest. These people had no idea about the danger that lurked in their presence. But he knew.

His teammates and superiors always tried to tell him he couldn't protect the entire world. But right now he'd be happy if he could protect just one woman.

THE FOLLOWING MORNING, Josh rose early to work out in the hotel gym and eat at the hotel restaurant. Then he settled in his room with his laptop whirring to life in front of him.

Drumming his thumbs on the keyboard, he gazed out his window onto the roof of another hotel. He had to compose a report to Ariel relaying the developments of last night without allowing his own suspicions of Gina to bleed into his words.

He dug his fingers into his scalp as he clutched his head. And what *were* his suspicions of Gina?

She seemed genuinely upset at the deaths of her father and husband. She'd seemed desperate to reconnect with Ricky Rojas. And she had secrets in her eyes.

Did she know something about the drugs and weapons? The DEA had originally thought so and had questioned her accordingly. They didn't break her, though.

Something told him Gina wouldn't break easily.

He flexed his fingers and began typing his message to Ariel. He stuck to the facts and kept his opinions to himself. He didn't even know if the men who'd tried to abduct Gina were from the cartel or the terrorist cell—or both.

When he finished his report, he clicked Send and heaved out a sigh. He never much liked paperwork, but he had to furnish one of these reports every day to Ariel—whoever that was. The name sounded female, but he couldn't even count on that. This assignment reached the upper echelons of power, and the people pulling the strings had tightened security to a suffocating degree. He had a few contacts in Miami for outside help and support, but Ariel expected him to manage this mission on his own, creating as few waves as possible.

He shoved aside the secure, encrypted laptop and powered on his personal one. He did still have a life outside this assignment and planned to take advantage of being back on US soil.

His sniper team unit was somewhere on the other side of the world right now, but two of his team members, Austin and Slade, had already fulfilled missions for Ariel and her covert bunch. His team had been singled out specifically because of their connection to Vlad, a sniper for the other side. Had Vlad really grown so powerful that he'd been able to assemble a band of terrorists with worldwide connections? Austin and Slade had been convinced of it.

Josh scrolled through his email and stuttered over one from the NYPD. He double-clicked on it and hissed through his teeth when he saw Detective Potts's name at the bottom of it.

Dragging his finger across the text, Josh read every word of the message and pumped his fist when he reached the end. He'd hit pay dirt with Potts, the new detective for cold cases in the fifty-second precinct.

Potts had reopened his mother's case and had come across some information that hadn't been investigated previously. He wanted to meet with Josh.

Too bad the detective hadn't let him know sooner— like when he'd been in New York a few weeks ago assisting Slade with his...disposal problem.

He responded to Potts, letting him know he was in Miami for a few weeks, but would tell him if he made it to New York again. Josh slumped back in his chair and scuffed his knuckles across his jaw. Would it be a few weeks? How long would it take to protect and secure Gina De Santos...or find out what she was hiding?

If this assignment went well, his superiors in the navy would have to give him a couple of days leave before he deployed. He'd spend them meeting with Potts in New York.

He skimmed through the rest of his emails, deleting more than he read.

As he closed the lid on his personal laptop, he eyed the file he'd been provided on Gina. He thought he knew her story but after meeting her, he couldn't figure out why a woman like her would give a punk like Rojas the time of day. He swept the file from the table and settled on the bed after punching a few pillows into submission.

He flipped open the file and scanned the details of her life. Her age surprised him. She seemed older than her twenty-six years, maybe because she'd been through a lot already—and had more coming her way.

He stared at the date she'd married Rojas, the birthdate of her son and the date of the day she'd become a widow, although he already had that date drilled into his memory. But those cold, hard facts didn't do a thing to explain why she'd married Rojas at the age of twenty-two or why she'd stayed with him as he climbed the ladder of the cartel.

She'd met him right after college, but the file didn't specify where. They'd opened a bar together a year later and had a son shortly after that.

He tossed the file off the bed with a grunt of disgust. Probably opened the bar with drug money and laundered it there. That had to be why the government took the place after the…assassinations.

She'd lost everything, and he'd been partially responsible for that.

He leaned over the side of the bed and gathered up the photos that had fanned out from the file. The first pictures showed Gina after the hits on her father and his associates, including her husband.

Josh squinted at the images. Gina seemed strangely detached. While everyone else scurried around in shock and terror, she comforted them. She alone knew exactly what had happened and why.

The next few pictures showed her in the interrogation room, her face strained but not a teardrop in sight. Did her composure indicate shock and disbelief or did it mean a new opportunity had just opened up for her?

A female head of a cartel would be different—and tricky. Had she taken over where her father and husband had left off?

He stacked the photos and turned them over. He needed a bottle of water to get the sour taste out of his mouth.

He rolled off the bed and reached for the mini fridge. As he twisted the cap off a water bottle, his phone buzzed.

Leaning against the window, he grabbed it from the table and swept his finger across the display to see the text message from Gina.

He read it aloud. "'I need to see you. I have something to confess.'"

Tapping the phone against his chin, he grimaced. If Gina De Santos thought she could play a New York street kid like him—she had another think coming.

Chapter Six

Gina pulled down the slat of the cheap blind at the window and squinted into the street. Her gun weighed down the purse strapped across her body, and she rested her hand lightly on the outside pocket that concealed it.

Two abduction attempts in one night called for extreme measures, although she couldn't help thinking if Josh hadn't come to the rescue that second time in the street, she might have this whole issue solved.

She'd lied to Josh about the driver of the sedan. She'd recognized his voice even though she'd been facedown in the back seat and couldn't see him. Pablo Guerrero had been one of her father's top lieutenants in the cartel. A bad cold had kept Guerrero home from the meeting the day her father and Ricky had been hit.

She'd given up his identity readily to the DEA, but that hadn't impressed the agents. They knew all about Guerrero, and she'd suspected they might have even been working with him.

Guerrero obviously had plans to resurrect the Los Santos cartel with himself as kingpin, and he figured he could start with her and those missing drugs and weapons.

He'd always seemed like a reasonable guy, as far as

drug dealers went. Maybe if she could just tell Guerrero she knew nothing, he'd leave her alone.

Of course, that would be a lie, and if she had to confess anything she'd rather do it to the hot navy SEAL who was the good guy in all this than a drug dealer looking to make fat stacks off other people's misery.

It had been a long time since she'd met a good guy.

Her heart stuttered when the silver compact wheeled in front of the house she'd told Faith she was showing to a prospective buyer. In fact, she was becoming quite the accomplished liar—must come from years of lying to herself.

Josh emerged from the driver's side, took a quick look up and down the street and strode up the driveway with a purpose that had her rethinking her decision.

He already didn't trust her. Why would he? The daughter and wife of drug dealers, who'd stayed even after she learned the truth about both. She would never be able to explain it to him. A man like that had control of every aspect of his life.

When he knocked on the front door, she huffed out a breath, misting a spot on the window before reaching for the door handle.

She threw open the door and stepped to the side. "Thanks for coming."

"How could I refuse to respond to a text like that? A confession?"

"Well, maybe I was being a little dramatic." She ducked her head.

"Everything about you has been dramatic from the moment I…met you." He locked the door behind them. "Are you sure it's okay to meet here?"

"Why not?" She shrugged. "I was planning on showing this dump today anyway, but the people looking canceled out on me. My coworker was none the wiser."

He peeked through the blinds just as she had done a few minutes earlier. "You weren't followed, were you?"

"I paid attention. Believe me, after having the CIA, the FBI and the DEA breathing down my neck for the past year, I recognize a tail when I see one." She patted her purse. "And I'm packing heat."

He held up his hands. "You sure you know how to use that thing?"

"Didn't I prove it to you the last time we were alone in a house together?" Tipping her head to one side, she dropped her lids, studying him out of half-closed eyes. "Besides, don't you think I'm some kind of drug moll?"

Josh tilted his head back and laughed at the seventies' popcorn ceiling. "What the hell is a drug moll?"

A smile tugged at her lips. That dry laugh seemed more natural than the grins and the winks, and transformed Josh's too-serious, tense face, lighting it up and making him look almost boyish.

"You know, like the women who hang around gangsters, but in this case, drug dealers."

His laugh evaporated as suddenly as it had burst forth and reminded her that he really didn't trust her at all.

She hoped to remedy that. She wanted Josh Elliott to trust her, to like her.

"Anyway, what I meant to imply is that there's a good chance someone like me with a father like I had is going to know her way around a weapon—and I do."

"I believe you." He rubbed the back of his neck with one hand. "What is it you want to confess?"

She waved her hand toward the two stools at the

kitchen peninsula, the only pieces of furniture left in the house. "Can we sit?"

Josh straddled the stool from behind and crossed his arms over his leather jacket. "Okay."

Perching on the stool across from him, she swept her tongue across her bottom lip. "I haven't been completely honest with you…or my father's associates."

Josh's Adam's apple bobbed in his throat and his nostrils flared. "Go on."

"I don't know anything about drugs or weapons, but I do know something about offshore accounts." She held her breath.

Josh blinked. "Offshore accounts?"

"Are you familiar with Isla Perdida?" She waved a hand in the air. "Of course you are."

"The Caribbean island that doubles as a playground for the rich and famous and a hiding place for their money." He uncrossed his arms and wedged his hands on his knees. "Does your father have an account there?"

"He does."

"You were able to keep that from the DEA?"

"I was."

He whistled through his teeth and settled back, giving her some breathing room. "You're good."

"It's not for me." She bolted up straight, hooking her feet around the legs of the stool so she wouldn't fall into his lap…again. "I don't use any of that money."

"Who does?"

He narrowed his eyes, and she willed the heat creeping up from her chest to stay out of her face. Nothing like looking guilty when she wasn't—not really.

"That's how my father has been giving money to my

mother for years. She has an accountant down there who facilitates everything."

Josh's eyelids drooped even more and she could almost believe he was asleep except for the way the muscles in his face twitched and shifted, as if his thoughts were running riot across his countenance.

"So, the ritzy condo in the ritzy building in the ritzy area…"

"Drug money."

"You're living there, living off that money."

"Not completely." She sucked in her lower lip and met Josh's hard stare. Who said confession was good for the soul? "When the US government seized all my assets—because Ricky's assets were mine and mine were his—I had no money, no property, nothing. I needed a place to stay and Mom offered. That's why I snatched at the first halfway decent job with career potential that popped up. I don't like selling real estate, but one of Mom's connections got me in and I need to make money so I can divorce myself from my mother and her blood money."

Josh cocked his head to one side, as if examining a rare bird.

"And why do you think this account in Isla Perdida is important? It sounds like it's money your father already made. Do you think it's enough to buy the weapons he planned to trade to the terrorists for their drugs?"

"Oh, no. I'm pretty sure that deal had already gone down before the CIA took him out. That's *why* the CIA took him out."

Josh shifted on his stool and raked a hand through his short hair. "That's what we figured, also."

"Then why did the CIA kill my father before they

knew where he'd stashed the drugs from the terrorists and the weapons he intended to pass off to them in exchange?"

"We... They thought they did know. The CIA managed to get to your father's driver, Chico Fernandez and wire him up. Chico recorded a conversation between your father and...your husband in the car. He mentioned a location then, and the CIA thought that's where he'd stashed everything."

Tapping one fingernail on the counter, Gina said, "Chico disappeared a few weeks before my father was killed."

"We don't know anything about that. He disappeared off our radar, too."

"D-do you think Chico's dead?"

"Maybe. Maybe your father discovered the wire, or Chico decided to hightail it out of your father's employ before he *did* discover it."

She rubbed the goose bumps from her arms. Her father's savagery never failed to stun her—even though she knew its real depths more than anyone.

Josh's eyes flickered at the gesture. "If you already know the money for the deal is not in the offshore account, why do you think it's so important to bring it up now after keeping it a secret all this time?"

"Because my father has more than just an account there. He also keeps a safe-deposit box at the Banco de Perdida on the island."

"Big enough for a stash of weapons?" His mouth twitched.

"Of course not." She brushed a strand of hair from her face impatiently. "But Isla Perdida was my father's safe place, just as it is for a lot of criminals. If there was something he wanted to protect, some information he wanted to keep hidden, he'd store it there."

"Do you think he was planning to double-cross the terrorists he was dealing with?"

"I don't know. Maybe he could feel the trap closing around him and took steps to avoid it. What I do know—" she leaned forward, almost touching her nose to his "—is that he went to Isla Perdida one week before the raid on his compound."

Josh shook his head. "No, he didn't. The CIA was watching his every move. He was in Bogotá that week."

Gina snorted. "That was Uncle Felipe."

"What?"

She pressed her lips into a neat smile. She got a certain satisfaction from his reaction—Mr. Know-It-All.

"Uncle Felipe, my father's brother, was his body double. My father used Felipe to throw off his enemies." She held up two fingers, side by side. "They were like this, only seventeen months apart, looked like twins."

"Felipe De Santos is in a Colombian jail right now, but he never said one word about the role he played in your father's organization."

"Why would he? My father had trained him long ago, even when they were children, to keep his mouth shut. He was a good soldier all those years."

"Except he wasn't at the house when the deal went down. Why?"

"My father never trusted him with important business." She tapped her head with one finger. "Always thought he was slow. He wasn't as clever as my father, but he wasn't slow. I guess his perceived dim-wittedness saved his life in the end."

"If I'm to believe you, your father sent Felipe to Bogotá to impersonate him while he staged a getaway to Isla Perdida one week before the raid."

"Yep, and I highly advise you to believe me. I have proof that he went."

"What proof?"

"A communication between him and his pilot. You don't think he hopped on a commercial jet, do you?"

"How did he manage to take a private jet out of the country?"

"How did Hector De Santos manage to do anything? Greased palms and payoffs." She clenched her jaw. "And threats."

"And you believe he went to Isla Perdida to protect information?"

"Yes. If the FBI, CIA and DEA can't find the drugs and weapons and if my father's own associates can't find them, he must've hidden them very, very well."

"I suppose if you give us the information about the account, the ops group I'm working with can go in and have a look."

"Uh-uh."

His brows shot up. "What?"

"I'm not giving them any information about that account, and I'll deny everything you tell them."

"Wait. I thought that's why you told me about the account."

"I told you about the account because I believe you might be able to find the information you're looking for, but that money belongs to my mother. I'm not allowing you or anyone else to take that away from her."

He spread his hands. "Then what are you proposing?"

"I'm proposing we do it my way."

"Which is?"

"We'll go down to Isla Perdida together."

Chapter Seven

The following day, Josh emptied the contents of his small bag into his big suitcase and dropped the empty bag on the bed. He'd reported to Ariel that he and Gina were taking a trip, but didn't mention the location.

When the truth came out that their jaunt had taken them to Isla Perdida, would it be enough to get him yanked off this assignment? His commanding officer in the navy had assured him nothing that happened on this assignment would impact his career as a navy SEAL— unless he died. That would impact it plenty.

Gina had been working all day while he finalized details of their trip tomorrow, and she'd be joining him for dinner in less than thirty minutes. Maybe they could have a real date tonight, free of suspicions and half-truths.

The half-truths would have to start back up tomorrow. They'd be traveling to Isla Perdida under assumed names, but Gina would have her ID on the island. She'd made another confession to him that she'd actually accompanied her father to Isla Perdida once, and he'd given her everything she needed to access his safe-deposit box.

Josh rolled up a T-shirt and tossed it into the bag.

Why would her father have done that if she hadn't given him some indication she was willing to learn Los Santos's operations and had every intention of continuing her father's evil legacy? Maybe she'd been playing both sides. Maybe she was playing both sides now.

He packed a few more items and as he hauled the bag from the bed, a knock sounded at the door of his hotel room. He strode to the door and put his eye to the peephole. He opened the door for Gina and swallowed as he took in her red dress that hit just above her knee and hugged her in all the right places.

Maybe she wanted to have a real date, too.

"Are you early, or did I lose track of time?"

"I'm five minutes early." She took a turn around the room and kicked his bag with the toe of her high-heeled shoe, red to match her dress. "Are you all packed?"

"Pretty much. Are you?"

"Threw some things in a carry-on when I got home from work."

"How'd work go?" Josh glanced down at his jeans, rethinking his clothing choices for the evening.

"Not great." She tossed a wave of dark hair over her shoulder. "Faith wasn't thrilled that I was taking off for a few days. I think I'm going to lose this job."

He knew the feeling.

He slid back the closet door and yanked a pair of black slacks from a hanger. "Doesn't sound as if you much like it anyway."

"I don't, but what am I going to do, be a spy for the CIA?" She snorted.

"I'm going to change." He held up the slacks, pretending he was going to wear them all along. He slipped into the bathroom and pulled off the jeans. Good thing he hadn't worn the slacks yet and they were still pressed.

When he walked back into the room, his personal cell phone was ringing.

Gina handed it to him. "Just started."

As he took it from her, he glanced at the display and his pulse jumped. He tapped the phone to answer it. "Elliott."

"Mr. Elliott, it's Detective Potts. In your email you indicated that you were in Miami. Well, I had to come out here for a case, and I thought I could kill two birds with one stone. I'm still here if you're free tonight."

Josh glanced at Gina, her eyes wide and questioning. "It's not the best time right now, Detective."

"You've waited over twelve years for this information and now's not the right time?"

"You said you found some uninvestigated information."

"I must've sounded too casual, Mr. Elliott, because it's more than that."

"More?" Josh's mouth felt dry and he couldn't swallow, couldn't breathe.

"Mr. Elliott, I have a good idea who murdered your mother."

"You're kidding."

"I'm not. Do you want me to lay it out for you tonight? Or I'll be here most of tomorrow. I think I can swing a breakfast meeting."

"I'm leaving tomorrow and going out to dinner tonight. I can meet you…after dinner."

"Give me the name of the restaurant, and I'll join you for coffee. One thing you can say for Miami, the restaurants stay open as late as the ones in New York."

Josh's gaze darted toward Gina, who was still watching him, her head tilted to one side. He hadn't told Gina anything about his family, but then why would he? He knew all about her family because it was part of his job. He'd never told anyone the full story behind his mother's death—not even his navy SEAL team members.

He inhaled a deep breath and gave Detective Potts the name of the Cuban restaurant where he and Gina would be dining and told him to be there around ten o'clock.

As soon as he ended the call, Gina asked, "What was that about? Not our current situation?"

"Something personal. I'm sorry. I know the timing couldn't be worse. I don't want to ruin our dinner, but this meeting has to happen tonight."

She folded her hands in front of her. "Are you going to tell me what it's all about? You'll have to unless you plan to send me home after we eat. When you first answered the phone, I thought you were going to fall over, and I'm sure it would take a lot to make you fall over."

He didn't plan to send her away after dinner. "It's about my mother."

"Is she okay?"

"My mother died many years ago."

"I'm so sorry. The phone call…?"

Clearing his throat, he stashed his phone in the pocket of his slacks. "My mother was murdered."

Gina crossed her hands over her chest. "That's terrible. How old were you?"

"Sixteen."

"And your father?"

"Long gone before then."

"What happened?"

"I never really knew. She was shot in the back of the head in an alley."

Gina had been approaching him slowly from across the room and when she reached him, she placed a hand on his arm. "That must've been horrible for you."

He met her dark eyes and couldn't look away from the compassion that made them glow. All this mess was going on in her own life and she had feelings to spare for him?

"I want to help you, Josh, like you've helped me."

"Help me? You don't have to, and I don't even know that you can. I've been living with this hell for twelve years."

"You've been living with it by yourself, haven't you? Tell me about it. Unburden yourself. You might feel a little better." She shrugged. "I'm going to find out about it after dinner anyway. I'd rather hear it straight from you than…?"

"Detective Potts."

"Detective Potts."

"It's an ugly story." He picked up her hand from his arm and kissed the inside of her wrist.

She took his hands and dragged him toward the bed. "Tell me about it, and tell me why you're meeting Potts tonight. Like you said, I was a little early and we have some time before our dinner reservation."

He sat beside her on the mattress while she kept possession of his hand, and he pinched the bridge of his nose. "My dad was out of my life by the time I was two and my brother, Jake, was four. My father was a junkie and my mom was, too."

Gina squeezed his hand but if she kept that up

through all the sad parts of his story, she'd cut off his circulation after about ten minutes.

"Where's your brother now?"

"Prison."

She blinked a few times and then pressed her lips together.

"When my dad left, my mom waitressed and walked the streets a little to make ends meet—feed us and feed her drug habit. She was still doing drugs and part-time hooking by the time I was a teenager. How she managed to survive that long and keep custody of us is beyond me, but she did. Then her luck ran out."

"Was she killed by one of her…johns?"

"That's what the cops thought, but Jake had his own theory. He was sure Mom's murder had to do with the guy she'd been seeing, Joey O'Hanlon. Joey O disappeared after the murder. Jake kept trying to tell the police about him, but the cops had their narrative and they were sticking to it."

"Did they have any good reason to stay with their story?"

"One of the working girls on the street saw my mother walk away with a guy who'd been trolling, swore he was a regular john. The cops focused on him but never found him. Unsolved murder, cold case."

"What happened to your brother? Why is he in prison?"

"He found Joey, claimed he killed him in self-defense but had to take a plea for second-degree murder."

Gina shook her head. "That's just all kinds of messed up."

"But I'll never forget what Jake told me. He said before he and Joey struggled over the gun, Joey claimed that Mom was murdered over drugs."

"She was? Was she selling or dealing?"

"No, but Joey O was." Josh skimmed a hand over his short hair. "We tried to tell the police, but they wouldn't listen to us."

"So, you'd already lost your dad, you lost your mom to murder and you lost your older brother to prison."

"Told you it was a sad story."

She trailed a hand down his back and he shivered. "What does Potts have?"

"He thinks he knows the killer, after twelve years as a cold case."

"Then you absolutely have to meet with him, and I'll gladly give over our dessert and coffee time so you can get some closure."

"Closure. I guess we all need some of that." He kissed the tips of her fingers and pushed up from the mattress.

Josh surveyed the restaurant and was glad he'd changed clothes. Plenty of men were wearing jeans, but they'd paired them with silk shirts in bright hues, unbuttoned to create a V on their chests and adorned with several gold chains. Not his scene, but his black slacks and white shirt fit in with all the peacocks.

Gina had ordered a mojito again but he stuck with beer. Josh liked his food—and his women—spicy, so the Cuban dishes—and Gina—made his mouth water. They both ordered the *ropa vieja* and spent most of the meal talking about Isla Perdida and RJ.

"I feel so blessed that RJ is a happy boy, and he

makes friends easily. We already had Diego, a little friend of his, over to Mom's for a playdate."

"Does he ask about his father?"

"Did you? You said your father was out of your life by the time you were two. RJ was about the same age."

Josh chased a kernel of rice around his plate with his fork. "I don't remember. I'm sure the questions didn't come until later, when I got to school and saw other kids with fathers. I think a boy will always miss a father figure in his life."

"Your mother never remarried?"

His lip curled. "She and my father weren't married and while she brought a lot of men around our apartment, she never married and I'd hardly call them father figures."

"RJ would look for his father, and his grandfather. He'd say their names. I tried to explain to him they were gone." She swirled her drink. "I don't know how much of that he took in. I'm gearing up for the questions later, and I honestly don't know how I'm going to answer them. How'd your mother handle it?"

Giving up on the rice, Josh stabbed a bean. "She told me and Jake that our father was a no-good bum and we were lucky he was out of our lives."

"That's one option." Gina pushed away her plate and asked a passing waitress for the dessert menu.

Rolling his wrist inward to check his watch, Josh said, "It's almost ten. Potts will be just in time to join us for coffee."

They ordered a key lime pie to share and two cups of Cuban coffee. Halfway through the pie and two sips into the sweet brew, Josh noticed the waitress leading a short, broad African American man with graying hair to their table.

Josh jumped up from his chair and extended his hand. "Detective Potts?"

"Good to meet you, Mr. Elliott."

"Josh. You can call me Josh and this is Gina."

When he was finished shaking Josh's hand, Potts engulfed Gina's in his clasp. "I hate to interrupt your dinner like this, but it seems like we're both on tight schedules."

"I'm glad you made it down here. Do you want some coffee? Dessert?"

"I ordered a cup of Cuban from the waitress while she walked me over here."

Josh crumpled up his napkin and tossed it next to his plate. "You know the name of my mother's killer?"

"It's a little more complicated than that."

"Complicated? Did Joey O'Hanlon have one of his dirtbag pals do it? I know he had an alibi, but my brother always thought he was to blame."

"Your brother's up for parole in a year."

"You sayin' you can help with that?"

"I might be able to, but Joey wasn't the one who ordered your mother's death, although he was indirectly responsible for it."

"I knew it."

"Joey O was a small-time drug dealer, which I'm sure you know by now. What you probably don't know is that Joey was stealing from his supplier, doing a little selling on his own."

"That's dangerous business."

"It's all dangerous business." Potts stopped talking and smiled his thanks at the waitress who delivered his coffee. He took a careful sip from the dainty cup. "Anyway, the supplier caught on and his boss caught on and so on and so on, and someone came out to pay Joey O a visit."

"He must've known what was coming down because he took off."

"That's right." Potts cradled the cup in his palm. "But your mother didn't. The hit man sent to take care of Joey couldn't find him, but he did find a substitute."

Josh's eye twitched. "Do you know the name of the hit man?"

"No, and we may never locate him, but we know who ordered the hit and you may get some satisfaction out of knowing that person is dead."

"Who was it? Who ordered the hit on my mother?"

"A big-time drug dealer—Hector De Santos."

Chapter Eight

Potts's words punched Josh in the gut but before he even had a second to react, Gina dropped her cup and it broke right in half, the dark liquid pooling in the saucer.

It was enough to distract Potts from Josh, giving him time to compose his features. So, he'd killed Gina's husband and her father had killed his mother...indirectly. A match made in heaven.

"Are you okay, ma'am?" Detective Potts reached across the table, picked up a piece of the cup and placed it in the saucer.

"I—I'm fine." Her face drained of all color, Gina grabbed her napkin and blotted up the drops of coffee dotting the table.

Josh coughed. "Hector De Santos. Isn't he the head of some big drug cartel?"

"He was. As I mentioned, he's dead now—no big loss."

"A guy like that was concerning himself with some small-time drug dealer in the Bronx?"

Potts spread his hands. "We all have to start somewhere. De Santos was still solidifying his empire twelve years ago, and that's one way he rose to power so quickly. He didn't mess around. You toyed with Hector De Santos, you paid the price."

"So, even if the NYPD back then had made this connection, there wasn't much they could've done about it. The triggerman was probably on his way back to Colombia within hours of murdering my mother."

"Could be and I'm sorry about that, but I thought you'd want some closure and I meant what I said about your brother, Jake. Tough rap for him when any one of us might've done the same thing to someone who'd wrecked our mothers' lives."

His mother had wrecked her life long before Joey O crashed onto the scene. "I appreciate the effort, Detective Potts."

"Allen." The detective pulled a card from his wallet and slid it across the table to Josh. "Let me know if you need anything and thank you for your service, chief."

The men shook hands, and the detective nodded at Gina as he pushed back from the table.

When Potts walked away, Gina folded her hands on the table, an incredible stillness falling over her as if she were resting in the eye of a storm.

There would be no storm.

Josh dabbed at a crumb from the pie plate with the pad of his finger. When he caught it, he sucked it into his mouth, meeting Gina's gaze for the first time since Potts delivered the bombshell.

She blinked her long lashes once but held his stare. "You don't seem very surprised."

"To hear your father's name from the detective's lips?" He hunched his shoulders. "It threw me for a loop, but it kind of makes sense. It's like some perfect circle." Gina didn't realize how perfect a circle it was.

"I'm—I'm so…"

He held up a hand. "Don't tell me you're sorry. It's

not your fault that your father was a drug dealer. It's what you do going forward that counts."

"I will do anything I can to help you, starting with Isla Perdida." She grabbed his hands. "Did it help seeing Potts? Did it give you that closure he mentioned?"

"It gave me...resolve."

THE NEXT DAY, Josh looked into the small, upturned face, dark eyes wide with curiosity, and cleared his throat. What were you supposed to say to a three-year-old? Was RJ too young to watch basketball? Too old for nursery rhymes?

RJ tugged on Josh's sleeve and pointed to a plastic truck on the floor.

"Is that your truck?" What a dumb question. Whose truck would it be? His mother's? His grandmother's?

RJ didn't seem to mind the stupid query as he nodded and smiled. He also tugged on Josh's sleeve again.

Josh dropped to his knees and placed a hand on top of the truck. He rolled it on the tile floor, and RJ scooted along beside it, tossing obstacles in its course. Josh dragged the toy over every magazine, coaster and pillow RJ put in the truck's way and even started making roaring truck noises in the process.

The heavy scent of musky perfume invaded his nostrils, and Josh twisted his head over his shoulder, his nose almost colliding with Joanna De Santos's kneecap.

She raised her penciled-in brows. "Getting to know RJ?"

"Just...uh—" he lifted the truck into the air, its wheels still spinning "—playing with the truck."

"You and Gina were awfully private about your dating. You've been seeing each other a few months and are ready to jet off on vacation together and this is the first time I'm even heard your name."

"Mom, I told you we wanted to keep things low-key." Breezing into the room, pulling a suitcase behind her, Gina nodded toward RJ, now constructing a full-scale obstacle course for the truck.

Joanna fluffed her dyed red hair around her shoulders. "When Gina told me you two were heading to the Bahamas together, I insisted that she introduce you to us before she left."

"A good idea and understandable." Josh crawled forward a few feet, pushing the truck ahead of him and aiming it at the tunnel RJ had created by propping up two cushions against each other.

"Yeah, well, Gina doesn't have the best taste in men."

"Mom!" Gina rolled her eyes at Josh. "This is exactly why I didn't bring him around. Would you please let me tell my own life story in my own way?"

"Sure, sure." Joanna flicked her long fingernails at Gina. "You two go off and have fun. God knows, you deserve it."

"Remember, just take RJ to his daycare like usual. I talked to the mother of Diego, his friend, about a playdate, so you can follow up with that. Remember, she brought him over here a few weeks ago." Gina leaned over and kissed her mother's cheek. "I'll text you when we get there, but let's not do any video chatting with RJ. I don't want him to be confused."

Crossing her arms, Joanna said, "Check, check, check."

Josh completed the obstacle course as RJ coached him. Then he ruffled the kid's hair and pushed to his feet just as Gina crouched down next to her son.

She touched noses with RJ before dragging him into her lap. "Be a good boy for Mami, and I'll bring you a present."

RJ curled his arms around Gina's neck and said, "Can I play with Diego?"

"I think so, and I won't be gone long so if Mami doesn't take you to Diego's, I will when I come back."

RJ cupped a hand over Gina's ear and whispered.

She smiled and kissed him. "I think he'd like that."

RJ jumped to his feet and scampered into the family room.

Earlier Josh had poked his head in that room, with its multitude of toys and a big-screen TV with bean-bag chairs and game consoles—a little boy's paradise. Grandma must be footing the bill for that, too.

Two seconds later, RJ bolted out of the room, clutching something in his small hands. He raced to Josh, arms outstretched.

"Whaddya got there?"

"A truck." RJ opened his hands where a red truck balanced on his palms. "A toy for the airplane."

"Thanks, RJ. That's just what I need."

He heard a soft snort behind him. Joanna didn't trust him for some reason—not that she should, but they couldn't tell Gina's mother the truth. If Gina's mother knew who he was and what he'd done, she would be doing more than snorting at his back.

Gina came up behind her son and combed her fingers through his messy hair. "That was thoughtful of you, RJ. Now, give me a big kiss before I leave."

She scooped him up in her arms and they traded kisses back and forth.

Whatever else Ricky Rojas had done, he'd given

Gina a son and she obviously didn't regret that. Did she regret anything about that marriage? She'd said very little about Rojas, and Josh hadn't wanted to encourage her in case it led to the truth of what had happened that day in Colombia. Even after Potts's revelation last night, Josh wasn't ready to reveal he'd been the one looking at Ricky through the scope.

"Are you sure you don't want me to drop you off at the airport?"

"No, Mom. We're good. Just take care of RJ."

"Of course."

Ten minutes later, they were clambering into a taxi, their bags in the back. Josh collapsed against the seat, feeling as if he'd just navigated through an obstacle course—just like that truck. "Your mom really didn't like me, did she?"

"She's just…protective of me."

"Protective?" Joanna's criticism of Gina had left a sour taste in his mouth—not that he didn't agree with it. "Your mother doesn't have much room to talk about bad taste in men."

"Mom's just speaking from experience." Gina poked him in the ribs and jerked her thumb toward the driver in the front.

Josh doubted the guy could hear one word they said, but he sealed his lips and spent most of the ride to the airport making sure they didn't have company on their way.

He wouldn't admit it to Gina, but the scariest part of that condo encounter was meeting RJ. Josh didn't have any children in his life and didn't have the first clue how to act with them, but RJ had gone easy on him.

The chaos in RJ's life had produced a seemingly

well-adjusted, social kid. How had RJ escaped un-scathed? Josh and his brother sure hadn't.

The taxi driver confirmed their airline with them and then navigated through the traffic of airport departures before pulling up to the curb.

They had their boarding passes and carry-on luggage only, so they sailed up to security. Josh held his breath as he presented his fake passport and ID in the name of Josh Edwards. The navy didn't want him traveling under his own name for this assignment, and that order extended to any side trips.

Whoever had provided the fake documents excelled at his or her job, and Josh eased out a breath as he passed through security.

Thirty minutes later, juggling their coffee cups and carry-ons, they found seats in the small boarding area for Carib Air. It would take about ninety minutes to get to Isla Perdida.

Josh took a sip of coffee and scanned the other passengers over the lid. He pegged the couple in the corner of the waiting area, who couldn't keep their hands off each other, as newlyweds. The couple across from them must have a few more years of married life under their belts, as they paid more attention to their phones than each other.

Did marriage have to play out that way? He slid a glance at Gina, on her own phone, texting her mother, no doubt. Had the flame died out between her and Ricky? Or had they been as passionate at the end as those two newlyweds? Maybe she never discussed him because she couldn't bear the pain of his loss.

She leaned toward him and whispered to him, her

words tickling his ear. "I'll bet you anything those two over by the window are newlyweds."

"I was thinking the same thing." He rolled his eyes toward the preoccupied couple. "Probably married awhile longer."

A giggle bubbled from her lips and she covered her mouth. "Lots of single men, most likely businessmen checking on their assets."

Josh's gaze darted among the six men, all solo, all on laptops or some sort of device, all well dressed. His nerves jangled, and he took another sip of coffee. He'd been leery about a tail ever since he planned this trip. Any one of those guys could qualify.

He'd kept an eye out the back window of the taxi on the way to the airport but he hadn't noticed any cars following them—that didn't mean anything. Drug dealers, terrorists, spies all had ways of tracking people.

Another couple wandered into the boarding area, and Josh's muscles relaxed an inch more. He didn't want to have to keep tabs on more than the six guys.

Gina chattered in his ear about the island. She told him again of her time there with her father, and once again his suspicions about her flared in his gut.

"It's beautiful but small." She swept her arm to encompass their fellow passengers. "As you can see, not a lot of young people go because there's very little nightlife, and not a whole lot of families go either since the attractions are mostly scenic—no zip lines, no swimming with dolphins, no catamaran cruises."

"A quiet getaway…or a place to fondle your money."

"You could say that."

Josh's gaze jumped back to one of the men. Had the man been watching them? He was accustomed to watching the nuances of a person's actions through a scope. It was harder to pick up on someone's movements from across a crowded room.

He asked Gina, "Are you done with your coffee?"

"I'm going to hang on to it and bring it with me on the plane."

"I'm going to visit that trash can next to the man in the red tie."

As he eased out of the seat, Gina exclaimed behind him. "Wait, what?"

Josh stretched and ambled toward the trash can, and the man sitting two seats from it. When he reached his destination, he lowered his eyelids and shifted his gaze to the man's body, below his neck. He didn't want to make eye contact.

Neat slacks and a tucked-in, striped button-down with one leather loafer resting on his knee made him fit right in with the other businessmen on the flight.

When Josh had approached the trash can, the man had stopped talking on his phone, and the device, encased in a leather holder with embossed gold letters in the corner, rested in his lap. Josh flipped the coffee cup into the can, brushed his hands together and turned away.

A quick glance at the man near the restrooms confirmed that he, too, had stopped talking on his phone.

Josh ducked next to Gina's chair. "I'm going to the men's room. Why don't you engage that nice couple in conversation while I'm gone?"

She nodded, her eyes wide but alight with comprehension.

As Josh walked toward the men's room and the man

stationed in front of it, he heard Gina say, "Is this your first trip to Isla Perdida?"

Josh passed the man near the restroom, his nose twitching at the guy's spicy cologne. Josh's gaze trailed to the cell phone the man clutched in one hand, and the blood thundered in his ears.

The man had the identical phone case as the man with the red tie. The embossed gold letters curled out from beneath the guy's fingers where they were wrapped around the case.

Josh stepped into the bathroom, but had no intention of sticking around in case the man outside decided to pay him a visit at the urinal. He joined another man at the sink and splashed cold water on his face.

Noticing the man's Miami Heat cap in the mirror, Josh nodded to him. "The Heat had a great season, huh?"

"Should've been longer."

Josh followed closely on the heels of the Heat fan out of the bathroom, brushing by the man with the leather cell phone case and giving half-hearted responses to the fan's enthusiastic analysis of the Heat's last play-off game. What did Josh know? He was a Knicks fan.

He parted ways with his newfound friend and took his seat next to Gina, who was still talking with the couple. He texted her.

The man with the red tie is talking to someone standing near the bathrooms with the exact same cell phone case. Don't look now.

When Gina's cell phone buzzed, she pulled it from her pocket and excused herself from the conversation with the couple.

She leaned into him, resting her head on his shoulder as she pretended to show him something on her phone. She said in hushed tones, with a smile on her face, "What does that mean?"

He pointed a finger at her display and laughed. "It means we're being followed. I'll wait to see who gets on the plane with us."

She tilted her face toward him, her smile wiped away. "How did that happen?"

"Not sure."

The loudspeaker interrupted their conversation with an announcement about boarding.

Josh grabbed his bag and pulled up Gina with him, and then positioned himself where he could keep an eye on both men. With the second boarding announcement, the two cell phone buddies got on their phones at the same time.

Oh, yeah. They were in cahoots.

The man with the red tie joined the end of the line. So, he was on his way to Isla Perdida. The man near the restrooms stayed at his post, making no move toward the boarding gate. Maybe he had been stationed there to try to take Josh out in the bathroom and give red tie unimpeded access to Gina.

Like he'd ever let that happen.

They shuffled toward the gate, and Gina pressed her shoulder against his arm. "Are we doing this?"

"Don't worry. I'll take care of him."

"I don't think the flight attendants are going to let you throw him off the plane."

"Wouldn't dream of it." As he handed his boarding pass to the attendant, he took one last look over his shoulder at the man by the bathrooms. At least he wouldn't be joining them on the island.

They shuffled onto the small plane with no seat assignments and Josh pinned his gaze on the empty seat behind the man, willing every other passenger away from it. Someone grabbed the seat before Josh could get to it, so he settled for a seat two rows behind the guy with the tie, allowing Gina to scoot in first and grab the window seat.

She raised her dark brows at him, but he just smiled.

The man with the red tie turned his head just once to see where they were sitting, and then settled into his seat, probably figuring his job was done until the plane landed.

Josh's job was just beginning.

Once everyone boarded and the flight attendant recited the safety instructions, the plane taxied and lifted off the runway. It cruised above Miami and out and over the deep blue sea.

Josh pulled his laptop case from beneath the seat in front of him and felt for the pen in the side pocket. He slid it out of the compartment and tucked it into the seat back in front of him.

When they reached cruising altitude, the flight attendants broke out the drink cart. As much as he could use a Bloody Mary right now, Josh ordered some orange juice.

Gina, still nursing her coffee from the terminal, passed on the drinks and ducked her head. "What are you going to do?"

"He may have gotten *on* the plane with us, but I'm going to make sure he doesn't get *off* the plane with us."

The plane bounced and Gina dug her fingers into

her seat's armrest. "I guess since we're here and they're here, I can't claim ignorance anymore."

"They wouldn't have believed you anyway." He drained his juice and placed the empty plastic cup on Gina's tray table. Then he plucked the pen from the seat back and released his seat belt. "I'll be right back."

The bathroom was in the back of the airplane, but he'd have to improvise.

He staggered into the aisle and made his way toward the front of the plane…and the man in the red tie. The plane dipped again, and Josh grabbed someone's seat back.

Just as he drew level with the man's row, a flight attendant came up behind him. "Sir, are you looking for the lavatories?"

"Yes."

As soon as he answered, the man with the red tie whipped his head around, but Josh had anticipated his response.

In one fluid movement, Josh gripped the side of the man's seat, pressed the release for the needle embedded in his pen and jabbed it into the back of the man's neck.

The man bolted forward but before he could utter an exclamation, he slumped back into his seat and his head lolled to the side.

No point in sedating someone if the drug wasn't fast acting.

"The lavatory is in the back of the plane, sir."

"Thanks." Josh cupped the needle in his hand and backed up to let the flight attendant squeeze past him.

She didn't give a second look to the man sleeping in his seat like so many others.

Josh maneuvered to the back, weaving with the turbulence common on these smaller planes. As he passed their row, Gina glanced up at him and he winked.

He locked himself in the bathroom and rolled back his shoulders. That was easier than he thought it would be…and badass.

He flushed the needle down the toilet, washed his hands and exited the lavatory, nodding at the woman waiting to use it. Then he slid into his seat and snapped on his seat belt.

"What happened? I didn't hear any commotion."

"I put our friend to sleep. He's not going to be getting off this plane for a long time."

Chapter Nine

As they exited the plane, Gina inched past the man in the suit and red tie as his seatmate nudged him.

"Sir? Sir, we've landed."

What would the flight attendants do when they couldn't wake him? Probably call an ambulance. Served him right.

She stared down into his face, but she didn't recognize him. Who were these strange people who had taken over Los Santos?

"Miss? Miss? This man is sleeping and won't move."

Gina exited the plane with Josh right behind her, propelling her forward with a hand at her back.

He said, "I doubt anyone saw me deliver the sleeping aid, but let's get out of here. He may be meeting someone else on this end."

Dragging her suitcase behind her, Gina quickened her pace to keep up with Josh's long legs. The humidity of the island had seeped into the terminal, and the light blouse she wore stuck to her back.

Josh's employers—whoever they were—had paid for the trip, or at least they would once they got the bill from Josh Edwards's credit card. Josh had assured her that money was no object, so he'd booked them into the most exclusive resort on the island—the same one she'd stayed at with her father on that fateful trip—the one that had changed her life.

Since they had no checked luggage, they sailed through Customs and snagged a taxi at the curb.

The driver placed their bags in his trunk and slid into the driver's seat.

Josh leaned forward and said, "Perdida Resort and Spa, *por favor*."

The cabbie adjusted his rearview mirror. "First visit to the island?"

Josh answered for both of them, squeezing her knee while he did so. "Yes, first time."

"I have a cousin who can show you around the island. Good price just for you."

"Thanks, man, but we're doing more business than pleasure."

"Money, money, money." The driver grinned, displaying his gold front tooth. "Isla Perdida has so much to offer but everyone sees the money."

Josh laughed. "We'll take some time to enjoy the resort if that makes you feel better."

"It does, senor. I'll give you my cousin's card just in case."

Thirty minutes later, the taxi pulled in front of the lush Perdida Resort and Spa. After he delivered their bags to the curb, the driver fished a card from his front pocket and extended it to Josh. "Just in case—for anything. They call him Fito, and he knows the island inside and out. Tell him his *primo* Robbie sent you."

"Gracias, Robbie." Josh pocketed the card and waved off the bellhops hovering to take their two small bags.

Gina's gaze swept the lobby. "Did you notice anyone suspicious?"

"Everyone looks suspicious to me now."

"Me, too." She pinched the ends of her blouse and fanned it up and down. "I could use a dip in the ocean."

Josh tapped a framed menu of spa services on the counter. "I could use a massage. My muscles are tied in knots right now."

"I guess navy SEALs aren't accustomed to the cloak-and-dagger stuff, huh?"

She drew her brows over her nose. What *were* SEALs accustomed to? She still didn't have a clue what Josh was doing at her father's compound. Protecting the CIA? Didn't seem like those CIA agents with the sniper rifles needed much protection. Maybe the SEALs had gotten the CIA in and out of the region.

She'd often wondered how the CIA had gotten into position around her father's compound. Must've had something to do with the SEALs. So, indirectly, Josh was responsible for her father's death—and Ricky's. And her father was indirectly responsible for his mother's death.

"Checking in?" The hotel clerk tapped the keyboard of her computer.

Josh slid their phony passports across the counter. "Josh and Gina Edwards."

Gina couldn't stop the butterflies that took off in her belly when she heard their names linked. They'd be sharing a room, pretending to be husband and wife.

Pretending was the key word. Behind closed doors they'd revert to…whatever it was they were. Partners? Coworkers? A couple linked by fate?

She watched his strong fingers grip the hotel's pen

as he signed the registration form. Not that she'd mind continuing the pretense in their hotel room. Josh exuded strength and confidence—must be his military bearing. Josh didn't have a weak bone—or muscle—in his body.

After witnessing her father's machismo, Gina had convinced herself she wanted a softer man, but in Ricky's case softer didn't equal better.

"Take the elevator past the lobby restaurant to the sixth floor and let us know if there's anything we can do to make your stay more comfortable."

Gina had a fleeting thought. *Can you keep drug dealers off our tail while we're here?*

Josh swept the key cards from the counter and took Gina's arm. "Will do, thanks."

When they got to their room, Gina glanced at the king-size bed on her way to the sliding doors to the balcony. She stepped outside, and the moist island air caressed her cheek. She called back inside. "We have an amazing view—the pool below and the ocean beyond."

Josh followed her outside and braced his hands against the railing. "Wow. This sure beats any other place I'd be right now on deployment."

She pointed to the right. "Do you see that cluster of buildings over there? That's where the bank is."

"They know you as Gina De Santos, right?"

"Yes. My electronic thumbprint is on file. It's the only way we're getting into my father's safe-deposit box."

"I'd say that's secure."

"And that's why I'm confident anything my father wanted to keep from his associates would be in that box."

"If the deal was going through, why would he keep it from his associates?"

"Maybe that's just it—the deal wasn't going through, or he wasn't sure or he didn't trust a bunch of terrorists. Imagine that?"

"That's kind of a case of the pot calling the kettle black, isn't it? Or are you going to try to tell me your father and husband were really honorable men."

Gina jerked away from him. Why did Josh always have to come back to that accusatory tone? He'd assured her that he didn't blame her for his mother's death at her father's orders. Was he lying to her? To himself?

She turned away from the beautiful view with ashes in her mouth. "I call dibs on the bed, but the sofa looks comfortable."

She slid the balcony door closed, leaving Josh out there by himself. Two could play that game. She was helping him, helping him and the US government, which had taken away everything she owned and had worked for in her life.

The money she'd used to start her restaurant hadn't come from her father. It had been an inheritance from her maternal grandmother, who'd been disgusted by her daughter's marriage to a drug dealer. Mami hadn't lived long enough to see her granddaughter make the same mistake—thank God.

The DEA hadn't cared about any of that. They'd seized everything after Ricky's death.

She dragged the zipper across her bag with such force, it broke. She cursed, which she never did around RJ. She cursed again.

The sliding door opened behind her. "Trying to keep the air-conditioning inside?"

"Yeah, that's it." She kept her back to him and pulled her toiletry bag from her suitcase. "We're too late to go to the bank today, so I'm going down to the beach to take that ocean swim."

"Closing at noon is really what I call banker's hours." He flicked the lock on the door. "I'll join you."

"We don't have to pretend to be married. You don't even have to pretend to like me." She stood up, clutching her skimpiest bikini to her chest. "I can handle a dip in the ocean by myself."

"I'm not going to allow you to run around Isla Perdida by yourself. They know we're here. I couldn't exactly murder the guy on the plane, so he may be showing up as early as tonight. Although the fact that we made him is going to make it hard for him to carry out his original assignment."

Josh unzipped his own suitcase and yanked out a pair of board shorts. "And I don't have to pretend."

"What?" She scowled at him over her shoulder on the way to the bathroom.

"I don't have to pretend to like you. I like you...a lot."

She'd closed the bathroom door on his last two words. Had he meant for her to hear them? Probably just playing her like every other man in her life had done.

She leaned into the mirror, the red bikini clutched in her hands giving her face a rosy stain. She dropped the bathing suit to the floor.

Nope—that pink flush was totally due to Josh Elliott, damn him.

If he liked her a lot, why did he keep needling her about her father? Did he think she didn't know her father was a dirtbag? She knew better than anyone else.

Of course, she'd never told Josh that, but he had to know. Didn't he?

She stripped off her sticky clothes and kicked them into the corner. Then she shimmied into her bikini bottoms and clasped the top around her neck. She nabbed a plush towel from the shelf beneath the vanity and wrapped it around her body.

Exiting the bathroom, she stumbled to a stop as she saw Josh tying the strings of his board shorts. "You changed out here?"

He spread his arms. "Is there a problem? I knew I'd be done before you."

She swallowed as she took in his hard muscles and washboard abs. *No problem at all.*

Her nose in the air, she dipped beside her suitcase and pulled out a beach cover-up. "Maybe you should just wait next time. I wouldn't appreciate surprising a naked man in my hotel room."

Liar.

Josh's mouth turned up on one side as he folded his clothes neatly, telling her that he totally knew she was lying.

Whistling, he brushed past her on the way to the bathroom, a plastic bag filled with men's toiletries tucked beneath one arm.

Was he flexing his muscles?

As soon as he disappeared into the cavernous bathroom, Gina whipped off the towel and pulled her black cover-up over her head. Just because he enjoying flaunting his assets, he couldn't expect her to feel the same way.

She was a mother, damn it.

The third curse word from her lips within the space

of fifteen minutes gave her a reckless thrill, which she recognized all too well. She hadn't been this excited about being with a man since she'd first met Ricky, even though this man infuriated her most of the time.

Josh strolled back into the room, pointing at the towel she'd dropped on the bed. "I'm pretty sure the hotel will have beach towels by the pool and cold water and food. Maybe after we come in from the ocean, we should make a pit stop at the pool. The pool practically spills into the ocean."

"Sounds good. I'm getting hungry." Gina placed a hand on her stomach.

"I'll take my key and put it in my pocket." He held up his key card. "Everything else we can just charge to the room, so we don't have to leave anything on the sand when we go in the water."

"Actually, Isla Perdida has a low crime rate."

"That's because all the crime is the white-collar variety and taking place at the banks in town." Josh crouched next to his bag, rummaging through it.

"You have a point." A shiver ran through Gina as she remembered their purpose on the island. If they didn't find any clues in her father's safe-deposit box, would Josh suspect her of finagling a trip to Isla Perdida for her own reasons?

Why did she feel she had to make him trust her? He was here on some secret assignment and he had orders to protect her, whether or not he trusted her. But to have a man like Josh Elliott really and truly on her side? That would go a long way to restore her self-worth, which various government agencies had been tearing down since the assassinations last year.

Of course, Josh was one big, fat government representative, wasn't he? US Navy, CIA, FBI. Who knows what other acronym he supported?

Josh waved a bottle of sunscreen in the air. "We're both gonna need this."

"Bring it." She stuffed her feet into a pair of flip-flops. "I'm ready."

They made their way down to the lobby, which was open to the outdoors and the pool area. Gina waved to the honeymooning couple, who'd come over on their flight, now draped over a couple of chaise longues.

Her flip-flops smacked against the pool deck as she followed Josh to the private beach, for resort guests only.

As soon as Josh's toes touched the sand, three or four hotel employees swarmed them asking if they needed chairs, towels, a cabana, a drink.

It all sounded good to her, and Gina agreed to everything. If the US government was paying, they owed her anyway.

Josh straddled his chaise longue beneath the shade of a tent, inches away from the turquoise water lapping at the fine white sand. He squirted some sunscreen into his palm and smoothed it over his chest.

The glistening oil highlighted the flat planes of his pecs even more, and he resembled a photo in one of those hot navy SEAL calendars—not that she knew if those calendars even existed, but if they did, Josh could be April.

He finished rubbing his hands all over the front of his body, and then he tossed the bottle to her. "Can you get my back?"

Was he kidding?

She cleared her throat. "Sure."

He stood up and turned his back to her. "I already got my shoulders and my sides. If you could just hit my shoulder blades and below, that would get me covered."

She shook the bottle and squeezed out a puddle of white goop into her hand. She rubbed her hands together and dragged them down Josh's back, his warm, smooth flesh marred by a gnarly scar on his lower left side.

Her fingers trailed across the uneven ridges of skin. "What happened here?"

"Bullet wound."

She gasped, but pressed against the scar even harder. "I guess that's a hazard of the job."

"Happened before I was in the navy."

The words hung in the air as she waited for an explanation. None was forthcoming.

"Thanks." He spun around and zigzagged his index finger in the air, over her body. "I'll wait until you get oiled up."

"Oh, right." She still had on her black beach cover-up, which hit just above her knees. She dropped the sunscreen bottle onto her chaise longue and yanked the billowing garment up and over her head.

She immediately regretted packing her smallest bikini when she got a load of Josh's eyes, practically bugging out of his skull.

It was not like she was a skinny girl. She could fill out a bikini with the best of them, but why'd she have to choose this particular trip to do so?

She was a mother, damn it.

She grabbed the bottle and applied sunscreen over all the bits that had been covered up from the Florida sun these past several months.

After his initial gawking, Josh had appointed himself

towel monitor, shaking out their two towels and placing them on the loungers.

Gina did her best to hit the spots within reach on her back, but if she didn't ask Josh for help she'd have red blotches all over her flip side from the intense Caribbean sun.

"Would you mind?" She held out the bottle. "Same, I got my shoulders and sides, just need those hard-to-reach places covered."

"You got it."

She presented her back to him and nearly jumped out of her skin when his rough hands skimmed over her flesh.

He rubbed his hands in circles, rough enough so that her body kept swaying forward. She didn't object to his strategy for turning the application of sunscreen into an athletic event rather than a seductive one.

Then his fingertip tripped over the edge of her bikini bottoms, and heat that had nothing to do with the island surged through her body.

"That's good, thanks." She stayed turned around to compose herself and scoop her hair into a ponytail.

When she peeked over her shoulder at Josh, he'd returned to business by placing the sunscreen bottle on the table between them and straightening out his towel.

"Okay, ready for the water?"

"Absolutely." Gina took a few steps into the crystal clear ocean and continued stepping lightly until the water enveloped her waist-high. "Ah, perfect temperature."

Josh dashed past her, splashing and kicking up droplets of water, until he dived headfirst into a gentle wave.

A few snorkelers' tubes stuck up from the surface

as they paddled with their fins on their search for sea life. A couple was swimming out to the reef that created a semicircle around their private beach, and a boat bobbed lazily just beyond the reef.

Josh's head popped up. "Feels great. It's not too deep and the waves are mild."

The water crept up to Gina's chest and she pushed her toes off the sandy bottom and dog-paddled toward Josh. If she were wearing a more practical bathing suit, she'd take a swim along that reef.

Josh ducked his head beneath the surface and came back up, sluicing his dark hair back from his face. "Maybe we should've picked up some snorkeling gear by the pool."

"We're not exactly on vacation." Gina tipped her head back and kicked out her legs so that she was floating on her back. Closing her eyes, she fluttered her hands at her sides to propel herself backward.

The sun warmed her cheeks and the salt water beaded on her body. The motion rocked her back and forth, and the tension in her muscles melted away. Why hadn't she taken a vacation since the raid at her father's compound? She'd needed one…badly.

After the deaths of her father and Ricky, she never felt as if she deserved a vacation. The people who'd questioned and accused her had made her feel lower than dirt…even when she'd explained her situation to them.

That's why she hadn't told Josh anything about that time. She wouldn't be able to stomach the disbelief and contempt in his eyes.

She eased out a breath, the warm ocean water bubbling at her lips. As she blew out another breath, a pair of firm hands encircled her waist from below and she found herself airborne, flying over the surface of the water before landing several feet away with a splash.

Gurgling and sputtering, she flailed her arms to regain her balance and dug her toes into the sand to gain purchase. When she rubbed the water from her eyes, a view of Josh laughing materialized a few feet in front of her.

"That was not funny."

"Sure it was. You looked so peaceful, I couldn't resist."

"You're sadistic. I could've drowned or had a heart attack thinking you were a shark."

He snorted and started paddling toward her. "We're in about five feet of water with no rip current, and I'm pretty sure there are no sharks inside the reef."

"Really? You're pretty sure?" She tugged at her bikini beneath the water to make sure everything was back in place.

He swam up next to her and put his hand vertically on his forehead to mimic a shark fin. "Well, I wasn't a shark, was I?"

"You'd better watch your back, SEAL."

He spit some water past her left ear. "Did you get your suit back on?"

"What does that mean?" She hit the surface of the water with her palm to splash water in his face. "Is that why you did it?"

He chuckled. "That's not why I did it, but it did turn out to be a side benefit."

What exactly had he seen? Those butterflies took flight in her belly again and a warm ache crept lower than that.

"You're…desperate."

"Honestly, that red bikini doesn't leave much to the imagination anyway."

"What are you talking about? It's just a bikini. It's a lot more modest than a couple of suits we passed on our way across the pool deck."

"Yeah, but those women… Let's just say they don't fill those suits out quite the way you do."

A tingling sensation raced all across her skin, and she crossed her arms. She had to gain control of this situation, of herself. "We're here under dangerous conditions with dangerous people after us on a dangerous mission."

Josh lifted his shoulders, water trickling down his bunched muscles. "Then it only makes sense that I'm with a dangerous woman with some seriously dangerous curves."

She didn't know how it happened. The water must've carried them closer together, but all of a sudden she and Josh were face-to-face, chest to chest even, as her breasts, safely back in their little triangles of red material, brushed the solid ridge of his pectoral muscles.

His hand rested on the curve of her hip, and the buoyancy of the water helped him to lift her up and draw her even closer.

Her toes bumped his shins and she could see droplets of water sparkling on the ends of his stubby black lashes. Her gaze dropped to his lips, parted and moist and she wanted nothing more than to taste the salt on his mouth.

His hand skimmed down her back and clutched one side of her buttocks to hold her in place as he angled his mouth over hers.

She sipped the salt water from his lips. Even his tongue tasted of the salty sea as he probed her mouth with it.

His fingers curled into the soft flesh of her bottom as he dragged her closer, his erection poking against her thigh.

She sucked his tongue harder and undulated her hips, so that his fingers slipped beneath the material of her bikini bottoms. The rough pads of his fingertips abraded her bare derriere, and she let out a breathy moan.

She could wrap her legs around him, right here in the ocean and let him take her. In fact, that's exactly what was going to happen. She hooked one leg around his hip, opening herself up to him.

He made a strangled noise as he broke their lip-lock and with one hand, reached under the water between them. He shoved aside the thin material of her bikini bottoms and swept one finger across her swollen flesh.

If he did that one more time, she'd come right here in the water, in view of...

"Hey, hey! Help!"

Josh jerked his head around and released her so abruptly, she sank before she started kicking her legs to tread water.

She looked over Josh's shoulder at the small motorboat beyond the reef and the man standing in it, waving his arms over his head.

"Looks like he's having trouble with his boat."

Gina launched forward in the water and swam toward the reef. As she turned her head to take a breath, Josh grabbed her ankle and she rolled onto her back. "What are you doing?"

"Take it slow. We don't know who this guy is."

"He's a tourist who needs help." She shook off his hand and backstroked closer to the reef and the sputtering boat. "You took care of the guy on the plane."

Josh pulled up beside her with a powerful stroke. "Let me go first. You wait here on the other side of the reef. Maybe he's just stuck and needs a lift from below, if his boat isn't damaged."

Gina allowed Josh to pass her but paddled after him. There was no way the man with the red tie's replacement was in Isla Perdida so soon and she found it hard to believe someone had already been here waiting for them, even though Josh had sounded that warning.

She squinted at Josh as he drew up to the reef and shouted something at the stranded tourist.

Two seconds later, Josh twisted his head around and yelled, "Duck! He's got a gun."

Chapter Ten

Josh dived beneath the surface, and a bullet whizzed by his head, slicing through the water. Through the clear Caribbean water, he could see Gina's legs kicking. Was she still upright?

He had a suspicion that a different fate awaited Gina once the phony tourist did away with him, but a bullet wound to her shoulder or arm would incapacitate her enough for the guy to scoop her up.

Josh snapped his legs hard in a breaststroke to reach Gina. He wrapped his arms around her legs and dragged her down.

With her eyes wide and bubbles spewing from her mouth, Gina joined him below and powered her arms through the water.

The man in the boat wouldn't be able to get his craft around the reef before Josh and Gina made it to shore, but he could climb onto the reef with his weapon to improve his aim. Somehow, Josh didn't think the man shooting at them would be bothered by the fact that disturbing sea life was a crime in Isla Perdida.

With his lungs ready to explode, Josh continued toward the beach, his arms and legs burning with the effort, Gina right beside him, matching him stroke for stroke, kick for kick.

She tugged on his board shorts and pointed toward the surface with her thumb.

He'd probably surprised her by dragging her under and she hadn't had time to take a deep breath. He wasn't going to allow her to surface on her own. Positioning himself between Gina and the man with the gun, Josh took her by the arms and rose through the water with her.

They broke the surface together and as he filled his lungs with air, Josh cranked his head over his shoulder. The boat that had feigned trouble had disappeared, and the small sailboat from earlier was now swaying behind the reef in its place. Had the sailboat scared off the shooter?

Josh wasn't taking any chances. He tapped Gina on the shoulder and she gave him a quick nod and ducked below again.

When the water became too shallow to completely cover them, Josh stopped swimming and stood up, planting his feet in the silky sand.

On her knees beside him, Gina coughed and sputtered.

"Are you okay?"

"I am now."

Josh swiveled his head from side to side, looking out for the motorboat, allowing Gina to gulp in some air and get her bearings. The few people in the shade of their cabana tents didn't even look up when he and Gina had staggered to the shore. Nobody had noticed the action in the water.

He swallowed as he glanced down at Gina, kneeling

in the surf, her chest heaving, the water glistening on her skin. No wonder he hadn't been able to resist her out there in the sea. Couldn't stop himself from touching her, from kissing her, from wanting her.

And he'd put them both in danger because of it.

He crouched beside her and brushed a strand of wet hair from her cheek. "Do you need me to help you up?"

"I'm good." She coughed and allowed one more swell from the ocean to wash over her before pushing up to her feet with one hand, tugging at her bathing suit bottoms with the other.

The honeymoon couple strolled past them hand in hand, and the woman waved. "How's the water?"

"Lovely." Gina smiled and murmured under her breath, "If you like bullets with your salt water."

Steps away in their cabana, Josh collapsed in his chaise longue. "I'm sorry. We should've never gone near that boat."

"Why are you apologizing?" Gina clutched her towel to her chest and dabbed her face with one corner. "I'm the one who insisted the guy was a hapless tourist who needed our help. I should've listened to you."

"I shouldn't be letting you insist anything. I'm supposed to be protecting you, and I never should've allowed you anywhere near that boat." He smacked his hand on the table between them, and knocked the bottle of sunscreen to the ground. "I was letting my other head rule."

Red flares claimed both of her cheeks. "What does that mean?"

"You know damned well what it means, Gina. I allowed my…lust for you to overrule my common sense."

She dropped to her chaise longue, wrapping the towel

tightly around her body. "That's ridiculous. Even if we hadn't been...uh...kissing, that boat would've come at us anyway."

"Not if I'd been paying attention to our surroundings instead of how damned hot you looked in that little bikini."

"Should I have worn a one-piece suit up to my chin and down to my knees?" She tilted her head and squeezed water out of her ponytail.

"You shouldn't have been wearing anything at all."

"Really?" She raised one eyebrow. "I think that would've made things worse...or better depending on your perspective."

"You know what I meant. You should've never changed into a swimsuit, and we should've stayed in the room." He shook his head. "We were just tracked into the ocean somehow and someone's taking potshots at me and you're cracking jokes."

"Technically, that wasn't a joke and he was taking potshots at both of us."

"I wouldn't be too sure of that." Josh toweled off his head and when he emerged, Gina was staring at him. He asked, "What?"

"He was just shooting at you?"

"You tell me. I approached the reef, he turned a gun on me and I ducked. I saw the bullet plunge through the water. Did he shoot again? Did he shoot at you?"

"No." She nibbled on the end of one of her fingers. "He took another shot at you in the water, and then he stood there with his weapon raised waiting for you to surface."

"He wanted to take me out to get to you. Who knows?

He may have had another weapon for you—one that shoots tranquilizer darts instead of bullets."

"You think so?" She hugged the towel more tightly around her body.

"They don't want you dead. They want to march you into that bank and have you give them access to your father's safe-deposit box, or whatever it is they think you're after on this island."

A waiter ducked his head beneath their awning. "Drinks, senor?"

"Sure, I'll have a cerveza, the island brand."

"Tequila sunrise for me—heavy on the tequila."

When the waiter left, Josh raised his brows. "Still need to take the edge off, huh?"

"Look at this." She held out one trembling hand. "I can't believe how stupid I was to trust a stranger like that."

"I can't believe how distracted I was to let you." He put on his sunglasses and reclined his lounger. "That can't happen again, Gina, and I apologize."

She smacked his calf. "You have nothing to apologize for. Sun, surf, skin—we just got carried away. This island could put a spell on you if you let it, and we've been under a lot of pressure."

"Back to business then. The bank opens at nine o'clock tomorrow morning. Make sure you bring everything you need to prove your identity and leave the fake ID at the hotel."

"I've been through the routine before with my father. I know what to do."

"Can I ask you a question?" He crossed his right index finger over his left in a protective gesture because every time he asked her anything about her father or his business, she got defensive.

"Yes."

"What were you doing here with your father, and why did he take you to the bank?"

She blew out a breath and shoved her sunglasses up to her head. "He wanted to prove a point to me."

"Which was?"

"You have to promise me you won't relay this information to anyone you work for—not the CIA, not the DEA."

"Is it going to get anyone killed?"

"No."

He held up two fingers. "Scout's honor, even though I was never a Boy Scout."

"Didn't think so." She chugged some water from one of the bottles the waiter had placed on the table while taking their order. "He wanted to show me where my mother's money was coming from."

"Why? You didn't know?"

"No. My father's family in Colombia had money. Mom had always told me that the settlement she received from my father for the separation had come from his family's money."

"That didn't turn out to be true." Josh had scooted forward on the chaise longue, digging his feet into the sand on either side of it.

When the waiter appeared with their drinks, Josh almost tossed him out for interrupting the flow of Gina's thoughts. She'd never told him this much before. Maybe kissing her in the ocean *hadn't* been such a mistake—his body hadn't thought so at all.

He thanked the waiter and scribbled the room number and his signature on the check. Wrapping his fingers around the beer bottle, Josh turned to Gina and waited.

She put her lips to the straw stuck in her glass and took a sip of the orange concoction inside. Then she bit off the point of the pineapple slice that was balanced precariously on the edge of her glass.

Josh held his breath.

She licked her fingers and then wiped them off on the towel still encasing her body like armor. "My father's family shunned him and disinherited him when they learned he was a drug dealer. He and my mother didn't get a dime from them."

"Why did your father want to show you where your mom was getting the money?"

"To control me."

Josh finally took a sip of his own drink. "Why did he need to control you?"

She pinned him with her dark eyes, flashing fire. "Why do you think? By this time, I'd figured out what he did for a living, and I wanted nothing to do with him. I wanted to walk away from it all, from him... from my marriage."

Josh's pulse jumped. *Her marriage.* Had she wanted to leave Ricky? It's what he'd wanted to hear from her all along. "Did your father think you'd rat him out?"

"I don't think so." She shrugged. "I probably wouldn't have gone that far. I didn't know anything the DEA hadn't already figured out."

"Your father didn't realize that?"

"My father was a man who took very few chances... even with his daughter."

"So, he showed you the money, and maybe how it was laundered for your mother, to prove your mother's complicity in his crimes. If you ever told anyone about the money or any of his business deals—" Josh drew a finger across his throat "—he'd either cut off your mother or she'd go down with him—at least for the financial crimes."

"That's it. My father knew I'd never do anything to disrupt my mother's life."

"Why didn't he let you walk away after that? He'd just assured your silence. Why were you still visiting him at his compound at the end?"

She sighed and sucked down half of her drink. "It's so complicated—*familia*."

Josh's heart sank. "You mean no matter what your father, your mother or your...husband did, you could forgive and forget to keep it in the family?"

Gina snorted and tossed back the rest of her drink. "No. It was my father who had a warped sense of family loyalty and what that means.

"I wasn't at his compound that day or any other day to find comfort in the bosom of my family."

"What then?" Josh pressed his cold, sweating bottle against his forehead.

"My father wanted—no, demanded—to see RJ."

"That's what he wanted from you? That's why he wanted to keep you close?"

"RJ is his only grandchild. He was afraid I'd take him away and he'd never see him again."

"Would you have done that?"

She blinked. "In a second."

"Your father threatened to take your mother's money away from her or turn her in if you didn't bring RJ around?"

"It was worse than that, Josh." She dropped her chin to her chest and shook her glass so that the ice tinkled.

"Worse?" Josh licked his dry lips and switched his beer for a bottle of water. Since Gina had turned toward a confessional mood, he wanted to find out the truth behind her marriage to Ricky Rojas.

He had to know how Gina felt about the man he'd killed.

"What was your husband's take on all this? He was okay with your son being in the company of a drug kingpin?"

She flicked her wet ponytail over her shoulder. "Ricky did whatever my father told him to do. In fact, he married me to get in with my father."

Josh could think of a million reasons why a man would want to marry Gina, but getting in good with her father wasn't one of them.

"Ricky knew all about Hector De Santos and Los Santos when you two started dating?"

"Ricky knew about my father *before* we started dating. He knew about my father before I did." She rolled the slender glass between her palms. "Ricky targeted me. He managed to get a job in the same restaurant where I worked and then really laid it on thick. I was such an idiot."

"Why would you even suspect Ricky's motives?" Josh shifted forward, walking his feet in the sand, and grabbed one of her hands, chilly and wet from the glass. "I'm sure a smooth SOB like Ricky knew just what the ladies wanted to hear."

"He knew what *this* lady wanted to hear." She jabbed a thumb at the towel still covering her chest. "I remember my father from when I was a child—the fights with

Mom, the violence, the swaggering machismo. I wanted none of it, and Ricky played into that. He was a poet, a musician…an aspiring crook."

"How long into your marriage before he made the move toward your father?"

"Long enough for me to be pregnant with RJ. Ricky knew that would be the glue, the true way into my father's heart—and his cartel."

"So, that's what you meant by worse. You were all tied up with your father, your husband, your child. I'm sure you had your reasons to stay." Josh released her hand and skimmed a palm across the top of his head.

He understood her apprehension about taking RJ and leaving, but the words from her mouth still sounded like excuses to him—just like the excuses his mother used to make.

"That is *not* what I meant." Gina put her glass down on the table with a click. "You think I stayed with my husband and brought my precious son to visit my murdering, psychotic father because of family ties and some money of my mother's?"

She sloughed off her towel and straddled the chaise longue, her shoulders back and her spine straight. "I brought my son around because my father threatened to take RJ and keep him away from me forever, bringing him into the business."

Chapter Eleven

Through the shade of her sunglasses, Gina watched the emotions play across Josh's face. Did she see relief in there somewhere?

Would her story finally convince him that she'd wanted no part of her father's drug empire and no part of her marriage with Ricky?

When Josh spoke, his words came out in measured, dull syllables as if he were suppressing a great rage. "How did your father intend to keep your son from you?"

"Really?" She shook her glass of rapidly melting ice. "My father had money and power in Colombia—politicians, judges, law enforcement officials—all in the palm of his hand. He gave me a taste of that power once, took RJ right away from me for a week."

"Your husband was okay with it?"

"My husband aided and abetted my father, and was handsomely rewarded for doing so. Even if I had initiated divorce proceedings against Ricky, my father would've seen to it that Ricky would win sole custody of RJ and I would've been shut out completely." Gina shivered in the heat.

A muscle ticked in Josh's tight jaw. "Is that why you were so anxious to find out if Ricky was alive?"

"Did you think I was anxious to reunite with my dead husband to rekindle our great romance?" Her lip curled. Ricky the poet and musician had completely morphed into something unrecognizable once he'd wormed his way into her father's organization. She never let him touch her again.

"I'm sorry. I shouldn't have made any assumptions."

The waiter showed up at their cabana again and while Josh waved him off, Gina held up her glass. *"Uno más, por favor."*

Josh wasn't finished with her yet. "Did you tell the DEA about your father's threats?"

"Yeah, but I don't think they believed me, and of course I didn't say anything about my mother's money or this bank account."

"Maybe that's why the agents didn't believe your story. They sensed you were lying about something."

"They were right." She collapsed back in the chaise longue, a great weight sloughing off her shoulders. "Do you trust me now?"

"Trust you? It was never about trust, Gina."

"Oh, yeah, it was. Sometimes you looked at me like…" She scrunched up her nose. "Like I was a bug to be squashed, and that was even before you found out about your mother."

His eyebrows jumped to his hairline. "I never thought of you as a bug—to be squashed or otherwise."

She waved her hands. "Okay, well, maybe we can just put that behind us. I wasn't in league with my father or my husband or any of Los Santos. I was just trying to protect my mother, my son. Now I'm trying to help you."

"I'm supposed to be helping you."

"Can't we help each other? You seem like a guy who needs help."

The waiter ducked beneath their awning with another tequila sunrise on a tray. Josh signed for the drink.

Toying with the swizzle stick loaded with fruit, Gina took a sip of the sweet drink but had lost her desire for it once her confession had ended.

"This—" Josh spread his hands "—isn't personal for me, you know. I was sent here on assignment by my superiors, and I obey orders."

"Hmm." She dragged her sunglasses to the tip of her nose with one finger and studied him over the top of the frame. "Not personal, huh?"

"You mean what happened in the water between us? That was… What did you say? Sun, surf and skin? You're a damned attractive woman, Gina, sexy as hell. I'm a red-blooded, American male, and I made a mistake."

She flicked her fingers at him. "I'm not talking about the…heat between us. There's something about this assignment that has gotten under your skin. Taking down Los Santos and making sure they stay out of business—" she thumped her chest with her fist "—means something to you, now more than ever."

He lifted his broad shoulders. "Law, order, truth, justice and the American way."

"If you say so, SEAL." She sucked down some more tequila.

"Are you ready to pack it up?" He leveled a finger at her half-full glass. "Or are you going to finish that?"

"They're pretty strong. That first one did the trick, took the edge off after our mad swim to shore." She dipped her head and scanned the ocean. She could just make out two heads bobbing close to the reef—*must be the honeymoon couple.* "Where do you think he went?"

"Back where he came from. My guess is that he lives here. Could just be a gun for hire, or maybe he's on retainer with the cartels to take care of business. There's no way Los Santos got someone to this island before we even arrived."

"Is it just Los Santos I have to worry about?" She stood up and pulled her beach cover-up over her head. "There were two parties screwed in that deal, right? If there are missing weapons as well as drugs, the people on the receiving end of those weapons must be just as invested in finding them as Los Santos is in finding the drugs."

"That's true."

She wedged a hand on her hip. "So, what are we talking about here, SEAL? Terrorists? Are you telling me I have a terrorist cell on my tail?"

He picked up her drink and downed it. "Yeah, you do. *We* do."

WHEN THEY GOT back to the hotel, Josh decided to pay a visit to the harbor to inquire about boat rentals and to see if he could get a line on anyone who'd rented a small motorboat that afternoon.

He paused at the hotel door. "You're not planning to take any more swims in the sea, are you?"

"Nope. I'm going to take a shower and sit on the balcony with my book, feet up."

"Good. Don't leave the room and don't open the door. Don't order room service or anything from housekeeping and keep the chain on."

"You're making me nervous." In fact, she'd been more than nervous once Josh admitted what she'd suspected deep down all along—she had some very bad guys after her.

"That's not a bad thing, to be nervous." He smacked the doorjamb. "I'll be waiting outside until I hear you lock and chain the door."

She turned from the window and crossed the room. "I'm on it."

Stepping into the hallway, Josh pulled the door closed behind him and Gina locked the top bolt and hooked the chain across.

She shut and locked the balcony doors for good measure, even though their room sat on the sixth floor, the top floor of the hotel. Then she grabbed her toiletry bag and headed for the bathroom.

She dropped her cover-up on the floor. She peeled off her bikini and stuck it in one of the sinks, running cool water over it. What had possessed her to pack that suit? She had a one-piece that covered a heckuva lot more, but what fun would that have been?

"Face it, girl." She braced her hands against the vanity and leaned in for a close look at her flushed face. "You wanted that SEAL before you even knew he was a SEAL."

She couldn't even explain her immediate chemistry with Josh to herself. Of course, he had the dark good looks she loved in a man and a body that wouldn't quit for days, but there had been some connection between them from the get-go.

Maybe it had to do with the fact that he was there in Colombia when her life had changed forever. What he was doing there, she still wasn't quite sure. It was all kind of strange and mysterious.

She yanked back the semicircular curtain on the shower and walked into the huge, tiled space that sported two showerheads. Perfect for showering with someone, but Josh had made it clear that what had happened in the ocean between them wouldn't happen again.

Sighing, she cranked on both faucets just because she could, allowing the dual jets to spray her front and back at the same time. Decadence.

She finished showering and put on a sundress— loose, modest, comfortable. She grabbed a book and padded out to the balcony with bare feet. Hanging over the railing, she watched the people at the pool, spotting the older couple from the plane but not the newlyweds. They were probably making out in one of the cabanas—lucky.

She sat in one of the chairs, her face shaded and her legs stretched out into the sunshine. Closing her eyes, she wiggled her toes.

She'd been confident her father had left something in his safe-deposit box relating to this deal, but what if she were mistaken? That's another reason why she'd told Josh about her past and the way her father had controlled her. If they found nothing in the safe-deposit box, Josh wouldn't suspect her of ulterior motives in suggesting the trip to Isla Perdida.

After seeing the swimsuit she'd packed, he might suspect her of other ulterior motives—and he wouldn't be far from the mark. The guy had it all in the looks department, but he was no pretty boy. His broad shoulders looked like they could carry the worries of the world... or at least her worries. Even the scars on his body were sexy because she knew he'd gotten them in the commission of good and not evil. Although there was the scar from the bullet wound he'd claimed he'd gotten pre–active duty days. He'd probably gotten it jumping in front of someone else.

A loud knock at the door made her start, and she scrambled out of her comfortable seat and rushed across the room. She peered through the peephole at the man of her recent daydreams.

She unchained the door and opened it. "Any luck?"

"A little." He squeezed past her and turned, holding a gun by the barrel.

Covering her mouth with one hand, she asked, "Where did you get that?"

"Remember Robbie, our taxi driver? He mentioned his cousin?"

"You got a gun from our taxi driver's cousin?"

"Robbie mentioned he could get anything for us."

"So, you naturally assumed that meant a weapon?"

"I read between the lines. His cousin is a go-to guy on the island—drugs, women, weapons. After today's… excitement in the water, I figured I'd need a piece for tomorrow's visit to the bank."

"The bank has metal detectors. You won't get in with that."

"I will if I'm your bodyguard. I already checked with Fito."

"Fito is Robbie's cousin?"

"Yep."

"I feel so—" she spun around with her arms outstretched "—useless. All I managed to do was take a shower and sit on the balcony, enjoying the view."

"That's all you needed to do." Josh crouched in front of the hotel safe in the closet and stashed the gun inside. "I'm going to get cleaned up, and we'll have some dinner."

"You didn't find out anything at the harbor about someone renting a boat?"

"No, but my new best friend, Fito, might be able to help me out there, too."

"If this guy's so darned helpful, maybe he helped the other guy get the boat and the weapon he used to shoot at us." She chewed her bottom lip. "Can you trust him?"

"I can trust him as much as the next payoff. I have no illusions about him, but I'm going to use him when I can." Josh closed the closet door and brushed his hands together. "I'm going to take a shower. You can return to the balcony and continue doing what you were doing out there."

Thinking about Josh Elliott.

"You'll like that shower." She slid open the door to the balcony and closed it behind her. She didn't need to hear that water running and imagine Josh's perfect form getting wet under two sprays of water.

She hung over the side of the balcony and spotted the honeymoon couple by the side of the pool, sitting across from each other at a table, not even talking. Were they sick of each other already?

She shifted her gaze from the pool to the sea beyond. She remembered those heady newlywed days. She'd been so young…and stupid. Ricky had been insistent upon starting a family immediately. She'd been touched by his enthusiasm until she realized the baby was a way to cement her to him and cement him to her father.

She didn't regret one day of RJ's sweet life, so she had a hard time looking back and wishing things had been different. Everything had changed anyway when the CIA decided to assassinate the leading members of Los Santos once they'd gotten in bed with a terrorist cell. That action had probably saved her life…and RJ's.

The door slid open behind her, and Josh put his hands on her shoulders. "Doing okay? How's the view?"

No regrets at all.

She inhaled his fresh scent and straightened up. "I'm fine, and the view is beautiful, as long as it doesn't contain any boats bearing men with guns."

"Pool area still crowded?"

"Plenty of people down there, including our honeymooners from the plane even though they seem to have gotten a little tired of each other." She turned, and Josh dropped his hands from her shoulders. "Where are we having dinner? I'm starving."

"I know there are plenty of five star restaurants on this little island, but would you mind if we just ate in the hotel restaurant? I'd prefer we keep a low profile here."

"I don't think the hotel's restaurant is too shabby either, so that's fine with me." She gave him the once-over in his cargo shorts and light blue button-down shirt.

He tugged on the hem of his shirt. "Too casual?"

"I'm sure it's fine. Most people at the hotel seem to wander from the beach to the pool to the restaurant without breaking their stride."

"Then I'm ready."

"Just need my shoes." She walked back into the room and slipped on a pair of sandals while Josh locked the doors to the balcony.

By the time they got down to the restaurant, people were crowding the edge of the pool area to watch the sunset and had already nabbed all the tables in the dining area.

Josh scanned the packed restaurant. "Should've figured this would be a popular time to eat. We can come back later or maybe order room service."

"I can't wait." Gina patted her stomach.

A woman popped up at one of the prime tables, outside on the patio and facing the sea, and waved. "Over here."

"It's the couple from the plane. I don't think they ever went up to their room."

"Maybe because they already knew what a madhouse it was here at sunset." Josh touched her elbow. "Should we go over?"

A hostess dressed in a flowing pareu floated toward them. "Excuse me. The couple at the edge of the patio would like you to join them for dinner. We are fully booked, otherwise."

Gina shrugged. "Why not? We can eat and run if they bore us."

Josh turned to the hostess. "Yes, we'll join them, thank you."

The hostess guided them to the best seats in the house, and Gina and Josh greeted their newfound friends.

Gina introduced Josh to Tara and Roger, as they'd exchanged names at the airport.

Tara smiled and squeezed her husband's arm. "We were warned about getting in early to watch the sunset."

Gina smiled. "Thank you so much. I was about ready to faint from hunger."

"I can imagine, since you had quite a swim in the ocean today."

Josh nudged Gina's toe with his foot. As if he had to warn her.

Nodding, Gina said, "Yeah, it was, uh, invigorating."

"I'm glad I'm not the only one going casual." Josh tipped his head at Roger, still dressed in his board shorts, although he'd topped them with a green polo shirt.

"We didn't want to miss out on getting a table. Lucky for you we didn't go back to our room or wander around the waterfront."

Josh kicked her under the table, and Gina slid a quick sidelong look at him. Did he think she was going to tell Roger about the taxi driver's cousin and the gun?

"Yep, lucky for us. Thanks again for asking us to join you. Have you ordered yet?"

"Just drinks." Tara picked up the menu. "But the waiter told us about the specials."

A waiter arrived with a tray bearing two margaritas.

"Those look good. I think we'll have a couple of those."

"That tequila sunrise I had on the beach was pretty good."

Josh kicked her again and chuckled. "But now it's sunset. In fact, we'll have a pitcher, please."

If he didn't stop kicking her, he'd get a glass of water in his face. Why was he so set on margaritas and an entire pitcher of them?

They exchanged more small talk about the island until the waiter returned with two more glasses and a pitcher of icy margaritas. The waiter poured drinks for Gina and Josh, and then took their orders.

After another fifteen minutes of chitchat, Josh grabbed the handle of the pitcher and held it up. "Top those off for you?"

Before Tara or Roger could answer, Josh was tipping the pitcher over their glasses, filling them to the top. "We've had a stressful day. I need this right now."

Josh wrapped a hand around his glass and gestured in the air as half his drink sloshed over his hand. *"Salud."*

Now it was her turn to kick him under the table.

Why was he telling good old Tara and Roger about their stressful day? Did he *want* them to start prying?

Tara eyed him over the wide rim of her glass. "I thought Isla Perdida was paradise? You mean you actually experienced stress here?"

Josh sputtered and clamped a napkin to his mouth. "Gina told you we were combining a little business with our pleasure? Well, it's the business part that's stressing us out."

"We wouldn't know about that, would we, Tara? It's strictly pleasure for us." Roger kissed his wife's hand.

"Then drink up."

Gina had no idea what game Josh was playing, but he ordered another pitcher and poured another round of drinks for everyone. Tara and Roger seemed reluctant to imbibe any more, but didn't want to offend Josh so they kept sipping away.

She didn't blame the honeymooners. She'd tossed the contents of at least one glass into the bushes to her left, but pretended to be drinking along with the rest of them.

The food arrived and Josh continued to get louder and louder. He liberally sampled food from the other couple's plates and ordered a third pitcher of margaritas.

Tara had indicated that they were from New York and without ever revealing his own connection to the state, Josh asked Roger questions about it as if he were planning on taking a vacation there.

Gina giggled along with his antics, while casting apologetic looks toward Tara. Roger didn't seem to mind at all. While Tara's heavy lids drooped over her eyes, Roger's speech began to slur and he had trouble retrieving his napkin from the ground.

"I have an idea." Josh snapped his fingers for the

waiter. "Let's hit one of those cabanas on the beach and finish the night with a few cocktails in the sand."

Tara waved her napkin as if waving a white flag. "I'm really tired."

Roger shot his new wife a very unnewlywed glance. "We'd be happy to, mate."

Josh scribbled on the check. "This one's on us."

"Very generous of you." Roger had to help his wife out of her chair.

Josh stumbled for good measure, but Gina didn't think for one minute he was drunk. She grabbed his arm and the four of them tripped out to the sand.

Josh kept prodding them on to the last cabana on the beach, even though it seemed as if Tara and now Roger could barely lift their feet from the sand to take their next step.

When they reached the tent, Josh helped Roger into a chaise longue and then poured Tara into hers. Within minutes, the two newlyweds were passed out cold.

Gina turned on Josh and, in a harsh whisper, asked, "Why in the world did you get those two drunk, and what are the odds that they'd both pass out?"

"Shh." Josh crouched beside Roger and transferred some items from the comatose man's pockets to his pockets. Then he plunged his hand in Tara's purse.

"What are you doing, robbing them?"

Josh held up a key card. "Let's hurry. We'll have a couple of hours to search their room."

"S-search their room?" Her eyes widened as her gaze shifted from one passed-out person to the other.

"What did you think was going on in the restaurant, Gina? These two are the enemy."

Chapter Twelve

Gina's feet felt rooted in the sand, and her jaw dropped open. The handsy newlywed couple, the enemy?

"What did you do to them?"

"Slipped a little something in their margaritas."

"You're a regular walking pharmaceutical repository. People are just dropping in your wake."

Completely sober, he took her arm. "I'll explain on the way to their room. Tara conveniently left her key card in the little envelope with their room number. She's no pro."

When they reached the hotel, Josh took her hand and they skirted the restaurant. No sense in having anyone wonder where the other drunken couple went.

As they raced through the lobby and into the elevator, Gina asked, "How did you know?"

"Tara let it slip that they were from New York. When she did, Roger shot her a look that could kill. Seemed odd, so I brought up something about New York later and it was clear they'd never lived there. Something you said earlier struck me as odd, too. A honeymooning couple that stays at the pool all day, and then the beach and then back at the pool where you said they hardly spoke to each other, let alone kissed?

"Wouldn't a honeymoon couple who were all over

each other like these two were want to spend more time in their hotel room than at the pool? And why were they going down to the water just after we'd been ambushed? To see that the job had been done on me and to help out with you?"

Gina shivered and hunched her shoulders. "But they seemed so...normal."

"And did you catch the *mate* business from Roger when the drug started taking effect on him? No New Yorker I know uses *mate*."

"Do you think they were working with the red tie man on our flight?"

"I don't know, Gina." He squeezed her waist.

Her blood ran cold, and she tripped to a stop as they exited the elevator. "You think both groups are here, don't you? Los Santos and the terrorist organization. They're both after us at the same time."

"Could be." He rubbed a circle on her back. "C'mon, we're almost there."

She scooped in a deep breath and hooked two fingers in the belt loop of Josh's shorts. They didn't see anyone else in the hallway.

When they reached the room, Josh slid the key home and held out a hand to keep her back. "Hang on. We don't know what we're going to find in here."

She hung back in the hallway until he waved her inside. The faux newlyweds' room was much like their own with one interesting detail—two beds.

Josh pointed at the beds. "An odd sleeping arrangement for a couple of honeymooners, wouldn't you say?"

Gina nodded. Either Tara and Roger weren't as committed to their deception as she and Josh were...or they weren't as attracted to each other.

"I'm going to search their suitcases. You look through the closets, drawers and bathroom."

Gina tiptoed to the closet even though she knew Tara and Roger were out cold on the beach with little chance that anyone would discover them until morning, unless they came to in the few hours that Josh gave them. She slid back the door and ran her hand along a few shirts and blouses neatly arrayed on hangers. Careful not to disturb any shoes, she crouched and inspected the floor of the closet.

"Their safe is locked."

"Don't worry. I have a surefire way of getting in there."

"That does not make me feel very confident about hotel safes." She stood on her tiptoes, her gaze sweeping across the iron and a few extra pillows on the closet shelf. "I don't see anything in the closet."

Josh came up behind her. "I found a few interesting items."

She glanced down at his hands, cupping an assortment of bottles and vials. "Looks like you're about to add some inventory to your pharmacy."

"Matches the pills I took from Roger's pocket." He shook one of the bottles. "If I hadn't drugged them first, it would be us passed out on the beach…or worse."

"That's probably why they were so eager to go with us. They hadn't figured out that we—you were onto them and they planned to slip something in our drinks on the sand."

"Exactly. Of course, they weren't thinking very clearly by that time." Josh knelt in front of the safe and after many beeps and clicks, the door swung open. He reached inside the small space and pulled out a couple of passports.

Gina leaned over his shoulder as he flipped them open and read from the passport page. "Roger Nealy and Tara Nealy. Are those fake?"

"As fake as ours." He replaced them in the safe, closing the door but not locking it.

"Shouldn't you lock it up again?"

"I would if I knew how to reset it with the code they used—I don't."

"They're going to figure out we got the jump on them."

"That's okay. They won't pretend to come at us like the hapless honeymooners anymore. The more of them we expose, the less likely they'll be able to surprise us."

Crossing her arms, she said, "Good. I don't like surprises."

Josh's height allowed him to get a better look at the closet shelf, and he lifted the pillows and checked out the iron.

"The iron isn't some kind of secret weapon?"

"I have no idea. I'm a sniper not a spy."

She tilted her head and scrunched up her face. "You…"

"Bathroom? Did you check it out yet? We need to get a move on."

"No."

Chewing her bottom lip, she trailed after him as he strode to the cavernous bathroom, sporting the same dual-head shower as theirs.

"Check her bag." He tipped his head toward a toiletry bag hanging on a hook as he pawed through a masculine version on the counter.

"Do you think they have any weapons in the room?" If Gina hoped to find any poison or hypodermic needles among Tara's stuff, the department store makeup and cleansers were a disappointment. At least this particular spy was thrifty.

"They weren't carrying any, and we know they couldn't have brought them on the plane. Maybe their cohort, the guy on the boat provided them with some guns.

"Tara has nothing."

"Roger either. Nothing in their suitcases with contact info either."

"You didn't expect to find a to-do list, did you? Number one, incapacitate the SEAL. Number two, kidnap the drug kingpin's daughter."

He tugged on a lock of her hair. "Not quite like that."

A cell phone buzzed and Gina patted the pocket of her purse. "Not mine."

"Not mine either." Josh dipped his hand into his shorts pocket and withdrew a vibrating cell phone. "It's Roger's."

"You got Roger's phone?"

"Lifted it from his pocket." He held the phone in front of his face. "Even better. This is a text message, not a phone call."

"You're not going to...?"

"Pretend I'm Roger?" He skimmed his finger across the phone's display. "Watch me."

"What does it say?" She squinted at the words on the display.

Josh read them aloud. "'What's going on?'"

"Good question. What are you going to respond?"

"I'm going to give this texter the good news. My lovely bride and I have the couple in question passed out in a couple of lounge chairs on the beach."

"You're going to send him right to Tara and Roger?"

"I'm going to send him right to me."

Gina grabbed his wrist. "What does that mean?"

"I'm going to direct this guy to the cabana, and I'm going to lie in wait and get some answers."

"That's…dangerous." She tried to swallow but her dry throat made her gag.

"Don't forget. I have that little piece from Fito."

"Josh, you can't shoot someone on Isla Perdida. You can't leave a dead body on the beach."

"Who said anything about any dead bodies? Tara and Roger will still be conked out. This man won't be expecting me, so I'll have the element of surprise. I'll get him at gunpoint and start asking a few questions. I'll be okay."

He twisted his arm out of her grasp and started tapping the phone's screen. "There. Forty-five minutes should give me enough time to retrieve that gun and conceal myself in the cabana with the newlyweds."

"Me, too."

"No way."

"I'm going with you, Josh."

"You're going to stay in the room with the door locked. I don't want you anywhere near this man or this situation."

"You just said it wasn't going to be dangerous."

"I didn't say that." He cupped her face with one hand. "Let me face the danger. You've faced enough—all your life."

Her nose tingled and she blinked her eyes to dispel the tears gathering there. Nobody, not her mother, not Ricky, not the DEA, CIA or the FBI had ever once acknowledged the fear and danger she'd lived with since finding out about her father.

She thought it had come to an end that day at her

father's compound, but she couldn't have been more wrong. Only now she had Josh Elliott to protect her and if he thought she needed to stay in the room for this encounter, she'd do it.

She nodded and sniffed. "All right. I'll wait in the room, but you'd better be careful."

"This is what I do."

Was it? Then what had he been doing at her father's compound?

THEY MADE THEIR way back to their room and Josh had to stuff his hands in his pockets so he wouldn't be tempted to put them all over Gina. He'd expected her to put up more of a fight about being left behind, but she showed a lot of common sense and restraint.

She must've realized that her presence would've added nothing to the trap. She didn't have a weapon of her own, not that he wouldn't have trusted her with one, and he didn't need for her to cause a distraction or have his back. He just needed to know she was safe in the room.

He closed and locked their hotel room door behind them and dived for the safe in the closet. Cradling the gun, he sat on the edge of the bed next to her and loaded it.

"Can I see it?"

Josh extended the butt of the gun to her and she gripped it, testing its heft and weight. "Nice little piece."

"Not bad."

"Please be careful. I shudder to think what the Isla Perdida *policía* would do to you if they arrested you for murder."

"That's not going to happen." He leaned forward and

kissed the top of her head. Then he took the gun from her and stuck it in the waistband of his shorts.

She wiggled her fingers in the air. "Shouldn't you change clothes? Black? Camouflage?"

"And stick out like a sore thumb in this resort? This will work." He pushed up from the bed and stood by the door, his fingers on the door handle. "Remember, stay in this room and don't open the door for anyone. I'll be back before you know it and hopefully somewhat wiser about who's here and why."

As he turned toward the door, Gina jumped from the bed and threw her arms around his neck. She planted a hard kiss on his mouth.

"Come back in one piece. I can't do this, any of this, without you."

On his way to the elevator, Josh brushed his fingers across his tingling lips. Gina had found a surefire way to get him to come back in one piece…as long as he could get the jump on this guy.

Once again, he made a wide berth around the pool deck and restaurant on his way to the beach. The resort had strung mini LED lights along the path to the beach and had stationed electric torches every few feet along the sand.

Josh kept clear of all the lights and hung back in the shadows as he ducked behind each cabana he passed until he reached the last one. He dropped to his hands and knees and lifted the edge of the tent where it met the sand, surveying the inside of the cabana.

Two inert forms lay sprawled across two of the chaise longues, and Josh released a slow breath.

He shimmied beneath the edge of the tent and army-crawled to the corner near the opening of it. Then he pulled the gun from his waistband and crouched...and waited.

This, he knew.

When rescuing damsels in distress and drugging spies, he was winging it. Lying in wait with a weapon in hand was second nature.

He'd let it slip tonight in that couple's hotel room that he was a sniper. He could tell by the look on her face Gina hadn't known that or thought about it before, but he could see the wheels start turning. Had he distracted her enough to stop the path of her thoughts?

He could probably tell Gina, without ramifications, that he'd been the one who had taken out Ricky. The way she'd felt about her husband had put him in the clear. She might even thank him, but how did you tell someone you'd killed her spouse? Taken away her child's father?

Josh tensed his muscles at the sound of scuffling sand. His hand tightened on the gun, as a shadow passed by the outside of the cabana.

The intruder led with his weapon, using it to push aside the flap of canvas covering the entrance.

Josh acted on instinct and training. He grabbed the barrel of the gun close to the handle and yanked down. The man grunted. His own instinct to hang on to his weapon caused his wrist to twist and his finger to lose its place on the trigger.

Josh brought home his advantage of surprise by driving his shoulder against the man's kneecap.

The intruder's legs buckled and as he dropped to the ground, Josh brought it home with a jab to the man's windpipe with his elbow. The guy released his gun.

Sputtering and groaning, the man only managed to suck dry sand into his mouth. He gagged and coughed.

Finally, Josh brought his own gun level with the man's forehead. "Now, you're going to tell me everything you know about who's on this island, what you want with Gina De Santos and what you think Hector De Santos hid."

The man's lips curled into a snarl. "Go to hell."

"Let's start with you." Josh kicked the man in the thigh. "Sit up."

He struggled to a seated position, and Josh patted him down, withdrawing a knife from a holster strapped to the man's leg.

"Who are you working for?"

"Not some low-life, cheating drug dealer." The man spit into the sand.

"Yeah, because a terrorist organization that targets innocent civilians is so above all that."

"There are no innocent civilians." The man's teeth gleamed in the darkness. "You should know that better than anyone. You're a sniper for one of the most lethal SEAL teams in the navy."

Josh's blood ran like ice water in his veins, and he narrowed his eyes. "Who are you? Are you working with Vlad?"

The man laughed so hard he choked. Raising his hand to his mouth, he met Josh's eyes. "He'll get his revenge. You'll never stop him."

Then he bit down on a heavy ring on his middle finger and collapsed in the sand.

Chapter Thirteen

The warm breeze lifted the ends of Gina's hair as she squinted at the ocean and a line of whitecaps flashing across its inky blue surface. Gentle chatter from the pool bar rose through the night air against the backdrop of the rolling sea's rush.

She hadn't heard any gunshots, screams or general pandemonium so whatever Josh was doing down there, he was doing it quietly. Or he was dead.

She pressed her folded hands against her lurching stomach. Why had she allowed her mind to go there? Josh knew what he was doing. He had a weapon, and he knew how to use it.

In fact, he'd mentioned earlier when they were searching the hotel room that he was a sniper, a navy SEAL sniper. Had she heard that correctly?

Something bumped against the hotel room door, and Gina spun around, her heart thumping, rattling her rib cage. She turned from the balcony and crept back in the room.

As she drew close to the door, someone tapped on it, making her jump. She pressed her eye against the peephole and released a noisy breath while flipping back the chain.

"Why are you banging around out here?" She gasped as Josh stumbled across the threshold, shirtless, his clothes and hair wet.

She slammed the door shut and threw the lock again. "Are you all right? What happened out there?"

Sluicing a hand across his hair, he tried to steady his breath as his chest heaved. "He's dead."

"The man you went to meet? How?" She knotted her fingers in front of her. If anyone saw Josh, he could be in big trouble. Isla Perdida didn't fool around with criminals, no matter what their nationality.

"He killed himself."

"I don't understand."

"I got the jump on him. He was never expecting me, and I got him at gunpoint. He…he knew who I was. When I started asking him questions, he downed some poison. He died immediately."

"Poison?" Gina took a turn around the room. "What? Where did he get poison?"

"He had it in a ring on his finger. He must've had orders to off himself if he ever got captured. I suppose if he hadn't, he would've been killed anyway. There is no way a terrorist organization is going to believe that a captive is not spilling his guts about everything he knows."

She doubled over, her hair creating a curtain around her face. "I can't believe this is happening."

"That ring? That's some serious stuff. They're prepared for anything, including death." He touched her back. "Are you okay?"

She straightened up. "Me? I've been cooling my heels in here all evening. What about you? How come you're soaking wet?"

"I couldn't leave his body there in the cabana. Maybe Roger and Tara would've taken care of business, but maybe they have similar orders. I didn't want to take any chances, so I dragged him down to the water. I hauled him over the reef. I'm hoping the current will take him out to sea, although he'll probably wash up somewhere."

"Just hopefully not before we leave. What happened to your—" she waved her hand over his glistening muscles "—shirt?"

"I figured this way, I'd just look like I went out for a late-night swim or a dip in the pool in case anyone noticed me."

"Do you think anyone did?" How could any woman in her right mind *not* notice him?

"I stayed away from the populated areas of the hotel. I avoided the lobby and the elevators and took the outside stairs."

She ducked into the bathroom and grabbed a towel for him. As she tossed it to him, she asked, "Did you get anything out of him before…?"

"Not much."

"But something?" She tilted her head to one side. Josh's face had gotten that tight look.

"He said something that confirmed a suspicion I had, that the CIA had."

"Which is?" She sat on the edge of the bed, pinning her nervous hands between her knees.

"The leader of this terrorist group is someone we know, someone I know."

"You *know* a leader of a terrorist group?" Her legs started bouncing.

"I guess *know* isn't the right word." He swiped the

towel over his short hair and draped it around his neck, hanging on to it with both hands. "There was a guy, a sniper, for the other side. He was deadly accurate, and he seemed to be everywhere we were."

"By *we*, you mean…?"

"My sniper team."

She dropped her chin to her chest, letting his words sink in. She'd been right about what he'd said before. He was not just a navy SEAL; he was a sniper—not that it made a difference. Did it?

"We got to know him, to recognize his style. We started calling him Vlad because he used a Russian sniper rifle, but in truth, we don't know what nationality he is or where his loyalties lie."

"You don't know his real name?"

"No. We know what he looks like, sort of. We've seen him, probably in disguise. He's been involved in the planning of attacks on US soil. So far we've thwarted him, but it's more than that."

Josh took his time pulling the gun from his pocket, wiping it with the towel and placing it on the credenza holding the TV. He unbuttoned the top button of his shorts and then seemed to remember where he was. He bunched up the towel and tossed it toward the open door of the bathroom.

"It's more than what? Finish the thought…out loud, please."

"I told you the man on the beach realized who I was, knew I was a SEAL."

"Yes."

"It all seems so…personal, not just this assignment but a couple of others."

"Personal? Like Vlad is devising these plans just to get to your team?"

"Yep."

"But if Vlad is the one who was working with my father to supply drugs for arms and passage into the US, he wasn't doing that to get at your team."

"No, I didn't say that. I think Vlad is going about his evil business but when his business clashes with ours—" Josh snapped his fingers "—he's ready to take his revenge."

"In a way, Vlad must feel as if you're dogging his every step."

"Tough luck for him—we are." He shrugged. "I'm going to get out of these wet shorts."

Her gaze trailed after him as he disappeared into the bathroom. He ran the shower for a few minutes, probably to rinse the sea salt and sand from his body, and she was sitting in exactly the same spot when he emerged with a whoosh of steam back into the room, a pair of running shorts hanging low on his hips.

She nibbled on the side of her thumb as she watched him dump some stuff in his suitcase and lock the gun back in the safe.

Straightening up to his full height, he glanced over his shoulder. "Are you okay? No disturbances while I was gone?"

"Everything was quiet." She crossed her legs beneath her body. "Are we ready for tomorrow?"

"I play the bodyguard, and you do what you have to do to access your father's safe-deposit box. Hopefully, we'll get lucky and find a clue to where he stashed the weapons, the drugs or both."

"I have a good feeling about this. I feel lucky."

He cocked an eyebrow at her. "After the day you just had? That's lucky?"

"Yeah, welcome to paradise." She kneaded the back of her neck with her fingers. "But I figure our luck has to change. I think it already has. If you hadn't caught on to the honeymoon couple, they would've drugged us or murdered us first."

"That's looking on the bright side." He flexed his fingers. "Do you want some help with that massage? I'm pretty good at working out the knots. God knows, my muscles get stiff when I'm watching a target for a long period of time. I've become a master at the quickie."

She hoped he meant quickie massage and not another kind of quickie because making love with Josh Elliott should be slow and languorous.

She swung her legs off the bed, perching on the edge. "Give it a try."

The mattress dipped as he sat next to her, and she turned away from him, offering him her back. Still shirtless, he exuded warmth from his body as he placed his hands on her shoulders.

"I'll start with your neck and work my way out and down. You tell me what works."

She bounced on the bed when he dug his thumbs into the sides of her neck. It hurt...and then it hurt so good.

Closing her eyes, she tilted her head to one side. "So you sit for long periods of time watching a target?"

The magic fingers stopped and she jerked her shoulders up and down to get him to start again, which he did.

"Yes, watching a target or watching a particular location for a target to appear."

"Snipers aren't in the midst of the battlefield?"

"Not generally, or you could say we're in the midst of the battlefield but doing a different type of job. We make sure areas are clear so that marines and other personnel can get their jobs done. We keep watch over them."

"And you take people out."

This time the magic fingers dug in deeper, and she winced.

"Of course, but the more bad people we take out, the more good people we save. I've always looked at it that way. It's what we do."

He stroked her shoulders, and she melted beneath his touch.

"That's what you were doing in Colombia?"

"What?"

"Making sure the area was clear for the CIA?"

Josh sighed and his warm breath tickled the back of her neck.

"Why would you do that? There was nobody to clear out of that area around my father's compound, except the people inside the compound." Her spine straightened and she jerked beneath Josh's touch. "In fact, why would a bunch of navy SEAL snipers be watching over CIA agents as they took out a group of men on the patio?"

"Gina…"

She jerked forward and whipped around. "What did you do at my father's compound, Josh?"

"I killed your husband."

Chapter Fourteen

Gina caught her breath as her heart fluttered in her chest. *Of course.*

The confident hands on her shoulders paused, the fingers entangled in her hair.

Her gaze met Josh's, unwavering, unapologetic. She'd known. She'd always known. Why would a bunch of navy SEAL snipers stand by and allow CIA agents to take down the prized targets?

She didn't even know if CIA agents killed people... but snipers did. Snipers had killed her father and her husband. Josh had killed her husband.

Confusion reigned in her mind. She opened her mouth but couldn't form one word. She slid from beneath Josh's touch and wandered to the window. Glancing at his reflection in the glass, she banished it by sliding open the door and stepping onto the balcony. She shut the door behind her, placing a barrier between them.

She inhaled the sweet scent on the air, hibiscus and jasmine mingling with the salt of the sea.

But another smell invaded her nostrils—the smell of blood and flesh and fear on the patio of her father's compound. The sounds of the servants' screams and terror echoed in her ears.

Gina covered her face with her hands. She didn't know what to feel. Why had this shadowy organization sent Josh out to monitor her? Did they figure he'd be the one to take her out if he discovered she'd picked up where her father had left off?

The way he'd rescued her from the man in the alley and the guy on the boat told a different story. He'd done nothing but protect her since the day they met… and even before.

She might not know how to feel now, but she remembered very clearly how she'd felt the day the leadership of Los Santos had been eliminated. *Relief.*

While everyone had been falling apart around her on that patio, a serene calm had descended on her shoulders. She'd felt free for the first time in months—and she owed it all to that man behind her in the hotel room.

The door slid open behind her.

"Gina?"

She dropped her hands and gripped the edge of the balcony.

"I'm sorry I didn't tell you sooner. I didn't think it was…appropriate, especially after I met RJ."

She cocked her head to the side and the lights at the pool below blurred as tears pooled in her eyes. She'd felt relief, but RJ had lost his father and his grandfather. Whatever else Hector De Santos was, he was a doting grandfather.

She smacked the balcony with her palms. Would a doting grandfather threaten to rip his grandson from his mother's arms? Would a doting grandfather make plans to inculcate his grandson in the ways of the cartel so he could take over for him in his dotage?

And what about Ricky? He'd never been an involved

father. He'd always seen RJ as a pawn, a way to ingratiate himself into Hector's good graces and a solid position of power within the cartel.

Josh shuffled behind her but kept his distance. "That was always the worst part for me, depriving a child of his parent. I saw RJ before…before. I saw him with you on the patio. I wish I hadn't."

She cleared her throat. "Ricky wasn't much of a father."

"Sometimes that doesn't matter. My mother wasn't much of a mother, and I still wanted revenge for her death or at least answers."

She drew her brows over her nose and sniffed. "I think RJ's better off without his father, without his grandfather in his life. Do you feel that way about your mother?"

"I suppose. I don't know. Was Ricky abusive toward RJ?"

"If by *abusive* you mean did he smack him around? No. But if you mean did he threaten to take him from me, did he use him to get close to my father, did he bring him into dangerous situations with dangerous people? Then, yes. He was abusive, and so was my father…and I guess I was, too."

Josh was beside her in a minute. "That's not true. You didn't have a choice. If you had refused to bring him around your father, Hector De Santos would've made sure you never saw RJ again. You and I both know he could've made good on his promise. You did what you had to do."

Josh's hand rested next to hers on the railing of the balcony, and she shifted her little finger over so that it touched his. "And you did what you had to do."

He expelled a breath. "I'm thinking I should've told you sooner. I shouldn't have left it for you to figure out on your own. I guess I'm a coward."

"A coward?" She twisted her head to the right to take in the fearless man at her side. "That's not the first word or even the hundredth I'd use to describe you, Josh."

"There's no other word to explain why I didn't tell you from the start."

"Really? How about *sensitive*? I mean, who would walk up to someone and say, 'Nice to meet you, I'm the guy who killed your husband'?"

"That would be awkward." He hunched his shoulders. "But I'm not usually the most sensitive guy in the room."

"You do a pretty good impression of one."

"I didn't tell you because… I wanted you to like me. I thought maybe you still had feelings for your husband, and you'd hate me for being the one who ended his life. I didn't want you to hate me."

"Hate you?" She covered his strong hand with her own. "You saved my life. You saved RJ's life. My father planned to initiate RJ into the cartel as soon as he was old enough."

Josh cursed. "What kind of grandfather would do that? What kind of man? Your husband was on board with this?"

"Of course. Ricky figured RJ would cement his own unbreakable bond with Los Santos. That's why Ricky wanted to have a baby with me so quickly." She snorted. "I thought it was true and undying love and the desire to create a family."

"Some people should never have children."

Josh's voice sounded hollow and she wanted nothing

more than to ask him more about the mother he'd lost, but she squeezed his hand instead.

"I can't regret having RJ. He's the light of my life."

"I'm glad my role in the assassinations is out in the open." He slipped his hand from beneath hers and hunched over the balcony, folding his arms. "I'm glad you didn't love Ricky anymore."

"I stopped loving him the day he informed me that we were taking RJ to Colombia to visit my father—and RJ hadn't even been born yet. He told me then that my father had reached out to him and they'd been meeting in secret, all while I was pregnant."

"I'm sorry he betrayed you."

"You see now why I believe you saved me?" She stroked his bare back. Although Josh's role in the assassinations had come as a shock, she didn't ever want him to think she blamed him or had any regrets about Ricky's death.

His spine had stiffened beneath her touch, and her fingers played along his smooth flesh. She knew what she *would* regret at the end of this adventure with Josh. It had been a long time since she'd felt safe with any man. She needed that now.

Scraping her nails lightly along his side, she whispered, "You saved me, Josh Elliott, and you saved my son."

He turned to her and cupped her face with one hand. "Then I did my job."

She twisted her head to the side and kissed his rough palm. Then she stood on her tiptoes and kissed the base of his neck where his pulse throbbed against her lips.

His hand slipped to the back of her head, his fingers

gathering her loose hair. He tugged her head back and slanted his mouth over hers.

His kiss was just a taste. It felt comforting. She didn't want comfort. She wanted the passion they'd ignited in the water this afternoon. She needed to obliterate the memory of her dead, deceitful husband. And what better way to do that than to make love with the man who'd killed him?

She hooked her arms around Josh's waist, pulling herself closer to him, her hips meeting his. She pressed against him, wanting to feel the proof of his desire for her…and he didn't disappoint.

At least below the waist, he didn't disappoint. His kiss had waned, his touch had slackened.

She sucked in his bottom lip and nibbled on it, hoping to show him she meant business…or pleasure. She slipped her hands beneath the waistband of his shorts, digging her fingers into the muscle of his buttocks.

He groaned in her ear and then growled, "Do you know what you're doing here?"

"Here in Isla Perdida or here on this balcony with a hot SEAL in my hands?"

"Either, both…ah."

His words and hopefully his reasoning trailed off as she cupped his backside with both hands and undulated against his erection.

"I know what I'm doing, and I know what I want."

He hooked his hands beneath her thighs and hoisted her up. Hiking up her dress, she wrapped her legs around his waist as he took possession of her mouth again—this time like he meant it.

With one arm braced against the balcony railing and

one supporting her derriere, Josh invaded her mouth with his tongue.

She welcomed it, demanded more. She sucked on his tongue with the same rhythm that drove her hips against his, over and over.

Her thin panties, damp with sweat and desire, chafed against her skin.

Josh reached between them and ripped them free from her body, as if sensing her discomfort...or his own.

The soft cotton of Josh's shorts stroked and tickled her bare flesh. She broke away from their kiss to gasp for breath as her blood heated up.

He rolled to his back so that the balcony railing supported him, then he gripped her thighs with both hands, his fingers sinking into her soft flesh, centimeters away from her pulsing pleasure zone.

He ran his tongue up one side of her neck and nibbled on her earlobe. His voice, harsh with pent-up desire, exploded in her ear. "You're not doing this out of gratitude, are you?"

"I can bake cookies to thank you, SEAL." She loosened her legs and yanked down his shorts, gasping at the feel of warm skin against warm skin.

During her repositioning, Josh's fingers had resettled closer to her core. Taking advantage of his new outlook, Josh plunged one finger inside her.

She threw her head back with a whimper. A burst of laughter erupted from a gaggle of late-nighters at the pool bar below and excitement flooded every cell of her body.

She'd been weighing the best time to move this party to the bed, but now her passion flamed with the thought of making love with Josh on the balcony. Nobody could see them, but just the thought of being claimed by Josh in a semipublic place had her senses on fire.

He pulled his finger out and strategically stroked her, stoking her onto heights of passion. Her belly fluttered and her toes curled. As every muscle in her body tightened in anticipation of her release, she dug her fingernails into Josh's shoulders.

Her orgasm hit her like a wave and she trembled beneath its awesome power. As it receded, she shivered with pleasure and her limbs grew heavy and boneless until her legs slipped from Josh's body.

She had to lean against him to keep from sliding to his feet, and he caressed her backside to ease her transition from heaven to earth.

He dipped his head and kissed her jaw. "Are you ready to try out that bed?"

"I want you to take me right here." She stroked his erection, cupping him below with her other hand.

"When you touch me like that, I'll give you anything you want. But I can't do this with you all wrapped around my body—as amazing as that feels."

He encircled her waist with both hands and did a little dance so that she was the one against the balcony, facing outward to the pool and the sea beyond.

He pulled her dress over her head and dropped it on one of the chairs. "I don't think anyone can see us up here."

He cupped her breasts with his hands, pinching her nipples, and she wriggled her bottom against him, feeling the hard tip of his erection brushing against her.

His hands played across her body, smoothing, caressing, tweaking, until her knees were trembling and she had to hold on to the railing with both hands.

He placed a hand flat on her back. "Bend forward."

She folded her arms on top of the wooden railing and gazed out at the deep blue of the water, the whitecaps drawing lines across the surface.

Josh parted her thighs and poked at her from behind, easing her open, filling her up, inch by inch. When he reached his hilt, his thighs pressing against the bare skin of her bottom, he pulled out almost all the way.

Just when she was missing him, he plunged into her again. Slow and fast he went, following some rhythm in his head, but it must've been her rhythm, too, because her passion grew with every thrust.

He slipped a hand in front of her, between her legs, and teased her again. It didn't take more than a few flicks from his fingertips before she reached her peak. This time, Josh extended her ride at the top as he plowed into her.

Her moans soon turned to cries of release and unabashed euphoria. Could they hear her down there? She didn't care. She felt alive and free for the first time in forever.

As she clenched around Josh, his thrusts grew more frenzied until he stopped and shuddered. When he was done, he wrapped his arms around her, pulling her against his chest, still inside her.

He kissed the back of her head. "Was that uncomfortable for you? I gave you what you wanted."

She pulled away from him and then turned in his arms. "You gave me more than I wanted. Was I...? Did you...?"

He put his finger to her lips. "You were everything I wanted."

He traced the pad of his finger along the red line

across her belly. "It's a good thing I didn't flip you over the balcony."

"It would've been a heckuva way to go." She smoothed her hands across his chest. "I'm ready to try that bed now."

Josh wedged a finger beneath her chin and kissed her bruised lips. "After you."

When he stepped aside, Gina pushed off the balcony. A commotion from the pool deck halted her next step and she tripped into Josh.

He took her hand and they peered over the balcony, side by side. A crowd of people had formed a semicircle around a man, wet from the sea, waving his arms and pointing back toward the water.

Josh whispered, "Looks like that dead body washed up after all."

SHOWERED AND FULLY CLOTHED, Josh sat on the edge of the bed and gently prodded Gina. "Gina, it's time to get up."

It was past time, but he hadn't the heart to wake her earlier. She'd had a restless night beside him, tossing and turning and twitching in her sleep.

They hadn't made love again, although before some nighttime swimmer had discovered a dead body in the water, he'd had every intention of doing so. The reminder of what they were doing here and the high stakes involved had put a damper on their libidos.

And then the reality of what he'd succumbed to hit him full force. He was pretty sure his assignment didn't include sleeping with the widow of the man he'd killed over a year ago.

He'd been saved from making this very mistake yesterday by the man in the boat. Looked like that same man in death hadn't come along soon enough last night to prevent the same mistake.

He brushed his hand along the length of her smooth arm. How could he call what had happened between them a mistake? It had felt so natural, so right.

He'd been concerned once Gina found out he'd pulled the trigger on her husband, she'd reject him, push him away. Instead she'd turned to him in gratitude.

As much as she'd denied her motivation, he could sense it in the urgency of her touch. It made sense—for her. He didn't have to go along for the ride. He traced the curve of her ear with his fingertip. But what a ride it had been.

No red-blooded American male would've been able to resist a hot-blooded Gina De Santos. He didn't claim to have any willpower in that area.

Maybe Ariel and the folks pulling the strings already knew that and were counting on it. How much easier would it be to manipulate a woman once you'd gotten her into your bed?

Somehow *he* felt like the manipulated one. He'd been dreading tears and anger when he'd broken the news about his role in Ricky's demise. When she'd responded with relief and understanding, he still felt he owed her something. If she preferred her payment in the currency of his kisses, who was he to deny her?

But it was back to business today.

"Gina?" He brushed the hair from her face and kissed her sweet mouth.

Like Sleeping Beauty, she roused, blinking her eyes and rubbing a hand across her mouth. "It's morning?"

"The bank opens in thirty minutes."

She bolted upright, the covers falling from her naked shoulders. "Thirty minutes? Why didn't you get me up sooner?"

"The bank's open for four hours. We have plenty of time." His gaze lingered on her perfect breasts, so soft and full they made his mouth water all over again.

She yanked the sheet up to her chin. "I have to get ready."

"The bathroom is all yours." He flicked the collar of his white button-down shirt. "As you can see, I'm ready to roll."

"We won't have time for breakfast."

"We'll get some later. Our flight isn't until late afternoon."

She rolled from the bed, dragging the covers with her in a sudden attack of modesty.

He'd seen—and touched—it all last night. She wasn't hiding anything from him now. Did she have regrets, too? Maybe she'd paid her debt and wanted to move on.

She rummaged in her suitcase, grabbed a few items and headed for the bathroom, calling over her shoulder, "I won't be long."

Josh shook out his jacket and draped it over the back of the chair. Isla Perdida might have its tourist and resort areas, but the island took its business very seriously.

He cranked on the air-conditioning and closed the door to the balcony, throwing a cursory glance at the pool. He'd meandered downstairs for coffee this morning and had picked up a few bits of info. A guest at the hotel had found a man floating in the sea, several yards from the beach. No immediate evidence of foul play had led to initial reports of a drowning.

Josh could live with that story for the rest of their

stay on the island. The toxicology report would soon refute a simple drowning, but the authorities just might rule suicide—and they'd be correct.

If his followers preferred suicide to capture and questioning, Vlad must have some devoted minions—devoted or terrified.

The bathroom door banged open behind him and Gina squealed, "It's freezing in here."

"Wait until you put on your bank duds. I don't want to melt out of the suit before I even leave the room."

"You have a point." She eyed the white dress hanging in the closet with something like trepidation in every muscle.

She dropped the towel she'd been hugging to her chest to reveal a snow-white set of bra and panties. She yanked the dress from the hanger and stepped into it, reaching around to her back to pull up the zipper.

"Let me." He crossed the room and slid the dress closed over her smooth mocha skin.

Gina had needed just one day in the blistering, relentless sun to sport an even tan across her body. He'd enjoyed tracing her tan lines last night, and had enjoyed exploring beyond the tan lines even more.

"Thanks." She stepped away from him and into a pair of beige high-heeled sandals. "At least *I'm* not expected to wear a suit."

"Lucky." He planted himself in front of the mirror and buttoned his top button. Then he reached for the tie hanging over the lid of his open suitcase.

"Do you need help with that?" She pointed at the blue tie hanging from his fingertips.

He raised his brows at the image he presented in the mirror, noticing the way his white shirt bunched around his shoulders and arms. Last time he wore this getup was for a buddy's funeral. Thank God, he hadn't needed it since, but he'd pumped up a bit more since then.

"Don't I look like the suit-and-tie type?"

"You look…just fine."

He held it out to her. "I could use some help."

She looped the tie over his head and tucked it beneath the collar of his shirt. "I know just one knot, so I hope you like it."

He dropped his gaze to hers. "I like everything you do."

She pressed her lips together but they twitched at the corner. Then she lodged the tip of her tongue in that same corner as she fed one end of the tie through an opening and flipped it over the other end.

"I think I got this." She turned him toward the mirror. "What do you think? Straighten it out a bit from your angle."

"Looks great." He tightened the knot. "Are you ready?"

"I need some makeup and I'm going to do my hair, so cool your heels for another fifteen minutes."

"I can't imagine how your face could look any more beautiful with fifteen minutes of makeup application."

This time her lips turned down in a frown. "You're very free and easy with the compliments this morning."

He sucked in his bottom lip. He'd never been accused of that before. The flattery just seemed to spring to mind, but whatever was prompting him to sing her praises, Gina didn't seem to like it.

Had Ricky Rojas laid it on thick? He'd probably wooed and schmoozed her as if his life depended on it. He'd seemed like a smooth SOB, just the kind of guy women would fall for—especially young and inexperienced ones like Gina had been.

"I'll zip it if it makes you uncomfortable." He held up his hands. "Wait. That didn't come out right."

She gave him a nervous giggle. "That's okay. Who doesn't like compliments?"

"Nobody likes them if they're not sincere." He drew a cross over his heart. "I swear, mine are completely spontaneous and sincere. Can't you tell by how clunky they are?"

"They're not." She nudged him away from the mirror and pulled her hair back.

He retreated to a chair and sat on the edge, watching Gina as she wound her luxuriant dark hair into a severe bun at the back of her head. "Are you nervous?"

"A little, but I have all the valid qualifications to get into my father's safe-deposit box." She stuck a pin in her hair and smoothed her hands over the skirt of her dress. "We should be fine."

She held up a small leopard-print bag. "Just some makeup and I'll be ready to go."

For this particular operation Gina went into the bathroom, and he stood up and lifted his jacket from the chair. They'd take a taxi for the ten-minute ride into town.

When Gina emerged from the bathroom with her war paint on, she did look ready to do battle—beautiful, sophisticated, just a little brittle.

"You look…ready."

"Let's do this."

"If it all comes to nothing…"

"It won't." She sliced a hand in the air right in front of his nose. "I got to know my father pretty well in those last months of his life. I had to study him to figure out a way to escape my predicament. This is what he'd do. This is where he'd keep his secrets."

"We'll soon find out, one way or the other." He draped his jacket over his arm, feeling for the gun in the pocket.

They made their way down to the lobby and as they traversed the gold-threaded marble, Josh made a detour to the front desk.

He ducked his head and asked the hotel clerk, "Is it true there was a dead body on the beach last night?"

Gina tensed beside him.

"Yes, sir, but no violence. No violence on the island. It looks to be a drowning." He shrugged. "Some shouldn't go out swimming at night in the dark."

"I'll keep that in mind." He rapped on the counter. "Thank you."

Gina let out a breath. "That's the word, huh? A drowning?"

"It is until the coroner runs a toxicology report, but we'll be long gone before those results come in."

"They're going to have a hard time finding his next of kin since he probably was using a fake name, unless the newlywed couple wants to claim him."

"Not likely."

The front doors of the hotel whisked open at their approach, and a bellhop jumped to attention. "Taxi, sir?"

"Yes, please."

The bellhop whistled and waved, and a hybrid car rolled up to the curb.

Josh gave the bank name to the driver. No address was necessary.

The taxi silently sped along the main road that wended its way around the island. Unlike Robbie from the day before, this driver made no small talk. In a place like Isla Perdida, small talk with people heading to the Banco de Perdida could get you in trouble.

At the end of the short drive, the cabbie hopped out of his car and opened the back door. Josh paid him and added a generous tip—in case anyone came around later asking about their destination and conversation. It was standard practice on the island.

Josh kept his hands to himself as he followed Gina into the bank, just like any good bodyguard would do. Any good bodyguard would decline to sleep with his charge, too.

Guess he was a failure as a bodyguard.

Josh opened the door of the bank and the cold air blasted his face. Were they afraid all their money might melt in the island heat?

An armed security guard stepped forward. "Your business, please?"

Gina flashed the passbook, green leather embossed with gold, from her father. "I'm here to visit my safe-deposit box. This is my bodyguard."

Josh placed his hand inside the pocket of his jacket just so there were no misunderstandings later.

The security guard nodded and gestured toward one of the small teller windows at the end of the row.

Gina's heels clicked on the marble floor and echoed among the hush of soft whispers emanating from the edges of the room.

Josh inhaled the scent of what had to be pure money…or maybe it was the smell of gold bullion.

Gina parked herself in front of the window and he hovered to her right as she whipped out various forms of ID, including pressing her thumb to an electronic pad.

She must've had everything in order because the

teller at the window told her to proceed to the gated entrance to the left of the windows.

Josh followed Gina to the locked doors and they both waited while someone on the other side released a series of locks and opened the door.

Gina jerked her thumb over her shoulder. "He's my bodyguard."

The bank official nodded and stepped aside. It was even more hushed on this side of the windows and more discreet. The black-suited official led them to the safe-deposit area and entered a code on the door. Gina then entered her code, which she'd memorized from a card in the taxi, and the door clicked open.

"Take your time, Ms. De Santos." The clerk melted away instead of sticking around like most bankers did for safe-deposit boxes in the United States.

When the door swung shut behind them in the dimly lit room lined with boxes of various sizes, Josh said, "I suppose it's better for the people who work here to be kept in the dark as to the contents of these boxes."

Gina released a breath as if she'd been holding it since they walked into the bank. "That's why the rich and crooked bank here—total privacy."

"I suppose your father didn't have a box big enough to hold drugs and weapons."

"I don't think so." She floated past the wall of boxes, trailing her fingers along their gleaming brass fronts. "I remember being in here with my father like it was yesterday. I was terrified then by the implications, but now I'm glad he entrusted all this to me."

"You're going to have to entrust this to the DEA when this is all over."

She shrugged. "I'll have to tell my mom first. She may lose everything."

"It was never hers to lose, Gina. Does she want blood on her hands?"

"My mother wants cash in her hands, whether it has blood on it or not. Do you really think she didn't know my father's profession when she married him? She did." She stopped about two-thirds of the way down the row. "Here it is."

She wiped her palms against the skirt of her dress, and then punched in a code. The lock on the box clicked, and Gina pulled the box from its cavity.

She placed it on the table in the middle of the room and flipped up the felt lid.

Josh leaned over her shoulder as she picked up a folded batch of papers and dropped them on the table.

Whistling, he hooked his finger around a diamond necklace and two matching bracelets. "I'm no expert, but these look like they could fund a few small wars."

"I have no idea why these are in here." She picked up a stack of American bills. "Or these."

"No secret tapes, computer disks, DVDs?" He dropped the necklace and bracelets on top of the papers and stirred his finger among a few other pieces of jewelry in the felt-lined box.

"Doesn't look like it."

"What about these?" Josh tapped the papers that had been on top.

Gina picked up the batch of papers, tipping them to the side, letting the diamonds slide to the table in a glittering pool. She unfolded them and flattened them on the table with her palms.

"I don't know what this is supposed to be." She

leaned over the eleven-by-fifteen sheets of paper and ran her fingertip along the lines on the page.

Josh bumped the side of her hip with his own to get a closer look. "These are plans, some kind of building plans with measurements and calculations."

"My father was never into real estate or buildings as far as I know. Why would he even be interested in building plans? It's not his compound in Colombia, is it?"

Josh squinted at the numbers, and then dug in his pocket for his phone. He entered some of the figures on his phone's calculator, and drew his brows over his nose. "This can't be a building. Those numbers are too small. The ceiling's barely six feet tall."

"My father was not a tall man, but the ceilings in his place were super high—cathedral."

"Are these more plans?" Josh shoved aside the top page only to find another odd set of figures. "We're going to need an architect to look at these, or at least someone with more building experience than I have."

He thumbed through the next few pages. When he came to the last one, his heart flip-flopped. "Gina, it's a map."

"Like a buried treasure map?" Bending forward, she dug her elbows into the table and peered at the squiggly lines on the page.

"It's Mexico." Josh's adrenaline started pumping, and a bead of sweat ran down his face despite the arctic temperatures in the room.

Gina wrinkled her nose. "Why Mexico?"

"Think about it." Josh jabbed the map with his finger. "This is the border with the US."

Gina's mouth dropped open, her eyes alight with understanding. "The crossing."

"Right." Josh scrabbled back through the other pages and grabbed the edges of the first set of plans. His gaze darted from one side of the page to the other, as calculations whirred through his brain.

Then he dropped the plans on the table with a pump of his fist. "This is it. You were right, Gina."

"I was? What do you think you figured out?"

"I don't *think* I figured it out. I *know* I did. Your father commissioned the construction of a tunnel between Mexico and the US and that's where he hid the drugs and the weapons. And they must still be there."

Chapter Fifteen

Josh's words acted like a switch to a light bulb over her head. How else would her father be able to secure passage for the terrorists and their weapons in exchange for drugs?

"You're right. It's all here in front of us." She picked up the edges of the map and read off some of the names. "It's at the border with Arizona. Can you figure out the exact location?"

"I'm sure we can once we compare this map to another. When I turn this over to the team, to Ariel, the CIA and the DEA can move in and confiscate the drugs and the weapons and destroy the tunnel. I wonder if it's been used yet. There are dozens of these tunnels on the border. I wonder what makes this one so special. I'm sure Los Santos has used tunnels before to ship their drugs to the States."

"I'm not sure. I wasn't aware of any tunnels before." Gina chewed on her bottom lip as Josh laid out each of the pages on the table. "Once this tunnel is located and if the drugs and weapons are there, do you think these people—Los Santos and this Vlad guy—will leave me alone?"

Josh looked up from taking his first picture of the plans with his phone. "They should. They tried to abduct you to get information from you and get you to turn it over to them. They failed."

"Thanks to you."

"Don't get too warm and fuzzy. I was sent to Miami, to you, to get the exact same information."

"Yeah, but you're the good guys." She wedged a hip against the table, watching Josh as he finished taking his pictures. "If I hadn't had the info or wouldn't turn it over to you, I don't think the US government's response would've been the same as Los Santos's or Vlad's."

"You sure about that?" He shifted his gaze from his phone to her face. "If we knew you had information that you weren't coughing up? It could've gotten ugly."

Gina narrowed her eyes as Josh collected the papers and folded them along their original seams. Could've gotten ugly or very, very friendly? Had Ariel and the powers that be told him to get to her using any means possible?

Her lips twitched at the idea of Josh as some kind of Mata Hari using his masculine wiles to woo information from her. She'd been the one who'd been all over him last night anyway. She doubted he would've made a move if she hadn't come on to him.

Of course, he could've just made it seem that way.

It didn't matter. She always planned to give him any information she had about her father and she'd wanted his body anyway. It was a win-win-win for everyone.

If she could only shake this feeling that finding this tunnel wouldn't be the end of the threat against her. She'd been living under a noxious miasma of evil for so long, she didn't feel as if she'd ever be free of it.

Josh pocketed his phone and handed her the plans. "Stick these in your bag. We'll get them to the right people when we hit stateside."

She shoved the papers in her bag and picked up the diamond necklace, dangling it from her fingertips. It threw rainbow sparks around the room. "Should we leave this here for the DEA, or do you have some woman in your life who needs a fabulous gift?"

He raised his eyebrows at her. "I have no woman in my life. Didn't I make that clear last night?"

Two spots of heat lit up her cheeks. "I didn't mean… I meant like a mother or… I'm sorry."

"Like an aunt or sister or grandmother? I have no one…like that."

She dropped the jewels in the safe-deposit box. "Then the DEA gets them."

Josh scooped them back up and dropped them in his pocket. "Maybe your mother wants them. Maybe they belong to her."

"You just said none of my father's money belonged to her."

"Forget what I said. Put the box away and let's get out of here. We have a flight to catch at four o'clock and I'm never gonna feel so happy to leave paradise as when that plane lifts off."

Fifteen minutes later, after going through the steps of securing the safe-deposit box and exiting the bank, they emerged onto the sidewalk.

Blinking in the harsh sunlight, Gina shook out her sunglasses and put them on. She surveyed the empty street. "Maybe we should've called for a taxi inside the bank."

As if by magic, a yellow cab glided up to the curb. The driver wasn't as attentive as the one who'd dropped them off, staying securely behind the wheel as Josh opened the car door for her.

Josh leaned forward slightly. "La Perdida Resort and Spa, *por favor*."

As the taxi rolled into the street, another taxi pulled up behind them, horn honking.

Their driver cursed and made a rude gesture out the window.

"What is that guy's problem? We didn't cut him off." Gina twisted her head around to glare at the other driver, who was still gesticulating and honking.

Josh had turned around, too, and his body stiffened, the muscles in the thigh beneath her hand coiling.

She jerked her head toward him, and he leaned in to kiss her cheek. Before he drew away, he whispered in her ear. "We need to get out of this taxi the next time he stops or slows down."

She blinked. Slows down? Josh expected her to jump out of a moving car in a white linen dress and high-heeled sandals?

He did. His right hand rested on the door handle of the car, his left gripped her wrist. He'd drag her out if he had to.

What had he seen in the other taxi that had led him to that conclusion? The car was still behind them, the driver tailgating them.

She scooted closer to Josh, her thigh pressing against his. Reaching down, she flicked off the ankle straps of her sandals and tucked them into the big bag at her feet—right next to the map of the tunnel. She pulled the bag into her lap, and hooked the strap over her shoulder.

Josh nodded.

Their taxi slowed to take a curve to the right, and Josh pinched her wrist. As soon as he opened that door, it was go time.

Go time arrived within a nanosecond as Josh pushed open the door, yanking on her wrist. She didn't need any more prompting than that.

Josh jumped out of the taxi while the driver yelled. With Josh still holding on to her wrist, Gina hoisted herself into the space right behind him, squashing her bag against her chest.

Josh had timed their exit well. They both tumbled into a patch of crawling vines on a soft shoulder, rolling just a few feet.

Their taxi screamed to a stop several yards ahead of them. The driver bolted from the car, a gun clutched in his hand.

Gina didn't know whether to make a run for it or stay down.

Josh shoved her behind his body as he reached for his own weapon and made the decision for her. "Stay down. Burrow beneath these vines if you can."

As Josh raised his gun, the taxi that had been dogging them screeched to a halt, cutting off their view of the driver with the gun.

Before she had time to think, Josh grabbed her upper arm and practically dragged her to the waiting taxi. A sharp report and the sound of cracking glass accompanied her into the back seat of the other taxi.

With the back door still gaping open, their new ride swung around in a wild U-turn and lurched into high speed, the sound of another gunshot behind them.

Once the taxi had gained traction and Gina had shoved the hair from her face, the driver turned around with a gold tooth gleaming in his big smile.

"*Dios mío*. Some crazy business you two are involved in."

Gina fell back against the seat. "Robbie? What are you doing here? How did you know that driver had a gun?"

Robbie looked in his rearview mirror and made a quick right turn. "I remembered Josh telling me about your appointment today at the bank. I was in the area and thought I'd roll by to give you a lift. When I saw you get into that rogue taxi, I knew you'd be in some kind of trouble."

"You have no idea." Josh clapped Robbie on the shoulder.

Gina asked, "Rogue taxi?"

"Like any place, Isla Perdida has unlicensed taxi drivers. They're especially common around the banks. They do a pickup—" Robbie made his fingers into a gun "—and then they rob you of the valuables you just collected at the bank."

Gina hugged her bag to her chest and slid a glance at Josh. "You mean that driver was just trying to rob us?"

"Just?" He shook his head. "He had a gun, senorita. He was serious, but this problem isn't something you're going to read in the guidebooks or in your business plans. The island keeps such things quiet."

"Thanks for the rescue, Robbie." Josh entwined his fingers with Gina's on the seat between them.

Robbie laughed. "I think you could've handled things, Josh, especially with the little beauty *mi primo* sold to you last night, but tourists don't want to be involved in any shootings in Isla Perdida."

"We appreciate everything you've done for us, Robbie."

"It was nothing." Robbie waved his hand at the mirror. "Now, I take you to my home so my wife can look after your injuries."

"Injuries?" Gina looked Josh up and down and except for a missing button on his jacket and a few leaves stuck to his hair, he looked just fine.

"You, not me." Josh touched a finger to her cheek and showed her the blood on the end of it.

She gasped. "Is it bad?"

"No worse than your hand and arm."

As soon as the words left his mouth, she felt stinging prickles on the palm of her left hand and noticed the red abrasions for the first time. "I honestly didn't even feel those. I'm sure I'll be okay."

"Perhaps, senorita, but it's better not to return to your hotel looking like you jumped from a moving car."

"You're probably right." She tilted her head back against the seat and rolled it to the left where she saw a different type of scenery flashing by.

Tangled roadside bushes had replaced the manicured landscaping. Old clunkers were rattling down the road instead of the gleaming taxis and high-end rentals of the city streets. People were lined up at shacks with thatched roofs and smoke rising from the back instead of four-star eateries.

She hadn't seen this side of Isla Perdida on her previous visit.

"If you're hungry, I'm sure my wife has some lunch prepared for my break."

Josh said, "We don't want to put her out."

"No trouble, senor. Since our three oldest left the island for Miami, she's been complaining she has nobody to cook for."

"Well, I'm starving." Gina brushed some dirt from her dress and then clutched the wrinkled material in her fists. "That other driver is not going to retaliate against you, is he?"

"I'd like to see him try. The *policía* don't look kindly upon the rogue drivers. Gives the island a black eye." He swung down an unpaved road with palm trees and lush vegetation on either side.

He parked the taxi in front of a tidy clapboard house with abundant fruit trees on one side and neat rows of vegetables and herbs on the other.

When Gina stepped out of the car, the moist earth squished between her toes as she inhaled the sweet scent of the blossoming fruit trees. "Now, *this* is paradise."

A petite, dark woman opened the door with a smile as big as her husband's. "*Hola, hola.* Robbie, you brought guests for lunch?"

Robbie introduced them to his wife, Fernanda, and then spoke in rapid Spanish to her, explaining about the rogue taxi driver.

She clicked her tongue. "Thieves. Come in, come in. Look at your pretty dress."

"I'm afraid it's a mess."

Fernanda tended to Gina's cuts and scrapes and then fed them a hearty meal of arroz con pollo.

An hour later, Josh tapped Gina on the shoulder, just as she'd launched probably the fiftieth picture of RJ on her phone to show Fernanda. "We should be getting back. We have a flight to catch."

Robbie stood up and stretched. "I'll take you back to the hotel and wait for you, Josh. Then I'll drive you to the airport. We need to get you out of Isla Perdida alive."

His light tone and chuckle at the end of his sentence didn't match his somber expression and tight mouth. Had Josh told him more, or had he figured it out on his own?

They said their goodbyes to Fernanda, promising to return for a visit.

Robbie got them back to the hotel without incident, and they hurriedly packed and changed clothes.

Gina turned to Josh. "You don't believe that rogue taxi driver was working for his own interests, do you?"

"Not a chance. They know we got something out of that bank, and they want their hands on it."

She snapped her suitcase shut and placed a hand over the knot in her belly. "All we need to do is get on that plane and get back to Miami."

"That's all. Easy."

Robbie made good time to the airport and also took precautions that they weren't followed. Even if Josh hadn't given him any more details about the purpose of their visit, Robbie knew there was more to their troubles than an island thief.

He stopped his taxi in front of their terminal and hauled their bags from the trunk.

Gina gave Robbie a hug and Josh slipped him some cash with a handshake.

As Robbie started to get into his car, Josh jogged around to the driver's side. "Forgot your tip."

He plunged his hand into the pocket of his cargo shorts and pulled out his fist. Then he poured the diamonds into Robbie's hand.

Robbie's eyes bulged out of their sockets. "Josh, Josh."

"Keep them." Josh hustled back to the curb and took Gina's arm. "Let's get out of here."

As they waited in the boarding area, Gina glanced around but didn't see anyone suspicious. The honeymooners hadn't looked suspicious either.

She and Josh passed the uneventful flight back to

Miami reading and studying the various passengers. The calm put her nerves on edge.

Resting her chin against Josh's arm, Gina asked, "Why aren't they coming at us now?"

"We don't know that they aren't. Stay alert. Roger and Tara didn't look like much of a threat, did they?"

She snorted. "They didn't end up being much of a threat. *They* should've stayed alert. Amateurs."

He pinched her chin. "Let's hope you don't become a pro at this."

"It's too late." She rubbed her eyes. "I thought my life of looking over my shoulder and walking on eggshells was over when my father and Ricky died."

"Your father left you some legacy by taking you into his confidence. Others must've known or Ricky blabbed. Otherwise, you wouldn't be in this predicament. These two groups who are trying to get to the drugs and weapons would've looked elsewhere for their answers."

"Hector De Santos—the father who keeps on giving." She tugged on the sleeve of his T-shirt. "Do I have to tell the DEA about my mother's account in that same bank on Isla Perdida?"

"I'm not here to do the DEA's job. You do what you think is best."

She covered her face with her hands. "There's what's best for my mother and what's right."

The plane touched down in Miami just thirty minutes late, and they moved through Customs with their fake IDs without incident. As the escalator brought them down to the baggage claim, Gina jerked her head in the direction of a brightly colored commotion to her right.

"What the heck is my mom doing here?"

"Where?"

Gina pointed to her mother, swathed in a hot-pink ensemble, her red hair permed and coiffed, and waved. "God, she probably wants all the details of our trip."

"Maybe she just wanted to bring RJ to meet you."

Gina scanned the area around her mother and her chest tightened. "Except RJ's not with her."

"Playdate?"

"You're right." Gina huffed out a breath. "I think that was scheduled for today, even though it's a little late for that now."

The escalator deposited them onto the linoleum floor, and Gina's mom rushed toward her, hands outstretched. "Gina, Gina."

Gina's heart dropped, and the blood rushed to her head. "What's wrong, Mom?"

Her mother looked over her shoulder. "Not here."

"Where's RJ?"

Mom practically dragged her toward some plastic chairs lined up against the wall across from the baggage service windows.

"Mom, you're scaring me. Just tell me RJ's okay and we can get to the rest."

"That's just it, Gina. RJ's not okay."

Gina sank to a chair and would've missed it if Josh hadn't guided her into it.

"I-is he hurt? Mom?" She felt like screaming as a cold dread crept through her body.

"No, or at least I don't think so."

"Just tell me what happened."

"Oh, Gina, they took him. He's gone."

Chapter Sixteen

Gina doubled over and the beige floor rushed toward her face. Once again, Josh caught her by wrapping his arm around her and pulling her against his side.

"What happened, Joanna?" He reached out and pulled her mom into the chair next to him. "Start from the beginning."

"I'm so sorry, Gina. I—I don't know what I could've done differently. You said it was okay."

Gina parted her dry lips but no sound came out.

Josh's low voice sounded very faraway. "What was okay? Try to focus, Joanna, and tell us what happened."

"It was the playdate. It was just a playdate, Gina. You told me it was all right, didn't you? To arrange a playdate with that boy, Diego? He'd been to our house before."

"Is that where he is, Joanna? With Diego's parents?"

"I called the mother, Rita, very nice lady. I even dropped RJ off at their house. Diego was right there to meet him."

"Do you have the address of the house?"

"Of course, I do, but it won't do you any good. There's nobody at that house now."

Gina took a few short breaths. "Did they contact

you, Mom? Or did you just go back to the house to pick him up?"

Her mother licked her frosted lips. "They contacted me before the playdate was even supposed to be over. They told me... I don't know. Craziness. They wanted me to meet you at the airport and break the news right away, but they told me not to call the police or..."

A sob bubbled up in Gina's throat. "Or they'd kill him?"

"They're not going to do that." Josh squeezed the back of Gina's neck. "If they did that, they wouldn't get what they wanted."

"Money?" Mom grabbed Josh's wrist. "I have that. I have plenty of that. They can have it all. Jewelry, too."

"They don't want money, Mom." Gina pinned Josh with her gaze. "They want something Dad left behind."

"That bastard. He just won't go away, will he?" Mom caught a tear on the end of her manicured nail before it ran a course through her makeup. "I'm sorry, sweetie. What can I do?"

"You're going to give us all the information you can about this couple or this woman and the house." Josh pushed to his feet and offered his hands to both Gina and her mom. "You didn't call the police, did you, Joanna?"

"You think I'm stupid?" She brushed his hand aside and stood up, tottering on her five-inch heels. "Let's go get RJ back."

They piled into Mom's car, but she couldn't drive and talk at the same time because she kept getting too excited and veering into other lanes.

Josh, his skin a few shades paler than when they'd stepped off the plane, grabbed the steering wheel at one point. "Joanna, pull over. I'll drive. You talk. Gina, are you doing okay back there?"

"Just great. My son is missing and it's my fault." Her stomach lurched and she felt like she was going to be sick.

Mom pulled over, and she and Josh switched places.

At the wheel and in control, Josh started the interrogation. "What's the address of the house where you dropped off RJ? We're going there right now."

"Sh-shouldn't we take my mother home first?"

"No way. She's our guide. She can tell us everything that went down. It might lead to something."

Joanna twisted in her seat. "I want to go back, Gina, and I don't know why you're blaming yourself. How could you possibly know that woman was with Los Santos? She had such nice shoes."

Gina rocked back and forth. "You don't understand."

Josh interrupted them, "Joanna, the address."

Mom swiped a finger across her phone and read out an address.

After Josh had Gina put the address in her phone's GPS, which momentarily stopped her thoughts from sinking into the dark corners of her mind, he continued with Joanna, "What did Diego's mom look like?"

Gina nodded as her mother described the tall Latina with a short, dark chestnut bob.

"That's the same woman I met at Sunny Days."

"You tried her phone number again, Joanna?"

"Out of service."

"Was there anyone at the house besides Rita and Diego?"

"A maid." Joanna described this woman, but Gina had never seen her before at the daycare.

"Only Rita ever picked up Diego. How did Diego seem? Scared? Weird in any way?"

"How would I know? That's the first time I ever saw the kid since I wasn't home when he came over. Seemed like a normal kid to me, happy to see RJ. I wasn't there long enough to observe his interactions with the two women, but he did seem to hover around the so-called maid more, so maybe that's his real mother. That Rita didn't seem like much of a mother to me."

"You just said she was nice, Mom."

"That was before the bitch took my grandson."

"Josh, Diego started just a few days after RJ at that daycare. They must've been planning something like this as a backup."

"A backup to what?" Mom drummed her long fingernails on the dashboard. "What's going on here, and who are you, Josh?"

"I'm… Let's just say I'm working for the government. I'm trying to help Gina."

"Haven't done a very good job of that so far, have you? But then if you're with some government agency, that doesn't surprise me."

"Mom." Gina rolled her eyes at Josh in the rearview mirror. "Josh has done more than enough to help me. You have no idea. And now he's going to help us get RJ back. Isn't that right, Josh?"

"We'll find him, and whoever took him is going to pay."

Gina pressed her forehead against the window. It had remained unspoken between them, but there was no way right now that they could turn over her father's map and plans to the tunnel to Josh's superiors. How RJ's kidnappers would even know whether or not they found the information and turned it over, she wasn't sure, but she wasn't willing to take any chances with RJ's life. She hoped Josh wouldn't either.

Following the GPS directions, Josh pulled to a stop in front of a white Mediterranean with a manicured lawn and landscaped gardens.

"Looks like Rita and her pals spared no expense." Gina tapped on the window.

Josh cut the engine. "Did they come out to greet you?"

"Yes. Rita came out first, and then the maid holding the little boy's hand. He broke right away from her when he saw RJ. I said goodbye to him, and then the maid ushered them into the house." Joanna sniffed.

"Mom, what made you think this other woman was the maid? Was she wearing some kind of uniform?"

"No. I don't know why I thought that. She didn't look anything like Rita and we weren't introduced, so I didn't think she was a relative and she was too young to be Diego's grandmother."

"Let's see if we can get inside the house." Josh opened his car door.

Gina shot out of the back seat and ran to the front door. She banged on the double doors and laid on the doorbell.

Joanna put one foot on the bottom step, tapping the toe of her sandal. "Do you think I didn't try that?"

Josh cupped a hand over his eyes and tried to peer through the frosted glass next to the door. "Did you ever get inside the house, Joanna?"

"No." She twisted the rings on her fingers. "I suppose I should've. I should've demanded to see where they were going to play and who was going to be there."

"That's just hindsight, Mom." Gina sat heavily on the

top step. "I don't think I would've done that at a play-date where I'd already seen the mom and some nanny or housekeeper with the kids. Don't blame yourself."

"That's the first time you've ever told me not to take the blame for everything that went wrong in your life. You even blamed me for liking Ricky Rojas. I'm not the one who married that pretty boy."

"No, you just married a drug dealer."

"So did you."

"Ladies." Josh held up his hands as if he were ref-ereeing a prizefight. "We don't have time to open old wounds right now. I'm going around to the back of the house. You can join me or sit here and argue on the front porch."

Joanna jabbed her finger at Josh's back. "Listen to this one. He's no pretty boy."

Gina rose to her feet with a flounce, mad at herself for taking her mother's bait and appearing immature in front of Josh.

He was right. They had no time for this. RJ was gone and she knew exactly what would be asked of them to get him back. She was more than willing to hand over the plans, the map and even the diamonds if Robbie didn't have them.

But was Josh?

She knew the people pulling Josh's strings didn't give a hoot about RJ or her…but Josh did.

As she followed Josh along the side of the big house, she paused each time he checked the windows or stud-ied the moist ground.

He opened an unlocked gate to the backyard and held it open for her and her mother, who'd slipped out of her high-heeled sandals.

Gina shivered when she caught sight of the shimmering pool, no safety gate surrounding it. Even if this playdate hadn't been totally fake, this would not have been a good environment for RJ. She'd been so vigilant about RJ ever since his birth, it had felt so normal and natural to slack off a bit and give the kid some breathing room—but she'd been too negligent.

"Here we go." Josh had crouched down in front of the sliding doors to the patio.

Gina hovered over him, his fingers tracing a neat square of cut-out glass. "They broke into this house? Isn't that taking a huge risk?"

"They probably knew it was vacant." He reached his arm inside the space and flicked the inside lock on the door. He slid it open and gestured to Gina to stay back.

He crept into the house while she and Mom waited outside.

Her mother put her hands on her hips. "Are you gonna tell me who he is now?"

"He told you."

"Is he DEA? Are you working with them now?" Her mother narrowed her eyes. "Where did the two of you go? I know it wasn't some romantic getaway in the Bahamas."

Gina's cheeks prickled with heat when she recalled making love with Josh on the balcony. It had been the most romantic and passionate thing she'd done in years... And while she'd been throwing all caution to the wind, someone was planning RJ's kidnapping.

"I can't tell you anything, Mom."

Josh poked his head outside. "It's all clear, but it doesn't look like they left anything behind."

Gina followed him inside with her mother trailing

after her. Her gaze darted around the sparsely furnished room. Even if Mom had come inside, she might not have noticed anything amiss.

"It looks like show furniture. When Realtors are selling a house that's vacant, they furnish it just for show."

"I should've demanded they let me in." Joanna dropped her shoes to the tile floor and kicked one. "I would've smelled a rat."

"Maybe, maybe not." Josh stepped into the kitchen and opened the refrigerator, the empty shelves glaring back at them. "Did you notice a car out front?"

"Black Mercedes, but don't ask me the model or license number."

"Gina, did you ever see the car at daycare?"

"Never noticed."

Mom flapped her arms, looking like a giant, exotic bird. "Are you going to call…whoever?"

Gina's eyes darted toward Josh, her tongue sweeping her lower lip. Josh hadn't had a chance to tell anyone about the tunnel plans yet. If he did so now, it would be game over…for RJ and for her.

"We're going to wait." Josh leaned against the fridge. "RJ's abductors want something from us in exchange for RJ, and we're going to give it to them—on our terms."

Gina folded her arms across her queasy stomach. She didn't like the sound of that. Terrorists had RJ in their clutches. As far as she was concerned, they could dictate any terms they wanted and she'd follow through with every one of them.

"D-do you think they'll call?"

"They have your phone number. They've made that clear already. They'll be in touch."

Joanna stamped one bare foot. "Who is *they*? Are

you talking about Los Santos? Did Hector leave you something they want?"

"Something like that, Mom, but it's best you don't know anything. Can you stay with your boyfriend for a while until we get this sorted out?"

"You're kicking me out of my own home?"

"Since when did I have to twist your arm to spend time with Tom?"

As they walked back to the car, Joanna grabbed Gina's arm. "Tell me you don't blame me for this."

Gina squeezed her mom's hand. "Not at all."

She knew where the blame lay, squarely on her own shoulders.

JOSH LET OUT a breath when he loaded the last of Joanna's many suitcases into the trunk of her car, and Joanna pulled away with a wiggle of her manicured fingers.

Massaging his temples, he walked Gina back into the pastel-colored building.

"I'm sorry you had to witness all that between us." Gina stabbed the elevator call button until it arrived and they got in. "We get at each other's throats sometimes."

"It's totally understandable. You're both under a tremendous amount of stress."

"That's a nice way to put it." She rested her forehead against the mirror inside the elevator. "I should've known they'd come after RJ. I should've never left him."

"They had other opportunities to get him, and never made an attempt. They decided to make a move once they figured you'd gotten your hands on the information they wanted. How were you supposed to know that?"

When the elevator doors opened, Gina walked silently to the door of her mother's place and then turned to him, grabbing handfuls of his shirt. "We're going to give it to them, aren't we, Josh?"

"I'm going to get RJ back for you. Count on it. They told your mother to meet us at the airport and break the news to you immediately, didn't they?"

"Yeah, that's what she said." She unlocked the door, and they entered the empty condo.

"They wanted to make sure we knew they had RJ before we turned over the information to the CIA. They don't want to hurt him. They wanted to give you that chance."

"What if they've already hurt him?" She swept up one of RJ's trucks from the floor and collapsed onto the sofa, hugging it to her chest.

"Of course, they're going to have to show some proof that he's okay before we even deal with them." He leaned over the back of the sofa and massaged her shoulders.

"When is that going to be? What are they waiting for?"

"The right time. I know it's hard, but try to be patient."

She spun one of the wheels of the truck. "You're not just going to hand over the plans, are you? They're too important. They're what you came for, why the government sent you here in the first place."

"I'll work something out. RJ's safety is the most important thing right now."

"It's the only thing to me."

"I know that." He twisted his head around. "Where's your phone? Keep an eye on it since you could be contacted at any time."

She patted the pocket of the sweater she'd hugged around her body since they'd returned, like she was trying to warm up. "Right here. Believe me, I'm not going anywhere without it."

"I suppose it won't do much good for you to get information about Diego's family from the daycare. It'll all be lies anyway, and we don't want to alert his kidnappers that we're probing."

"Josh." She placed the truck on the floor and wandered to the window, twisting her fingers in front of her. "How would the terrorists know that we gave the info to the CIA? They don't even know what they're looking for. They don't know the weapons are in a tunnel. They don't even know about the tunnel. What if we just turned over the plans to your superiors and pretended to give Los Santos's and Vlad's people vital information that was actually worthless?"

"First, they're not going to release RJ without some solid proof that you know where the drugs and weapons are. Second, don't discount the idea that they're not going to know what the CIA is up to. Computer hacking, leaks, moles—these are all real concerns in the intelligence community. Just as we monitor their chatter, they monitor ours."

"I thought as much." She burrowed back into the sofa. Hunching her shoulders, she buried herself deeper into her sweater.

That was not the answer she'd wanted from him, but he wasn't going to risk RJ's life…and he wasn't going to let the CIA or Ariel risk that child's life either.

He couldn't watch her sitting comatose in the corner of that sofa just waiting and worrying.

"Let's order something to eat. We haven't had anything since Fernanda fed us lunch, and that seems like a lifetime ago."

"We can't leave. I'm not walking out of here with RJ missing to have a meal."

"I said *order*. Pizza?"

She flicked her fingers. "Whatever you like. I can't stomach the thought of food."

He crossed the room to pick up Joanna's landline, holding up the buzzing receiver. "Any recommendations?"

"Supreme Pizza." She pulled out her cell phone. "The number's in here."

Not wanting to tie up her phone, he punched in the number on the landline and handed Gina's cell back to her. When he gave the pizza place Joanna's phone number, the guy on the phone already knew the address.

"Extra-large pepperoni and a house salad, Italian dressing." He glanced at Gina and she shrugged.

While they waited for the pizza, Josh typed up some notes on his laptop and Gina watched TV without seeing a thing. Josh shot a few worried glances her way. He almost wished she'd wail and gnash her teeth in her grief. It would be easier to comfort her.

Right now she looked as brittle as a dried stalk of wheat that, once touched, would break apart and scatter. If that happened, he'd lose her for sure.

He didn't know what Vlad's people were waiting for, but he was almost certain it *was* Vlad who had RJ and not Los Santos. The drug dealers were much less discreet than the terrorists—and not as highly trained.

The buzzer for the front door of the building startled them both, and Josh shoved away from the counter where he'd been working to press the speaker button. "Yeah?"

"Pizza delivery for Joanna."

"Stay there. I'll be right down."

Gina looked over the pillow she was hugging to her chest. "My mom usually lets him in and invites him up."

"Not this time. I'll be right back."

Josh stuffed some cash in his pocket and dashed downstairs to the lobby, waving at the security guard on duty. He opened the door for the pizza guy just as a couple was coming through the front door.

"Thanks and keep the change." Josh handed the kid some money and put the bag with the salad on top of the big pizza box and carried it to the elevator.

Back in the condo, he dished some salad into bowls and tossed a couple of pieces of pizza onto two plates. "Come and join me at the counter. I'll even throw in a glass of red wine."

"I couldn't…"

"What? Eat or drink while your son is missing?" He pulled out one of the high stools tucked beneath the center island in the kitchen. "C'mon. You'll need your strength when that call comes through, and a little wine will help you relax while we wait."

She tossed her security pillow to the side and shuffled to the counter. "Why haven't they called? Where is he?"

"They'll call. They want that info and they're not going to jeopardize that by harming RJ." He poured a glass half-full of a red wine he'd found on a small wine rack beneath the island counter. "Drink."

She sipped the wine, closing her eyes. Then she took a bigger gulp and set down the glass with a sigh.

"Already unwound a few of those muscles, right?"

Cupping the glass with both hands, she said, "I'm scared."

"I know you are, Gina." He brushed his fingers along her arm. "You'd be crazy not to be worried, but we got this—and then they'll pay. I'll make them pay."

A cell phone buzzed and he and Gina locked eyes for a few seconds.

She plunged her hand in her pocket, bobbling her phone and almost dropping it before holding it in front of her face. "Unknown number."

"It's them. Speaker."

She nodded and swallowed. "Hello?"

"What did you collect from that bank, Gina? And is it worth your son's life?"

Chapter Seventeen

Gina's heart hammered so loudly in her chest she could hardly hear her own response. "I have the information you want. Where's my son?"

"He's fine. Playing with his companion, Diego."

"I need to speak to him. I need to see him."

The man spoke away from the phone. "Isabella, bring the boy here."

A woman's voice cooed in the background. "It's your mama. Say hello."

"Hi, Mama."

Gina's throat closed with tears, which overflowed from her eyes. "RJ, how are you? Are you having fun?"

"Playing with Diego. We ate hamburgers."

"Lucky." She dashed a tear from her cheek with a balled-up fist. "Where are you?"

"At Diego's."

The sound of a clicking tongue came over the line. "Did you really think RJ was going to give you directions? As you can tell, he's fine. Now, what did you pick up at the bank?"

Josh tapped her phone and then pointed to his eyes.

"I—I want to see RJ."

"For God's sake. The boy is fine." After some noise in the background, the man heaved a heavy sigh. "All right."

A minute later, a picture of RJ holding a French fry and smiling came over the phone, and Gina traced his precious face with her finger.

The man growled, "Well?"

Josh had been writing on napkins and shoved the first one at her.

She read from the napkin. "'The weapons and the drugs are in a tunnel.'"

There was a sharp intake of breath over the phone. "A tunnel, where?"

Josh tapped the paper and she read the words he'd written. "'A tunnel beneath the US–Mexican border.'"

The man cursed in a language other than English, other than Spanish, and Gina gripped the phone tighter. Los Santos didn't have RJ, the terrorists did.

"Where is it? Do you have a map?" He paused for a few seconds. "You didn't already turn this information over to that navy SEAL or the CIA, did you? Because if you did…"

"No!" She knew the end of that sentence and didn't want to hear it, didn't even want to think it. "I mean, my… The SEAL knows because he was there with me. He's here now."

Josh leaned toward the phone. "What should stop us from turning this over to the US government? Why wouldn't we, and just lie to you about it? How would you know one way or the other?"

"Oh, we'd know. That's why this kid is still alive. We haven't heard anything, otherwise."

"You have a mole?"

"Where's the tunnel?"

"Where's Gina's son?"

"She'll get him back, safe and sound, once we get

our weapons, the weapons her lying, cheating father stole from us. If the CIA hadn't killed Hector De Santos, we would've done it for them. We'd upheld our end of the deal and delivered the drugs and he didn't turn over the weapons, as planned. You can blame your father for all of this."

Gina covered her eyes with her hand. She blamed them all.

"Listen—" Josh picked up the phone "—you're not getting this information until RJ is in his mother's arms. We'll meet you in Mexico. We'll guide you in from there once Gina has her son."

Lifting her hand, Gina peeked at Josh. He was serious. They were all going to meet out by this tunnel in Mexico.

The man on the other end of the line grunted. "That could work, but if you call in the CIA, the FBI, the DEA, the US military, we'll know about it—and the deal is off and things won't end well for Hector De Santos's grandson."

Gina put her hands to her ears and suppressed a moan that had started deep in her gut.

Josh stroked her hair. "I believe you. We won't call anyone."

Josh spent the rest of the conversation telling the man, who called himself Yuri, where to meet them in the Sonoran Desert and working out a plan for an exchange.

When Josh ended the call, Gina folded her arms across her stomach. "What are you going to do? You're not going to allow a band of terrorists to walk away with a cache of weapons, are you?"

"No. I don't think Los Santos is going to allow it either."

"What do you mean?"

"I told the scumbag on the phone that I wouldn't tell any government agency and I won't, but I don't think the terrorists have a mole within Los Santos. Do you?"

"You're going to tell Los Santos to meet us there, too?" She put one hand to her throat where her pulse was beating wildly. "That could put RJ in so much danger."

"RJ's already in danger. We have to have some element of surprise on our side."

"Why would Los Santos trust you? They can't possibly believe you're going to allow them to keep the drugs once they take out Vlad's people—*if* they can take out Vlad's people."

"Maybe we broker our own kind of deal with Los Santos. Vlad knows who I am, but the drug dealers don't. They don't know you're working with anyone. You can play them off."

"Me?" She jabbed an index finger at her chest just to make sure. "How can I play them off? What does that even mean?"

"As far as they know, you're Hector De Santos's daughter and Ricky Rojas's widow. You were more than eager to meet up with them when you thought Ricky might still be alive. I'm the jealous boyfriend who wouldn't allow it."

"You want me to contact the cartel, don't you? You want me to make some kind of deal with them."

"You can turn to them. Tell them the terrorist group has kidnapped your son, Hector De Santos's grandson and the heir apparent to Los Santos. You want your son back, you want revenge and you want those drugs."

She had to take another swig of wine for this one. "What about you?"

"Like I said, they don't know who I am. Why wouldn't you seek the protection of Los Santos? The last remaining members heard of you, you were at your father's compound in Colombia when he and your husband were shot and killed. You were grilled by the DEA and never gave up anyone or anything."

"That's because I didn't know anything."

"They don't know that. Besides, you knew about the accounts on Isla Perdida and kept mum about those."

"How are we going to pull this off without endangering RJ?"

"We'll keep RJ safe. We'll have to arrange some kind of ambush by Los Santos after you have possession of RJ."

"Los Santos will get away with the drugs. You know that, don't you? How could you live with yourself if you allowed that to happen, after all you've been through, after what your family went through at the hands of my father's cartel?"

"The DEA can always go after the cartel. Stopping Vlad is more important right now. Los Santos is the lesser of two evils. We know the location of the tunnel, and the DEA can come in and shut it down.

"It'll work." He popped a pizza crust in his mouth. "We'll make it work."

"Will it satisfy the people you report to?"

"It will hinder Vlad, and that's what they care about."

"Los Santos will want those weapons back."

"They're not going to get them. That I can't allow."

"You have a plan for those, I suppose?"

"Oh, yeah. Think about it." He crumpled a napkin and fired it into the lid of the pizza box. "We have a huge advantage over both Vlad and Los Santos—we're the only ones who know the location of that tunnel."

"What do we do next?"

"Before we fly out to Tucson tomorrow, you're going to contact Los Santos. Reply to the number they used to text you. Tell them you need their help and are willing to turn over Hector's drugs to get it."

"I hope they believe me."

"Why wouldn't they? You were afraid of them before. You thought they were going to kill you for information you didn't have—now you do have it."

"The people in Isla Perdida—were they Vlad's or the cartel's?"

"I think the man in the red tie who conveniently passed out on the plane was Los Santos. The couple and the assassin in the boat were Vlad."

"And you?"

"I'm just the jealous boyfriend who wants a little piece of the action."

Licking the taste of spicy pepperoni from her lips, Gina eyed her cell phone. "Should I do it now?"

"Send them a text."

They worked out the text together on the napkin first, and then Gina entered it into her phone.

I know where the drugs are. They have RJ. I need help.

She held her breath as the message zipped through. If this didn't work, she could die. RJ could die. She had to trust that Josh wouldn't let that happen. She had to trust the man who had killed RJ's father.

Gina stared at the display on her phone until her eyes grew tired and dry, until Josh had cleaned up all the dishes and wrapped up the pizza, until her wine-glass was full again.

"Go to bed." Josh brushed a finger across her lips. "They're not going to answer any faster with you staring at the phone."

She dragged her gaze away from the cell. "What if Los Santos doesn't answer at all? What if they don't believe me?"

"They want those drugs. That haul represents millions and millions of dollars to them and their street cred. If Los Santos wants to ride again, they need to prove they have the goods and the guts to carry on without the brains behind the operation."

"I hope you're right, or we'll be going out to Mexico tomorrow to face Vlad's people with nothing." She cupped her phone in her hand just as it buzzed, and she jumped.

Josh raised his brows at her, but she shook her head. "It's a text from Mom. Should I tell her I talked to RJ?"

"Don't tell her anything."

She responded to her mother and then dumped the rest of her wine in the sink. She needed a clear head to confront what was coming her way.

As they both turned to face the stairs, she grabbed Josh's hand. "Stay the night with me? I can't be alone."

"You're not alone." He placed his hands on her hips and followed her up the stairs.

Later in bed, she nestled her back against Josh, whose arm was draped around her waist. "I wonder if RJ is afraid. I wonder if he knows something isn't right."

"His captors are going to do everything in their power to make him comfortable. They have to bring him to Mexico, and they don't want an uncooperative subject. I'm sure they're telling him he's going to meet you there. He's probably still with Diego."

"Whoever that child is." Gina squeezed her eyes shut, trying to block out the guilt she felt for sending RJ into the unknown.

Just as she started to drift off, Josh's arm still securely around her, the cell phone in her hand buzzed.

She jerked awake and Josh said, "Is it them?"

Peering at the screen glowing in the dark, she read aloud from the text. "'Welcome home, *paloma*.'"

THE NEXT DAY, Gina stood in the middle of the Sonoran Desert as the wind whipped her hair across her face and sand pelted the back of her neck.

While they were in Arizona, Josh had called upon a buddy of his, a retired marine who'd worked bomb demolition. Josh had explained that Connor Delancey not only knew how to take apart explosives, he knew how to put them together.

Gina squinted through the binoculars at the rocks guarding the cave's entrance and said a little prayer for Josh and Connor as they rigged explosives among the weapons and drugs that were tucked inside the miles-long tunnel beneath the earth. Without her father's map, the location would be completely hidden.

She hoped RJ was miles away from that tunnel when it blew. They were counting on Los Santos to provide a diversion and some chaos so that Josh could get away from the tunnel and trigger the explosion.

Movement near the entrance of the tunnel had her tightening the grip on her .22. When Josh waved his arms over his head, she sagged with relief even though they still had a long way to go.

Five minutes later, the two men were back in Connor's four-wheel drive.

"Did everything go okay? Do you think it's going to work?"

"As long as this guy does his job as well as I've done mine." Connor jabbed Josh in the ribs with the end of a stick he'd picked up on his way into the tunnel.

Gina grabbed her hair with one hand, holding it in a ponytail. "How long?"

Josh checked his watch. "Two hours before I give Vlad's people their final directions to this spot in the desert."

Connor clapped Josh on the back. "Do me a favor, dude."

"Let me guess—pictures?"

"You got that right." Connor framed his hands in the air. "Just the moment it all detonates."

"Hopefully, we're going to be too far away to get any good pictures."

"C'mon, man. You're going to deny an artist his moment in the sun."

"You've got issues, Connor. I'll do what I can."

Josh shook Connor's hand, and Connor pulled him in for a one-armed, manly hug. "Hope it works out for you. If you need anything else on the other side of the border, let me know. And remember—" he winked at Gina "—I was never here."

Gina threw her arms around the big man. "Thank you so much. We couldn't have done this without you."

He took her by the shoulders. "I'd do anything for Josh Elliott. The man saved so many lives, including my own. Take a life, save a life."

She nodded, tears pricking the backs of her eyes. That's exactly what Josh had done for her.

Several minutes later, Josh took her hand as they stood side by side watching the dust from Connor's four-wheel drive disperse across the desert sand.

"It's just us now." She pressed the side of her head against his arm.

"Us and—" he walked to their Jeep and lifted a huge case from the back "—this. I'm going to set up now."

"Should I go with you?"

He pointed to some rock outcroppings in the distance. "We're going right there. Your father couldn't have picked a better place for his tunnel."

"That's driving distance, especially in this terrain."

"That's the point. Nobody can see or figure out what we're doing from that distance." He leveled a finger at the rocks.

"What if…?"

He held up a hand. "We'll work through anything that comes up."

She swung into the Jeep beside him and they bounced over the uneven ground, heading for a pile of rocks that resembled the discarded building blocks of some playful giants.

Josh parked the Jeep at the base of the outcropping and hauled his sniper rifle from the back. She followed him up and over the granite until he reached a flattop.

"Are you going to be able to get here in time?"

Josh ignored her question, and Gina perched on a rock, watching him pull pieces of his weapon out of the case and set it up on the flat base of the rock. Had he gone through the same motions on a hillside outside her father's compound in Colombia?

His eye to the scope, he tweaked and shifted the rifle several times before letting out a long breath. "Got it."

"What if there's someone standing in the way? What if they notice the trigger wire at the tunnel's entrance and yank it out?"

"I doubt anyone's going to be yanking any wires, even if they see them. They'll take off running before they do that. And I'll make sure nobody is standing in the way."

"You do this sort of thing all the time? Set up these types of ambushes?"

"I'm an old pro."

"How much time?"

"Just enough time to get you up here and show you what to do."

Gina froze. "What are you talking about?"

"I'm going to train you to be a sniper in fifteen minutes."

She blinked. She stood up. She plopped back down on the rock. "You're not serious."

"I'm deadly serious." He held out his hand to her. "Do you really think Vlad's people or Los Santos for that matter, are going to allow me to leave that tunnel?"

"Th-they're not going to kill you."

"Vlad would like nothing better than to kill me." He cupped his fingers and gestured her forward. "You have to do this, Gina. It's all set up for you. I've done the hard part. All you have to do is pull the trigger."

"You're crazy." She shook her head back and forth, hoping to clear it.

"I'm not gonna lie. The kickback on the rifle's gonna be a bitch, but you're a strong woman and you can handle it. If it knocks you on your ass after you take the shot, that's okay. You just need the one shot, and then you take RJ and get the hell out of here."

"You mean, after I pick you up."

"Yeah, yeah. After you pick me up."

"Josh…"

He took her hand. "C'mon up and let me show you what to do."

Gina spent the next several minutes with her eye to the scope, her finger on the trigger of the big rifle and a knot in her stomach. Josh actually expected her to shoot the sniper rifle at the trigger he and Connor had propped up between two rocks, setting off an explosion in the tunnel.

And then he expected her to, what? Leave him behind? Knowing his life could be in her hands gave her more courage and determination than she'd ever had before in her life.

After he had her run through the instructions with him for about the hundredth time, she collapsed on a rock and stretched out her fingers.

"I think you've got it down. You can do this." He sat beside her and rested his hand on her thigh.

She glanced down at his hand and trailed her fingers along the corded muscle of his forearm. She wasn't ready to lose Josh yet. There was too much she had to tell him.

The pressure of her touch increased as a sudden panic rushed through her body.

Josh's head shifted slightly to the side as he raised his eyebrows. "You okay?"

"Whatever happens today, just know that I love you, Josh Elliott."

He grabbed her face with both hands and pulled her close. "God, and I thought it was just me who'd fallen in love with you."

Chapter Eighteen

Josh's muscles tensed as he spied the headlights in the distance. Nighttime hadn't fallen in the desert yet, but any minute now it would come on fast like a curtain dropping on a stage.

Gina sat up in the passenger seat of the Jeep. "Is that them?"

"Can't imagine who else it would be out here," Josh mouthed the words around the toothpick in the side of his mouth, and then spit it out. "Are you ready?"

"I'm ready to see RJ."

Tugging on her hair, he pulled her close and kissed her hard on the mouth. "This is gonna work."

"I know. I believe that with all my heart."

"Then it's showtime." He launched out of the Jeep onto the desert floor and called back to Gina. "Two vehicles."

She exited the car and stood beside him, crossing her arms. "One of those cars better have RJ in it."

"They passed the rocks where the rifle is stationed." He rolled his shoulders. One victory at a time.

The two off-road vehicles came in hot, kicking up a dust storm in their wake. The first truck carried a man, standing and pointing a rifle at them.

The knots in Josh's gut tightened as he spread his arms out to his sides. He'd already disarmed himself, his weapons, except for the sniper rifle hidden in the rocks, displayed on the hood of the Jeep.

A bright white light mounted on the first truck bathed the area in an eerie glow. The vehicles squealed to a stop, and Josh huffed out a breath when he saw a woman lead RJ from the second vehicle.

Gina cried out and rushed toward her son, but the man with the rifle waved her off.

"When we say you can."

Gina stopped, her arms stretched out before her. "RJ, are you okay?"

The boy nodded, his eyes wide and glassy. Fun time with Diego must've ended and confusion had set in.

Josh curled his fists at his sides. This had to work.

A man stepped forward and Josh recognized his voice from the phone call. Yuri. "Where is the tunnel? How do we get to it?"

"Release the boy to his mother now, let them both leave as planned and I'll take you over. It's not gonna happen before that and you'll never find the entrance to that tunnel without me."

The ringleader nodded to one of his minions, and he grabbed Josh and patted him down. Then the man took the gun and the knife on top of the Jeep and pocketed them. "You won't be needing these."

The woman, who had to be the one who called herself Rita, said something to RJ and relinquished her grip on his shoulders.

RJ took off like a shot and barreled into his mother's waiting arms.

She stroked RJ's hair and whispered to him.

"Take the Jeep, Gina, and get out of here."

She raised her head and met his gaze. Her eyes were dark pools in her face, but he knew she could do it.

Yuri motioned with his gun. "The tunnel?"

"This way." Josh didn't give Gina another look as she piled RJ into the Jeep beside her and made a U-turn, kicking up sand with her wheels.

He didn't want any of this bunch to realize what Gina meant to him. Hell, he hadn't realized how much she meant to him until she told him she loved him.

Josh wiped a drop of sweat from his brow and picked up his flashlight. "This way, about a quarter of a mile."

He scuffed through the sand toward the tunnel Hector De Santos had constructed for the purpose of allowing terrorists and weapons to enter the United States.

Vlad would never give up something this valuable, so Josh put a little insurance into place to at least give himself a fighting chance to get out of here alive…in case Los Santos didn't follow through.

As he approached the entrance, obscured by the two boulders, Josh turned suddenly to the three men following him. "If Vlad thinks he's going to have use of this tunnel after you remove these weapons, you can set him straight."

Yuri narrowed his eyes. "What do you mean?"

"Before you got here, I videotaped the location of the tunnel on my phone and sent it to my email address. I have an email message set to send automatically in two days, and if I'm not alive and well to stop that message, it will go out to a friend of mine with instructions. You can imagine what those instructions are."

"What's to stop you from sending out that message anyway when…if we let you go?"

"Nothing except my word and your word that Gina De Santos and her son will be safe as long as you get what you want here tonight."

"We intend to get what we want, and Vlad will get what he wants."

The corner of Josh's eye twitched. What Vlad wanted was to kill one of the navy SEALs from the team that had dogged him all over the Middle East.

Josh continued to the two innocuous-looking rocks and aimed his flashlight at the entrance, careful to keep the light away from the two rocks that held the trigger box.

"I see it, Yuri. I see how to get into the tunnel." One of Yuri's henchmen pushed Josh to the side where he stumbled against the two rocks. Perfect—now he could stand in front of the trigger mechanism, blocking it from view.

Yuri stood back as the man shoved aside one of the boulders, already leveraged to move with ease.

"Watch him." Yuri ducked inside the tunnel and one of the men followed him, while the other stayed at the entrance with Josh.

Out of the corner of his eye, Josh detected movement by the vehicles. Rita and one other had stayed behind with the cars, but they would be no match for the members of the cartel, intent on getting their drugs.

The man holding Josh at gunpoint hadn't noticed the commotion yet, didn't know what to look for in the rapidly darkening desert.

The tunnel interested the guy much more. He cupped a hand around his mouth and yelled, "Are they there? Are the weapons there?"

Yuri called back, "Everything De Santos promised

and even all the drugs we gave him…and I'm guessing this tunnel leads straight into Arizona."

Finally the man guarding him noticed the three figures slipping toward them in the shadows.

"What the hell?" Those were the last words out of his mouth—forever. He dropped in front of Josh, and Josh leaped over the rocks housing the trigger box and started crawling through the sand.

"Hey, hey!"

Someone else shouted in Spanish and a gunshot rang out.

Josh was not waiting around to see who was shooting at what. At some point they'd reach a standoff, and both parties probably figured they'd be able to catch up with him and kill him out here in the desert.

But they weren't figuring on Gina De Santos.

PANTING, GINA REACHED the lookout. She'd left RJ snug in the back seat of the Jeep, wrapped in a blanket.

She put her eye to the scope of the sniper rifle, and it framed exactly what it was supposed to frame. She had to stop herself from moving it to look for Josh to make sure he was out of the way.

He'd assured her he'd be long gone, but he would've told her that anyway. He was only half expecting to make it out of this desert alive. He was willing to sacrifice himself to destroy the weapons and the drugs, to destroy that tunnel…and to protect her and RJ.

She licked her lips. She planned to get Josh out of here in one piece and it started with one shot.

With her eye pressed to the scope, just as Josh had taught her, she curled her finger around the trigger. The night vision on the scope made everything at the tunnel as clear as day, and she saw two men disappear into what looked like the solid face of a rock. Another man had a gun pointed at Josh. She couldn't look at that.

All her focus, and the rifle's, was on the box wedged between two rocks at Josh's feet. He'd instructed her to shoot when she saw Los Santos on the scene, regardless of where he was or what he was doing.

Fat chance.

The man holding Josh at gunpoint dropped. Two flashes of light flared near the tunnel entrance. She could no longer see Josh's feet near the two rocks. Did that mean he'd gotten away? Followed the men into the tunnel? Gotten himself shot?

Josh's voice growled in her ear. *Don't think. Take the shot.*

With a sob she braced her feet against a boulder behind her and pulled the trigger of the sniper rifle.

The kickback on the rifle almost ripped her arm from its socket and she stumbled backward, the boulder catching her fall. She made a hard landing on the rock just as the night sky exploded with a red-and-orange cloud.

Staggering to her feet, she gaped at the flames and smoke cascading up to the desert sky.

"Mama!"

Leaving the rifle, she scampered down the rocks to the Jeep and vaulted into the driver's seat. "Are you okay, RJ?"

"Look. Fireworks."

"You're right. Someone set off some fireworks, all right."

She mumbled a few prayers as she cranked on the

Jeep's engine. Josh had told her to wait here for him after the explosion, and he'd make his way back.

Not one chance in hell.

She flicked on the high beams and followed the well-worn trail back toward the original meeting place, a gun on the passenger seat beside her. If Los Santos hadn't taken out Rita and whoever else stayed behind, Gina would be ready for them.

And if any of Vlad's men had Josh in their clutches, she'd be ready for them, too.

Her lights picked out a figure running, the orange glow behind him, the sand dragging down his every step. Holding her breath, Gina slowed down and grabbed the gun.

"Are we going to the fireworks, Mama?"

"Maybe we are, little frog."

The figure waved his arms and Gina let out a sob as she recognized Josh's handsome face with the biggest smile she'd ever seen plastered on it. She made a U-turn and then pulled up alongside him.

He'd stopped, bending over with his hands on his knees, gulping in air.

She leaned over and opened the passenger door. "Goin' my way, SEAL?"

Epilogue

Gina stretched her arms toward the sun and then adjusted her red bikini top. Cupping one hand over her eyes, she yelled toward the pool, "Not so close to the edge."

Josh, with RJ on his shoulders, turned and then both of them splashed water at her at the same time.

"You two!" She laughed and tipped up her sunglasses. "RJ, come and eat your lunch."

"C'mon, big guy." Josh swam to the edge of the pool, towing RJ behind him. "Time to eat lunch. We can go out again, unless you want to visit the turtles on the beach first."

"Turtles, turtles!"

"You got it." Josh lifted RJ out of the pool and placed him on the deck.

Gina patted the chaise longue to her left. "Come and dry off."

RJ clambered into the chaise longue, pulling a towel around his wet body, and a minute later the poolside waitress delivered lunch.

Gina made sure RJ had everything he needed and then took a sip of her tequila sunrise. She held up the glass to Josh toweling off his hair on the other side of her. "Kind of decadent to have a froufrou drink in the middle of the afternoon."

"We're on vacation, and you deserve it."

Once Josh's superiors had received his report and were satisfied that the weapons Hector De Santos was once going to deliver to Vlad's terrorist organization had been destroyed, along with the drugs he'd gotten in exchange for those weapons, they sent Josh on a short leave before he had to return to his deployment overseas.

They'd decided to join Gina's mother and Tom in the Bahamas, and RJ couldn't have been happier with the arrangement. For having no father as a role model, Josh had picked up the part quickly.

Josh clinked his beer mug against her glass. "Don't get too comfortable behind that sniper rifle. My commanding officer just might send you out in the field."

"Where you're going." She smoothed a hand down his shoulder. "I'm going to worry about you."

"That's the hard part—for you. It's almost easier being out there than sitting at home waiting." He kissed the inside of her wrist. "I hear that all the time from the guys who have partners. Their wives and girlfriends are the ones who do all the hard work."

"I don't want you to be thinking about that, about me. I'm going to have plenty to keep me busy, finding a spot for my new bar now that the DEA released my grandmother's money to me."

"Impossible for me to not think about you, but I'll be imagining you starting your new venture and not worrying about me. Deal?"

"Works for me. Everything about you works for me, Josh."

"Was Joanna upset you turned the accounts in Isla Perdida over to the DEA?"

"No—resigned. When I told some of what we went through and what Hector had been planning, she didn't want the money anymore. Besides, Tom has enough for the both of them. What about Vlad?"

His jaw tightened. "What about him?"

"Did all this bring the CIA…or Ariel any closer to finding him?"

"No. He has his minions do the dirty work. He pulls the strings behind the scenes. But more and more, he's making his presence known and he's going to slip up. When he does—" Josh snapped his fingers "—we'll be there."

"With so many people on his trail, it's bound to happen. Was the CIA able to bring in any of the people who followed us to the island?"

"They picked up Roger and Tara—surprisingly not their real names. The man in the red tie?" He shrugged. "Melted away."

"But they did get Rita. Poor Diego. His own mother used him to get to RJ."

"Diego is safe with his grandmother now."

Gina shivered. "RJ could've wound up like Diego if my father and Ricky had lived."

"But they didn't." Josh raised his glass and took a sip of his drink. "Let's try to enjoy these few days we have together. Joanna promised that she and Tom would stay with RJ tonight while I take you out for some dinner, dancing and a moonlit stroll along the beach—and RJ's staying in their room."

"I can't wait." She'd enjoy every second with Josh until he had to leave her, and then she'd send him off with love and the belief that he'd do his job to the best of his ability and come home to her.

Josh held up the sunscreen. "Can you get my back?"

She winked. "I'll always have your back, SEAL."

And she knew he'd always have hers.

* * * * *

Look for the next book in Carol Ericson's
RED, WHITE AND BUILT *series,*
POINT BLANK SEAL, *on sale next month!*
And don't miss the first two books in the series:

LOCKED, LOADED AND SEALED
ALPHA BRAVO SEAL

You'll find them wherever
Mills & Boon Intrigue books are sold!

He was close enough to see the tears streaming down her cheeks.

Ah, hell. He hadn't meant to cause that.

"You want to know what my life was like?" she pushed.

"Imagine the worst day you've ever had..." Her eyes were wild; he'd never seen her like this before. "And then imagine people were getting hurt all around you and you had no power to stop it."

"Tell me what he did to you, Melissa," he said. He needed to hear the words.

"Right now all I can think about is staying alive so that I can take care of my little girl. I get that you hate me. I hurt you and I probably deserve whatever anger you hurl at me. But my life has been hell and I just want this nightmare to end. Nothing else matters until it does."

Colin couldn't think of one positive thing to say to calm her down so he threw all caution to the wind, pulled her into his arms and kissed her.

TEXAS WITNESS

BY
BARB HAN

MILLS & BOON

First Published in Great Britain 2017
By Mills & Boon, an imprint of HarperCollins*Publishers*
1 London Bridge Street, London, SE1 9GF

© 2017 Barb Han

ISBN: 978-0-263-92915-7

46-0917

Our policy is to use papers that are natural, renewable and recyclable products and made from wood grown in sustainable forests. The logging and manufacturing processes conform to the legal environmental regulations of the country of origin.

Printed and bound in Spain
by CPI, Barcelona

USA TODAY bestselling author **Barb Han** lives in north Texas with her very own hero-worthy husband, three beautiful children, a spunky golden retriever/standard poodle mix and too many books in her to-read pile. In her downtime, she plays video games and spends much of her time on or around a basketball court. She loves interacting with readers and is grateful for their support. You can reach her at www.barbhan.com.

Many thanks go to Allison Lyons, who makes every book better! A deep well of gratitude goes to Jill Marsal, who really is the best of the best and a dream to work with.

Brandon, Jacob and Tori, the three of you light up my life in so many bright and colorful ways. I love each of you even more with every passing year, and it is my greatest pleasure to see the beautiful people you've become.

Babe, we're watching another one of our babies test his wings. We get to enjoy a few more years with our youngest before she does the same. Then it'll be the two of us again, just like in the beginning... And a whole new set of adventures await. I love you!

Chapter One

"I didn't approve her. I would never do that. She shouldn't be here." Cynthia Stoker, the Cattlemen Crime Club's event coordinator, paced in the kitchen. Her fingers were a braided knot. She was responsible for the guest list at the Spring Fling, the annual end-of-spring fund-raiser hosted by the O'Brien family.

"I know." Colin O'Brien folded his arms, hiding just how much the thought of seeing Melissa Roark—correction, Melissa Rancic—again twisted his gut. Being the fourth son of the wealthy O'Brien family and with good looks and charm to spare, he hadn't seen a lot of rejection in his life. Until her. And she'd ripped his heart out. "How'd her name get past security?"

"She asked to come as Carolina Jordan's plus-one, and since she wasn't listed as a threat they approved her," Cynthia said, throwing her hands in the air, worry lines bracketing her mouth. She'd worked at the ranch for a little more than five years. She'd become close with his family and knew that the subject of Melissa was off-limits. "Honest. I thought she moved away a year ago. I had no idea she'd resurface."

"She did." The thought that she'd returned to Bluff, Texas, let alone be bold enough to show up at his family's fund-raiser riding on someone else's invitation, sat hot and heavy. The heels of his boots clicked on the tile floor as he paced. The last time he'd seen her had been when she'd handed him the engagement ring she'd been wearing—the one he'd given her—and then married one of the biggest jerks to ever blow through town, Richard Rancic. The guy was all flash and no substance, splashing local businesses with his money before taking what he wanted—Melissa—and breezing out of town. The newlyweds had disappeared after the quickie wedding. Apparently, Melissa couldn't get away from Colin fast enough.

He'd moved on, dated plenty of interesting women since then. The thought of seeing her again shouldn't hurt this much. And just to prove to himself that it didn't, he planned to march right into the ballroom and show her just how freakin' fantastic he was doing since she'd told him that she didn't love him the same anymore and then walked out of his life.

Cynthia stalked toward the kitchen table, where Colin had seen her cell phone.

"I'm calling security. Don't worry about a thing. You don't even have to look at her. I'll have her escorted out. She shouldn't be here and Carolina should've known better than to bring her. I'm putting them both on the Never Allow list." Her voice had that *shaming* quality.

"No need. I'll walk her out myself and then deal with Carolina personally," Colin bit out in a low growl.

Cynthia tensed, reacting to his sharp words.

Well, he hadn't meant to make her do that. He'd apologize later. Right now, he had an important matter to take care of. He didn't want one of his brothers seeing Melissa first and ushering her out of the building before he got a chance to have his say. No, he wanted to handle this little *problem* on his own. Carolina might've been Melissa's girlfriend but she'd become close with his family. Colin considered Carolina a friend, too, until now.

Colin stalked out of the room and toward the Great Hall. The place was decorated to the nines for the Spring Fling. Paper lanterns hung from the forty-foot tented ceiling. White candles contrasted against the dark oak beams and wood floors. Round tables with white linens covering them surrounded the dance floor. The place, fixed up, gave a nod to its heritage as an old horse barn and had rustic charm in spades.

Colin's blood pressure spiked with each step inside the room as he searched for his target. George Strait's "Baby Blue" filled the air as pairs of boots shuffled around the dance floor in a two-step.

And then he saw her. His gaze fixed. His heart fisted.

Melissa Rancic stood in front of the buffet table, nervously searching the faces in the crowd. At least she had enough sense to be worried even if she also had a whole helluva lot of nerve showing up at his family home.

Colin didn't want to acknowledge how damn good she looked. Her wavy auburn hair hung just past her shoulders. She'd cut it since the last time he'd seen her when it fell mid-back in large ringlets. She had on a cream-colored sleeveless dress that smoothed along the soft curves of her frame and flared below the waist with two layers of ruffles.

The dress fell mid-thigh, showing off those long legs of hers. Her fingers toyed with the necklace that hung in the middle of her chest, and the huge rock on her wedding finger sparkled in the dim light. She wore light brown boots with blue inlay. The fact that she still owned them at all made him believe she'd stayed somewhere in Texas. Although, she could live anywhere. He wouldn't know. After the way she'd left things unfinished between them, he'd refused to talk about her again. She'd made her choice and he'd closed up inside, telling himself that he needed to cowboy up and move on. Of course, he'd spent plenty of couch time licking his wounds before he'd had enough of the lovesick-puppy routine.

Memories of her in his arms, her warm, naked skin against his, tried to break through his thoughts as he stared at her. The way she smelled like early morning on a sunny day in spring, all flowers and warmth. Her intelligence. The way she laughed...

Those thoughts had about as much place in his mind as she had in his house. To be clear, there was room for neither. It was about time she knew it.

As he stalked closer, he realized there was more than worry going on in her head. She was anxious, stressed and those weren't the same things. She had to know this was the last place on earth she should be. Since it had been so easy for her to walk away from him last year and shut him out of her life completely, he figured her apprehension had nothing to do with the possibility of running into him. Was she afraid Carolina had disappeared on her? She was looking for someone. Or *looking out* for someone. Watching. Weary.

Her weight shifted from side to side like when she was nervous. She kept toying with that necklace, too. Was that a gift from *him*, from Richard?

Rather than sneak up on her or come at her from the side, Colin took a straight-on approach, and he didn't bother to hide the intensity in his glare. If she had the guts to come to his house, she could take it.

The second she saw him, her body language changed. Her posture tensed and she stood stiff and uncomfortable. A look of panic crossed her features as her gaze darted around, probably looking for an escape route. With the buffet table behind her and the only other exit to Colin's back, she was trapped in between.

As he neared, he could see that her pulse pounded at the base of her neck—a neck he had no business looking at in the first place, especially not the exact spot that made her mewl with pleasure when his mouth covered it.

When he was close enough to see the violet streaks in her brown eyes, she tried to duck right.

"Not so fast," Colin ground out, catching her by the arm.

"Let go of me, Colin O'Brien," she said, facing toward the east wall, refusing to look at him directly.

Colin wasn't about to let her get away with that. It was high time she learned that sidestepping a problem didn't make it go away. He spun her around to face him. They were almost nose-to-nose and the movement brought her scent washing over him, memories crashing into him. His heart double fisted.

"Why are you here?" he managed to bite out, clenching his back teeth.

"I shouldn't have come." Her eyes were pleading for him to let go now.

He couldn't. He wanted—no, *needed* to understand what he'd done wrong to make her run out on him in the first place. His pride kept him from asking as she shook out of his grip, the diamond on her wedding ring scratching his arm as she jerked free.

"Hold on, Mel—"

Before he could finish, she was gone. She'd dashed across the dance floor, pushed open the double doors to the lawn and fled. All the lines he'd practiced in his head a million times over were a distant memory. He stood there, mute and stupid. Frozen. Just like before.

Dancing had stopped even though the music played on. All eyes were on him now. From his peripheral vision, he saw two of his brothers making a beeline toward him.

Colin wasn't in the mood for a family meeting, so he reversed course and then ditched them out the back door.

HEART POUNDING, MELISSA ran to her sedan. She should've known better than to show up at the O'Brien's ranch. Yet, she'd had to see Colin one more time before disappearing into her new identity in witness protection. She glanced at the clock on her dashboard. She had little more than two hours left before saying goodbye to her past life. At midnight, Melissa Rancic would no longer exist. Richard Rancic, her husband and a hardened criminal, had escaped custody and was on the loose. According to her US marshal handler, Tim Davis, Richard was last seen making a run for the Canadian border. That he was so far away had given her the confidence she'd needed to come back to Bluff and see Colin. She'd expected it to hurt but also to comfort her. To give her the strength she would need to do what had to be done in order to protect her daughter.

Hands shaking, she managed to retrieve her purse

from the backseat and locate her keys. Getting the right one in the ignition proved a frustrating challenge. After several attempts, she had the engine purring and the Great Hall in the rearview. Not long after that, the entire O'Brien ranch disappeared.

Head spinning, she thought about the fact that Colin hadn't changed one bit, unless it was possible to look even better. That old saying about absence making the heart grow fonder proved true. His jet-black hair and those intense dark eyes still had the power to make her weak-kneed with one look. There was a deeper emotion present in his eyes now, too, and it looked a lot like hurt.

The past year of living without him had been like living in an Arctic cave…brutal, dark, cold. There'd been no sun. No laughter. No joy. And yet, day after day, she'd had to put on a brave face with her husband and pretend that she loved him. Both her and her daughter's survival had depended on delivering a good show. A shiver raced through her as she thought about what her life had turned into and the dangerous man she was running from.

Life, like spring weather in Texas, could change in a flash.

The gravity of just how big a mistake it had been to come back to Bluff, to see Colin, had shifted the ground beneath her feet. This whole idea had been a stupid mistake no matter how badly her body had reacted at the thought of never seeing him again, and the panic attack had been almost crippling. Her chest had squeezed until she thought it might burst. When release finally came, her heart filled with an ache so deep she could scarcely breathe.

Even so, it had been rash of her to think that she

could get away with slipping into the dimly lit Great Hall and catch one last glimpse of him before someone recognized her and kicked her out. Based on his expression, he would have her thrown out himself.

Memories of spending time at the ranch assaulted her. She and Colin had been so happy, so carefree, so in love...

A sob escaped before she could suppress it. Her eyes blurred as she navigated onto the main road into town. At least she had their daughter. She'd have to hold on to that piece of Colin for the rest of her life and let it be enough. Angelina touched a piece of Melissa's heart that could belong to no one else. She thought about how unfair it was that her daughter had never met her real father, would never meet him.

But then, this was the way it had to be, she reminded herself. Melissa's father was old and sick. He'd made his mistakes and they were both paying for them. If Richard had followed through on his threats, her father would live out the rest of his life in jail. She couldn't allow that to happen no matter how angry she'd become at him for his unethical business practices. And then there were the threats Richard had made about Colin and his family. The man could destroy the O'Briens if their secret was revealed. The bedrock of the family had been their parents' unwavering love and devotion. If Richard had gone public with the photos he had, the ones of Mr. O'Brien having an affair, the family would've been crushed. Colin would've been devastated.

In order to save her father and Colin, Melissa had done as Richard had said. Break off her engagement with Colin and agree to marry Richard instead. Save two families. Melissa had naively believed that all she needed was time to figure out how to back out of the arrangement with Richard. It had all come at her so fast. How simple had she been to think that man wouldn't force her to go through with the wedding or a loveless union?

And then she'd missed her period. Once she'd realized she was pregnant and that Richard would stop at nothing to destroy her if she walked out on him, she'd been too frightened to put up a fight. Scared he'd force her to give the baby up for adoption or, worse yet, do something more sinister, she'd convinced Richard that Angelina was his. She hadn't realized how a small snowball of a lie could grow and build, gaining momentum until it became an avalanche and destroyed everything in its path, destroyed her.

In her heart, she'd known all along that Richard would've moved heaven and earth to find her if she'd left him before the feds became involved. Then he'd destroy everything she loved. The worst part about her whole marriage was that she'd had to persuade her husband that Colin meant nothing to her. Her and her daughter's lives had depended on Melissa being convincing.

Three days after Angelina had been born, the feds had shown up and told Melissa they were building a case against Richard and his family. She'd been given an ultimatum: help the government or lose her daughter. She'd negotiated to have her father taken into protective custody. He was living in an undisclosed facility. Melissa had secretly helped gather evidence against her husband, living in daily fear of being discovered. And that wasn't the worst of it. The true hell that she'd lived had been wondering what her life would have been like if she'd married Colin instead…

There was no time for doubts now.

Melissa had done what she'd had to do in order to protect those closest to her, including him. Regretting the past or her actions now wouldn't change a thing. Witnessing the pain in Colin's eyes had her second-guessing everything.

Tears streaked her cheeks as, once again, she drove away from the only man she'd ever loved.

Chapter Two

"Thank you so much, Mrs. Klein," Melissa said as she held out a couple of twenties in her fist, not realizing she was clenching her hand until she noticed her white knuckles.

The older woman glanced at Melissa and smiled before waving her hand. She'd retired and moved to Bluff after thirty years of teaching in the Houston ISD. Her husband's family was originally from the area, and the two of them had returned to live out their retirement in a small town. She was the perfect neighbor because she didn't know everyone yet and had no idea about Melissa's past in Bluff.

"I can't take all that and especially not for—" Mrs. Klein glanced at her watch "—an hour and fifteen minutes' worth of work."

"Please do. I didn't realize I'd be back so soon and I've messed up your whole evening." Tears free-fell down Melissa's cheeks now, and they had nothing to do with the words coming out of her mouth.

"Don't worry about it, dear. Seriously. There's still time to catch CSI with Bernard if I hurry." Mrs. Klein's brow furrowed and she had a mix of pity and kindness on her face. She really was a sweet woman. "The baby was no trouble. She's been asleep the whole time."

Melissa told herself to get it together. She would. It had been easier to leave town when she thought she was saving everyone she loved. With everything that she'd been through in the past twelve months, she figured she could endure most anything. Seeing Colin again was too much. She'd been naive to think that she could see him again and then walk away a second time without a few tears. He looked good… unbelievably good. Different, but good. His quick smile and easygoing charm had been replaced by distrust and cautious eyes.

The way he'd looked at her, so angry, so hurt…so final.

For Colin, there wasn't a lot of gray area. Life was black-and-white. She should've known that once she'd left him, he'd be done. Having her fear confirmed hurt. The only consolation was that she'd always have a piece of Colin with her in their daughter.

"At least take something for your time," Melissa managed to get out before Mrs. Klein could walk out the door.

Melissa flipped on the front porch light. Nothing happened. The electricity in this old house was about as reliable as the cell coverage in town. Both were spotty.

"Oh, great. Now what?" Melissa asked rhetorically as more tears streamed.

"It's really okay, dear. Don't make yourself sick over it," Mrs. Klein said, patting Melissa on the shoulder. "Are you going to be all right?"

Melissa suppressed a sob. "I'll be fine. It's been a long day and I just need a good night of sleep. That's all."

She wished a few hours of rest could fix all her problems. Instead, she'd be meeting with her handler in a little more than an hour and a half. Her world would never be the same again.

"Whatever's going on will get better with time. I promise," Mrs. Klein soothed.

The woman had no idea how complicated Melissa's life had become.

"At least take something for your trouble." Melissa held out the fistful of twenties toward Mrs. Klein.

"If it'll make you feel better." The old woman peeled off the top twenty and tucked it inside her pocket. She winked. "I'll take Bernard out to breakfast with that money in the morning."

"Thank you for everything," Melissa said. She closed and locked the door after watching Mrs. Klein walk across the street to see that she was safely home. She texted Carolina that she'd left the party.

Melissa was relieved that the older woman hadn't pressed to find out what was really wrong with her. She'd been mute for twelve long months, save for the conversations she'd had with the feds, and she wanted to shout from the rooftops now that she was free. But she wasn't really free. Richard was still out there. Somewhere. Melissa shivered at the thought. She was about to leave everything she'd ever known behind for witness protection because of that man. And there was a very real possibility that she would never see Colin again. A sob tried to escape. She suppressed it.

The feds had said that Richard should be somewhere near the Canadian border by now. Melissa had been under so much duress, especially in the past two months since talking with the agents, that she could barely think straight. She told herself that was the reason she'd been misguided enough to think seeing Colin one more time would somehow fill the ache in her chest.

Everything had spun out of control. Her relationship with the feds hadn't exactly been a friendly alliance. The only reason she'd collected evidence against Richard was because they threatened to take Angelina away from her. Ever since they'd approached her while she picked up the mail that cold January morning, she'd been walking a tightrope.

Richard had been good at covering his tracks, so culling evidence against him had been difficult. She'd eventually gathered the proof needed for the feds to get an arrest warrant. She'd risked her life, not to mention her daughter's. And what had they done with Richard? Allowed him to escape. No one could save Melissa now if Richard got to her. If it wasn't for Angelina, for that smiling angelic face, Melissa would've lost hope a long time ago.

Melissa was weary, lonely, and part of her felt like she'd never live a normal life again. At least her father was in protective custody. His health was sketchy but he was in a decent facility in the Pacific Northwest. That's the only information she'd been given and that's all she needed to know. She wasn't ready to forgive her father for what he'd done to ruin both of their lives, but she'd felt the need to protect him. And now, she and Angelina would be Bethany and Claire soon. A new life, a fresh start, shouldn't feel like such a death sentence. But it would be because they'd be living a life without Colin.

Head pounding, heart aching, she closed her eyes before leaning against the door and then sinking until her bottom hit the hardwood floor. She twisted off her wedding ring, noticing the red marks on her finger it left behind because it had always been a little too tight, and threw it across the room. Relief flooded her at getting that thing off her finger. She'd put it on so no one would question her about it. The only reason she'd held on to the ring was because she figured she could sell it if times got tight. The government had made promises to her, but who really knew if they could be trusted? They'd allowed Richard to slip through their fingers and that wasn't exactly reassuring.

Seconds turned into minutes and Melissa had no idea how long she'd been sitting there when she finally opened her eyes again.

Her father was safe. The baby was safe. Colin was safe. And she was exhausted.

She blocked out thoughts of how much Colin hated her now. She'd seen it in his eyes as he stalked toward her. The anger was so palpable that she'd had to turn her face away. Right then, she knew that he would never forgive her for leaving. And what had she really expected? For him to tell her everything would be okay? A hug?

Maybe it was good that Melissa Rancic would no longer exist in less than—she checked the clock—an hour. Maybe it was time to turn over a new leaf. Maybe it was time to make a new life for herself and Angelina. The thought of causing Colin any more pain was like a knife to her heart anyway. He deserved so much more.

She pushed up to stand as a knock sounded on the door from behind. She jumped. Her heart leapt to her throat and her chest squeezed. That same old feeling of panic, of the walls closing in and the air thinning, threatened to debilitate her. And that same question burned through her mind…had Richard found her?

No. That was impossible. He was probably in Canada by now.

The knocks sounded again, a little louder, a little more urgent.

Her mind spun. All the anxiety crashed down around her, freezing her limbs and making something as simple as taking a breath hurt.

Hold on a second. Richard wouldn't knock at her front door nor would anyone he sent. That was way too direct. He would slip in during the night and slit her throat.

She glanced around the room, searching for a purse or jacket. Mrs. Klein most likely forgot something and she was returning to get it. The simple explanation was usually the right one no matter how much her brain protested and fear overtook her.

Melissa flipped the switch to the porch light and checked out the peephole. The light was out. Had it been like that before? Melissa couldn't remember. This was an old house. It belonged to her cousin's best friend. It had a lot of quirks.

Yes. It had. She remembered a little while ago when Mrs. Klein had gone home that the porch light hadn't been working. No way was Melissa opening that door without confirmation.

"Mrs. Klein?" Melissa said softly, and then waited for a response.

A high-pitched murmur of acknowledgment came.

As Melissa opened the door, she said, "What did you—"

And then froze.

She gasped as panic roared through her. She quickly regained her bearings and pushed the door, trying to shut it quickly even though it wouldn't budge. There was something wedged at the base. She glanced down. The toe of Colin's boot stared up at her.

"Not so fast, Melissa." He pushed open the door a little too easily and brushed past her.

"YOU SHOULDN'T BE HERE," Melissa said with more panic than anger, and he noticed that she'd positioned her body between him and the stairs. Was she blocking him for a reason? Was someone up there? Richard?

"I almost didn't come." Colin had followed Melissa on a whim. And then he'd sat at the end of the street trying to decide if he should knock or not. Seeing her with Richard would knife him, but maybe he needed that reinforcement to be able to finally let go. He'd been stuck in a place between still loving her and the kind of pain he wouldn't wish on his worst enemy for the past year. Seeing her dredged up feelings he thought he'd learned to live with, or live without, depending on how he looked at it.

"Why did you?" she asked.

"Is *he* here?" Colin motioned toward the base of the staircase, ignoring her question. That old anger from her leaving him for a flash-in-the-pan guy like Richard renewed.

She looked down and then shook her head.

He didn't realize he'd been holding his breath until that moment. Forcing himself to exhale slowly, he also noticed that she wasn't wearing her ring anymore and she looked completely wrung out. Had the two of them been in a fight?

Colin shouldn't want to interfere with a married couple's business, but part of him needed to know that she was okay. "Did he do anything to you? Hurt you in any way?"

"No," she said quickly. He couldn't help but notice how her body was trembling.

He made a move toward her and she flinched. Another sign he didn't like.

"Why did you come to the ranch?" He pinned her with his stare, letting his anger show in his words. He couldn't afford to let her get inside his head or his heart.

"I wanted to see you," she said, looking like she'd had to force the words out. She didn't budge or invite him in, and she kept glancing toward the door like she expected her husband to walk through at any minute.

"Why?" he asked.

"We're moving out of the country and I guess I got nostalgic for the past." The corner of her mouth twitched. She was lying.

"Where are you going?" he asked.

She flashed her eyes at him but didn't speak. Her body trembled as she brought her hand to her chest, signs that she was in a panic.

Nostalgia? This seemed an over-the-top reaction to being a little homesick.

"Everything going okay between the two of you?" Colin asked, a piece of him hoping she would say it wasn't. There was so much off about her, he noticed. From her reaction to him to the way she talked about her husband, Colin didn't know where to start with questions.

She nodded that it was. And that should be enough for Colin. He should walk right out the door and never look back. She'd broken his heart once, and this little visit was reopening old wounds that he had no doubt were going to sting for a long while after she left. If his heart was a muscle, it was memory causing his body to have this reaction to seeing her again, the one where he felt like the world was going to tumble down around him as soon as he walked out that door.

None of those feelings were welcomed. He stared at her, trying to read her to see if he could figure out why she'd really shown up at the ranch earlier. There was a time when knowing what was on her mind would've been second nature. But she'd changed. Colin might not be able to tell what she was thinking but he knew fear when he saw it. And she was afraid of something. If not her husband, then who? Him?

"So, he's treating you right?" he asked, unable to stop pushing for the answers he really wanted but his pride wouldn't allow him to ask. Like why she'd really ditched him for Richard in the first place.

"I said he was," she said, and her body language changed. She folded her arms and gritted her back teeth in the way that she did when she was shoring her strength.

"You're the one who came to see me and now you act like you can't stand to be in the same room," he said.

"Time for you to go," she shot back.

Was she there to torture him? To remind him of what he'd lost? Did she really hate him that much?

A piece of him had to know if she'd walked away because she'd really stopped loving him like she'd said. He stalked toward her and she walked backward until she was against the wall. The stairs were to the left and the hallway to the right would take him into the kitchen.

Melissa's hands came up in defense and she turned her face away, shutting her eyes.

This close, her heart thumped at the base of her throat wildly. The air changed and electricity pinged between them.

Their sexual chemistry hadn't dimmed. Were her feelings for him really dead?

"You're not getting away so easy this time." Colin used his thumb on her chin to guide her face toward him. His other hand wrapped around the base of her neck. Being this close took a toll on him, on his body. He took in a sharp breath and, by accident, breathed in her scent. At least one thing hadn't changed about her. She still smelled like sunshine after the first spring rain. All flowers and fresh air. "Why'd you take off your ring?"

She kept her eyes shut.

"I'm not leaving until you look at me and give me an answer." She'd never been able to do that and lie. A piece of him dared to hope she was done with her marriage, that she could admit it had been a mistake and that she'd never stopped loving him. Colin knew it was his bruised ego wishing for that. Because he had enough pride to realize that he would never love her in the same way again no matter what excuses she gave for walking out. That innocence had been shattered into a thousand tiny pieces along with his heart, and he doubted he could ever love anyone in that same way again, especially not her.

Melissa opened her eyes, slowly, and it was like the sun cresting on the horizon. Those violet streaks like rays, bathing darkness with light. His heart clenched and his muscles corded as her hands came up to his chest. He expected a jab or for her to push him away, but instead she double fisted his shirt and tugged him toward her.

All rationale flew out the window as Colin's pulse kicked up a few notches. He shouldn't want to dip down and claim her heart-shaped pink lips again. He shouldn't want to pull her body flush with his. He shouldn't want to get lost inside her.

And that's where he stopped.

Because he could never trust her enough to close his eyes again.

He pulled back, a little stunned at how easy it was to get trapped in old habits. How many times had they been in a similar position? Eager to rip each other's clothes off and let the feelings they had for each other consume them in a splendid, heated flame until they lay gasping for air, their arms and legs tangled. How easy it had been to talk to her, to laugh with her.

And look where that had gotten him. Rejected. Hurt.

Anger flooded him because she was messing with his mind and the future they would never have—a future he shouldn't want.

All he needed was to regain his sanity because Melissa was bad for him, and he knew that even if his body said otherwise.

She seemed to quickly regain her composure, and then she ducked out of his grasp.

"How did you know where to find me?" she asked.

"You weren't hard to follow speeding through town," he said.

"I have somewhere to be," she said. "You need to leave."

Colin glanced at his watch. "At eleven forty at night?"

"Yes," she said with too much conviction. She was either lying or hiding something.

"Seems late for an appointment," he said.

"I'm meeting up with someone…with *him*." Her face morphed for a split second like it did when she felt guilty.

"Why did you come back?" he asked.

"Doesn't matter. I'm not staying," she responded.

"Carolina said you wanted to talk to me," he pressed.

"She's mistaken."

He shot her a look.

"I'm the one who made a mistake. I shouldn't have gone to the ranch. Richard will be livid if he finds you here, so you need to go."

"Fine." Was she lying to protect Colin because he could see that she wasn't being truthful? There was no way to shield him now. Not after what she'd done to him. No one could convince him that she cared for his feelings.

"I didn't see your parents earlier. Would you tell them happy anniversary for me?" she asked, and he'd almost forgotten about that. They would have been married forty-two years next week.

But, wait, she hadn't heard the news? Sheriff Tommy Johnson had done a great job of keeping the murder investigation out of the papers, but Colin assumed that everyone knew his parents had died. He glanced down and back before shaking his head. He still had a hard time finding the right words to talk about it.

"What?" She searched his gaze as if what he was about to say would be stamped there.

"They're gone," he managed to say.

"Oh, no," she said with a little more alarm than

seemed appropriate under the circumstances. She shouldn't care about him or his family anymore. "What happened?"

"Tommy's investigating their deaths," he said, and a curious look overtook her features. Sheriff Johnson was a close friend and grew up with all six of the O'Brien boys. He was more like family and was taking the murder investigation even more personally as a result of how much he cared for the O'Brien family. Colin couldn't pinpoint what was pinging through her thoughts but he could almost see the wheels churning. What was that all about?

"I'm so sorry," she said, and she looked stunned. Maybe a little guilty, too.

Colin had every intention of figuring out why.

"Are you telling me that you didn't know?" he asked, surprised, his curiosity getting the best of him.

"No." She shook her head as though for emphasis. Did she really hate him so much that she'd completely cut herself off from any news about Bluff? About his folks? She'd cared about them once. "How long have you been here?"

"Not long. This is just a quick stop on my way to—" she paused and he figured she was about to make something up. "Galveston." She raked her teeth across her bottom lip. "I'm so sorry about your parents."

She'd been especially close to his mother. His mom had made sure that Melissa was included in all their family celebrations, saying over and over that it was about time there was a little more estrogen at the table. Mom had said that after being surrounded by six boys— boys that she adored—for most of her life that she couldn't wait to have a girl in the family.

For a minute, she looked shocked and a little frail, which was unlike Melissa. She must've figured out what he was thinking because her defenses flared. "I always cared about your parents, you know that. Especially your mother. I would've sent something if I'd realized."

Her voice broke and a look passed behind her eyes that he couldn't quite pinpoint when she said that last word.

Did she know something about the murders?

No. No way. She didn't even know his parents were gone before he told her.

Chapter Three

The only things keeping Melissa upright and on her feet were sheer determination and willpower. The second she'd heard the news about Colin's parents she'd almost buckled. Had her worst fears been realized? Had Richard gotten to them because of some sick need to punish her? So many other questions swirled. If Mr. O'Brien was having an affair, could that be connected to the murders? Melissa quieted her internal thoughts. It was dangerous to give away her reaction to the news. She couldn't risk Colin having any suspicion about Richard.

The news would spread soon enough that he was a criminal on the run, and Melissa would be long gone. Her handler, Marshal Davis, had been keeping the situation out of the news until Melissa could disappear. Speaking of which, it was almost time to meet him. If she didn't show at their rendezvous point, he'd start looking for her and she didn't need him asking around or giving more cause for concern. There were enough red flags in the air and she'd done enough damage on her own coming to Bluff.

An immediate problem of six feet two inches of raw masculinity stood in front of her. Melissa needed to think of a way to get him out of there so she could grab her sleeping infant and run. A wave of guilt assaulted her at thinking how much Colin had missed—how much he would miss—of his daughter's life. But with Richard on the loose, it was even more important to keep Colin and the baby separate for both of their protection.

If Colin knew about his daughter, it would be impossible to keep him away or stop him from fighting for custody. Once things settled down, the ranch would be an obvious place for Richard to look. As long as he was on the loose, Angelina was in danger.

But it was Colin's parents. She had to know if there was even a slight possibility that Richard could've been involved. "Like I said, I'm truly sorry to hear about your parents, Colin. When did it happen?"

"They were killed September of last year." His words were a sober reminder of how dangerous Richard could be. A thought struck. Could she leave Angelina with Colin? The ranch was probably safer than the US Treasury.

No. It wouldn't work. Richard believed Angelina was his daughter. If he heard or saw her with Colin it would be too easy to put the pieces together. Until Richard was safely locked away or dead, she couldn't risk it. She mumbled an apology under her breath and a prayer for forgiveness.

"What happened to them?" she asked.

"At first, we believed Dad had a heart attack while driving and wrecked with both him and Mom in the car. Something felt off to Tommy so he ran labs. Toxicology report came back with poison in their systems," he said.

"That's awful. How on earth could they be poisoned?" Melissa's heart broke at hearing the details.

"Tommy doesn't know. It would have to be someone

who had access to both of them. Mom had hosted their annual party for local artists earlier that night, so a few people had admission to the ranch," he said.

"I'm guessing Tommy already checked everyone out at the party, including staff," she said, still trying to absorb the news. It was selfish to think about the fact that Angelina would never know her grandparents. There was always some small part of Melissa wishing things would magically work out and she and Colin would end up together. It was a crazy notion that had given her the tiniest sliver of hope in what had been the worst year of her life save for the birth of her child.

"He did. All he has so far is the poison. He doesn't know how it got in their systems or what the motive for murder could be," Colin said. "There's a slight chance that they ingested the poison accidentally."

"Except what are the chances they both ingested the same thing at the same time?" she said out loud, not meaning to. She shouldn't add fuel to the fire. Colin might find out the truth about his father and that would crush him. She still could scarcely believe that the man would have an affair. She'd argued with Richard, putting up more of a fight than she knew better to, refusing to accept his accusation at first. And that had led to an even bigger fight between them when he'd accused her of defending the O'Briens because she still loved Colin.

In order to survive, she'd had to swallow her emotions and convince Richard that she loved him. Only him. If someone had told her that she'd be able to sell that lie a year ago she would've laughed. Finding out she was pregnant had changed her priorities. Nothing mattered more to her than keeping Colin's baby safe.

As a mother, she'd found a new well of strength to

draw from than she had ever known existed inside her. Angelina's safety took precedence over everyone and everything.

"It's late, Colin. I need to go," she said, using all the courage she could muster to speak those words. Being with Colin again was taking a toll on her, body, soul and mind. She was grateful that Angelina was a sound sleeper. Melissa had a prayer of getting out of this situation without doing any more damage.

Coming back to Bluff had been a mistake. Seeing the pain in Colin's eyes was heartbreaking. And that would be the last image she would have of him to hold on to. She had hoped to see him happy, to see his charismatic smile. His sexy half grin that had been so good at making her pulse race and her body ache in that perfect way. She hadn't counted on seeing him still so miserable. Or wanting to touch him so much that she physically hurt.

Blocking out the pain, an act she'd mastered in the past twelve months, she pushed past him and then opened the front door wide. She needed to meet her handler so she could disappear. The thought she was running from her problems struck. She pushed it aside.

Yes, the man standing in front of her was an issue. Yes, he deserved to know about Angelina. Yes, his daughter deserved to know about him. Not now. Not if it meant putting their little girl in danger. Even Colin would agree that Angelina had to come first.

She pushed the door open as wide as it would go.

"Please, Colin, don't make me ask again." She prayed he didn't pick up on the desperate note in her tone.

COLIN SAT IN his vehicle contemplating the conversation he'd just had with Melissa for a good twenty minutes.

Something about the way she'd asked him to leave didn't sit right. Forget the electricity they still shared, sex had always been a whole other experience with her, and it was muscle memory causing the heat between them to sizzle like it was yesterday. He'd felt the chemistry, loud and powerful, when her back had been against the wall and there wasn't more than a foot of space between her full breasts and his chest.

She was married to someone else and Colin would never act on his impulses. He'd stopped having sex for sex's sake when he became old enough to fight for his country. He'd done a tour and then returned home. His reputation for dating around might be true, but he was selective when it came to who he spent time with and even more so with women he slept with.

Colin had an ironclad commandment about not messing around with another man's wife. Even if he and Melissa had belonged to each other at one time, his rule was etched in stone and applied no matter how much his heart tried to protest. Or tell him that she was still his after all this time.

Logic ruled. It was time to move on.

Then there was the reaction she'd had to the news about his parents and the questions that had followed.

What was the point of worrying about it? She'd said that she was about to move and was homesick. Colin needed to accept it and move on. He was just about to start his ignition and drive off when he saw twin headlights exit the alley. Curiosity got the best of him, so he followed Melissa's car. All he needed was to see her with Richard to imprint the new reality of her being married to someone else into his brain. Colin was visual and he needed that image in order to stamp out all those other thoughts that kept creeping in. Thoughts of how sweet she still smelled, all floral and sunshine. Thoughts of how soft her skin still was when he'd touched her arm. Thoughts of how rapid her breathing had become when they were standing too close. All of which was dangerous for Colin to acknowledge.

Melissa was married to Richard Rancic. The words sat bitter on his tongue as he cut right, allowing enough distance between cars so that she wouldn't realize she was being followed. She'd made her choice. She was Melissa Rancic now. It was high time his mind caught up.

Cutting right a few seconds after she did, he was flooded with memories—memories he fought to keep from overtaking his thoughts. Letting go of her wasn't going to be easy but he'd find a way. He had to. Because a little voice, the one that still knew her, said that once she left town she wasn't coming back this time. Colin's heart fisted again. He reminded himself that it was a good thing to acknowledge and accept the situation for what it was.

Melissa made another turn into the parking lot of the lawnmower store at the edge of town. It was located at the edge of the last neighborhood in Bluff before hay bales and country roads dotted the landscape. The lots were one-to-two acres in this area.

On three sides of the parking lot were woods, basically mesquite trees with two feet of underbrush. It was most likely Colin's military training that had him checking the perimeter for any signs of danger and not the hairs that pricked on the back of his neck. Why would she meet her husband after midnight in an empty parking lot?

Scenarios started running through his mind as he pulled past the lot, turned off his headlights and then made a U-turn. Was it his heart and not his logical mind saying that she wanted out of the marriage? If there had been abuse she would be smarter to meet out in the open in a busy place, like a restaurant. This would be the worst possible spot. Empty, abandoned for all practical purposes. Images of her being abducted against her will assaulted him. And that was most likely his training taking over. Now he really needed to stick around to make sure she was okay.

There was a street lamp in the middle of the empty parking lot, and that was the only light around. The building was completely blacked out. All of Colin's danger radar flared. He wanted her to park under the light at least.

She didn't.

Melissa parked at the far corner of the lot with woods to each side. What was she thinking? He thought he'd trained her better than that in personal safety in the time they were together. She might be meeting her husband but any whacko could take advantage of this situation.

Did she really not have sense enough to think this through? Or had he rattled her? He blamed himself for that, figuring their conversation had upset her more than she'd wanted to let on. Seeing her again had certainly done a number on him.

Colin pulled over to the side of the road where he could see vehicles as they entered and exited the lot. There was only one other place a car could turn in and it came from a country road that ended at Sander's farm a half hour down the road.

He wanted eyes on Rancic. And then he could finally convince himself to let her go.

A light blue sedan turned right into the lot fifteen minutes later. Colin exited his vehicle and moved stealthily along the tree line in order to get a good look at the exchange, telling himself that he needed to be close enough to see their faces. Maybe he was a glutton for punishment, and it seemed his heart would agree with that statement as a knifelike pain stabbed through him with each forward step. He told himself that he was making ground on being able to let go of the grip she had on him, still had on him. That thought carried his steps forward.

The headlights illuminated Melissa's car and Colin could see her clearly from his position as she exited her vehicle. She should be happy to see her husband, shouldn't she?

All Colin saw clearly was fear as Rancic parked and cut the lights. Colin moved to get a better look. Melissa's attention shifted from Rancic to the backseat of her car as she backed away from him.

What was that all about?

Colin's fear that their marriage had gone sour seemed to be playing out in front of him. Based on her expression, she was scared to death of the guy.

All his instincts told him to walk away. Melissa had made her choice and it wasn't his place to interfere with a husband and wife. And yet he knew without a doubt that he was about to do just that…interfere. She could thank him or curse him later.

As Colin broke out of the tree line, the sheriff's cruiser sped across the lot. Melissa used the distraction to lock herself inside the vehicle. Smart. He'd hang back behind her car and let Tommy do his job.

Rancic dove into his vehicle and managed to come up behind the wheel. He gunned the engine in reverse, burning rubber. His tires finally gripped the concrete and he sped backward.

Tommy must not've seen the barrel of the shotgun poking out from the driver's side an inch or two as he hit his brakes, no doubt ready to turn around and give chase. Fire shot out the end as the blast split the air, burning through Colin's ears as he pushed off the back of Melissa's vehicle and bolted toward the sheriff's SUV.

Rancic was out of there by the time Colin reached Tommy.

He pulled his friend from his vehicle and laid him out on the cement. Blood was everywhere as Colin scanned Tommy's body, assessing the damage.

"Damn shotgun," Tommy said, and his voice was a little too calm. No doubt, he was in shock.

Colin knew enough about weapons to know just how dangerous shotgun shells were to bulletproof vests. They weren't rated for those because they didn't have a consistent velocity. Tommy had taken a bullet to his left side and blood covered his shirt. A red dot flowered. Colin needed to stop the bleeding.

"How bad is it? Be honest," Tommy said as he searched Colin's face, no doubt looking for a reaction so he could gauge his injury.

"You're going to be just fine." It was the lie every soldier had told no matter how grave the damage looked.

He maintained his game face and could only pray that no major organs or arteries had been pierced as he shrugged out of his T-shirt and then used it to place pressure on the wound.

Suddenly Melissa was there, too, and sounds of a baby crying came from a distance.

"It's getting colder out here," Tommy said, already shivering.

"Stay with me, man," Colin said.

"What can I do?" Melissa asked as Colin looked up at her.

"Call 911. *Now*," he said.

Chapter Four

Colin paced in Bluff General's waiting room after giving his statement to Deputy Garcia. The deputy had gone to speak to hospital staff, leaving Colin to wait alone for updates.

Blue carpet, blue chairs and stark white walls couldn't erase the bloody images scrolling through Colin's mind. There was blood on his shirt, Tommy's blood. Tommy had been shot by Melissa's husband. *Estranged husband*, a little voice in his head clarified. Colin could hardly wrap his thoughts around what had happened even though he'd seen it with his own eyes.

Tommy had been immediately taken into surgery, and Colin had called his brothers to deliver the news. His eldest brother, Dallas, was on his way to the hospital. The others would soon follow. Tommy needed all the family around him that he could get, and the O'Briens were a tight-knit bunch.

Personally, Colin had seen the inside of the county hospital a few too many times recently. As far as desirable places to end up went, Bluff General bottomed his list. In the six months since his parents' murders, several of his brothers had ended up in a room not unlike the one Tommy was in now. Many of his siblings had also found the loves of their lives in recent months, but that was a whole different subject. Colin had believed that he'd found his in Melissa.

If that weren't enough to make his head spin, Melissa had a baby. Colin didn't want to acknowledge the anger burning through his chest, considering she'd been adamant about waiting to have children with him.

He forced himself to stop pacing and take a seat.

The thought of Melissa having Richard Rancic's child hit Colin harder than a battering ram. It made her marriage to another man feel very real. Thinking back to the way she'd acted so cagey at the house and how quickly she'd ushered him out the door had him wondering if she'd wanted to hide her baby from him. Richard Rancic was a criminal and a jerk. For the life of Colin he couldn't figure out why she'd marry the guy, let alone have his child. Colin stabbed his fingers through his dark hair. Speaking of Melissa, she should be there by now. He glanced around.

Dallas should arrive any minute. Tommy was more like a brother than a friend and he was fighting for his life. Going over the scenario again and again was about to make Colin's head explode.

Caffeine. He needed a giant cup of black coffee about now.

Colin pushed off the chair as Melissa rounded the corner. A pink blanket swathed a small bundle cradled in her arms. Melissa's baby was somehow tinier than he'd expected. The child must be asleep because she didn't move.

"How's Tommy?" Melissa's eyes were wide and stress lines bracketed her mouth. She glanced down at her baby and another emotion flickered that he had trouble pinpointing. Guilt?

"He's in surgery," Colin said, noticing how she kept one arm underneath the little bundle and her other hand on the baby's back. How much did it blow his mind to think that Melissa had a daughter?

Damn.

"What happened back there? You told me that you were meeting your husband and then you looked scared to death when he showed. What aren't you telling me?" Colin asked, taking note of the dark look that passed behind her eyes when he said the word *husband*.

"It's nothing. A misunderstanding," Melissa said, and the corner of her mouth twitched in the way it did when she was scared.

"That's impossible. Tommy's lying on a bed being cut open right now and that sure isn't because of nothing," Colin said, his voice raised in frustration.

"I didn't mean—" The little girl stirred and panic washed over Melissa's features.

He needed to take a minute to calm down.

"I can't talk about it right now," she said quietly, motioning toward the baby.

Colin rubbed his chin and turned to face the other direction. He couldn't help but notice how natural Melissa looked holding her daughter and he shouldn't want the child in her arms to be his. She wasn't. That reality crashed around Colin like a rogue wave, unexpected and all-consuming. It caught him off guard, but he couldn't afford to care right now. Not with Tommy down the hall in surgery and Melissa tight-lipping his questions about her husband.

Part of his anger had to do with his pent-up emotions about Melissa. He'd have to figure out a way to make peace with the fact that she'd married someone else and was now a mother. The thought was going to take a minute to sink in. Seeing the little girl made good strides toward acceptance.

"Have you been happy?" He surprised himself with the question.

"About her?" she asked, and then answered before he could respond. "Absolutely."

There was so much conviction in her voice that he didn't question her answer.

"What was all that about back there, Melissa? I saw Richard. I know he shot Tommy," he said. Her husband's name sat bitterly on his tongue. "What's he doing that you won't talk about?"

She turned away from him.

"The man just shot a sheriff, Melissa," Colin said, his anger on the rise again. He shouldn't be frustrated at thinking about a time when there were no secrets between them. She'd betrayed him, he reminded himself, needing to gain his bearings again. Because his heart stirred while standing this close to her, and he didn't want to care this much about anyone ever again. He told himself that his reaction had to do more with her safety than his own out-of-control emotions.

Melissa bounced her little girl gently, continuing to ignore him while the baby slept. Curiosity was starting to get the best of him. He couldn't see the baby's face, which was just a distraction anyway, and he wasn't sure he could handle seeing the product of Richard and Melissa together. More proof that Melissa had never belonged to him in the first place. Then again, maybe that's exactly what he needed: a reality check.

"I can't talk about it with you," she said.

"Can't or won't?"

"Does it matter? Either way I'm not talking, Colin."
Again, hearing his name on her tongue brought an on-
slaught of feelings he needed to ignore.

"Why not, Melissa?" Did she hate him that much?

"It's complicated," she said on a sigh, still bouncing
as the nervous tick returned.

On closer look, there was so much stress and worry
in her eyes.

"What's going on between you and your husband?"
Colin asked a little too loudly, causing the baby to stir
again.

"Shhh. You'll wake her." Melissa patted the little
girl's back and started humming.

Colin didn't want to disturb the baby. From what
he knew about little ones, which wasn't much until recently, once they were awake all grown-up discussion
ceased.

Maybe he needed a minute to clear his thoughts. His
emotions were riding high after watching one of his best
friends take a bullet. Seeing Melissa at the ranch earlier
had sent him to a dark place to begin with, and watching her now wasn't improving the situation.

"I need coffee," he said, stalking out the door, needing to walk away and gain some perspective. He didn't
want to notice how much she was trembling or how
hard she was working to put on a brave front. Her eyes
had always been her tell, and right now hers said that
she was terrified. Of Colin? No way could she think he
would hurt her. Her husband was another story and one
Colin planned to hear in detail before he let her walk

out that door again. And especially now that Richard had tried to kill a sheriff.

The coffee was just how Colin liked it, strong and hot. He took a sip to clear his head. Took another when that didn't work. There were too many residual feelings coloring his thoughts, not to mention the stress that came with not knowing how Tommy was doing yet. Colin had already checked three times in fifteen minutes before Melissa had arrived.

"Any word on Tommy?" Dallas asked as he walked inside the break room.

"All I know is that he's in surgery." Colin gave his brother a bear hug before shaking his head. He poured a fresh cup and then handed it to Dallas. "It could be a while before we hear anything."

"Well then, no news is probably good news." Dallas took a sip, worry lines etched in his forehead as he gave Colin a once-over, his gaze fixed on the large red stain centered on Colin's shirt.

"It's all his blood. I'm fine," Colin reassured.

"I might have an extra shirt in my truck if you want to put on something clean," Dallas offered.

Colin had washed his hands not long after arriving at the hospital when a nurse had tried to put him in a wheelchair and take him into the back for a check. He'd had to lift his shirt to show her there were no marks on his body to convince her.

"I may take you up on that," he said to Dallas.

"You said Tommy was in the parking lot of Zahn Lawn Mower Supply. Any idea what he was doing out there so late?" Dallas asked. Colin had only given his brother essential information. Tommy had been shot and he was at Bluff General. Richard Rancic was armed and dangerous.

"Good question." There was another one that would follow.

"What were you doing there?" Dallas didn't wait long to hit him with that one. That was an even better question. Colin was still trying to figure that out. Dallas didn't ask about Melissa, but the questions about her were written in his tense expression.

"She ran away so fast at the Fling," he finally said.

Dallas compressed his lips and gave a nod, saying he understood. It was good that someone did because Colin was still scratching his head over the night's events. Talk about an evening going haywire. His friend was fighting for his life in a hospital bed and the woman he'd wanted to marry had a child.

"What did she say when you showed up?" Dallas asked.

"I parked to the side, trying to decide if I was going to talk to her or not." It wasn't entirely untrue. "Then, I saw her husband pull into the lot and she seemed real uncomfortable. I thought she was supposed to be meeting him." Colin's voice hitched on that last word.

"Why would a husband be meeting his wife in a parking lot at midnight?" Dallas asked, and then sipped his coffee.

"I'd like to hear the answer to that question for myself, but she's not talking." Based on her terrorized expression when she saw Richard, he was the last person she'd expected to show. It was clear to Colin that she was scared to death of the guy, which made even less sense. Rancic was a jerk and his business reputation said he was cutthroat. Didn't make him a criminal. So, why did the guy show up and then shoot a sheriff? Obviously, there was a lot going on. Had Melissa left her husband? Was Richard so determined to get her back that he'd shot a sheriff, realized what he'd done and then fled the scene?

"So, she's here?" Dallas asked.

Colin nodded.

"Have you spoken to her?" Dallas's eyebrow shot up.

"There hasn't been much time. She stayed back with officers at the scene. I've been busy giving all the information I could to the hospital workers since I was the one who'd been stemming the blood flow and administering CPR. And then I gave a statement to the deputy," Colin said.

"Garcia?" Dallas asked.

Colin nodded again.

"Melissa just showed up here a few minutes ago and it didn't exactly go well between us," he said with a shrug. "Guess I needed a minute to clear my head before taking another go at it with her."

"It's hard when you have so much history," Dallas agreed.

When Colin had been standing close to her at the house, he hadn't noticed anything unusual on her body. There was no bruising, no other marks of any kind indicating abuse. She still had that same rosy skin, a combination of cream and silk. And yet she was terrified of her husband and that made Colin believe their relationship had been abusive.

"She has a kid now," was all Colin said. He took a sip of coffee.

"You okay?" Dallas asked. "I can take things from

here if you want to go cool off somewhere. Go get cleaned up and come back."

"I'll be fine. Me and Melissa were a long time ago," he said, mostly for his own benefit. "A lot's changed since we went out, and let's not forget that she's married to someone else."

Dallas did the "tight lip/nod" thing again. "That's probably a healthy way to look at it."

"Not much choice, is there." It wasn't a question. He didn't repeat the fact that she and Richard had a child together. Colin could've lived the rest of his life without knowing that detail.

Dallas shrugged with an apologetic look.

"Here's what else I know. Tommy comes roaring through the parking lot soon after Rancic, no lights or sirens. And then I'm really confused about what's going on," Colin continued. "The next thing I see is Tommy being shot. Rancic squeals out of the parking lot and I'm trying to save my friend's life."

"That's a lot to have coming at you at once." Dallas shot a look that said he was talking about more than the incident in the parking lot with Tommy.

Colin studied his coffee cup before taking a sip.

"For the record, I still think it's a good idea to get some fresh air," Dallas added.

"I'm not leaving until I know Tommy's going to be okay and I get a few answers out of Melissa. Who knows when she'll take off and I might never see her again." Colin ground his back teeth. He gripped the coffee cup a little too tight.

"You sure about that last part?" Dallas's brow lifted.

"As sure as the sun rises in the east," Colin said.

Another one of Dallas's concerned looks creased his brother's forehead.

"It might help that you're here. She always liked you and she never did anything to put a wedge between the two of you," Colin said.

"Hell yes she did," Dallas said without hesitation. "She hurt my brother."

Colin topped off both of their cups before urging his brother out of the lounge. "Let's go get some answers."

MELISSA TEXTED HER handler for the sixth time since the incident in the parking lot and an ominous feeling settled over her. Where was Marshal Davis? And how on earth had Richard found her? He was supposed to be in Canada by now. If Tommy and Colin hadn't shown when they did she'd be dead.

Her body trembled no matter how hard she tried to settle down. A thought struck. Was there any possibility that Richard was the reason Marshal Davis hadn't shown?

The US marshal was most likely a victim of Bluff's spotty cell coverage, but being without contact after everything that had happened caused a cold chill to trickle down her spine. That uneasy feeling gripped her again as she rocked Angelina.

Tommy Johnson was shot and she couldn't help but blame herself. If she had stayed away from Bluff none of this would be happening. Her stress levels were climbing through the roof and another big part of that had to do with the man down the hall. Colin would be back any second with questions she couldn't answer. And especially not without speaking to Marshal Davis first.

Angelina whimpered in her sleep.

"It's okay, sweet girl," Melissa soothed, wishing it were that simple in all areas of her life.

Thinking about the possibility of Colin realizing the little girl was his daughter sent another tremor racing through Melissa. She couldn't allow him to put the pieces together, to know about Angelina. She'd done a great job of hiding the little girl's face so far. Could she keep it up until Marshal Davis showed? He *had* to show. He was her ticket to a new life, a safe life.

Melissa needed to get out of Bluff and disappear. Witness protection never sounded better. Although, there was no way she could leave without knowing Tommy was going to be okay. And she didn't dare risk Angelina's life by walking out the hospital door alone. Melissa was no fool. Richard was out there, somewhere. He would make good on his promise to destroy her and everyone she loved if he saw her.

Suddenly, the walls felt like they were closing in because if Colin figured out that Angelina was his, there'd be no walking out that door without him.

Okay, breathe.

The world seemed like it was crumbling down around her. All she had to do was let her baby sleep while Melissa obstructed the view of her face until her handler called. She could do that. She'd been through so much more in the past year. Melissa wanted to run, to escape in her car and disappear. She wasn't fool enough to go outside without protection.

Richard had nothing to lose. He was already wanted by the federal government. And now, a sheriff who happened to be her childhood friend lay on an operating table because of Richard—*because of her*. Icy tendrils gripped her spine as her pulse raced. She checked her cell's screen again. No messages.

Melissa stood up and then crossed the waiting room. Maybe she could find another place to sit and still be safe? On second thought, she seriously doubted it. The hospital had security but not the caliber she needed to keep Richard at bay. There was no place to hide from him except here with the O'Briens, where Colin could protect her and Angelina.

A panicked feeling made Melissa pace even faster. Everything inside her wanted to run out that door and keep going, except her heart. That stubborn organ wanted to be near Colin because he was the only person who'd ever made her feel safe. She'd taken that for granted when they'd been together before. But then, what had she had to run from? She'd had no idea what kind of monster lurked in Bluff a year ago. Any creature that she could conjure in her mind paled in comparison to Richard. He was worse than a monster. He was pure evil.

The scuffle of boots sounded in the hallway and she didn't need to turn around to know that Colin had entered the room. She faced him.

"Dallas," she said, startled. In an attempt to recover, she added, "It's good to see you again."

"You, too, Melissa." Dallas stood behind his brother.

Melissa hoped he couldn't hear her heart thudding against her ribs at the thought of two O'Briens in the room. If either one of them got a look at her daughter it was over.

It wasn't a selfish desire that had her wanting to keep Angelina a secret. Although she had that, too. It was survival. Either of them figured out paternity and

Colin would follow her to the ends of the earth to find her and his child. But then, she hadn't really thought this through because this whole room would be filled with O'Briens soon.

Her chest squeezed thinking about it. She was trying to move away from danger, not put everyone in front of the firing squad. As long as Angelina was resting, Melissa should be able to hide her true identity. *Sleep, my little angel. Sleep.*

Melissa couldn't allow herself to think about anything but Tommy being okay. Finding her handler ran a close second.

"I take it no one's come in with an update?" Dallas asked as Colin moved by the window and stared outside.

She desperately wanted to ask him to move away from there.

"Not yet," she said. "I'm really sorry about what happened to Tommy."

A few tears free-fell despite her attempts to force them back.

"It's not your fault," Colin said under his breath.

She wasn't so sure.

"I can help you with your daughter if you'd like a break," Dallas said, offering to hold her.

"No," Melissa said too quickly. "I just don't want to take a chance of waking her with everything going on."

The blanket slipped with movement and she secured it back in place. With Dallas standing close and Colin on the other side of the room, it was going to be a challenge to keep Angelina's face concealed.

Dallas's right brow raised but he didn't immediately comment.

"I never knew how little sleep any of our parents

must've gotten until my son, Jackson, came into my life," he finally said, and then motioned toward chairs near Colin. "At least sit down."

"You have a child?" she asked as she glanced at the chairs and then at Colin. Angelina stirred and Melissa's heart dropped. *Please, little angel.*

"And a wife," Dallas said.

"What?" Melissa didn't mean to sound so shocked. She smiled at him as she moved to the farthest wall and took a seat.

"A lot has changed since you left," Dallas said with a glance toward Colin.

"Well, congratulations," she said. "You looked very happy when you mentioned your family."

Dallas smiled and took a seat next to her.

"What's her name?" He motioned toward the baby.

"Angelina," she said quietly. Out of her periphery, she saw Colin's reaction as his entire body tensed. It had been a moment of weakness that had her needing to use that name—the name that she and Colin had said they'd use if they ever had a daughter.

Dallas seemed to pick up on the added tension when he changed the subject by asking if Melissa wanted anything to drink.

"No, thanks," she said. "I'm still shocked at hearing you got married. It's good. And I think it's amazing that you have a son."

"It's funny how everyone tells you that you won't sleep when you have a baby, but no one says that you won't mind," Dallas said, that O'Brien pride written all over his features.

"I couldn't be happier for you, Dallas." She would bet any one of the O'Brien boys would make a great father, and her heart especially believed that about Colin. A wave of sadness crashed into her. She checked her phone again. The sooner she heard from Marshal Davis, the faster she could leave.

"Thank you. He's a great kid. I hope you'll swing by the ranch and meet my wife, Kate," he said, and that comment netted a harsh look from Colin.

"I'd like that," she said, even though the words were hollow. Liking the idea wasn't the problem. She'd be Bethany soon enough and would never be allowed to look back. And especially not while Richard was a free man. Probably not after, either, considering he managed a network of ruthless criminals.

Speaking of the devil, she really needed to update Marshal Davis about Richard being in Bluff. She hoped Davis wasn't waiting at their meet-up, but how could he be? She hadn't thought about it before but there'd been cell coverage in the parking lot. She'd used her phone to call for an ambulance and yet she hadn't heard from her handler.

Her cell buzzed, causing her to jump. She checked the text. Relief washed over her and through her when she saw the initials from her handler along with a text message. The second blessing was that Angelina didn't wake.

New meet-up location: Bluff Motel.

"I have to go." Melissa dropped the phone into her bag and felt around for the car keys.

Colin moved in between her and the door.

"You're not leaving without explaining yourself."

Chapter Five

The baby stirred at Colin's booming voice. Melissa's heart dropped. This time, Angelina whined and Melissa knew that her daughter was about to cry.

"Shhh, baby. It's okay," Melissa soothed. She needed to get out of there fast before Colin saw her daughter's face—correction, *their* daughter's face. All Melissa's plans at keeping everyone safe while starting a new life were being threatened. O'Brien men were too honest and too much about family for Colin to stand by while she took his daughter on the run without him knowing where they'd gone or if they'd return. Coming to the hospital had been a huge risk, but what choice did she have? She'd had no idea where her handler was and her daughter needed protection. The storm that had been brewing inside her was developing, swirling, threatening to devastate her.

There was a ray of sunshine, though. Marshal Davis had finally contacted her. He was okay. Melissa needed to get to the checkpoint so she could disappear. Wow, she didn't expect that word to hurt so much.

"I'll give you some privacy," Dallas said. He stopped as he rounded by Angelina and all Melissa could think was, *Keep walking, Dallas.*

Melissa feared he'd have questions, especially if he made a quick calculation and estimated Angelina's age. Her heart dropped as one of her worst nightmares threatened to play out before her eyes. She held her breath, waiting. Dallas gave her a look as he passed by but he didn't say a word.

She let out the breath she'd been holding.

"What's going on?" Colin's tone was harsh, his words like daggers being thrown at her.

"Colin, I can't do this right now," she shot back under her breath, trying to will her body to stop shaking. "I need to take care of my daughter and I have to go."

"Not until you tell me where," he said, and his athletic frame blocked the exit. "And not until I know you'll be safe."

"Richard is in trouble with the law and I'm going to meet with a US marshal. Everything will be fine," she said, her voice breaking on the last few words. Everything wasn't going to be fine. It hadn't been fine in a very long time. And Melissa feared that it would never be fine again.

"What has he done?" he asked.

"I can't talk about it. I told you what you wanted to know. Move out of the way," she said. Angelina took in a deep breath.

Colin folded his arms across his chest. "Not good enough, Melissa."

"Don't do this, Colin. I have to go. He's waiting for me," she said, and then it seemed to dawn on him why she'd be meeting with a US marshal.

At the same time, Angelina popped her head up and the blanket dipped. Melissa covered her as her daughter tried to follow the new voice…

Every muscle in Colin's body seemed to harden as shock and disbelief formed brackets around his mouth and creased his forehead. Did he know?

"Melissa..." was all he seemed able to get out as Angelina belted out the saddest-sounding cry.

"I can't right now," was all she said as she started pacing and soothing her daughter. Colin figuring out that Angelina was his daughter would cause all kinds of wrinkles in Melissa's plans. He'd turn the world over to find them if he allowed her outside that door in the first place.

Melissa's legs felt like rubber as her carefully constructed world crumbled around her. She was going to have to tell him at some point. *Not now*, a little voice said.

"Richard is armed and dangerous. There's no telling where he is, and I can't let you walk out that door if I don't know you're going to be protected. Period," Colin said.

"He's not going to hurt us," she countered, but there was no life in those words. She might be feeling defeated at the moment, but her determination would kick in soon and she'd recover. She'd get her life back on track. Richard did not get to win.

"What if you take us to the meet-up point?" she asked. Before she could answer Dallas stepped into the room with a man in uniform behind him. She recognized Deputy Garcia.

Angelina had settled on Melissa's shoulder again, and if Colin realized he had a daughter he didn't show it.

"Deputy Garcia has news that I think you need to hear," Dallas said.

After perfunctory greetings, the deputy said, "A US

marshal was found shot on Highway 287. He was pronounced dead at the scene."

The air *whooshed* from Melissa's lungs and she was almost knocked back a step. This couldn't be happening. This couldn't be real.

"When?" she asked, her knees buckling.

Colin caught her before she went down and helped her over to a nearby blue chair.

"His distress call came in just before midnight. Tommy had received a call for aid and he was following the gunman when he was shot," Deputy Garcia said, his voice anguished.

"Midnight?" she repeated, her voice trailing off. *How could that be?* She blinked up at Garcia. "This can't be real. You must be mistaken. He just texted me. He has to be alive."

"It couldn't have been him," Colin said, his gaze intense on her. He redirected, looking at Garcia instead. "Was the marshal's phone at the scene when they found him?"

"Hold on while I check." Garcia excused himself to make the call.

"If Marshal Davis didn't text me, who did?" Melissa asked, too stunned to accept that the marshal might be dead. He had a wife, kids. He couldn't be gone.

Garcia returned a few minutes later. "We don't know where his phone is. It's missing along with his laptop and the weapons in his trunk."

Richard had shot Marshal Davis. Richard had shot Tommy. And he'd shoot Melissa if he had a chance. Her only question was why he hadn't fired on her in the parking lot.

He didn't want to risk killing his daughter, a little

voice in the back of her head said. She glanced down at her angel—the child that Richard believed to be his. Melissa couldn't even think that anything could happen to her.

"There's more. I just learned that the suspect's vehicle was last seen in this area. I need to take you into protective custody," Garcia said to her.

She was already shaking her head. If a US marshal couldn't keep her safe, how could Garcia? He didn't have half the resources available to him that the federal government would.

"I have to get her out of here," Colin said with a glance toward her. She could tell by his expression that he was expecting some kind of acknowledgment or agreement.

She was still too shocked to react.

"How do you plan to do that?" Garcia said. "I have a US marshal supervisor waiting to hear from me that she's okay and on her way in."

"They can't guarantee her safety. I can," Colin said emphatically.

"If we can get her to the ranch we should be okay," Dallas offered.

Colin was already shaking his head again.

"We're going off the grid. I don't want anyone to know where I take her," he said to Dallas. "Not even you guys."

"Can I refuse protective custody?" Melissa asked. So far, her handler was dead and her childhood friend was fighting for his life in surgery down the hallway.

Richard had followed and then shot a US marshal in order to find her. He'd stop at nothing and allow no one to step in his path because at this point he had nothing to lose.

The way she saw it, Colin was her best chance to survive, especially when he figured out that Angelina was his child. And he would figure it out soon at this rate.

Garcia nodded. "I can't advise that, though."

She looked to Colin. "Can you keep me and my daughter alive until they locate Richard and lock him away?"

She didn't even want to think about his brother or the others working in the organization who could come after her. Right now, she focused on Richard.

"He won't hurt either one of you on my watch." His words, steady as steel, carried a vow, a promise, and Colin had always delivered on his word.

"Then, I'm refusing your offer for protective custody," she said to Garcia. All Melissa cared about was keeping Angelina alive at this point. Nothing mattered more to her than her daughter and she couldn't even fathom anything happening to her little angel. There was no worse thought for a parent than losing a child. It was unfair, unthinkable and no one deserved it.

"We'll get farther if Dallas takes your daughter to the ranch and keeps her there while we go on the run," Colin said to her. His word choice made her realize that he hadn't figured it out yet.

"No way. She goes with me or no deal," Melissa said, holding on to her baby a little bit tighter to her chest.

"Listen, if we lead Richard away from here she'll be safer," Colin said, but there was no conviction in his words. He knew her well enough to know that this would be a losing battle. Colin had never been one to waste energy on lost causes and he'd see the threat to her by now.

"We'll send Fisher with you." Dallas also seemed to understand that leaving her baby behind wasn't an option. He was referring to Gideon Fisher, head of security at the ranch.

"No extra protection. We're more nimble if it's just us." Colin pulled his cell from his pocket and then handed it to his brother. "And no cell phones. I don't want to take a chance of anyone being able to locate us using the GPS in those."

He indicated that Melissa should do the same. She fished hers out of her handbag and stared at it. She'd become so dependent on her phone that the thought of handing it over—especially with so many other unknowns in her situation—brought on a wave of anxiety. But Angelina's life was on the line.

Melissa passed her phone over, her connection to the new life she was supposed to be making. Instead, she was going on the run. Life changes were like stray lightning. She never knew when a bolt was coming that could change her life forever. She'd learned not to depend on making plans in the past twelve months.

Right there, she made a silent vow not to rest until Richard was locked behind bars where he belonged. Angelina didn't deserve this life. And Melissa was prepared to do whatever it took in order to make sure her daughter never had to suffer because of that man again.

COLIN ONLY GOT a glimpse of the little girl's face and yet that one second had frozen the blood in his veins. There was no way that little girl could be his. Period. And this wasn't the time to discuss it. Although, he planned to have a conversation with Melissa as soon as he could allow himself to think about something besides Tommy healing and stopping Richard. For now, everything else was on hold.

The look on Melissa's face when Colin had asked her to let Dallas take her daughter was an image he wouldn't soon be able to erase. She'd been mother bear and desperate and heartbroken all at once. Colin had fought against the urge to comfort her. For reasons he couldn't explain, he had every intention of keeping Melissa with her daughter, together, where they belonged, and helping her put this entire mess with Richard behind her.

"Are we good?" Colin asked Deputy Garcia. Colin had been in plenty of volatile situations before but never with a kid. Part of him thought he should've put up a stronger argument for Dallas taking the youngster to the ranch, where she'd be tucked away and safe. Colin didn't have to be a father to understand Melissa's need to keep her daughter in her arms, to protect her above all else. Melissa had had that desperate, determined look in her eyes. The kind only a devoted mother could have. So, he'd figure out a way to take them both on the run and keep them safe. He needed to account for the baby being with them because that complicated the situation. Based on his knowledge from the kiddos at the ranch, the younger the baby, the more the feedings occurred. It would be more difficult to travel with one so little.

Garcia nodded. "I can't force anyone into protective custody. It's her choice. It's my job to advise against this course of action. Obviously, I won't stop you from leaving. I'm planning to get some air myself. I'm going to step outside via the…?" He looked at Colin.

"ER bay," he said. Colin understood the insinuation. Garcia was giving them an out while he watched over them to make sure they made it safely out of the parking lot.

"My truck will be waiting," Dallas said with a nod, emptying the cash from his pockets and handing over a stack of twenties. "This should help. There's a baby seat inside the truck that should work fine for the little one."

Colin was grateful for the help.

Garcia checked his watch. "If I head out now I'll be back in five minutes or so."

"Thank you," Colin said. Leaving Tommy while he was in the hospital fighting for his life was a tough blow. The image of his friend being shot and bleeding out in a parking lot would stick with Colin for a long time.

Being negative and fearing the worst wasn't the energy he wanted to put into the situation. Thoughts were powerful. Colin replaced the image with the two of them fishing together this summer, smiling, drinking a cold brew. Tommy would pull through, *had* to pull through.

"Make sure he has everything he needs when he wakes from surgery." Colin nodded toward the hallway, thinking that he needed to stop off at a gas station so that he could pick up a prepaid phone—one that couldn't be traced back to him—so that he could check on Tommy.

"Will do." Garcia tipped his hat before walking out of the room.

"You ready?" he asked Melissa.

She nodded. "Angelina's diaper bag is in my car. It has everything I need to get through a couple of days."

"I'll put it in the truck if you tell me where you're parked and give me the keys," Dallas said.

Melissa's hand trembled but she managed to locate her keys and hand them over. "I'm parked in the visitor lot. Front row. White car. I don't know the license plate and I can't remember if there's more than one."

"I can use the auto-lock button to locate it," he said. "Give me a head start, a couple of minutes."

Colin drained his coffee cup and then set it on the counter.

Melissa had given her baby a pacifier and that had settled her down. Melissa's nerves, on the other hand, were raw. She never paced and she was practically wearing a hole in the blue carpet.

"Let's do this." Colin took Melissa's free hand and led her toward the stairs. He ignored the frisson of heat, figuring it was residual attraction left over from more than a year ago. He chalked it up to unfinished business between the two of them. Spending a few days with her while the feds caught up with Richard would be just what Colin needed to gain closure. He had to admit that seeing Melissa with her and Richard's daughter was going a long way toward helping him realize that she'd moved on. Did he have questions about Angelina? Yeah. This wasn't the time or the place to ask.

He led her to the ER bay, where the king cab truck waited, engine purring, keys inside.

"Keep your head down and walk with purpose," he said from the sterile white hallway. "No matter what happens, don't look up. I'll stand behind you as you buckle your daughter into the car seat and I'll make sure no one's taking notice of what you're doing. Do the best you can to act casual."

Colin tucked his chin to his chest so that the brim of his Stetson would cover his face. He stood behind Melissa, his hand on the small of her back, as she tucked her little bundle in the car seat.

Soon after, she opened the front passenger door and climbed inside the vehicle without drawing unwanted attention. Knowing that Deputy Garcia had eyes on them to prevent any problems or in case things went south to give them extra time was a comfort. Dallas was no doubt keeping watch, as well. That was even more reassuring.

Pulling out of the lot, Colin kept vigilant watch on anything that moved around them. At this time of night, there was very little activity on the roads and that would make it a little more challenging to get out of town unnoticed. He needed to get them onto the highway pretty darn quick where they could blend in with the other vehicles. There were more trucks in this part of Texas than sedans, so being in Dallas's truck would help.

"Where are we going?" Melissa asked, fighting back a yawn.

Colin ignored the reaction his body had to the sadness and defeat in her voice. No doubt, she was exhausted. It was the middle of the night and there was no telling how long it had been since she'd had a good night's sleep. Her lack of rest most likely had more to do with the man she'd lived with than the baby sleeping in the backseat.

"Where's Richard from?" he asked, his eyes focused on the road ahead. He was already making his way toward the highway.

"Oklahoma City, originally. Why?" she asked, sounding surprised at the question.

"His family still there?" he asked, not ready to answer just yet. He meandered onto the highway, grateful for the thick traffic. He'd kept vigilant watch in the rearview mirror to make sure no one had followed them.

A cursory glance at her and he saw that her head was leaned against the headrest and her gaze was fixed out the front windshield. Her fingers pinched her nose like she was trying to stem a headache.

"Yes," she said.

"Then, we're headed to Oklahoma City," he said.

"What? Why?" she asked as she turned to face him.

"Because it's the last place he'll expect you to be while we formulate a plan," he said.

"Shouldn't we be running anywhere besides his hometown?" she asked.

"He won't expect us to go there. And he needs to know we're not in Bluff anymore. Word will get around." Colin checked the rearview again to see if any cars were following them. "I'll need to find a place that we can bunk down with a baby for a few days. We'll need more supplies than what's in your diaper bag."

Dallas had a gun permit so there'd be a gun in the locked glove compartment. He'd cleared out his shotgun from the backseat once he'd had a baby.

Colin always carried cash, and he had a couple hundred dollars in his wallet plus what Dallas had given him.

"We'll have to stay off the grid, which means no credit cards. I have enough money to get by until we figure out a plan of attack. First step is to get us to a secure area and far away from Bluff. A place that your husband will least suspect to find you."

"Should we figure out a way to let Richard see us leaving?" she asked.

"Too risky," he said.

Melissa got quiet like she did when she was churning something over and over again in her mind. Reasoning with her when she was doing that wouldn't do any good, so Colin focused on his own thoughts.

When he was sure they were in the clear, he stopped off at a gas station to buy a cell phone.

A little while later, Colin wasn't exactly sure when, Melissa settled into her chair. She leaned back and rubbed her temples. A short time after that, her breathing became steady and even.

The baby in the backseat stirred but didn't cry. He thought about her curly black hair and that face...

Colin pushed the image of the little girl out of his mind as he made the rest of the almost four-hour drive. He veered east to Lake Stanley Draper and then located a boat dock. After scouting for a good place to bunk for the night, he parked the vehicle just inside a few trees in order to keep the truck out of sight. The sun would be up soon and he'd watch the dock throughout the next morning to see who came and went. This time of year and with rain in the forecast, he hoped no one would show and they could have their pick of houseboat rentals to "borrow."

His brain hadn't had time to process the fact that Melissa was in his life again, even if it was temporary. He looked over at her and his heart fisted—not the reaction he was hoping for.

Since they were going to be around each other 24/7, at least for a few days, he needed a mental headshake to stay on track. Because seeing her asleep and looking so vulnerable was threatening to crack the walls he'd constructed around his heart.

She was resting peacefully and he didn't want to disturb her, so he took care in leaning her chair back and then pulled a blanket Dallas kept in the backseat and placed it over her. She rolled onto her side but didn't open her eyes.

His military training made it easy for him to sleep anywhere, anytime. Working the ranch had reinforced his need for very little shut-eye. A couple hours of quality time would be good enough for him. The sun would be up soon and that would make it harder to rest. He closed his eyes and the image of Melissa's little girl immediately popped into his thoughts.

Curly black hair. Those round cheeks. The name, Angelina.

Couldn't be his, he thought as he settled in so he could nab a few hours of shut-eye.

Chapter Six

All Colin would've needed was a couple hours of sleep and he'd be good to go. He got forty-five minutes before the little angel in the backseat stirred, waking him. He sat up and surveyed his surroundings. The wind was picking up. Other than slight movement in the trees, all seemed quiet.

And that's when his brain decided to loop the notion that Angelina looked a lot like him from his own baby pictures.

With effort, he pushed aside the image. Didn't need that distraction this morning. Besides, Richard had dark hair and Angelina was his daughter.

Melissa was still asleep but Colin needed coffee. There was no way he could wake her even though he suspected the little one would be up soon enough for a feeding.

Caffeine would go a long way toward clearing the cobwebs in his head. Colin shook his head to see if that would do any good. Maybe going over what he knew so far would get his blood pumping. Just the thought of Richard Rancic was enough to heat Colin's blood. There was enough residual anger there to do the trick, and the notion that the man had targeted Melissa stoked the flames.

Colin couldn't go there without questioning the circumstances under which Melissa had walked out on him in the first place. Had she known what she was getting into when she'd made that choice? Richard had been all flash and charm as he'd rolled through town, and Colin had been beyond shocked when Melissa had fallen for it, for him. He'd believed that the two of them were solid, that nothing could come between them, which seemed pretty naive now.

Apparently, money could. There was no way Melissa could have had real feelings for Richard, was there?

Sure, her father had been having some business troubles. That much was common knowledge. Had Rancic made promises to Mr. Roark, to Melissa after going into business with him? Mr. Roark loved his daughter and his lack of business acumen was well-known in some circles. Had he played a role in the sudden turn of events last year? Had money?

Those were questions that Colin wouldn't allow himself to consider. He'd made his decision to move on that rainy spring day when she'd thrown his ring at him. Afterward, he'd shut down all communication between them, which wasn't too difficult given that she'd moved and he'd never been on social media. Besides, he wasn't one to hang around where he wasn't wanted.

The way Richard had made his family's wealth so obvious had turned Colin's stomach. Sure, Colin had money, too. To him, his family fortune amounted to a bunch of zeroes in a bank account. Security was nice, don't get him wrong, but he didn't need much beyond the basics of oxygen, water, food, shelter and sleep.

Three of those cost nothing, considering his water came from various wells on the ranch. Then, there was the obvious need for companionship, for building a life with someone.

Colin looked at Melissa, the woman who felt so much like a stranger. Change was inevitable. More than a year had passed since he'd last seen her. She was a mother now. And yet what he'd seen in her eyes last night was the result of something totally different. She'd been in what he could only guess was an abusive marriage. There were no physical marks that he could see but that didn't mean much. His charity work with victims had given him insight into what went on behind closed doors in toxic relationships. He'd listened to countless victims talk about how good they became at hiding bruises. And then there was emotional abuse, the kind that left no visible trail but did as much, if not more, damage on the inside. He found it painful to watch people stay in unhealthy relationships. He wanted them to know there was a way out, but he knew they'd see only when they were able to, if at all.

And what about the baby? A man who would strike down an officer of the law didn't seem like the type to let his child go. No matter what else happened, Richard would always be the girl's father. The little bundle in the backseat would bind Melissa to Richard for the rest of her life.

Even if she hadn't seen through Richard right away, how could Melissa be so careless as to have a baby with someone she barely knew? Then again, the same wisdom carried over to her choice to marry the man in the first place. Colin wouldn't understand it in a hundred years. Melissa had been clear with him. She'd thought they were too young to have a child when he'd thrown the idea out. She'd said that she wanted to have time together to build memories of the two of them before expanding their family. He'd argued that they'd been dating for two years already. He knew enough about her to realize that she was the one, the only one he wanted to spend the rest of his life with. He didn't need a marriage certificate to have a baby. Although, he knew that she did and respected it. A blow, like a physical punch, nearly knocked the wind out of him at thinking about her having a child with Richard.

Where'd that come from?

It's exactly what he deserved for rehashing the past, he thought wryly.

What's done was done. There was no going back and no changing it. Colin accepted that logically even if his heart had some catching up to do.

Melissa rolled onto her side and then opened her eyes. Still that same honey-brown with violet streaks.

"Morning," he said quietly, not wanting to wake the little passenger in the backseat.

Melissa stretched and yawned, immediately checking behind her. "Already time to wake up?"

"Afraid so," he said.

"Where are we?" She pulled the lever on her chair in order to sit upright and then spun around to check on her daughter.

"East of Oklahoma City," he supplied, straightening out his own chair. Even the large cab in the vehicle had been uncomfortable for a man of his size and build. "I need coffee. Will it wake her if I drive to the store?"

"Car rides actually help her sleep," she said. "I can heat a bottle at the store when she wakes."

He rubbed his eyes as he started the ignition.

Melissa was quiet on the drive to the country market. The baby started shifting around and he figured it was only a matter of time before she started crying.

Fifteen minutes later, he pulled into a spot and parked.

"Should I wait here for you or can I take her into the bathroom to change her?" she asked, adding, "She'll need to eat soon, too."

"What do you need for that?" He'd been around enough babies in the past few months to know they ate different things at different times based on their ages.

"I have formula in her diaper bag, so maybe just clean water and a microwave to warm it up," she said, and then lowered her voice when she added, "I couldn't breastfeed."

The note of sadness in her voice at that last part struck him in a bad place. The main task of a mother, in his opinion, was to love her child unconditionally. Colin could see that wasn't a problem for Melissa. She might not have been ready to be a mother, but from what he'd seen so far she'd more than stepped up to the challenge. He'd seen the way she looked at her baby last night. The fierce protectiveness in her eyes. An irritating little voice in the back of his head said that she might not have been ready to be a parent *with him*.

Colin glanced around. "Since we're fairly close to his family home, you should stick near me while we're exposed."

He waited while she unbuckled the baby and the little girl's sleepy yawn tugged at his heart.

Inside, he bought a couple of travel toothbrushes and a tube of toothpaste and then waited for Melissa in the hallway leading to the restroom while she changed her daughter. He could hear her low voice as she sang to the infant.

A couple of minutes later, she opened the door. The baby was swaddled in a pink blanket and all he could see clearly was her sweet little face and those round eyes.

"I bought a few supplies I thought you might appreciate considering how fast we left town," he said, holding up the offerings, remembering how quickly she would hop out of bed to brush her teeth in the mornings. Then again, most of the time she hopped right back in afterward for a heated round of making love before she had to get ready for work.

"Can you hold her while I brush?" Her smile faded fast as she looked at him and then at the baby. There was a mix of emotions he couldn't readily identify brewing behind her eyes.

"Sure." He held out his arms. He'd had enough experience holding babies at the ranch in the past six months to make him feel comfortable enough with Angelina. Instead of focusing on the fact that this was Richard's daughter, he thought about her belonging to Melissa and a feeling of the world being right came over him as he took her. It was odd.

He'd always known that Melissa would be a good mother, even when she didn't have the confidence to believe in herself. From what he could see so far, Angelina was happy, content. Melissa had done well.

"Will you be okay?" she asked. Her desperate and panicked look was almost an insult.

It shouldn't make him smile, but it did. He also shouldn't feel a surge of attraction toward Melissa but he felt that, too. His heart warned that spending time with her was going to take a toll.

"I'm fine. Not sure how she feels about all this—" he glanced down at the baby and back "—but I'm good."

Melissa's eyes gave away her nervousness. She didn't leave. Instead, she shifted her weight from foot to foot and he could tell that she was analyzing her options. "Maybe I should just figure out a way—"

"I got this. Go brush," he said, nodding toward the restroom.

She chewed on the thought for a minute, glancing from him to her daughter.

"I'll be back in one sec," she finally said, holding up her index finger.

"Go," he repeated.

She blew out a breath and immediately disappeared into the bathroom.

The door flew open a few minutes later and she came out with her hair in a ponytail and a fresh face. "I'll take her back now."

She seemed especially nervous for him to be holding her daughter. He cocked an eyebrow but didn't call her out on it, chalking it up to being too close to Rancic's family home as he handed Angelina over to her mother.

Colin excused himself to go to the men's room and brush his teeth, and then bought two cups of steaming brew. Melissa liked sweeteners added to hers but Colin liked his straight-up black.

She smiled when she saw the cup meant for her. "That looks amazing right now. But she gets hers first."

"What can I do to help?" he asked.

She gave him a couple of instructions, so he went inside to use the microwave. When he mixed the warm water with the formula and it looked like milk, he let himself smile.

"You're actually pretty good at that," she said, bouncing her baby, who was sucking away on a pacifier.

There was a moment happening between them, a connection that he couldn't afford. He handed over the bottle. "Wait here until I come get you."

"Okay." She started the feeding.

Colin walked away, climbed into the cab and started the truck. He didn't move far. He repositioned the truck at one side of the parking lot where he could watch all the vehicles exiting the highway. It made him visible, too, so he slipped on his cowboy hat and shades even though the skies were starting to cloud up. He'd rather have Melissa and the baby as much out of sight as possible.

As he walked toward the convenience mart, Melissa met him halfway.

"Can you sit in the backseat and feed her?" he asked.

"Yes," she said. Once the baby was settled in with the bottle, Melissa said, "Colin."

There was something in her voice he couldn't quite pinpoint, maybe a warning, that had him thinking her next words weren't going to be ones that he wanted to hear.

"Yeah," was all he said, resisting the urge to look at her through the rearview mirror. His head already pounded and he didn't need to add to that.

"Thank you for everything you're doing for me and Angelina. I'm really sorry about what happened between us before," Melissa finally said.

There was a long pause. Another reason not to get too comfortable in their tentative…alliance. Friendship was too strong a word. He was helping someone who needed him. That's as far as Colin would allow his mind to go with this.

"It is what it is," he countered, not able to go there with her. Call it licking wounds or whatever, but he had no plans to use this time to "reconnect" their relationship. Richard had won. She'd married him instead of Colin. There was nothing more that needed to be said between them. "Let's just stay focused on what needs to be done and get you two moved on."

"Okay," she said, a little breathless.

Had he knocked the wind out of her with his cold shoulder? Maybe. It was nothing compared to the blow she'd delivered him a year ago.

"Where to next?" she asked after the baby finished her bottle and had been burped.

"We need to find a place to bunk down for the night and get out of the open," he said. "Then, I'll make sure we have enough supplies to get us through tonight since I plan on staying put."

He pulled out the cell he'd bought.

"Where'd you get that?" she asked.

"At a convenience store last night. It's a throw-away phone, meaning there's no way to trace it back to us. I paid cash for it so the transaction can't be tracked back to us, either," he supplied. Sticking to the facts and keeping conversation to a minimum should help keep her from confusing his help for still having feelings for her.

"I must've slept right through all of that," she said.

"I had to stop for gas and I wanted to call the hospital to check on Tommy," he said.

"And?"

"He made it out of surgery not long after we left last night. Everything went well and the doctor was able to remove all the bullet fragments from the shotgun blast," he replied.

"That's so good to hear," she said on an expelled breath. "I'm so relieved."

"He lost a lot of blood but, yeah, he'll pull through. He's tough," Colin said.

Tears streamed down her cheeks and Colin resisted the urge to reach over and wipe them away. It was muscle memory and nothing more causing him to want to do that.

"Richard doesn't want anything to do with Tommy. He just happened to get in the way, so he should be safe from any retaliation," she said.

"There will be enough eyes on Tommy's room to make sure of it. Plus, your husband killed a law enforcement officer. No one takes that lightly," he said with a little more intensity than he'd planned.

"It's good we left town. I don't want anyone else getting hurt because of me," she said. Was she blaming herself?

"It's because of Richard, not you. *You* had nothing to do with this." Colin gripped the steering wheel tighter.

"Yes, I did. I knew better than to come back to Bluff. Marshal Davis is dead because I didn't listen to him. He warned me against returning. I heard Richard was last seen heading to Canada, so I went against his advice. There's no way that his death is not my fault," she said, and Colin tried not to notice how much anguish there was in her voice. Shock still reverberated through him at just how dangerous the man she'd married seemed to be.

"Tell me about your husband, Melissa. What's he into?" he asked.

"I don't even know where to start. He's a career criminal."

"And you had no idea before you rushed into marriage with him?" Colin's voice was too harsh and she immediately went into defensive mode.

"Remember when I took you on that fishing trip to Big Bend?" he asked.

Her cheeks flushed and he realized just what part of the trip she'd focused on. Yes, they'd had hours and hours of great sex, but that wasn't where he was going with this.

"The sun was going down. You were sitting out on the porch and there was that baby jackrabbit that you thought lost its mother. You put tiny pieces of vegetables along one end of the porch. The jackrabbit came over and you thought it was the cutest little thing. You were so happy that you'd fed it and then so startled when an eagle swooped down and snapped up the jackrabbit. You made yourself sick over blaming yourself for that little creature's death."

"That was obviously my fault, Colin. If I hadn't fed the jackrabbit it would be alive today."

"There's where you're wrong. That eagle would've been flying around anyway. He would've seen the jackrabbit and swooped down to get him no matter what. That's his nature and you're not responsible for that," Colin said, hoping his words might offer some reassurance.

She gave a noncommittal shrug in response.

EVERYWHERE MELISSA HAD GONE, everything she'd done for the past year made her feel like she was the jackrabbit and her husband was the eagle. There was always the thought of him lurking in the back of her mind, ready to swoop down and take Angelina away. Even when he left on business—and those were trips that had kept her sane—there was never a feeling that he was ever truly gone.

The fear that he'd pop up around every corner had almost driven her beyond the brink. Once the baby had been born, Melissa had kept Angelina within arm's reach at all times. Always aware that Richard could put two and two together at any moment and deliver on his threats to destroy Melissa and everyone she loved if she betrayed him.

And now she really was the jackrabbit, seeking shelter, scrambling to get away from the eagle that was circling, ready to pounce the second she slipped. Any mistake and she'd be in the eagle's grip, where she'd be crushed.

Colin pulled into the spot near the trees where they'd been parked this morning. She sipped on her coffee, wishing it could give her more than a fleeting jolt of energy.

"What is he wanted for?" Colin asked.

"The feds are after him for money laundering and murder. Also, he was using his resorts as a shelter in order to harbor some very bad men, keeping them hidden from law enforcement and allowing them access to the US. His brother is involved in the business and I think his father is, too, but I couldn't find proof," she said.

"How do you know about his brother?" he asked.

"I recorded them during their Sunday night football games. They used to turn up the volume real loud so feds sitting out front in a white minivan couldn't pick up their voices when the two of them talked business. I sewed a recording device inside the collar of one of Richard's shirts. He always wore a button-down. Even on game day," she said.

"How'd you know which shirt he would wear?" he asked.

"I didn't. So, I sewed it into the collar of one of his favorites and waited." She didn't want to think about all those sleepless nights she'd spent waiting for him to wear the right shirt. There were too many.

"That was taking a big risk," Colin said with a hint of reverence in his voice. She didn't want to notice. She didn't want to think about how much she'd missed his deep voice—a voice that could soothe even the worst days. His easygoing style could lift her up the minute she saw him. He'd been her safe place. Her shelter from all the craziness of trying to stay on top of her father's affairs. Obviously, she'd failed at that, too, or she wouldn't be in this mess in the first place.

"I should've done more," she said, thinking of the mix of excitement and tension she'd had the Sunday morning she'd finally seen Richard wearing the shirt. The sense of freedom that was so close she could almost touch it. It had been like standing in the middle of a downpour with a bolt of sunlight on the horizon.

No matter what, she'd had to control her reaction. Even though she'd had a lot of training at stuffing her feelings down deep inside, nothing had prepared her for the mix of nerves on that day. She'd been so relieved that the nightmare was nearing an end and yet so anxious that something would go wrong and he'd figure her out before the feds could get what they needed to arrest him.

Knowing just how much was at stake made the task even more difficult.

"You played it right. You did the right things," he said. "I know it probably doesn't feel like it right now. But you did."

"Did I?" she asked, fierce and angry at the same time. "I was afraid, so federal officers had to put a lot of pressure on me to get a recording, or some kind of admission from him about his illegal activities. Talking to him about what he did when he left the house wasn't even a serious consideration for me. He would've known something was up immediately and I didn't dare risk Angelina's life. But my daughter's life is in danger because I failed her."

"Don't think like that, Melissa." His words brought little comfort when she thought about everything that could go wrong. "We'll figure this out. Her father will be in jail for the rest of his life. He won't be able to hurt her."

Hearing Colin say those words knifed her. She wanted to scream that Richard wasn't the father. This wasn't the right time to have the discussion that she needed to have with Colin about her daughter's paternity. She needed to change the subject. "How do we find shelter?"

"By being patient," he said.

"I don't know how much longer I can sit here and do nothing while my life crumbles around me. I've done too much of that already," she said, and then figured she'd said too much based on Colin's reaction. She made a move for the door handle.

"Where do you think you're going?" he asked.

"I can't sit here anymore," she said.

"You need to take a walk? Get some fresh air?" he asked, his voice rising in anger. "Then get used to someone being right on top of you because you're not getting out of my sight until this situation is resolved. You've run out of patience? Good. So have I, and I won't tolerate anyone stalking out on their own and disappearing on me, especially not since you've done it once already."

Chapter Seven

Melissa froze. Her heart thudded. Her chest squeezed. All Colin needed to add in order to complete the insult would be to remind her that it was her own fault she was in this mess. He could tell her that she should've handled everything differently. She should've trusted him and talked to him about it earlier. She should've...

Going down that road again was as productive as milking a bat to feed a horse. Another round of the blame game wouldn't change anything. All she'd be doing was wasting precious energy, and she needed every ounce to get her through this ordeal.

Out of her peripheral vision, she could see Colin chewing on his jaw like he did when he said something he regretted. He'd always acted on impulse and could rely on his charm to get him out of sticky situations. That was part of the reason she hadn't confided in him before. She couldn't be sure that he wouldn't do something they'd all regret.

He had no idea what she'd faced. And he had no idea the real reasons she'd married Richard. She almost blurted out that she'd made those choices in order to protect him and his family. What good would it do? Colin would never forgive her for walking out. He'd never get over what she'd done, especially not when he learned that Angelina was his daughter. So, there was no use in trying to pretend otherwise. Let him believe what he believed. The truth would only hurt him more.

Besides, she'd had her father to protect. He was finally in protective custody, being cared for in a nursing home. Once this was over, she and Angelina could settle into a little house. Bring her father there. She could get a job.

Part of her almost wished she'd skimmed money from the piles of cash Richard always had on hand. If she'd needed proof that Richard had been involved in illegal activity, it hadn't taken long to figure out. Who put tens of thousands of dollars out on the breakfast table?

She'd suspected foul play after the first couple of weeks of marriage, and it hadn't taken long to realize that he was knee-deep in illegal activity. Of course, there'd been no preparing her for just how demented her husband was or how far he was willing to go to keep his activities quiet.

"We'll camp out here for the rest of the day and keep an eye on the dock," Colin finally said, cutting into her heavy thoughts. He pointed to a spot between the trees.

Melissa focused. At first she didn't see anything but then it became clear. She saw several large boats. She had never spent much time in the water and she had a lifelong fear of drowning, so she had no idea what kind of boats she was looking at except to say that they offered shelter. A few were large. Houseboats?

"I can't sleep on one of those," she said. "You know I'm terrified of drowning."

"Did your husband know that, too?" Colin asked.

"Yes." Hearing Colin say the words *your husband*

sat heavy in her chest. In her mind, Richard had never been her husband.

"Then it's the safest place for us to be. He'd never look for you around water," he said, and he was right. It was smart and she hoped she could actually do it.

"That might be true but—"

"I won't let anything happen to you, but you have to trust me."

That was a tall order. She trusted Colin without a doubt. It was the water she didn't trust. Her pulse kicked up just thinking about it. How many times had she been startled out of a deep sleep with the nightmare that she was drowning? Too many. But if facing her fear meant protecting her daughter, there was nothing to think about.

"You're right about all of it," she conceded, glancing up at the skies that had darkened under layers of gray clouds. "How long do we wait?"

"Until nightfall. I have my eye on that one." He pointed toward a cream-colored boat with a blue zig-zag stripe down the side. "My guess is that it's a rental, which means we'll have to clear out around nine o'clock every morning just to be safe. We should be okay this time of year since there are no major school breaks. There'll be fewer vacationers to worry about."

"How do you know that?"

"It's the same on the ranch for the Rifleman's Club. We see the most visitors during school breaks in March. Other than that, we get a few stragglers, mostly honey-mooners and guys' trips."

"I never understood honeymooners going on a hunting vacation," she said. "To each his own, I guess."

"Women in Texas know how to handle a rifle," he

said, and there was a disapproving quality to his tone. "And they like to shoot."

"I know and I get it. But on your honeymoon? I can think of better things to do than shoot wild hogs," she said.

Out of the corner of her eye, she saw Colin's muscles tense. It dawned on her that he must be thinking about her own honeymoon. The one she never had and didn't want in the first place. "It's not like that. I..."

"Save it," he said under his breath. There was so much anger behind those two words.

How many nights in the past year had she stayed awake, wondering how much he hated her for what she'd done? The mystery was over. It was clear and so hard to see because she never stopped loving him, not even now. Her heart didn't care or seem to want to acknowledge there was no going back. Not with Colin. She'd known that when she walked away and yet seeing it written all over his expression and hearing it in his words made it seem so...final.

She'd done what she had to do in order to survive, she reminded herself. Repeating her mantra had gotten her through so many difficult times in her life.

Naively, she'd believed that given enough time she'd get over Colin. How young. How silly. Maybe there was one true love in life and if it didn't work out, that was it. She tried not to let the thought deflate her. Besides, Angelina was her heart now. Melissa had her daughter and a piece of Colin would be with her forever. That had been enough to get her through an entire year with Richard. It would be enough to carry her through the rest of her life, as well.

Angelina was already showing signs of her father's

personality. Smart. Stubborn. Independent. Sometimes a little intense. And her face? She had the face of an angel.

Melissa needed to change the subject.

"I hate not knowing what's going on in Bluff," Melissa said.

Colin took a minute to answer. "We'll find out when we call the hospital to check on Tommy in a little while."

"Can we do that?" she asked.

"Calls go through a switchboard, so the numbers are impossible to trace. One of my brothers will be in the room and should pick up."

"Tommy's safe, right? In case Richard changes his mind and goes after him for answers," she asked, giving into a moment of panic. "Richard can't get to him, can he?"

"Not with my brothers on watch and as we already covered Richard was never after Tommy. Besides, with him being spotted in the area someone will keep eye on Tommy at all times. I doubt Richard would be crazy enough to try anything else in Bluff. It'd be too risky and he's fixated on getting to you. He'd only make a move on Tommy's room if he thought you were there," Colin said. "I'm sure he's figured out by now that you're nowhere around town."

"How? He didn't see me leave," she said, and the thought of seeing Richard again caused her pulse to race.

"You haven't been spotted, either. You've had a run-in with him, so he's cunning enough to realize that you'd bolt. He's figuring that you're scared, so he's most likely having someone watch the ranch just in case you come running back to me."

"He knows that I wouldn't do that," she said in a moment of fear. The words came out a little too quickly based on Colin's reaction. She needed to make something up or he'd start asking questions, and she didn't have the heart to hurt him again with what she knew about his father. News like that would devastate the O'Briens and they'd always been good to her. There was no way she would deliver that blow to the proud family. "Richard was convinced that I was still in love with you when we married. So, I had to go to great lengths to prove to him that I'd gotten over you."

"And he believed you?" he said, staring out the front windshield, his arms folded across his chest.

"Of course he did. It took some time but I finally convinced him. I made sure there was no room for doubt." She left out the part where both her and her daughter's survival had depended on her putting on a convincing show.

"How soon did you figure out he's a criminal?" Colin asked. He'd recovered his game face and his voice gave away nothing of his emotions. This was a new side to him, a side that she couldn't read. Maybe it had been there all along but she'd never seen it. Before, she believed that the two of them had shared everything. With him, she could truly be herself. No pretense. No facade. Just Melissa. Imperfections and all. And he'd seemed to love her even more for them. But then he'd always been black-and-white. If Colin loved something, he went all in.

Pain gripped her. She had to breathe through it and not allow the walls to collapse around her like it had felt so many times in the past year. It was so much harder to construct barriers with Colin sitting right next to her.

"It didn't take long." She'd known since before the wedding that something was off with Richard, but it didn't matter because her priority had been to protect her father and Colin.

"And you stayed anyway?" he asked. The note of disappointment in his tone was a knife to her heart.

If she was going to get through this with him, and there was no other choice at the moment, then she was going to have to turn off her feelings altogether. She straightened in her chair and stared out the window. She hated the thought of lying. Period. And lying to Colin was even worse.

"I had a daughter to think about." That wasn't a lie.

"How soon did you get pregnant after leaving me?" he asked, and he didn't seem able to hide the bitterness.

"I'm hungry." She didn't dare look at him because he'd see the tears welling in her eyes. There was no way she could afford to give away her emotions now. "When's lunch?"

"We're not leaving until you tell me the truth. You said that you weren't ready to have a baby with me. And yet you seemed perfectly fine to have a child with a man that you knew was a criminal? None of this makes sense to me, Melissa."

"Can't we just leave it at that?" she asked. Her carefully constructed walls were cracking.

"No." The power of that one word struck her.

Colin had questions. She knew that. She'd seen it in his eyes from the moment he got a good look at her daughter.

"Well, I'm not talking about it," she said with as much authority as she could muster.

"Why not?" he asked.

"Because…"

"You hate me that much?" There was so much anger and pain in his voice.

"It's not that…"

"Then what, Melissa?" His gaze bore holes into her.

"Leave it alone." He would do the math at some point and realize…oh, no. He would figure out that Angelina was his daughter. And then what? Would he want to keep her and push Melissa away? He'd never forgive her. She'd seen the hurt and anger buried deep in his eyes and there'd be no coming back from that. Even so, a little voice in her head said that he deserved to know. That Angelina deserved to know her real father.

"What if I can't?" he said quietly and with so much hurt in his voice. "What if I need to know so I can move on? I need to hear it, Melissa. I need to hear that you loved him when you walked out. That you didn't leave me for some…rich jerk…with a bent for breaking the law."

"That's why you thought I left?" His words were daggers to her chest.

"What am I supposed to think?" he asked.

"I didn't have a choice. I was forced to leave. Does knowing that really make you feel better?" she blurted out, and then folded her arms across her chest.

"Maybe." His gaze flicked from Angelina back to Melissa and she could tell that he was about to ask the question she feared most…

"Is she mine?"

Melissa looked down at her angel. She needed to stay strong for Angelina, so she took a fortifying breath. This wasn't the way she'd imagined telling Colin that he was a father, but she didn't have it in her heart to lie to him anymore, either.

"Yes." She couldn't look at him.

All she heard was a sharp intake of air before the driver's side door opened and then closed.

In that moment she knew that everything had changed.

Melissa waited a full twenty minutes before she slipped out of the car. She cradled Angelina, who was happily cooing. She looked down at her baby, all big eyes and smiles. No matter the backlash she would face, it felt right to tell Colin. He deserved to know this angel belonged to him.

She found him sitting by the lake near the tree line, where he almost disappeared into the brush. He was staring out at the water, wearing an intense expression.

She almost didn't walk over to him.

But it was Colin. She'd just dropped a bomb on him and she deserved whatever backlash came with it.

"Can I sit with you?" she asked, stepping up beside him.

He didn't look up. His nod was almost imperceptible. She took it as a positive sign and sat down with enough distance between them to give him space.

If Angelina picked up on the tension between them she sure didn't act like it. She smiled and cooed at Melissa.

"I'm sorry that you're finding out like this," she said. "I'd planned—"

"What? To send me a postcard? From where? Was I ever going to get to know that I have a child?" It was obvious that Colin was keeping control of his temper because of the baby by the way his voice would start rising and then he'd glance at Angelina before pulling his emotions back into check. "I can read the writing on the wall, Melissa. The reason you were meeting with Marshal Davis was to go into witness protection to get away from Richard. I also know that you would never be able to leave the program. Not as long as he or his brother was alive. They'd hunt you down and—" he glanced at the baby "—let's just say there'd be no going back once you entered the program. And did you think about her growing up without a father? How could you do that to her? To me?"

This wasn't the time to tell him how often she'd wake from a dream crying because of how much she missed him. Or how many times her heart begged to see him in the past year. How much it had broken her spirit to walk away in the first place and then to be made to live with the charade that she actually had feelings for another man. She had feelings all right. As far as Richard went, none of them were good.

There was no way she could make hearing this news in this way right for Colin. When other words escaped her, she finally asked, "Do you want to hold your daughter?"

He shook his head.

Colin had stopped talking and that wasn't a good sign.

The truth was out and Melissa couldn't bring herself to regret it now. There was no changing it, no going back, no do-overs when it came to life. She'd done the best she could under the circumstances. Her decision had spared her father jail time in his last years. He was resting comfortably in an undisclosed facility. It had spared Colin's family shame and embarrassment. And their daughter was safe *for now*.

Chapter Eight

Storm clouds thickened as the day went on. The winds had picked up speed. It was obvious that a storm was brewing. Melissa wondered just how bad it was going to get. Thoughts of being on a boat during a bad storm weren't exactly warm and fuzzy.

Few words passed between Colin and Melissa for the balance of the day. He needed time to think, to process, and she understood that on some level. A bomb had been dropped and he was trying to get his bearings. She'd felt the same way. At first, she'd been shocked. And then, afraid.

When it came to Colin, there were worse things he could do besides give her the silent treatment. All things considered, this was good.

"The cream-colored boat with the blue stripe will work for us," he finally said, motioning toward one of the vessels.

The thought of staying on a boat shot Melissa's heart rate up. She had second thoughts as panic gripped her.

"I can't do it. I can't get on that thing," she said, cradling Angelina close to her chest. "There has to be somewhere else we can go."

"This is the best place for all three of us," Colin said evenly, his tone unreadable.

She looked up at the cloudy sky. "It's going to rain."

"Uh-huh," he said, his gaze steady on her.

"You know how I feel about being anywhere near water, let alone on a lake during a storm," she said.

"It could get pretty bad tonight," he agreed.

"Come on, Colin. You don't expect me to…"

"What? Inconvenience yourself?" He fired the words like bullets from a silencer, quiet but deadly.

Tears threatened. "You know it's more than that."

She'd been deathly afraid of water since she was ten and stood ankle deep on the beach as her mother was swept away by a current while swimming during their annual trip to Gulf Shores, Alabama. Her mother's body had been found two days later. Since then, Melissa didn't go near the water.

"You need to decide what you're going to do, but me and that little girl will be on the boat tonight," he said, pushing up to stand.

Melissa stood and backed away from the water.

"You coming?" Colin held his hand out.

"It's not ours," she said. "What if we get caught?"

"We're just borrowing it. I'll have it back and in better condition than before when this is all said and done," he said, still standing, hand still extended.

He was a man of his word, and Melissa had no doubt that the owners would end up with something even nicer for their inconvenience. She was stalling, praying for courage.

"It's the only place she'll be safe tonight," he said, and his voice was low, compassionate as he motioned toward Angelina.

Melissa stared at her daughter's sweet round face. She looked out at the water and took a deep breath. "Okay."

She followed Colin to the dock.

"This is a rental and I already checked that they have everything we'll need to take care of her," he said as he held out his hand.

She took a tentative step toward him and the ground swayed under her feet. "I don't know if I can."

"Don't think about it," he said, his voice calmer and more reassuring this time. "Take my hand and then take two steps forward."

The wood decking in the slip felt solid. The boat did not. Besides, the winds were picking up. Who knew how bad the storm might get.

"I can't. Not while I'm holding the baby," she said.

Colin repositioned until he had one foot on the boat and the other on the decking.

"You won't fall. Not on my watch," he said, and his voice was low. There was so much promise in his words that she took a tentative step forward, keeping one foot on land. The boat shifted and her stomach felt like she'd just dropped down the first hill on a roller coaster. She lifted her foot, anchoring herself with her back foot. Her foot hovered above the boat's decking.

No more being afraid.

With a deep breath and Colin's strong hand on her back, guiding her, Melissa made the short hop onto the boat. She hugged Angelina even closer as she navigated the shaky ground.

"There's a place to sit, cook and eat on board," he said, guiding her toward the open glass doors at the back. "There's also a shower and a bedroom for you and the baby. They have a bassinet for guests to use, so I can set that up."

"There really is everything here," she said, glancing around the space. The houseboat had a simple layout and felt a little bit like a wide RV.

"And those?" She pointed to stairs.

"Don't worry about them. The top deck is open and has extra space for people who rent this to catch plenty of sunrays. We won't be using it," he said. "The kitchen is stocked with pans, plates and glasses. We can easily get by for a few nights on here."

"Will we stay right here?" She glanced back at the sliders, which was not a good idea because it made her head spin.

"Steady," Colin said, his strong hands on her, helping her to the counter where she could lean. Much of his earlier shock and anger had dissipated. He had that focus in his eyes, that intensity, if not the spark. "We'll find a good spot and drop anchor for the night."

Her stomach flipped in part because of his eyes on her. "What about filling up the tank?"

"Most owners have a policy that these have to be returned full, so that's no worry. Everything should be ready to go," he said.

"Are you familiar with this lake?" she asked.

"No. There'll be maps on board. I'll find a good place for us to spend the night," he said.

"Do we have to leave the dock?" Another wave of panic rushed through her. At least she was close to shore as long as they were parked in the slip.

"Yes. Once I get you and the baby settled I'll run out for supplies—"

She was shaking her head as she held on to the

counter for dear life. Thankfully, Angelina was napping in her arms.

"Sit down." He guided her to the couch. "We'll need food for us and more formula for her," he said.

"You can't leave us alone on this...*thing*." Her throat was dry.

"Just for an hour or so while I get—"

"No. We're coming with you," she said. "After the baby wakes and has her bottle we can all go." She stopped herself from saying as a family. She wasn't even sure where the thought came from. They were Angelina's parents but they were far from a family. It was most likely just a blast from the past, a hope for what might've been. It was her nerves and the stress of the situation causing her brain to go there and not her heart's desire.

He must've picked up on how rapidly her pulse was rising when he said, "It'll be okay. We'll figure this out together."

"Promise me you won't disappear if I go into the bathroom or something," she said. She was being irrational but she couldn't help herself.

"I give you my word," he said with a look that said he absolutely meant it. There was something about that one look, those words that calmed her more than she knew better than to allow.

She nodded.

Colin checked drawers until he located a map of the lake and another of the surrounding area. He spread both out on the counter and then studied them with the intensity of a climber looking for a water source.

"She's quiet and she sleeps a lot. Is everything

okay?" he asked, and she picked up on the note of uncertainty in his voice. Parenting was new to him.

"She's a good baby," Melissa said, thinking she was three months ahead on the learning curve.

"Does Richard know that she's mine?" he asked.

"No," she said a little too quickly. "It was in our best interest for me to convince him that she was his."

Colin's gaze intensified on the map splayed out in front of him.

"You mean in *your* best interest," he said.

THE TRIP FOR supplies was uneventful. Dinner was quiet and the mood was heavy. Colin had set up the bassinet in one corner of the living room so they could keep watch over the baby while she slept. Melissa had washed the baby, fed her and then put the sleeping girl in her temporary bed. She turned around and faced Colin, who was doing a final review of the maps, no doubt ready to push off land soon.

"We need to talk," she said, motioning toward the chairs in the dining area near the sliding doors at the back of the boat.

Colin turned around and folded his arms.

"Teach me how to fight," she said.

"We don't exactly have a lot of time to train," he said, and his tense posture made her believe he was expecting a different conversation.

"We can use whatever time we have together," she said, determined.

"Our time will be better spent coming up with a strategy to deal with your husband," he said.

Hearing the word *husband* come out of Colin's mouth hit Melissa harder than a physical punch and yet she had married Richard. Technically, legally, she was still married to Richard even though her heart had never agreed.

But Richard didn't get to make her feel afraid anymore.

"I've had a lot of time to think about...*things*. I'm tired of feeling weak and like I can't defend myself. Surely, that makes sense to someone like you," she said, refusing to beg. If he didn't want to train her she'd figure out another way to learn. It was as simple as that.

"What do you think I'm here for?" he asked, a little indignant. "I'll handle whatever comes our way."

"I need to take care of myself." She stood and then stalked toward the door. "I thought you of all people would understand that."

Melissa stepped outside into the cool evening air and onto the decking. Seeing all that water around her made her nauseous and dizzy. She hopped onto stable ground and grabbed onto a beam that supported the overhead structure.

Emotions were a tidal wave building inside her. Thoughts of hiding, of playing along with Richard's plans for the past year ate away at her insides. Having to pretend everything was great when she was dying inside fueled the force of the crash that was to come. The waves were cresting and she needed an outlet.

Melissa glanced around before running onto the nearby bank. She crouched down and hugged her knees, looking across the water near the light from the boat dock. As her gaze traveled onto the waves she couldn't help but notice that there was so much darkness, so much unknown.

Richard had always liked to keep her guessing. He'd tell her that he was going on a business trip and would be away for a few days only to show up an hour later just to catch her off guard. There was always some excuse as to why the change in plans. Meeting canceled. Flight canceled. She knew the real reason was to check up on her and keep her on her toes. If she never knew when to expect him then she always had the feeling he could walk through the door at any minute. Too many months of her life had been spent in fear of that, of him.

Fury had her eyes burning with tears that needed release. It had been so very long since she'd allowed herself to really cry, to release all the pent-up emotions pressing against the dam she'd built inside. Twelve long months of trying to convince Richard that she loved him when her heart wanted to burst from the pain of leaving Colin. She'd had to hide the fact that she was mourning the loss of the only man she ever loved. Ever would love? She'd had to bury everything. Had that made her seem cold to the outside world? Probably. There was no denying the ice inside her chest—the ice wall that only Angelina had managed to crack, until seeing Colin again.

She thought about all the other times that Richard had said he was leaving for two days and then didn't return for a week or more. Those times were even worse. The persistent feeling that he could show at any second unannounced ensured that she wouldn't rest. She didn't dare pack or try to disappear because he could literally show up in a blink. A year. Twelve months. Every day had felt like a prison sentence, like being locked in solitary confinement. Protecting her father had been her initial marching order. And then Colin's father complicated the situation. Angelina had come along, giving Melissa a reason to live but also a reason to stay.

As long as Richard had thought the baby was his, she was given everything she could want. The best doctor in Tyler. The best care. And the best part was that he'd left her alone physically. But if he'd suspected for one minute that Angelina wasn't his...

Melissa couldn't even go there. She gave into the sobs racking her shoulders in sweet release. She would give herself a minute to mourn all that could've been and the horrible mess that her life had become. And then she would pick up the shattered pieces of her soul and move on.

Wiping tears from her cheeks, she rolled onto her stomach and started doing push-ups. Exercising had been her one haven and Richard had commented that he liked her body to be strong, so he didn't stop her.

If she had to figure out how to fight him on her own, so be it.

One. Two. She pushed off the cold hard earth. Three. Four. She continued, counting as she pushed up and then released down.

She went on like that...counting, pushing, counting, pushing until her arms burned and she could scarcely lift herself off the ground anymore. Melissa rolled onto her back, exhausted, and tried to catch her breath. Her chest rose and fell rapidly and her heart pounded in her chest. This was the first time she'd felt alive since leaving Bluff a year ago.

Movement out of the corner of her eye caught her off guard. She repositioned onto her belly again in order to get a better look, keeping her head low to the ground.

The figure moved toward her from the opposite direction of the boat.

She pushed to her feet. "Stop."

A male stepped into the clearing and she saw that it was Colin.

"Dammit, Colin. Why did you sneak up on me?"

"I didn't. You were emotional, angry and didn't pay enough attention to your surroundings," he said.

"How do you know what I felt?" she asked defensively.

He shot her a look that said he knew her better than that.

Melissa sat down on the cold earth and cradled her legs against her chest, watching the houseboat. "And?"

"That made you vulnerable. You think fighting is about hitting someone, but a bullet beats a fist every time," he said as he sat next to her. He motioned toward the boat. "Angelina is asleep. If she wakes, we'll be able to hear her from here."

Heat radiated off him and her body flushed with him this close. His scent washed over her, virile and musky and clean. His knee touched hers and an explosion of electricity sparked between them. He must've felt it, too, because he repositioned so that they didn't make contact.

"Tell me everything about your husband," he said. "The more I know, the better I can figure out how he'll come at us."

"First of all, I need you to stop calling him my husband," she said emphatically. "I was planning to divorce him."

It wasn't exactly the truth but she wouldn't have hesitated if the opportunity had arisen, and she'd been looking for an out from before she'd said *I do.*

"Why didn't you go to the police when you found out about his illegal activities?" Colin asked.

"I was afraid. He'd made it clear from day one of my pregnancy that if I ever went against him that losing my daughter would be the least of my worries," she said, keeping her gaze trained on the houseboat.

"So, he's the kind of guy who figures out what's important and then uses it against people. It also tells me that he isn't afraid to use his own flesh and blood to his advantage," he said. "Even though he thinks that Angelina is his, he would still use her against you."

If only Colin knew the extent to which Richard would make someone pay. Melissa nodded. "He has no soul."

"Then why get together with him in the first place?" he asked.

"My father. Richard threatened to have him jailed unless I married him."

"And you didn't think to come to me and talk about it?"

"There was nothing you could've done," she defended.

"We'll never know now." Colin paused. The flash of anger across his already intense features said that he was contemplating her words a little deeper. "Richard's desperate now. Anyone willing to shoot law enforcement doesn't feel like they have anything to lose. That will make him even more dangerous." Colin paused again. "On the flip side, since he shot and killed a US marshal and put a sheriff in the hospital, every single agency in law enforcement has eyes out for him right now. I'd put money on the fact that they want him as much as we do."

"Impossible," she said low, almost under her breath.

Colin didn't respond and for a second she thought that maybe he hadn't heard her.

"Agreed," he finally said, almost as quietly.

"He's smart and he has sophisticated channels to hide in," she said. "He's made it this far and he won't stop until I'm six feet underground and he has Angelina."

"First, he has to find you. Then, he has to plan his attack if he wants to get out alive and/or without spending the rest of his life behind bars," Colin offered. "Over my dead body he'll take my daughter away."

The words sat thickly in between them.

"I'm betting that he wants it all. Revenge and freedom. And I intend to complicate his plans even further. He'll have to get past me in order to get to either one of you," Colin said after a thoughtful pause.

"I hope you're right about him because that would give us more time. He's intelligent and can be very charismatic but his temper is his weakness. He believes that I wronged him when I betrayed him with the federal government and he'll want me to pay for that more than he wants to breathe. I've heard him say that he won't go back to prison," she said. How many times had he promised her that he'd kill their daughter in front of her eyes if she so much as spoke poorly of him to someone else? What she'd done to him was his worst nightmare come to life.

"A man who can't control his anger will make mistakes. He'll get too focused on revenge and miss an angle," Colin said. "That's where we capitalize."

"There was a man who'd lied to Richard about skimming money off the books," she said. "A week later that same man was found burned alive in his own home. His wife was bound to a chair secured to a wall post. If her mother hadn't been scheduled to come over for lunch the woman would've burned down with the house after watching her husband die."

"Did they have kids?" he asked.

"Three," she supplied. "They'd already left for school."

"Then, the wife must've been involved in the scam somehow," he said after a thoughtful pause.

"What do we do? Run forever trying to get away from him?" she asked, tamping down a wave of panic.

"I can't risk taking him on with you and Angelina here," he said. "For now, I keep you guys out of sight long enough for law enforcement to catch him. They will if we give them a chance."

"You don't think he'll get to my father?" she asked.

"Where is he?" Colin kept his gaze trained on the houseboat.

"All I've been told is that he's in a facility in the Pacific Northwest. That might not even be true." She rocked back and forth. "What if Richard figures it out and goes after my father to get to me?"

"We'll deal with it," Colin said. She wondered if he'd feel the same if he knew that her father was the reason she was in this situation.

"Maybe we should go there and pick him up to be safe," she said.

"Not a good idea," he quickly countered. "If you knew the name of the facility, I could send someone. But keep in mind he's in protective custody and they've most likely changed his name and location in anticipation of Richard finding the information from Marshal Davis."

He had a good point.

"There's no way for me to check in with the marshal's office, is there?" she asked.

"We need to stay focused on keeping you and Angelina safe," he said. "I'm sure they're doing everything in their power to keep your father protected and that's not who Richard wants anyway."

"He might use him to get to me," she said. "Or he could believe that my father was somehow involved in my decision to help the authorities."

Colin didn't immediately answer. "Those two were in business together, right?"

"Yes. My father got into trouble and Richard partnered with him to help out," she said.

"How?" Colin asked.

"Dad had a gambling problem and eventually it got so bad that he drained his company's cash. To keep business afloat, he started offering an investment opportunity to his suppliers," she said. Her dad had owned a successful auto repair business. "To keep them happy, he paid dividends using the money he'd get from new investors."

"He was running a Ponzi scheme?" he asked.

"Yes," she said. "Needless to say, it ballooned and he ended up in trouble."

"And Richard was there to help him out?" Colin asked.

She nodded. "Richard is smart. He figured out pretty quickly that I'd be willing to do most anything for my family."

Colin's jaw clenched and she suspected he was about to ask her something that she wasn't prepared to answer, like if that was the real reason she left him.

"The best thing you can do right now is keep a positive attitude. I know that can be difficult—"

"Try impossible," she said, thankful he'd moved on instead of pushing her.

"It's important, though. If we panic or lose focus a door will be cracked open for Richard to take advantage of," he said and, once again, he was making sense. "We can't afford to give him anything to work with. For now, we need to set our personal feelings aside."

"You're right." She said a little protection prayer for her father that she'd learned as a child. "I'll try not to dwell on what could happen."

"Good. We'll face what we have in front of us right now and deal with the rest as it comes, okay?" He glanced at her and she realized that statement covered so much more than hiding from Richard.

"I can deal with that," she said.

"I need to know more about Richard. What's important to him?" Colin asked.

"The first thing that comes to mind is his family. His mother probably sits at the top of that list. He puts her on a pedestal," she said, raising her flat palm high above her head. "I think she was suspicious of Angelina's birth. I mean, anyone who could do math and knew anything about pregnancy would have to have questions."

"Did Richard ever attempt the calculations?" he asked.

"He never went to doctor appointments or sonograms. I lied about the due date. Said she was born a month early," she said, remembering how much she'd wished that Colin could have been there.

"What about the birth?" he asked. "Surely the doctors would've given you away."

"I said that I wanted a home birth," she said. "I knew full well that he wouldn't have the stomach for that. He had no problem ordering the end of a man's life but he couldn't handle my morning sickness."

"What about his mother?" he asked.

"If she had questions she kept them to herself," she said. "I'm sure that she would've had suspicions in a few years. Angelina looks more and more like you every day."

"If his mother is important to him, we start with her." Colin stared at the waves battering against the shore. Winds had picked up and the spring thunderstorm was rolling in as promised. Some of the worst storms came late in the season after a cold winter. And this one had been freezing. Warm air clashed with frigid temperatures, causing all kinds of destruction where they met.

"She'll have protection around her 24/7," Melissa said as her hair whipped around her face, the intensity of the threatening storm growing.

"Is she in the family business?" Colin didn't budge. Not even when the first large droplets of rain splattered around them.

Before Melissa could respond, he launched toward her.

Chapter Nine

Melissa reacted quickly, rolling just out of Colin's reach. *Good.*

"Your reflexes are honed. I don't think I want to know why you automatically flinch when a man comes toward you, but I can work with your instincts," he said, lying chest down on the dirt.

Melissa threw a punch at him. He caught her fist in his hand.

"You're not fast enough to pull that off," he said. "We have to learn to work with what you've got."

"I thought we were using strategy to avoid confrontation," she said, staring at her hand.

Did she feel the same jolt of electricity pulsing through her hand and down her arm that he did? Colin didn't want to feel anything when he was around Melissa. "We are. And when that fails, you need to learn how to defend yourself long enough for help to arrive or to get away."

"You asked about his mother earlier. No, she's not in the family business, but that doesn't mean she's stupid to it. It's my observation that she accepts what they do and benefits from the lifestyle she gets out of it. It had never crossed my mind to enjoy a fortune that had been built on other people's blood as much as it had been built on criminal activity, but she didn't seem to mind." Melissa ran her finger along the dirt. "She has a driver, who is always with her. He wouldn't hesitate to shoot first and ask questions later."

"What about security at the family home?" he asked.

"It's rigged with a security system. I was never given the access code to his parents' house. There are dogs. It's probably not as good as the ranch but it would be hard to walk onto the property unnoticed," she said. "Someone's on foot at all times. I don't see guns but I'm sure the men are carrying."

"That could work to our benefit. If the weapons aren't visible then they'll be harder to reach. A few seconds could give us the advantage we need," he said.

"I can't go anywhere near the place without people knowing who I am," she said. "And I'm praying that you won't leave me and Angelina alone to fend for ourselves."

Melissa had brought up a good point. He couldn't exactly stash her and the baby somewhere while he walked into harm's way. He didn't know Richard well enough to be able to do proper risk analysis. The assignment to keep her and Angelina safe while the feds did their job was going to be challenging enough.

He needed to test her reflexes again now that she seemed relaxed.

Colin dove to his right.

Melissa flinched and then drew back but wasn't fast enough.

He was on top of her in a half second, pinning her to the ground. This wasn't the time to notice how good her body felt pressed against his. The outside of her legs were being secured by his thighs and warmth shot through him at the contact.

Out of nowhere a thunderclap of need caused his body to vibrate. He shut out the images of being in this position with her, her legs wrapped around his waist as he buried himself deep inside her.

The shock of that deep-seeded desire knocked him off balance enough for her to push him off her. He didn't resist because he'd been so caught off guard that he didn't know what to do with it. He wanted to keep on resenting her for what she'd done to him. He sure as hell didn't want to feel that same old fire that had been incredible while it burned bright and had threatened to consume him in its shadow.

"Colin, are you okay?" Her voice broke through the raging thoughts in his head.

"Yeah, of course." He finally looked up to see her leaning over him, her brows knitted in concern.

"What happened a minute ago?" she asked. "It's like you mentally checked out."

"It was nothing. That's enough for one day." He forced himself upright. Rain had started coming down faster and they needed to get inside the boat. "Time to get ready to bunk down for the night."

Melissa visibly shook. She'd always been scared of being near water. Colin didn't like putting her in this position any more than he liked the bigger situation they faced. He hoped she could take it. Plan B was to sleep in the truck but they'd get better quality rest inside the houseboat, so that was his first choice. And especially since Richard liked to exploit people's weaknesses. Anger burned inside Colin at what Melissa had had to put up with being with Richard.

Even though it had been her decision to pick Richard over him—and he'd licked plenty of wounds over her choice—he wasn't the kind of person who'd wish the life she'd signed up for on his worst enemy, and especially not on someone who'd meant so much to him at one point in his life. He refused to allow himself to think there could be any more to his feelings than that. And he sure as hell didn't want to think about what had happened back there on the shoreline as he helped her onto the boat.

"You can have first dibs on the shower," he said to Melissa. "I can keep an eye on the little bug."

She checked on her daughter. *Their daughter.*

"I'll just be a minute," she said, holding on to the counter so tightly that her knuckles turned white.

He and Melissa had a lot to talk about in the very near future. For now, all he could allow himself to think about was Richard.

Colin steered away from the slip and watched out the window as he navigated the boat to Buckner Cove. Lightning flashed sideways across the night sky. The tat-tat-tat of rain on the upstairs deck filled the room.

Colin idled the engine, doing his level best not to think about the fact that Melissa was naked in the shower not twenty away feet from him. He dropped anchor, shut off the engine and pocketed the key.

The houseboat was a rental so there were no clothes he could borrow on board. He'd have to hand wash his own in the sink and let them dry.

He rinsed out the basin and filled it with soapy water. Then he moved to the bathroom and knocked on the door.

"I need your clothes," he said.

"They're on the counter," came the shaky response.

Colin cracked the door open. His body reacted to the silhouette in the shower. He diverted his eyes before his imagination took over, focusing instead on the pile of clothes on the counter.

"Got 'em," he said, anxious to close the door.

Washing Melissa's pale purple silk panties by hand wasn't at the top of Colin's list of things he'd wanted to do today, but they needed clean clothes. He rinsed out her undergarments before placing a towel on the back of the sofa and laying them out to dry. Her blouse and jeans were next.

By the time she emerged from the bathroom, his clothes were clean, hanging to dry, and he was wrapped in a towel waiting his turn. Angelina was still sleeping. The gentle sway of the boat seemed to rock her into a deep slumber.

He was grateful for dim lights. He didn't want to see every detail of her body. As it was, he could see that the beige towel wrapped around her fell mid-thigh. Her long, silky legs were exposed.

"Your turn," she said, gripping the top of her towel like she was dangling from a ledge and the piece of cloth was the only thing between her and dropping to a certain death.

He grunted as he walked past, ignoring all the impulses firing in his body that told him to take her in his arms.

Once inside the shower, he blasted cold water and stood under the spout. His body might want what his brain knew better than to desire but that wouldn't stop him from cooling his jets. He wasn't a reckless kid anymore, and since he'd been old enough to drive a tractor he'd stopped thinking about casual sex. Good sex was another story altogether. He was up for that pretty much anytime. But he was also old enough to know that if he put his hand directly into a fire he'd get burned.

He'd done that once already.

After talking to Melissa about Richard, another picture was starting to emerge. It was probably just Colin's ego talking, but he wondered whether or not leaving him had been her choice. Had Richard done something to her? Threatened her? What could he possibly have over Melissa that would make her walk away from the life they'd planned? He already knew about her father but was there something else? Colin believed, at the time at least, that she'd wanted marriage and a family with him as much as he'd wanted those things with her.

Was he blinded to the reality that someone could swoop in and offer her more? That she could run toward more security?

All her words from a year ago wound through his thoughts... *I don't love you anymore. Not the way that I did when we first met. There's someone else.*

Once the writing was on the wall and she was determined to leave him, he'd closed off his emotions. What they'd had between them had been genuine and real. Or at least that's what he'd believed. What a lovesick fool he'd been. If their feelings had been genuine and equal on both sides—necessary for a shot at a good marriage—she wouldn't have been able to walk away so easily.

Thinking back, it had all happened so fast. Literally, the change in her had been like someone had flipped a switch. Colin remembered being the happiest he'd ever been with his whole life planned out with the woman he loved. He'd been so convinced that she'd been *the one*. And then, like a curveball slamming him in the face while he batted air, his entire world had been tilted on its axis and he had an empty hole in his chest. He'd been left with the burning question…how did he not see this coming?

Part of him wanted to step out of the shower and demand answers. The other part wanted to hurt her in return, let her see how it felt to have her world pulled out from underneath her in the blink of an eye. He was too much of a man to go that route. And he could see that had already happened to her even if he didn't understand the whole situation yet.

He finished his shower and dried off before wrapping the towel around his waist and returning to the other room.

Her gaze flickered across his bare chest and then she quickly turned to face the other direction.

"What's wrong? Afraid you'll offend your husband by seeing another man with his shirt off?" he asked, his anger having returned. It was a low blow but he'd been wallowing in self-pity in the shower. *Damn it, O'Brien.* He was a better man than that.

Before he could apologize, she whirled around on him.

"You want me to look at you?" she asked, all fire and sass. "You want me to admit that I missed you? Fine. I did, Colin. I missed you and I'm sorry that I hurt you, but the past year hasn't exactly been a picnic for me, either, so if you want to hurt me even more just know that you can't."

He was close enough to see the tears streaming down her cheeks.

Ah, hell. He hadn't meant to cause that.

"You want to know what my life was like?" she pushed. "Do you *really want to know*?"

He opened his mouth to apologize but she shut him down again.

"Imagine the worst day you've ever had…the day you found out your parents were…*gone*…imagine waking up every day and *that* moment replaying over and over again. That moment being your life." Her eyes were wild and he'd never seen her like this before. "And then imagine that whoever did that to them was after someone else you loved and there was nothing you could do to stop it. People were getting hurt all around you and you had no power to stop it."

"Tell me what he did to you, Melissa," he said. He needed to hear the words.

"If it would change anything, I'd be all for it," she said. "Right now, all I can think about is staying alive so that I can take care of my little girl. I get that you hate me. I hurt you and I probably deserve whatever anger you whirl at me. But my life has been hell and I just want this nightmare to end. Nothing else matters until it does."

Colin wasn't normally at a loss for words. Standing there in the kitchen, her body vibrating from anger, he couldn't think of one positive thing to say to calm her down. His own body was chorded with tension, strung so tight he thought his muscles might snap, so he threw all rationale to the wind, pulled her into his arms and kissed her.

Her muscles tensed against him and he half figured she'd pull away and throw a punch like she had on the shore. Instead, she leaned into him and popped up onto her tiptoes to deepen the kiss. Colin groaned against her mouth and then pulled back.

All he'd hoped to do was calm her down, not stir up a bunch of...*feelings*. That kiss was like a shotgun blast to the chest and stirred up an inappropriate reaction down south. He took a step back, put his hands behind him and gripped the edge of the counter to keep from doing any further damage. The thought that both of them were naked underneath their towels wasn't the one he wanted to have.

"That shouldn't have happened," Melissa said.

"Agreed."

"It won't happen again," she continued.

He crossed his arms over his chest and smirked. "Well, it shouldn't."

She laughed and it was the first real break in tension since seeing her again. Thunder cracked and she flinched. It was the same reaction she'd had to him making a move toward her on the bank. Another second ticked by and she recovered.

He wanted to ask her what that was all about but figured better of it.

"Now what do we do?" she asked, diverting her eyes from whatever she'd been staring at on his chest.

Colin located the throwaway phone and then held it up on the flat palm of his right hand. "First, we check on Tommy."

"Can we do that without giving away our location?" she asked.

"Yes." He held up his hand and nodded. He called the main number to Bluff General, a number he'd committed to memory when his parents had been admitted, a number he didn't want to have to know.

"Can you connect me to a volunteer on the second floor?" he asked when the operator answered.

"Yes, sir," the calm, pleasant and practiced female voice on the other end of the line said.

After a few seconds of elevator music, a chipper voice chimed in. "This is Renee. How may I help you?"

"I'm wondering if you can do me a huge favor," he said.

"Okay." Renee sounded excited.

Good.

"In Room 207 will be a visitor named Mr. O'Brien. If you could ask him if the package I sent made it to its destination, I'd sure be able to sleep a whole lot better tonight," he said. He didn't need to know which brother was in the room but he knew for certain one of them would be there. Giving the last name would cut down on any confusion because any of his brothers would be able to figure out the cryptic message.

"Who should I tell him wants to know?" she asked, ever perky.

"This is Cardin from Dan's Delivery Service," he said. All of his brothers would remember the nickname one of the twins gave him when they were little. Two-year-old Joshua had said *Cardin* instead of *Colin* and it had stuck for a few years.

"Okay, sir. Would you mind holding?" she asked.

"Not at all," Colin said.

It took a full five minutes for her to return.

"I'm sorry, sir. The room is empty."

Chapter Ten

"What do you mean the room's empty?" Colin asked. Those last three words echoed in Melissa's head as all the air was sucked out of the room in a whoosh.

News like that couldn't be good. Tommy was stable last night. He'd been moved to a recovery area.

Melissa centered herself by gripping the edge of the table.

"Has the patient been moved?" he asked, and then she heard him give Tommy's name.

The silence sent cold chills down Melissa's spine.

"Can you check at the nurse's stand?" he asked, his gaze intensely focused on a spot on the floor. "Yes, I'll hold."

Melissa moved next to Colin and then he tilted the earpiece so that she could hear.

"The patient was moved. I'm not authorized to give his room number but you'll be happy to know that your package arrived safely and all is well. We paged Mr. O'Brien and he confirmed receipt," she said with a self-satisfied tone.

"Thanks, Renee. It means a lot to have that confirmed," he said, and Melissa could hear the relief in his voice.

"You betcha. Anything else I can help with tonight?" she chirped.

"That's it for tonight," he said before wishing her a good evening and ending the call.

A flash of light was followed by a brilliant thunderclap that felt like it was directly on top of them.

Melissa flinched at the same time she gasped.

Colin looked at her and his gaze sent goose bumps up her arms—goose bumps that were totally inappropriate under the circumstances. Then again, so was that kiss, and she couldn't stop thinking about it.

"It's late and you should probably try to get some rest," he said.

Melissa released a deep breath. Relief was quickly replaced by anger. Richard had put her in this position in the first place. He'd tortured her for twelve long months. It was time to make it stop. She turned to face Colin. There wasn't more than a foot between them and she could see his pulse pound at the base of his throat no matter how calm his facade remained.

"What are we going to do to find that jerk?" she asked.

"We're not." Colin's shoulders were tense, belying his casual words.

"I know what you said about staying hidden until they catch him, but how long is that going to take?" she asked. "How much longer do I have to wait?"

"Good question," he said. "One I don't have an answer to."

"We can't just stay here and hide. He'll find us eventually," she said, hoping she was getting through.

"You're frustrated and I get that, but we have another priority right now." He stared at the bassinet. "I want to go after the guy more than—"

She shot him a look that said, "Impossible."

He put up a hand. "Okay, as much as you do. But we made the decision to keep Angelina with us and as long as she's here, we can't risk a direct approach."

Colin was making perfect sense and yet she wasn't ready to concede. Her body was chorded with tension and there'd be no break until Richard was behind bars.

"It's only been one day," Colin reasoned. Again, he was making sense that she wasn't quite ready to accept. "We have to give it a little more time, Melissa."

He'd made good points. The farther Angelina was from Richard, the safer she'd be. Obviously, her daughter was her first priority.

"I'm just so angry and frustrated," she said.

Colin launched toward her.

She ducked but not in time. His arms closed around her midsection and all kinds of unwanted sensations trilled through her body.

He pinned her against the counter with his large frame.

"You need to be ready at all times. When you let your emotions run wild, you lose focus," he said, and his voice was a deep growl that poured over her.

With his body flush with hers, his muscled chest against her breasts, it was impossible to think.

And then the rain pattering on the rooftop seemed to stop. The world felt as though it stopped spinning as everything stilled. All Melissa could hear was her heart pounding inside her chest. All she could feel was the heat and electricity pinging between the two of them. All she wanted to do was reach up and kiss Colin again.

Pupils large, lips compressed, he appeared to be as surprised by the instant change in chemistry as she'd been.

"You take the bed. I'll bunk down for the night on the couch," he said after a long pause.

COLIN LAY ON the couch, facing the ceiling. Thunder cracked in the sky overhead and he half expected Melissa to bolt through the door or the baby to wake. Neither budged. He flipped onto his side. The thin blanket covering him slipped off and landed on the floor. He picked up the tan piece of cotton and repositioned, trying to get comfortable. The material wasn't much bigger than the bath towel Melissa had been wearing earlier. Sleep was about as realistic as an ice storm in a Texas summer.

He sat up. Something was bothering him and he couldn't quite pinpoint what it was. Melissa wasn't telling him everything. It was clear that she was afraid of her husband—correction, her soon-to-be ex. And there was something else niggling at the back of his mind.

Obviously Rancic was a ruthless criminal. Figuring out how to find him wasn't as cut-and-dried, especially with Angelina in the picture. Taking care of a three-month-old was already a full-time job—forget trying to track down a criminal while keeping the baby out of harm's way.

Colin peeked inside the bassinet. The thought that he and Melissa had a daughter together sent his mind into a tailspin. At one time, this had been the plan. And then, like a tornado touching down, everything had changed. He'd done his best to move on in the past twelve months. Events of the past twenty-four hours already had his mind whirling.

He had questions, not the least of which was why she'd married Richard in the first place. It was becoming obvious there was so much more to the story, especially given how afraid she was of the guy. Colin told himself that the only reason he cared was because his daughter was involved and it had nothing to do with the feelings resurfacing for Melissa.

His daughter. Those two words would take getting used to. Angelina wasn't the problem. That little thing with big brown eyes and just enough curly black hair on her head to make her adorable was an angel. To be fair, he'd believed her to be a cutie even before he realized she belonged to him.

Colin had grown up around brothers. He had five of his own: Dallas, Austin, Tyler, and the twins, Ryder and Joshua. Then, there was Tommy. He'd grown up on the ranch as one of the boys. Colin didn't have the first idea what to do with a girl. He'd figure it out, though.

First, he'd deal with Rancic.

As far as figuring out the future, Colin hadn't given himself time to think about more than the next hour or two. One thing was certain. That precious girl deserved to have two parents with their acts together.

Another bolt of lightning lit up the room. A loud *crack* sounded.

This time, Angelina stirred. Colin moved even closer to her, standing over her bassinet. It was one thing to be handed a baby from someone else. How the heck did he pick her up without hurting her?

Her big eyes opened and she blinked up at him. Her whimper nearly cracked his heart in half.

There was no sign of Melissa and he had no idea how to fix the formula. He didn't want his little girl crying any longer than she had to.

After a couple of aborted attempts, he finally secured

her head with one hand as he bent down close enough to lift her to his chest with the other. She was wiggly and felt a little too loose in his hands. His heart squeezed at the thought of even the slightest possibility of dropping her. There was no way he would allow that to happen. He hugged her firmly and bounced up and down.

The boat was already rocking them from side to side, making Colin unsure about his footing. He didn't like that. Angelina was winding up for what promised to be a loud cry based on his limited experience with her so far. He took a few steps toward the bedroom pocket door that was closed.

Angelina's cries were heartbreaking. As much as he wanted to leave Melissa alone, he realized that he couldn't do this without her.

"I know you're hungry. Let's go wake up your mom," Colin soothed, wishing he was further along on the learning curve of taking care of his daughter.

He made it halfway to the door when it opened.

"Sick," she said. Melissa's face was white. On closer inspection, maybe a little green. She looked torn between taking her crying baby in her arms and being afraid she might throw up on her.

"Tell me what to do," he said.

"She likes singing," she said.

"Tell me something else to do. My singing will make her cry even more," he said, bouncing as gently as he could.

"A bottle." Melissa's hand came up. She covered her mouth. The weather wasn't cooperating. It had the boat rocking back and forth.

"Trash can's under the sink," he said.

She held on to the wall to keep her balance as she

moved. He followed her. Everything he needed for the baby was in the diaper bag and the kitchen, and he wanted to make sure that Melissa was okay.

The waves were big enough outside to make moving around on the boat a challenge. Navigating out of the cove in this weather wasn't a good option, either. They needed to stay the course. His only solace was Rancic was nowhere around. Keeping Angelina and Melissa safe was his first priority.

Melissa was getting sick in the bathroom. The baby was crying. The storm raged outside. It seemed intent on not giving them a break.

"I'm sorry," Melissa managed to say in between heaves.

"You're doing fine" he said calmly. She needed reassurance as much as Angelina needed her bottle. Both were urgent and he needed to be the calm in the storm for both of them.

"There's a formula packet in the diaper bag. First, you put the plastic liner in the bottle and then add the powder," she said. "I'll heat water in the microwave."

She worked quickly in between heaves.

Colin somehow managed to get the liner inside the plastic bottle and the packet of powder where it needed to go. That he managed to pull any of it off without spilling a speck of powder was nothing short of a miracle.

"How can you possibly be smiling?" Melissa asked and she broke into a smile, too, as she helped finish up the bottle.

He just shook his head and kept on grinning.

Angelina immediately settled down as soon as she started sucking on the nipple and the warm milk passed her lips.

"Hearing her cry is the worst," Colin said, situating himself on a chair in the kitchen so he could hold his daughter more comfortably without fear of dropping her.

"Believe me, I know," she said. "She sounds so pitiful."

He nodded.

"The first few weeks were awful. She'd cry and I didn't have the first idea how to handle it. I just wanted to comfort her but I felt like I was doing everything wrong. Then, I don't know, I guess I started getting more confident with being a mother," she said.

Melissa had been an only child and didn't grow up close to cousins. Colin knew that it had just been her, and she'd often commented about how lucky he'd been to have so many brothers around. Of course, he'd joke about how messy the bathroom had been but he wouldn't change his childhood for the world. Yeah, his family had money and they hadn't wanted for anything. But Dad had built his fortune from the ground up and had never forgotten his roots. And maybe that's why their family fortune was nothing but zeroes in a bank account to Colin. Looking at her now, he wondered if he'd placed more emphasis on giving her material things if she would've left him for Richard in the first place.

It was the pain talking. He chalked it up to wounded pride. In his heart he realized that he'd never want to be with a person who cared more about his bank account than building a real life with him. Money was important, don't get him wrong, but it didn't guarantee a person's happiness. Aunt Bea and Uncle Ezra were prime examples. Dad had given them both a small piece of his business so that they'd be taken care of in their later years and yet all the two of them ever did was argue. Money couldn't bring his parents back. Or give him more time with the people he loved. But he was also realizing that money was only part of the reason Melissa had left. She hadn't trusted him enough to tell him what was going on.

"You look much better," he said. Her color was returning and her cheeks were flushed.

She rinsed her mouth out and then splashed water on her face. "It's been a crazy few days, hasn't it?"

"Nothing we can't deal with," he said.

"So what made you smile before?" she asked.

"All of this. Being on a boat in a storm with you. The fact that I have a daughter," he said. "I guess this scenario amused me. This is pretty much the last place on earth I expected to be and the situation we're in is even more bizarre. I'm not exactly one to run the other way from trouble."

"No, you're not," she agreed.

"When she was crying a few minutes ago, I'd never felt so helpless in my life," he admitted. "She seems so little, so fragile."

"I felt the same way when I first held her," Melissa said, and she had a wistful look in her eyes. "I was pretty sure that I was going to mess up the whole parenting thing. Not being able to breastfeed was a big blow in that department. But then I started slowly figuring things out and we started to get into a routine. I think she likes a schedule, actually."

Colin glanced down. The liner was almost empty. "She was hungry."

"You should stop before she sucks air. It'll make her tummy hurt," Melissa said.

He gently pulled the bottle out of his daughter's mouth. Being able to feed her and give her what she needed brought on a surprising bout of emotions. It felt good.

"We should get her burped and changed, and then we'll be good for another four hours or so. Sometimes I get five or six," Melissa said, walking toward him. He handed over the baby and watched as Melissa placed their daughter against her right shoulder. She patted the little girl's back until she made a few gurgling noises and then belched.

"She has strong lungs. There's no doubt about that," Colin said as he followed Melissa into the next room.

"Can you bring a diaper and the package of wipes?" Melissa positioned their daughter as he grabbed supplies. Angelina was sound asleep and didn't stir.

He handed the items to her and watched her fluid movements as she changed the baby's diaper. There was something so natural about being with Melissa again. Seeing how much she loved their daughter. It had to be a sign that she'd given their daughter the name they'd picked out. Those thoughts confused the hell out of him when he considered what she'd done to him.

"I hear the moms on the ranch say the same thing about having their babies on a routine," he offered, trying to give some reassurance.

"She's doing really well considering the fact that our world has been turned upside down in a second," Melissa said.

Was she regretting turning over evidence on Rancic? Colin's defenses kicked in.

"Did you mean being on the run from your husband?" he asked, and she shot him a look when he said the last word. It was true. She was married to Richard.

"I wish you'd stop reminding me of that," she said under her breath. She placed the baby in the bassinet and stalked out of the room.

Chapter Eleven

By the time the sun came up, Colin needed a strong cup of black coffee more than he needed air. There was no way he was going to leave Melissa or the baby alone to get one, though.

He woke with the last words spoken between him and Melissa fresh on his mind. Seeing her and the baby together, knowing Angelina was his, threatened to chip away at his armor and leave him exposed. The two looked so natural together and they felt like his family.

Colin couldn't believe his own stupidity. He'd started tripping down the road that could only lead to disaster with Melissa. He mentally slapped himself for momentarily forgetting just how burned he'd been before.

Don't get too comfortable, O'Brien.

Darkness loomed on the horizon and Colin needed to focus all his attention on keeping his daughter and Melissa safe.

At least the storm had abated, if only for a little while. He'd checked the weather and it was supposed to be even worse that evening. Melissa had barely made it through last night. There was no way she'd survive worse. With severe lightning in the forecast, he didn't want to take a chance and stay on the boat. He'd have to scout a better location before the next round of storms rolled in.

Being on the run with a three-month-old wasn't exactly an ideal scenario. He'd thought about it all night and Melissa had had a point. They couldn't hide forever. Richard or one of his men would catch up to them sooner or later, and they were vulnerable while traveling with the baby. Colin couldn't even contemplate going after the man while Angelina was with them. They were stuck between a place of needing to protect their daughter and stopping the threat.

He stared at the dark-haired angel happily sleeping in her bassinet. The fact that he was a father was starting to sink in. There was no doubt that he'd do everything he could for his daughter. For a flicker, he thought about asking Melissa for custody, but he couldn't see her going for that after watching their bond last night. She wasn't an unfit mother. In fact, when he'd watched her feed the baby again at the crack of dawn, he'd been awed at how much she loved that little girl. She sang a soothing song and he'd pretended to be asleep to give them privacy.

Awe was great, but there was no way he was confusing that for real feelings between him and Melissa. As far as Colin was concerned, that ship had sailed. He needed to remind himself of the fact often because it was all too easy to forget when he saw her with his daughter.

The door to the bedroom opened at first light and Melissa walked into the room looking like she'd had about as good a night's sleep as he did.

"Storm passed," he said. In daylight he could really see the dark circles cradling her eyes.

"Yeah, about an hour ago," she said. Even though she walked like a zombie, she looked good. He tried not to think about the pale purple undergarments he'd washed yesterday—the ones she was wearing—as she checked on the baby.

"I figure I'll go into town for supplies early before folks are up and moving. Pick up some coffee," he said.

She plopped down on the couch next to him. It didn't help that when he'd tried to sleep there'd been a metal rod beneath the too-thin cushion that had poked his back all night.

"You didn't get any rest, did you?" she asked. "I can tell when you're tired. Your voice gets deep and your eyes are even darker."

"Don't need much sleep to function," he said, telling himself that he didn't care how well she knew him. "I got enough to do what needs to be done today. That's all that matters."

"Military training kicking in again?" she asked.

He nodded again and then rubbed the scruff on his chin.

"Coffee sounds like heaven right now," she said. "Did you check the cupboard to see if there was any?"

"At about four o'clock this morning," he said. "We can head out whenever you're ready."

"Just let me brush my teeth and wash my face," she said, pushing off the couch. "Then I'll need to wake Angelina, of course. She fed a little while ago so she won't need to eat again for a few hours. We're good there."

Colin had already brushed his teeth and was ready to go. His muscles were sore from the uncomfortable position he'd been in during the night. He moved to the hallway, took off his shirt and set it on the bench seat in the dining room. He dropped down for a few morning push-ups to get the blood pumping. There was someone in the next room who got other parts of him stirring by walking into a room.

Colin didn't need to think about her right now.

WAKING TO SEE shirtless Colin holding their daughter against his chest last night, sick or not, made Melissa's heart free-fall. They'd had a few good moments before he'd armored up again. She could understand if he couldn't have feelings for her anymore but she hoped that one day he'd be able to forgive her.

When her father had come to her with the proposal for her to marry Richard in order to get him out of a bad business deal, she'd laughed. In her mind, there was no way he could be serious. But then he'd sat her down at the table and fixed a pot of coffee. That was the routine saved for grave moments, like when he'd told her that her mother had gone to heaven and wasn't coming back. That the two of them were a team now.

Melissa's heart pounded against her chest just thinking about it.

Her father had poured two cups and set one down in front of her. He'd taken the seat across the table before clasping his hands and resting his elbows on the table.

"This is serious," he'd said with that same ominous tone he'd used on the warm summer morning, too low and too calm.

Melissa's chest had squeezed as she'd tried to force herself to breathe.

"I'm in trouble and I could go away for a long time if word gets out. Richard has offered an escape route."

Her father's face had looked so anguished. "I think we should take it."

Thinking about her own daughter, the strong need to protect her above all else, Melissa couldn't fathom taking away that choice for her. Because once it was out there that Richard was the only salvation, that it was about more than just getting the money to pay Richard back, she would have no other choice but to agree. Her father had been the first to say that he'd gladly swallow his pride and ask the O'Briens for help if that were the case. Colin had plenty of money even if Melissa didn't and they were known for being a generous family.

Maybe Melissa could've gone to her fiancé for help. Part of her never really could completely trust a man after some of her father's actions over the years. Another part didn't have the heart to go to Colin. Would it have been embarrassing? Yes. But she trusted their relationship enough to realize that Colin would've done what it took to bail out her father. But Richard had evidence against her father that would send him to jail.

Could she have talked to Colin? The problem was that he would've sought revenge if he'd known that it hadn't been her choice to leave. He would've kept coming back, and her heart couldn't take seeing him once she'd agreed to marry Richard. And in order to keep her father from going to jail, she'd had to marry Richard.

When she'd gotten cold feet at the last minute and said she needed more time, Richard's brother had visited her. He'd made it clear that no one hurt his family. And then there was the threat to Colin's family.

Her heart thudded.

Everything had happened so fast. In hindsight, she

might've handled things differently. But she'd done the best she could under the circumstances.

"I've been thinking about a few possibilities to bring the fight to Richard's doorstep. I keep coming around to one. We have to pull him out of hiding and get him back in the area. We have to—"

Melissa held her hand up. Richard could still play his card against the O'Brien family and they needed to be prepared.

"Before we go down this road any further, I need to tell you something, Colin." She left no room for doubt with the seriousness of those words. A lump was forming in her throat and she didn't want to be the one to tell him this news—news that could shatter him.

Colin motioned toward the small kitchen table with a three-sided bench seat, the back of which was attached to the wall. Talking to him while she wore an oversized T-shirt with the word *Bahamas* plastered across the front made her so much more aware of how vulnerable she felt being close to him.

"Give me a minute to get dressed and then we'll talk," she said. Was a part of her stalling for time? Probably. She'd need a minute to gather her resolve. Colin needed to hear this from her, not read it in the papers or be ambushed by the news or however Richard deemed appropriate to deliver it.

"Your clothes are still damp," he warned.

"I don't care." She gathered her garments and took them into the bedroom. She returned a few minutes later feeling more like she could handle what she needed to say. She knew how much he loved his parents, and hearing something like this after losing them would be a hard blow. But she'd rather be the one to tell him because if he planned to draw Richard out, then he needed to know exactly what weapons the man had in his arsenal. Information could be just as damaging as a knife.

She took a seat across from Colin, noticing that he'd put on his jeans. Maybe he'd picked up on her discomfort at being scarcely covered.

"I don't know how he knew this or why, but Richard will come after your family with something very damaging," she began, twisting her fingers together as she spoke.

"There's nothing he can do to hurt my family. The ranch is secure," he said, but she untangled her fingers and held a hand up to stop him. He needed to hear this. From her.

"I'm not saying that he'll physically attack or try to get past security. I know Gideon can handle whatever comes at him in Bluff. I just think that if we're considering going after his family, you should know the way in which he'll come after yours." She was dancing around the topic, stalling as long as she could. She needed to gather her strength. The problem was that she loved his parents. When she'd first heard the news she denied it, not wanting to accept that it could be real. But then he'd shown her the pictures and she couldn't deny it any longer...

"Richard has proof that your father was—" she took in a deep breath and looked him straight in the eye "—having an affair."

"Oh, yeah? What does he think he has?" Colin asked calmly, surprisingly unaffected by the bomb she'd just dropped.

"He had pictures of your father with another woman,"

she said, and her eyebrow must've risen because Colin smirked. "What?"

"If I had a nickel for every time a random person tried to accuse someone in my family of doing something wrong, I'd be a rich man," he quipped.

"I hate to point out the obvious, but you already are a rich man," she countered.

"I'd be even wealthier," he said, and then took a casual sip of water.

"So, you don't believe me?" Melissa balked.

"Oh, no. I believe you one hundred percent."

"Then fill me in because I'm confused," she said.

"Pictures don't mean anything. There are so many ways to doctor them with computer programs. Surely, you know that," he said.

"Nothing about these looked fake," she said. "I must've checked them a dozen times."

"Did you recognize the woman? We can track her down and ask if it would make you feel better," he said.

"These pictures get out and it'll hurt your family business if not your relationships with each other. This is your parents we're talking about, Colin," she said, not willing to accept that she'd sacrificed the past year and lost the love of her life over potentially fake photos. Obviously, there'd been more to it than that. Richard had been blackmailing her father and threatening him with jail. No matter what else was false, that was true.

But she'd gotten through more than 365 horrible days by reminding herself that she was doing this for Colin's family, as well. It had somehow eased some of the pain of being forced to walk away from him.

Of course, figuring out she was six weeks pregnant two weeks into her marriage had complicated things even further. Richard must've realized she could never have real feelings for him, and why he seemed content with a facade she would never know. Richard was a collector. He liked to buy shiny things and look at them on the shelves in his office. She was never more than another shiny object to him.

"If a couple of pictures could bring down the foundation of our business or our relationships with each other, they weren't strong to begin with." He shrugged it off, but his gaze intensified on her.

She could read between the lines. He was saying that if a little squall like Richard could destroy their relationship, it wasn't much of one.

"That's not true. Houses can be brought down by a ten-minute dust storm and you know it," she said a little too quickly.

"Again, it wasn't much of a house if it could be brought down by a couple of strong winds." He folded his arms across his chest.

It was pretty clear that he wasn't talking about his parents any longer. This conversation was at a standstill.

Her mind was bouncing all over the place, especially in contrast to how calm Colin was being. While he'd been the cool, casual brother for the most part, he'd also had a quick temper and could make snap judgments about situations and people. It was part of the reason she didn't want to drag him into the situation with her father. She'd feared that he'd go off half-cocked and make everything so much worse. It was hard to imagine life could become more complicated than it had.

Colin had changed in the past year. Grown up. He seemed so much more…centered and in control. Don't get her wrong, half the excitement of their relationship had been due to his unpredictable nature. She'd never known what to expect from one day to the next except that she never had to question how much he loved her. That part had been secure.

And they could talk for hours. He was the only person on earth who really knew her and understood her. His impulsive and unpredictable side had been so much a part of his charm and worked even better at seducing her.

But then that was the past. So much had changed in the last year.

"I guess I was wrong then," she said. "But what makes you so sure he didn't have an affair?"

"If he did, that was between my parents. Neither said anything to us and so I have to trust that they believed what they had was worth fighting for and they worked it out. Here's the thing I can be certain about. They had a strong marriage and that would be impossible to have without total honesty," he said so automatically, so naturally.

She wished she had half his confidence.

"I'm more concerned with why my parents' marriage would even come up in a conversation between you and your...ex," he said, those intense dark eyes staring right into her.

"We had a fight and I threatened to walk out," she said, and that was partially true. "He thought I was still in love with you and said that if I ran back to you he'd destroy your family. I didn't believe that he could so he showed me."

"You threatened to leave him from the beginning?" Colin asked, and she was glad that he left alone the part about her still being in love with him.

"It was early in our marriage," she said. "And like I said, we'd had a fight."

"What was the argument really about?" he asked.

She just stared at him for a long moment. And then she said, "You."

"Why would you and your hus…" he glanced at her with an apologetic look, "*ex* be talking about me at all? You were pretty clear with your feelings when you threw my engagement ring at me and walked out."

Those words were impossible to hear coming out of Colin's mouth. They were like daggers being thrown and it didn't matter how relaxed his tone came across— she knew there was pain on his side, too.

Melissa pushed off the table and walked into the bedroom.

"Hold on a sec," Colin said, trailing after her into the small hallway that lead to the bathroom and bedroom. His hand pressed to her shoulder and suddenly she was being whirled around to face him in the hallway. The space felt small a second ago and even more so now that she was standing there with Colin. His big frame blocked out all the light from the other room. The bedroom door was four steps behind her and the bathroom was to her left. Even though the boat had stopped rocking, it felt like the world tilted with him so close.

And she was trapped between two closed doors, a wall and Colin. Not that it mattered. Where could she go? She was trapped in the middle of a lake with him.

The boat was still but talking about the past, bringing up all those intense feelings she'd had when she'd left Colin, was starting to make her feel sick again. "I need to go. I have to get off here and figure something else out. This isn't working."

Chapter Twelve

Melissa didn't want to look Colin in the face or let him see that she was about to cry.

"Don't run away from me, Melissa," he said. "Not this time."

"Low blow, Colin," she shot back, trying to regain her equilibrium.

"Is it? You keep running and I'm just trying to help you," he said. "You're not telling me everything. I still know you well enough to know that. And that's fine if you don't want to talk to me. I get that there are things between a husband and a wife that other people don't need to know. I can see that you don't trust me. You didn't before and that's most likely why you walked out in the first place."

Melissa sucked in a burst of air.

"You don't think I believed in you?" She fired the words like buckshot. "In us? After everything I've told you? You still don't get it?"

"Don't worry about it. I've learned to deal. It's fine. I'm still going to figure out a way to get to Richard and take him down. I'm still going to figure out a way to make sure you and our daughter are safe from your husband," he said.

"Stop calling him my husband," Melissa barked. Anger and frustration got the best of her and she was shaking. Maybe it was the fact that her nerves were still fried from being on this boat in a storm last night. Wasn't that just her luck? Or maybe it was because she still had the same feelings for Colin that she did a year ago and seeing him, being this close to him but in such a different way, had been eating away at her from the inside out. She knew that they could never have what they'd had before. It was gone. Lost. And so was she except for that little girl not fifteen feet away, sleeping in a bassinet.

Melissa's anger was building and building until all twelve months of frustration boiled over. "He's not my husband. I didn't love him. I never loved him. Got it? And I don't need you to keep telling me how he was my husband because he wasn't. Not in my heart. Not in any way that mattered."

Her heart pounded her ribs and her breath came out in pulses. Her outburst seemed to silence Colin because he didn't speak a word.

"I don't need you telling me what my relationship was. I certainly don't want to talk about it with you. I can't stand him. He's a criminal and I…" She stopped herself right there. No way was she going to tell him that Richard had done nothing but repulse her.

Colin stood in front of her, contemplating her. His calm demeanor frustrated her even more.

"Move out of the way." She tried to push past him but her hand met a wall.

"It's clear to me that you had no intention of leaving him until the government stepped in. So, why did you name our daughter Angelina?" he asked, those intense eyes of his looking right through her.

And the air *whooshed* from her lungs.

"Because I love that name." It was true. She loved the name and everything it had represented, which boiled down to every day she'd spent with him. There was so much anger in his eyes now. She knew that leaving him would be the hardest thing she'd ever done. Little did she know that she'd had it all wrong. Standing in front of him, facing him, was by far the most difficult.

His expression faltered. "But that was *our* name. For *our* baby if we ever had a girl. And yet you were content to use it with another man."

"She's your daughter," Melissa quipped.

"He didn't know that and I wouldn't have, either," he said.

Was he trying to hurt her? What did any of it really matter? He'd been clear. He would never trust her again. Their "house" had been made of cards and the first strong wind had blown it down. He'd made excellent points. What did that really say about their relationship?

Melissa couldn't keep going if she opened that dam. She had to stay focused on finding Richard and making him pay for what he'd done to her and so many others.

She folded her arms, needing to get this conversation back on track.

"He was trying to buy a place in Colorado but he didn't want his name on it," she said.

A look of hurt passed behind Colin's steely gaze before he seemed to shore up his resolve, too. "Good. We can start there."

He turned around, his back to her, and walked to the

kitchen. Before taking a seat at the table, he rummaged around for a piece of paper and a pen. "Where?"

"Crow's Peak, Colorado. And there's another thing. I know he's made a lot of enemies just in the time I've known him." She was trying hard to think, which was difficult given the fact that water was everywhere, she was on a boat that had rocked all night and had turned her stomach upside down. She was trapped with a man who made her crazy and want things she shouldn't. Her heart was a mess. At least the storm outside had calmed down.

"Let's see. The Colorado deal sticks out the most in my mind. He appeared clean in almost every business deal but blackmail was his specialty. People were too scared to testify against him so he ended up getting whatever he wanted." She couldn't look at Colin when she said those words.

"Who did he blackmail?" he asked, and his voice was a study in calm.

"He tried to keep his business life separate from home for the most part. He never kept a home office. He and his brother, Ray, met at our home sometimes but they kept the volume of the TV turned up. Richard always assumed someone was listening. He was the kind of guy who covered his tracks," she said.

"Did he blackmail you into marrying him?" Colin asked.

Melissa didn't immediately answer.

"What do you mean?" she finally asked.

"You heard my question," he said.

"We're getting off track here," Melissa said.

Colin paused before asking, "Tell me more about the Colorado deal."

"One of his buddies planned to sell the hotel to him and they kept talking about using offshore accounts and a dummy company." Richard had set up several networks to help other criminals disappear. Any one of the men he'd harbored would help him in a heartbeat if asked.

"It would be a good way to launder money," Colin said. "Isn't that one of his forms of income?"

She nodded. It was one of many illegal activities that Richard managed to keep a hand in.

"Maybe we should start there," Colin said. "I have to say that I don't like the idea of getting close to Richard while we have Angelina with us."

"I agree," she said, her heart rate picking up again. "But I can't be apart from her. I have to be able to protect her, Colin. Especially after being so unsure that I'd be able to for the past year. From the moment I knew I was pregnant I've been a mess thinking about how much he could hurt me using her."

The baby stirred. A little cry sounded in the next room.

"I'll get her," she said quickly.

ANGELINA WAS AWAKE and it was important to keep positive energy between her parents, so he needed to shift gears. Colin was surprised at just how much the new babies on the ranch picked up on. If a situation was tense, they cried or acted out. If everything was calm, they responded with happiness.

"They say the storm is going to be worse tonight," he said. "I'd planned to stay on the boat for a few days. Plans have changed. We'll need dry land."

"Where will we go?" Melissa asked, her gaze darting around, and he could see real fear in her eyes. Talking about Richard brought out intense emotions in her.

"We can figure that out after coffee," he said with a slight smile. Too much conversation had already gone on without caffeine and he needed to dial down his intensity for Angelina's sake. It wasn't easy. But Colin would do anything for that little girl.

"I'll get the baby ready." Melissa had everything ready to go in five minutes, baby in her arms, diaper bag slung over her shoulder.

Colin steered the houseboat back to the bay slowly, making sure there weren't any law enforcement officers waiting for him. After all, he had technically stolen the boat. He parked and then took one of the rental brochures so he could reimburse the family who owned the Sea Fairy. He'd make sure the owners were more than compensated for "lending" their rental.

Melissa had changed. At more than one point during the storms last night he'd expected her to come out of the bedroom for reassurance. Being with Angelina made a difference. There was a sense of determination and purpose to Melissa's personality now. She was protective. The change looked good on her.

Now that Colin could set his emotions aside and think a little more clearly, he was also beginning to piece together a few possibilities of why Melissa might've really left him. He didn't like the scenarios playing out in his head. In fact, they made him want to put his hands on Richard and show him what it really was to be afraid.

From what Colin could gather so far, Melissa had been damn brave. She'd reacted big time to his question about being blackmailed. He had every intention of getting to the bottom of that later when the two of them could focus on something besides nailing Richard.

Colin pulled into the dock and then tied the boat down. He helped Melissa off, ignoring the frissons of heat prickling his hand where it touched hers.

"Mind if I give that a try?" he asked, motioning toward the baby's seat in the back of Dallas's pickup.

A reluctant look passed behind Melissa's eyes before she nodded her head and then handed Angelina over to him.

"Careful," she said as she stood, watching over his shoulder.

Melissa needed to get used to the fact that Angelina's father intended to be around to watch her grow up.

Balancing her head as he lifted her into the seat was going to be the tricky part, he decided.

"Don't worry," he reassured Melissa. "I'm not going to do anything that could possibly hurt our daughter."

"You're right." There was a note of resignation in her voice. She must've taken that wrong. He didn't mean anything by it. He really wouldn't do anything to hurt his daughter on purpose. It was that simple. He'd sort out that miscommunication later when Angelina was safely secured in the car seat. Besides, he had a few rounds of apologies to deliver once this was over. He'd been off since Melissa had returned. Thinking back, he'd practically bit Cynthia's head off at the Spring Fling when he'd found out that Melissa was there.

Colin thought about it. Maybe some of Melissa's actions last year had to do with his immaturity. She hadn't trusted him and that was a problem, especially since they'd planned to spend the rest of their lives together.

In hindsight, he could admit that there were situations he could've handled better.

He gently held out Angelina. Balancing her over the seat was nerve-racking. He could only hope that she wouldn't suddenly wiggle at the wrong time. Even though she was no bigger than a minute and his hands were decently large, he worried about dropping her. All his muscles bunched as he set her down. He released the breath he'd been holding.

The straps weren't too difficult to manage.

He stepped aside when he was finished with them. "How'd I do?"

Melissa inspected his work, tugging at the straps to make sure they were solid.

"Pretty darn good for your first time, soldier." The corners of her lips turned up but the smile didn't reach her eyes.

Part of him wanted to make her laugh, to regain that easy feeling they'd once shared. There'd been glimmers of it since their reunion. But that was dangerous and his heart wouldn't survive another blow like the one she'd delivered last year. He couldn't afford to let his guard down no matter how nice it would be for the time being.

Colin held open her door for her before moving around to the driver's side and settling into his seat.

"She always this easy to take care of?" he asked.

"Pretty much. She's a good baby. We had a few bumps in the road early on but I'm pretty sure that was my inexperience," she said. "I'm thinking these little ones feed off the emotions around them more than we realize."

"I was just thinking that earlier." He started the engine. He put his hand on the gearshift and then paused.

"I'm sorry about not being around during your pregnancy."

"That's not your fault," she said, sounding shocked.

He wanted to believe that was true. But that wasn't exactly the case, was it? If he'd acted more maturely she might've trusted him. He'd had no idea what she was going through. He'd been too busy licking his own wounds to realize that she might've been forced out of Bluff, out of her life by a ruthless criminal.

"Yeah, it was." He put the gearshift in reverse and backed out of his parking spot.

Melissa didn't respond. She didn't need to. Colin owned up to his mistakes.

The sky was layered with rolling gray clouds. On the ranch, Colin had learned to believe the weather. If there were thick dark clouds and the air was intense, that most likely did mean there was a bad storm on the way. Besides, his knees always let him know how much moisture there'd be in the air and they were creaking like he was 110 years old.

It took nearly a half hour to reach the nearest convenience store and they passed one car on the long, two-way road to the turn off for the lake. Storm or not, last night on the boat had been the perfect cover.

Every vehicle was suspect and traffic was picking up now that they were hitting one of the main roads in and out of the lake area. He was rethinking his idea to be in Oklahoma near Rancic's family home. It might be better to move on to Colorado and check out the place Rancic had been interested in. The one Melissa had told him about earlier. Having a place with no paperwork trail that could lead authorities back to Rancic was smart. There was a possibility that they'd find

Rancic there. Give Colin five minutes alone with the guy and he didn't need a gun. He'd take him with his bare hands. But he had to consider his daughter first.

He parked near the air pump of the gas station and pulled out the throwaway cell phone. "I need to touch base with Dallas."

"Will you check on Tommy again?" she asked, and there was so much concern in her tone. She exited the truck long enough to get their daughter and return to her seat, cradling the baby.

"Yes." Colin didn't want to notice the compassion in her voice when she spoke about their friend. He didn't want to notice how great of a mother she seemed to be to their daughter. And she sure as hell didn't want to notice that she was even more beautiful than the year before. For someone who'd wanted to put off mother-hood until a few years later, it sure looked good on her. It was impossible not to acknowledge how natural she was with Angelina. But then that little girl was an angel.

Melissa held their baby in her arms. Angelina's smiling face at such a contrast to the feelings going on inside him. What he had to say might tear Melissa's heart out.

"I was hoping that it wouldn't come to this," he started, "but I think we should take Dallas up on his offer to keep Angelina on the ranch. Before you say no, hear me out."

She nodded, her lips compressed together like she had to hold back her words.

"We need to go to Colorado and check out the place Rancic was looking at buying. What is it, by the way? Land? A hotel?"

"Both. The hotel is Mountain Trail Inn," she supplied.

"Okay. Say we check the place out. He might actually be there, which would put our daughter at risk. Besides, with the amount of care she needs, we'll be left vulnerable too often. If we're in a sticky situation and she cries at the wrong time, it's game over for all three of us. Rancic might not have put two and two together about me being her father but he might when he sees us together. At the very least he kills us and takes her, thinking that she belongs to him."

Melissa didn't answer right away and that was a good thing. It meant she was seriously considering his words.

"I'm not doubting my military skills but we have no idea how many men Richard could bring to a fight. My guess is that his brother is helping him at the very least," he said.

"The others in his organization probably won't," she said. "I'm pretty sure a few of them have been waiting for an opportunity like this. If Richard's out of the picture, they can handle Raymond a lot easier. But he's helped a lot of people and they might. Although, they tend to move through because they have problems of their own to deal with being on the run."

"I'm sure there's at least one more Rancic can trust and that's the best-case scenario. That would be three against one," he said. "Worst case, his entire network is looking for you."

She shot him a concerned look. "I can help."

"Fine, three against two, but you can't exactly handle a gun," he said. "And what little training I've been able to give you might not be enough. Not even with your instincts, which are strong."

She acknowledged his point with a nod.

"Those aren't bad odds if I'm full strength. With Angelina in the picture, it weakens both of our abilities to focus and we can't exactly stop to feed her in the middle of a gunfight. She cries, and she will cry, they'll be able to track us no matter where we go or how smart we think we are. She introduces too much of an unknown variable for me to have confidence I can keep you both safe. That has to be our top priority," he said. He was thinking solely on strategy and pushing his emotions aside. Even though he was professionally trained to do just that, the thought of leaving his little angel behind hit him square in the chest and harder than expected.

Melissa frowned and she hugged Angelina tightly. More proof that his words were making an impact.

"I thought the same thing last night on the boat," she said. "I was getting sick. You were trying to feed her and I figured if someone attacked us at that moment, there was no way we were coming out alive."

They sat in silence for a few more minutes. This wasn't the time to push for an answer. Colin would give her the space she needed to make a decision.

"I don't like the thought of being away from her," she finally said.

"Neither do I," he admitted.

"You've thought of every other possibility, haven't you?" she asked.

"Every scenario I can think of. Our best chance of staying under the radar was the boat. With the storms predicted to come through tonight, we have to stay on dry land. That will leave us exposed," he said.

"That's what I thought, too," she said.

Melissa hugged their daughter.

"Will Dallas be able to meet us somewhere for a handoff?" she asked.

Colin glanced in the rearview mirror. His gaze froze. "Change sides with me."

"What…*what* is it?" she asked, and it was obvious that she'd picked up on the adrenaline rush coursing through him.

"I want you to take the wheel," he said with a forced calm.

Chapter Thirteen

Melissa glanced up in time to see a pair of men in a truck staring at them from twenty feet away.

"Dallas's license plate must've given us away," Colin said. "I don't think they know we've figured them out so no quick moves."

Melissa looked at the cooing baby in her arms and then at Colin. "What am I supposed to do with her while I drive?"

"Give her to me," he said, holding his arms out. "And then slowly slide over to take the wheel."

She handed over the baby, regretting that she hadn't given Angelina to Dallas sooner.

Melissa eased over to the driver's side as Colin fluidly slid over the seat. Angelina was lying against his chest, giggling. The motion must've tickled her tummy.

By the time Melissa buckled her seat belt, Angelina was strapped in.

"Get ready to go when I say," Colin said.

"Maybe I should walk over to them and shock them. Then you can take off with the baby," Melissa said, panic swelling in her chest.

"No way," Colin said. "I won't risk you."

"I guess there's no chance they haven't seen us," she said.

"None."

She watched in the rearview mirror as Colin—who was facing forward—slid the rear window open enough to fit a gun barrel through the opening.

"Where'd you get that?" she asked.

"From the glovebox last night." Colin dropped into position, ready to fire on the truck. "Ready?"

"Absolutely," she said. She'd made up her mind that nothing could happen to her daughter. Her resolve was the only thing keeping her from losing it. As adrenaline coursed through her, her hands began to shake.

"Drive away slowly," he said.

Melissa took a fortifying breath, put the gearshift in drive and stepped on the gas. She pressed a little harder than she'd intended and a few rocks spewed out from underneath her tires.

"Sorry," she said.

"You're doing great," Colin replied, his voice a study in calm. "Don't worry about checking behind you. I'll take care of them."

Colin's head had disappeared. She prepared herself for the *crack* sound that would come next.

Her nerves were strung so tight she thought they might snap. Her chest squeezed and breathing was difficult as she pulled onto the road.

"I was hoping for a cup of coffee before we had to party," Colin said with that calm and casual tone he was so good at during intense situations.

She couldn't help herself. She laughed.

"Good. I was hoping for that reaction," he said.

"We're going to be fine. Believe that in your heart and it'll be true."

"Is that how you got through your missions in the military?" she asked.

"It is," he said.

"And it actually works?" she asked.

"Every time," he said.

She would absorb all the confidence that pulsed from him because her heart pounded wildly in her chest.

"What day is it today?" he asked.

"Monday, I think," she said, and she hated that her voice was as erratic as her pulse.

"What time is it?" he asked.

She glanced at the clock on the dashboard. "Seven forty-eight."

"Great," he said. "Take a left and then take the first on-ramp onto the highway."

It dawned on her why. "No stoplights?"

"That's right. We don't want to end up stuck at a light, plus it'll be easier for these guys to follow us in town," he said. "We have a better chance of disappearing in thick morning rush-hour traffic."

"Good point."

The men must've figured them out and realized they had a chance of escape because she heard a *crack*, the telltale sound of a handgun being fired.

Colin muttered the same curse she was thinking. Her heart stuttered. It was already pounding so hard it hurt.

Were they hit?

"Colin?" was all she could manage.

Another *crack* sound blasted in her ears.

Tires squealed behind them. She glanced in the rear-view in time to see the truck swerving. She nailed the gas pedal and the truck got smaller and smaller until she saw it drive onto the embankment and stop.

Colin was beside her in the next heartbeat, checking her over.

"Is she—"

"The baby's fine," he said. "Pull off at the next exit."

"Are you hurt?" she asked as she did what he said. She hadn't dared look.

"We're okay," he said. "But we need to get out of here fast. Those guys back there most likely have friends. I blew out their front tire so we've slowed them down, but I have no idea how many we're up against and we have to assume the worst."

She had enough possession of her mental faculties to put on her emergency blinkers as she exited the highway and then pulled onto the side of the road. "That noise was so loud."

"I took care of her," he said. His tone was all business as he traded seats with her.

Melissa climbed over to check on their daughter as he buckled in. A second later, he sped away.

The baby's toothless grin tugged at Melissa's heart. The white headphones she had on were huge, covering most of the sides of her head.

"Dallas keeps those in the back for when he goes to the firing range," Colin said. "Her ears are fine."

Melissa buckled herself in with a sigh of relief. She took off the baby's headphones and Angelina cooed at her.

Colin cut the wheel a few times. Melissa couldn't be sure how many. She was too focused on her daughter and on being grateful that her little girl was safe.

But for how long?

COLIN HAD BEEN driving for more than two hours before he'd said it was safe enough to run through a fast-food chain's drive-thru. He'd already been in touch with Dallas to arrange to meet.

"I never thought a plain old cup of coffee could taste so good," Melissa said, enjoying every drop of that first sip.

"Every single cup tastes like heaven to me," he said with a wry smile.

The tension was starting to break from their earlier run-in with Richard's men. Colin had been too focused on making sure they were far away to get too comfortable. His grip on the wheel had been tight and his gaze intense on the stretches of highway in front of them. He'd made several defensive maneuvers, moved from highways to roads and back before exiting and then pulling under the golden arches.

Since then, the baby had been changed and fed, and slept peacefully. She was safe. *For now.* Those two little words wound through Melissa's mind.

They sat in the parking lot, waiting for Dallas to arrive, so she figured they might be somewhere in Texas. She hadn't kept up and decided the less she knew the better. She'd only stress more and she was trying to maintain a sense of calm with the baby around.

"After what happened, I'm convinced that we're doing the right thing by sending Angelina to the ranch with Dallas," she said after taking another sip. This was the meet-up point that Colin and Dallas had agreed on. She had no idea what town they were in and didn't care as long as they were far away from anyone connected to Richard.

"We are," he said.

"I'm shocked that she isn't traumatized by what happened this morning," Melissa said with a little more tension in her voice than she'd intended. It wasn't going to be easy to shake off the stress from the morning's events. Heck, when she added what they'd gone through last night, she figured she was doing pretty darn well under the circumstances. "I know I am."

Colin took another sip of coffee before he spoke, and that made her believe he had something serious on his mind. "I can break out on my own to find Rancic. You can go with the baby to the ranch. It might be better that way for everyone involved."

"I never thought I'd say this but she's safer without me," she said. "He wants revenge and he won't stop until he destroys me."

"He hasn't figured out that the baby doesn't belong to him," Colin said after a brief pause.

"How do you know?" she asked.

"Those men are trained to use weapons. They missed the entire truck using a 9mm handgun. Do you know what the odds of that are?" he asked.

She had to admit that she could fit what she knew about guns in a thimble. "They must be pretty slim if you're bringing it up right now."

"So that means Rancic thinks Angelina belongs to him and he doesn't want anything to happen to her. You'll be safer if you stick close to the baby," he said, and she couldn't read his emotions. Did he want her to go? Did he not want her to go? She had no idea.

Melissa could admit that the sexual current running between them had been a distraction neither could afford if they wanted to stay alive. This morning was a stark reminder of how serious this situation was. Even if the men hadn't intended to hit the truck, they could've. She knew enough about guns to realize that some were more accurate than others.

Richard had used a shotgun on Tommy, and stray fragments could've hurt her and the baby. Granted, Tommy was in the opposite direction the whole time.

It suddenly occurred to her that the only reason she was still alive was most likely because she was standing in front of the car where Angelina was strapped in her car seat. If Richard had had a shot that couldn't possibly hit the baby, he would've taken it.

He must not've known whether or not he'd hit Tommy or he would've turned around.

So, all that really meant was that he really didn't want to get caught. He'd said that he'd never go back to jail.

The thought that the only thing keeping Melissa alive was her daughter struck hard.

"I'm sticking with you," she said. "Richard wants me dead, not Angelina. He'll deal with me first and then come after her later. Is there any chance he won't be able to figure out that she's still with me?"

"We can assume that he believes you have her or he wouldn't have ordered the men not to pull the trigger unless they had a clear shot," he said.

She'd overheard Colin asking Dallas to bring a baby doll earlier. Now, his request made sense.

A gray SUV pulled into the parking lot and then parked alongside them. Melissa had already noticed that Dallas was driving and Gideon was in the passenger seat.

Her heart pounded as she thought about being away from her daughter. They hadn't been separated since Angelina was born. Not to mention she was about to trust Dallas O'Brien with the most important thing in her life, her daughter. Somewhere down deep, and no matter how hard her heart wanted to fight it, she realized that it would be safer for Angelina to go with him—to be away from her—until law enforcement had a chance to find Richard or they had a chance to stop him.

Dallas slid into the backseat and they exchanged somber greetings.

"She eats every four hours during the day and five to six at night," Melissa said, immediately launching into how to care of her baby.

Dallas listened and nodded.

"She likes to have her back patted and get some tummy time after a shower but you have to be right next to her. A story at bedtime is her favorite and I usually play classical music to calm her down." It was her nerves doing that, causing her to spew out everything she could think to tell him about Angelina.

Neither O'Brien spoke. Both patiently listened.

"There's another option for you," Colin said to her when she finished. "I can keep both of you alive if you hear me out. But you're going to have to trust that I know what I'm doing. Richard knows how devoted you are to your daughter, right?"

"Yes, he does," she said.

"And so he knows you well enough to realize that you wouldn't separate from her, right?" Colin asked.

"Of course." Her heart still argued against the idea of being away from her child, even for a few days.

"We've had an influx of kids at the ranch so one more won't raise any eyebrows. Besides, everything she needs is right there. No need to leave the property

and you already know how tight security is. We won't
have to add any personnel or do anything that would
signal to Richard that anything's changed. He no doubt
has people watching since you're his primary target, so
they'll be extra careful."

Right again. Melissa nodded a third time.

"So, as soon as your location leaks he'll head directly
toward you," Colin said.

"What if…" She couldn't even bring herself to say
the words.

"I'll be there 24/7," Dallas offered. "She'll stay with
me and Kate while you guys lead Richard far away and
to his arrest."

"Unless you agree to go into protective custody right
now," Colin said.

Had he been saving this so he could drop the bomb
last minute? "I already told you how I feel about us
being separated. It's bad enough that I won't be with
our daughter, let alone be stuck in a strange city with
no idea what was going on."

She realized her mistake almost the instant the slip
left her mouth.

Dallas's gaze shot toward Colin, who gave a nod of
acknowledgment. The brothers were so close that they
didn't need words in a situation like this. Dallas now
knew that Angelina was Colin's daughter. If it bothered
him, he didn't show it. If he had questions—and who
wouldn't?—he didn't ask.

"Think about what I said because we're reaching a
point of no return here," Colin said.

Did he want her to go away from him?

She studied his expression and decided the answer
was *no*.

The US Marshals service had failed her already. The O'Brien brothers were her best chance.

"I'm not going to the law," she said as panic nearly tore a hole in her chest, thinking about handing Angelina over. "If anything happens to me or Colin, though, she has no one else."

Melissa looked directly at Dallas. He was the eldest brother and could be the most intense. He was tall, like Colin, and similarly muscled. His hair was blacker and his eyes a little darker. He smiled less than Colin and already had the worry lines to prove it.

"She has all of us and we're her family, too," Dallas said and then promised, "but we won't let it come to that. Richard is going to jail and both of you are coming home."

"That's my plan," Colin said.

"I'll get her safely to the ranch. There's no question about that," Dallas added. "Once we're there, no one will touch her so I don't want you to worry." He paused a beat. "I know that's probably a tall order but I want you to know that we'll take good care of her."

"I wouldn't trust her with anyone else," Melissa said. She'd always loved the O'Briens and her daughter couldn't be in better hands.

"Your truck has been made," Colin said to Dallas. "I know I already told you that but it bears repeating."

"We're ditching it a couple of blocks from here. Gideon knows someone who'll keep it in their garage while they strip it," Dallas said, and his expression changed as he looked at Colin.

"What is it?" Colin asked.

"You need to know that a story broke in this morning's newspaper about Dad," Dallas said, and his voice was steady.

"I'm sorry that I haven't had a chance to warn you. I figured that might be coming," Colin said. "I'm guessing there were some pretty damning pictures involved."

Dallas nodded.

"Richard used those to pressure Melissa into going through with a wedding when she tried to change her mind," Colin said.

Dallas muttered a curse low and under his breath. "We should've known something else was going on."

"I'm sorry I didn't tell you before," she said, tearing up. "There was so much going on and I thought I could protect your family if I just did what he said."

"We know now," Colin said. "And that's what matters."

"Agreed," Dallas said. "Now the SOB needs to pay for what he's done."

"If you're ready, we should go," Colin said.

Melissa got out of the cab and took her daughter out of the car seat, reminding herself that this was the best way to keep Angelina safe.

"Gideon packed the trunk of the SUV with a few supplies he thought you'd be able to use in the coming days," Dallas said. "A few of us will join you as soon as we can."

Colin walked over to Gideon and then shook his hand.

"Take her now," she said to Dallas, handing her daughter to him. "Richard won't expect you to have her since he knows I'm not in Bluff."

Dallas took the sleeping little girl.

"And Dallas. Please keep her safe," she said, shoving

down the ache in her chest at watching him preparing to walk away with Angelina.

"I understand what's at stake," Dallas said.

"Are you sure you want to do this?" she asked. "Richard is a dangerous man, and if he finds out you're involved with me in any way he'll try to destroy you and everything you love."

"I know the risk I'm taking," Dallas said. "My family doesn't shy away from doing the right thing because it's difficult."

She stood there, thinking how much a contrast Richard was to the O'Brien family.

"Thank you, Dallas," she said.

"It's time to get on the road," Colin said, moving next to her. His jaw was set. Determination darkened his eyes. And even though he tucked it down deep, she could see pain in his eyes.

Melissa knew that allowing Dallas to take Angelina away was the absolute right decision and yet her heart felt like it was being ripped out of her chest as she took the baby doll from Gideon. She couldn't allow herself to think that this was the last time she'd see her daughter. The thought nearly brought her to her knees.

No matter what else happened, Angelina was safe. Melissa repeated those words over and over again as Dallas turned and then walked away. With every step he took in the opposite direction, Melissa's heart ached a little bit more.

Before she had time to analyze her actions, she was reaching for Colin. His arms closed around her as the first tears fell. She buried her face in his chest, unable to watch the truck pull away and disappear as the sun kissed the western horizon.

"It'll only be for a couple of days," he said, and his voice was soft and warm against her neck where his face was nestled. She felt his heartbeat, steady and strong.

Melissa wrapped her arms around him, holding on like tomorrow was a question instead of a guarantee. Reality said that that was true. There were no more certainties while Richard was free. And the pain of being away from her daughter nearly impaled her. She tightened her grip around Colin.

"She's safe," he said, his lips moving against her skin. "He won't get to her. No one will ever hurt our daughter."

It wasn't the first time he'd spoken those last two words together. But this time was different. In them, there was hope for a future for the three of them. No matter what happened in the coming hours or days, Melissa would cling to that thought—the one where Angelina grew up with loving parents who were able to set aside differences and always put her first.

All they had to do was live long enough to see her again.

They stood there for a moment that stretched and extended around them. Cars and trucks zipped in and out of the parking lot; a busy place provided the best cover. None of the activity really registered. Her world shrank down to the two of them, together, in their own world as they looked into each other's eyes.

Melissa could pinpoint the exact second when her emotions turned from sadness and desperation to awareness—awareness of Colin's strong arms holding her upright, awareness of his muscled chest pressed against her breasts, awareness of him, male and virile and strong.

Colin repositioned his hands, cupping her face and tilting her head. He dipped down and pressed his lips to hers.

His eyes were closed, so she closed hers, too.

The taste of coffee was still on his lips.

Her body flush with his, she could feel his need—a need that matched hers. She wanted to be naked and tangled around him.

She wanted to feel his warm athletic body—all muscles and strength—molded to hers. She wanted to feel his weight on top of her, pressing her into the mattress.

She wanted to be happy again, if only for a short time.

And she wanted to get lost in that feeling.

Melissa couldn't be sure how long they stood there, kissing. Although, her body cried *not nearly long enough* when he pulled away.

He took in a sharp breath.

"We can't do this," he said in a low voice.

THE SUN DISAPPEARED across the highway by the time Colin took Melissa's hand and led her to the SUV. Melissa buckled up on the passenger side, ready for the long drive. The highway was flat for the rest of the drive through Oklahoma, Kansas and most of Colorado. It wasn't until they were close to Denver that the roads started winding up, down and around. Not that it mattered. She couldn't quiet her mind enough to get any rest.

Melissa missed her little girl. All she could think about was Angelina making it to the ranch safely. She tried not to overthink everything that could go wrong with their plans. One bright spot so far was how well

Tommy was recovering from surgery. And then there was kissing in the parking lot. For those moments in Colin's arms were the first in a year that Melissa felt like she was home.

The vehicle climbed and her ears started popping. By the time the SUV stopped, sleep was trying to take hold and she'd been dozing on and off for the last hour.

Colin moved the suitcase to the trunk after taking out and loading a handgun.

"I'll keep this under my seat, just in case," he said.

"Where are we?" she asked.

"At an old camp that I used to go to with the twins when we were young," he said, referring to his younger brothers Ryder and Joshua. "My uncle used to own and run the place. It closed years ago and nothing's been done with the land since. I know the area, which will keep us safer and it'll be easier to set a trap for Richard here. I wish you would've gone with Angelina, though."

"I know you do," she said. "You already made your position clear and so did I. He wants me dead. He'll come directly at me first. He would only use her if he couldn't get to me, which isn't going to be a problem. She's safer if she's not around me." Her voice broke on that last sentence. It was true. Colin knew it, too, or he never would've agreed to let her come along.

"Still, I don't like you being here," he said in a low growl. "I don't want him to get close to you."

"Then don't let him," she said. "But I'm sticking with you. We both know you're my best chance at staying alive."

Chapter Fourteen

The line between being there for the mother of Colin's child when she needed a shoulder to cry on or to feel safe in someone's arms and physically connecting with her was a fine thread. He'd be smart to remind himself to keep a safe distance, to keep in focus that Melissa was there so he could protect her for his daughter's sake. Losing her mother at such a young age would be a huge blow to the little girl.

That was totally being fair. Colin's feelings for Melissa ran deeper than wanting to keep her alive for their child's sake. He and Melissa had history. It was obvious they still had chemistry. There were too many times that he'd wanted nothing more than to take her into his arms and make love to her until she lay there exhausted like they'd done so many times in the past.

But that part of their relationship was in the past. Trying to recapture even a small slice of what they had would confuse an already complicated situation. Besides, a lot could change in a year. A lot *had* changed in a year, the annoying little voice inside his head reminded. And a whole lot more could change in the next twenty-four hours.

He needed to stay focused or they'd both end up

dead. There was no way he'd allow Angelina to grow up an orphan. Thoughts of those big eyes, round cheeks and her smile breathed new resolve into him.

"We'll bunk down for a few hours in the car for the rest of the night," he said, locating a blanket in the backseat. He placed it over her. "Lay your chair back and try to get in as much sleep as you can. I need you as well rested as possible come morning."

COLIN HAD BARELY closed his eyes when the first light peeked through the windshield. He'd scarcely moved when Melissa bolted upright, practically gasping for air.

"You're okay," he said, keeping his voice level so he didn't give away his true level of concern.

"He was here," she said, out of breath. Her gaze darted around.

"It's just me." Between her flinching every time he reached for her unexpectedly and the nightmare, he was beginning to see the true scars from the past year. Richard had to be stopped. Colin was starting to get a better picture of what her life must've been like.

Melissa relaxed on an exhale when she seemed certain that she was safe. She fumbled around for the lever on her right and then repositioned her seat in the upright position.

Colin grabbed the pack from the backseat and pulled out bottled waters, toothpaste and toothbrushes. Seeing Melissa's panic first thing didn't do good things to his blood pressure and made him want to punish Rancic even more. Colin also realized that Melissa had been living in a prison.

He held out her toothbrush. She took the offering

without saying anything. Mostly, she just looked shaken and Colin fought the urge to take her in his arms.

They exited the car and moved near a towering pine. It was still chilly this time of year in the mountains. Beautiful, but cold. Colin missed Texas, warm sunshine and the ranch even more as he brushed his teeth.

A random thought struck. Could he convince Melissa to live on the ranch? She would need her own place but there was plenty of land and spots to build. They could figure out a way to make it work. He'd offer his house to Melissa and Angelina while having something more suitable built.

After rinsing toothpaste out of his mouth using bottled water, he surveyed the area. He'd memorized the camp layout and these woods years ago but everything looked different now, smaller. He probably should've expected that.

Melissa was a quiet shadow as he walked the perimeter of the cabins. There were a dozen, half on one side of the main gathering area, half on the other, just like he remembered from spending time here with the twins. A couple of chaperones kept boys and girls separate. There wasn't much else needed at that age. Young boys mostly wanted to tease girls, tease and torture by pulling hair or toilet-papering cabins. The true spark wouldn't ignite for a couple more years. The cabins were set back and on either side of the mess hall.

A party room was to the left of the campfire, and an outdoor pavilion sat to the right. Behind the outdoor pavilion was a small shop to buy sweets and souvenirs. The campfire was a circle in the middle and the center of activity. Logs still circled the rocked-off area where they'd lit the flame and had heard stories of the Old West.

Two feet of weeds covered much of the area now, choking out grass and flowers.

The air at this elevation was dry, so Colin would have to be careful when he lit a flame. He moved to the fire pit and then pulled weeds. Melissa worked silently beside him, following his lead.

Colin lit a fire and took out camping supplies. He made coffee using an iron pot. The air was filled with purpose. There was a lot to do between now and tonight.

"When will your brothers be here?" Melissa finally asked. "Did they text to let you know?"

"Yes. Before the sun goes down," he said, handing her a tin cup filled with fresh coffee. "I don't have any sweeteners."

"I don't need any today," she said, taking the offering. She took a sip. "This is amazing."

"There's a PowerBar in the backpack if you're hungry," he said, motioning toward the green bag.

"Maybe later," she said. "I'm not awake enough to eat yet."

Colin suspected there was more to it than that. She still seemed shaken by her nightmare. He didn't press. She'd talk when she was ready. He sat back on his heels and drank the dark liquid. It wasn't too bad.

"Where are we sleeping tonight?" she asked.

"You and me will be in the souvenir shop," he said.

She stared at one of the buildings. Something was on her mind. He could tell by the way she chewed on the inside of her jaw.

"Can I ask you a question?" she finally asked, settling next to him.

He nodded, stretching out his legs.

"Before, when I told you about what Richard said about your father. You didn't hesitate to defend him and neither did Dallas earlier. I know you both love him, but you especially are not the kind of person to let that love blind you. So, how do you know he didn't have an affair?" she asked.

"I can't be absolutely certain about anything. I know one thing. Two people never loved each other more than my parents," he said.

"How do you know that?" she asked.

He looked straight at her, into those brown eyes with violet streaks, and took in a sharp breath. "Because that's the way I loved you."

A few tears streamed down her cheeks and he thumbed them away. "Don't do that. Don't cry."

"The only way I could get through the day that I married Richard was by picturing you standing there, not him," she said. "He turned my stomach but I had to help my father. I was so confused and I couldn't stand by and watch my father go to jail. He was wrong. He did things that were bad and part of me wants to condemn him for it. But the other part, the side that won, remembers how he used to sing those old bluegrass songs to put me to sleep after Mom died."

She stopped long enough to release a few sobs.

Colin put his arm around her waist and, in one motion, swept her beside him. Their outer thighs touched and he felt the same trill she did based on her reaction to the contact.

"He was all I had growing up and he did the best he could," she said, and her voice held less sorrow now. "Without him, I was afraid of being all alone."

"You had me, my family," he said in a low voice. He understood not being able to turn her back on her father. Colin was even more grateful for his own parents in comparison.

"I know. But how could I turn to you?" she asked.

"We were building a life together, Melissa," he said. "You don't think I would've understood about your father? Helped him?"

"Please don't be upset. I was embarrassed. I was marrying *you*. Your family is perfect. They have principles and do the right thing for other people even if it means they could get hurt. *You're* perfect. I'm not," she said. "Besides, I had no way out. This was about more than money. Richard had proof that my dad had doctored the books on the business he'd planned to buy from him."

"You should've trusted me enough to be honest about what was going on," Colin said.

"And then what? You're impulsive, Colin, and used to getting your way in life. Would you have honestly been able to step aside?" she asked.

He started to argue but she stopped him.

"You could never let an injustice like that stand without trying to do something to stop it," she countered.

Colin thought hard about what she was saying. The truth wasn't always the easiest thing to hear.

He picked her up and sat her on his lap, facing him. At this vantage point, they could see eye to eye, which was good because she needed to see the sincerity in his. "My family is far from perfect. See that tree over there? The one with the big branch? I let my brother fall off it because I thought he needed to learn a lesson."

"Doesn't exactly make you a criminal," she said.

"Except that he broke his arm in two places and I really did it because I was mad at him. Summer camp was over after that, like I knew it would be if something happened, and I didn't want to be here to watch my brothers anyway when I could be home, hanging out with my friends," he said.

"You were a kid," she said.

"I was fourteen. Old enough to know better," he said. "My girlfriend had broken up with me because she didn't want to be alone during the summer. I blamed my brothers so I rebelled and didn't take care of them like I should've."

"That's not the same as pushing him off the limb," she said, staring into his eyes. The air had changed and they both seemed aware of the position they were in.

"True. But I could've stopped him. I saw the danger. First week of camp a kid fell off that exact same spot and had to be sent home," he said. "All I could think about was getting back to Bluff so I could win Leslie back."

Melissa didn't speak for a long moment. She just looked into his eyes. It was the most honest moment he'd had in a long time. Being with her, spending time with her, cracked the casing he'd built around his heart. He didn't want to allow light inside the dark places. He didn't want to need anyone again the same way he needed her. That annoying little voice inside his head said it was too late. He'd reopened that wound and when this was over, he was going to feel worse than the last time if that was even possible.

"Melissa." He gripped her waist tighter.

"Colin." Those intelligent eyes of hers stared beyond the physical.

"Why did you really leave?" he asked. "Was it me?"

"You? It was never your fault, Colin. I'm all my father has and it's just been us. I never stopped loving you but I'm not good enough for you. Know that whatever happens in the next couple of days that my heart always belonged to you," she said. And then she kissed him.

Chapter Fifteen

"I wish you would've trusted me," Colin said wrapping his arms around Melissa tighter, pulling her body flush with his as she molded around him, still in his lap. Heat zinged through her as the current built inside her.

His hands roamed her body, erasing the past, the torment, making her feel alive and like a real woman again. In that moment, Melissa finally felt that the world had righted itself even though it wouldn't last. She tunneled her hands through his dark hair.

Shifting position, she ground her sex against his full erection. Her body cried out to touch him, to feel him moving inside her one more time.

Colin drove his tongue into her mouth. He tasted like coffee and peppermint toothpaste, two of her favorite flavors mixed together. She sucked on the tip of his tongue and his grip tightened around her hips.

He brought his hands around to the front and cupped her full breasts in his palms. Her nipples beaded and so much hunger welled up from deep inside that her hands shook.

She kissed him harder.

The next thing she knew, her shirt was being pulled up. She grabbed the hem and helped shrug out of it, aiding its removal. She tugged at his next and they managed to have it off and piled with hers a couple of seconds later. Her bra was a quick third.

"You're beautiful," Colin said, stopping long enough to take in her partially naked form.

She should be embarrassed by the fact that she was half-naked and in the middle of a campground. There was something about being with Colin that made everything seem natural, right, like life was just the way it was supposed to be, if only temporarily.

A breeze blew across her sensitized skin as her hands moved straight to Colin's zipper. He managed to remove his jeans and boxers without upsetting her position as she straddled him. The rest of her clothing followed suit just as seamlessly, as if this was a dance they'd rehearsed a hundred times. Maybe they had. Making love had always been a beyond-this-world experience with Colin. His easy charm, intelligence and dark good looks were so good at seducing her.

Melissa was tired of fighting her feelings for him, her attraction—an attraction that had her feeling so natural with him, naked and outside.

His erection pulsed against her and need engulfed her. She guided his tip inside her and he released a guttural groan. His fingers tightened around her hips, easing her down on top of him. His entire body was chorded as she took him in. And then his hands were on her breasts.

"You're perfect," he managed to say before their mouths fused together.

She bucked her hips and his hands fell back to her waist, driving her up and down until the pressure built and the emotions skyrocketed and tension reached a peak. She rocked faster and he thrust harder until both were on the edge, begging for release, their bodies in perfect motion. She tipped over first and then he followed.

"I still love you," Colin said quietly, his lips moving against her neck. "I can't lose you again."

"I love you, Colin." And those words changed everything.

COLIN'S BROTHERS WOULD arrive soon and there was a lot to do in order to be ready. He'd spent the balance of the day mapping the area around the cabins as though their lives depended on it. They did. He'd retraced his steps several times, memorizing every tree, every possible escape route, and every potential hazard.

There was a pond on the far east side of the site. A creek cut across the property in a near-straight line, running north to south. Just below camp, it pooled into a sizable swimming hole. Colin remembered the bright orange vests counselors had strapped on them before allowing them time in the water.

A set of teepees clustered on the west side of camp. The camp was straightforward, a throwback to simpler days. Or maybe it just seemed simple when all Colin had had to think about was keeping the twins out of trouble. The older he got, the more he was beginning to realize that life got a lot more complicated with age. He needed to change with the times, too. Maybe it was time to outgrow his black-and-white approach toward life and start acknowledging that it wasn't that simple. His feelings for Melissa would certainly fall in the gray area. In the past, he'd have looked at her actions as a flat betrayal, and he had done just that for the past year. There would be no coming back from that.

After what he'd learned, Melissa's situation couldn't have been more complex. She loved her father, and Richard had used that love against her to manipulate her. The man had also used her love for Colin and his family. He clenched his back teeth thinking about it.

To complicate matters, there was a child involved.

And then there were Colin's feelings for Melissa. He could acknowledge that he'd never stopped loving her. He could further acknowledge that her leaving him fell under the category of extenuating circumstances. The hardest part for him to swallow now was that she hadn't believed in him enough to tell him what was really going on. What kind of a life could they build together without trust?

Colin could go round and round on that question until his head spun. He glanced at his watch. His brothers should be arriving sometime within the next two hours.

"What's next?" Melissa asked. She hadn't strayed more than two feet from him since making love this morning. Not that he could say that he minded. He liked having her near, and it was more than just so he could watch over her. He wasn't ready to analyze what that meant.

"We clean out a cabin as a decoy. One of my brothers will be in a different one, close enough to watch," he said, walking into the first cabin. He wedged the door open to allow sunlight inside. Melissa stopped at the door.

"I'm not going in there," she said. Something moved in a dark corner. It was probably a field mouse but Melissa jumped anyway. "There have to be about a thousand spiders."

"Okay, this one's out." He linked their fingers and led her to the next one with a wry grin. "I'm guessing going inside one of these to make love again is out of the question."

She tugged at his hand to make him stop.

"We can make love again, just not in one of those," she said.

He didn't waste time hauling her into his arms. She pushed back.

"Hold on," she said. "Is that swimming hole safe?"

"Should be," he said.

He'd barely answered when she took off down the hill, stripping off clothes as she ran. The sun was out and it was warmer now.

Colin followed suit, both of their garments littering the trail behind them.

The water was cold but her skin was warm against his. He picked her up, she wrapped her legs around his midsection and he drove himself inside her, home.

With their bodies pressed together and her arms tangled around his neck, Colin shut out the questions in his mind and made love to her. This time, they moved slow and sweet, savoring every kiss and the feel of being completely connected. He'd missed this…the feeling of being one with Melissa…of being lost with her.

"That was amazing," she finally said, breathless from making love.

"Once this is over we have some decisions to make," he said, not quite ready to examine the implications of what was happening between them.

"Yeah," she said, "like how are we going to dry off and not freeze to death first?"

He squeezed her sweet round bottom and pressed his erection against her belly. "Who said we were done?"

WHETHER HE LIKED it or not, Colin had a shadow. Based on the way he stopped every once in a while to pull her into an embrace or plant a sweet kiss on her lips, Melissa didn't think he minded.

Her heart wanted to believe that what was happening between them was real again, that it was something they could build on.

"You should probably try to get some rest before my brothers arrive," he said. "There's no telling when Richard will show now that my brothers have put out word."

"What about law enforcement?" she asked.

"We'll get all that information when my brothers arrive, which should be soon," he said.

"It makes me nervous that we haven't been able to make contact with them," she said.

"They won't come if it's not safe," Colin said, setting up a sleeping bag and a rifle in the woods near the campsite. He'd located a spot below the campfire and above the spillway they'd made love in. "I'd feel better if you weren't here when this all goes down."

"Where else would I go?" she asked, her nerves set on edge.

"I'm not letting you out of my sight. You're safest with me," he said, glancing up from the scope he'd trained on the door of the decoy cabin. "I just wish I could tuck you somewhere safe."

"I just hope he falls for it," she said. "This is a lot to coordinate."

"That's true," he admitted, and she was glad that he wasn't sugar-coating the situation. "I know you're scared. We'll let law enforcement do their jobs as soon as we have Richard on-site and we make the call. Until they get here, I'll do what I have to in order to protect you. Two of my brothers will be awake, one inside that cabin." He pointed to the one directly across from the decoy. "The other will be in the mess hall. Both will be armed and ready to go. One will make the call to law enforcement as soon as Richard shows. All we have to do is trap and detain the man. They'll do the rest."

"A lot can go wrong and we don't know if he'll show or send someone else." She sat down on the sleeping bag. She hoped it would be as easy as it sounded.

"If he thinks you're here with a few of us and no law, he'll bite," he said, sitting up. He pressed a kiss to her temple. "Believe it or not, I've done missions like this before."

"But what if things don't go as planned?" she asked.

"I've thought through all the possibilities, even the ones that include me not making it out alive, and believe me, Richard won't go free," he said with so much sincerity, so much confidence, that she almost believed it, too.

She couldn't even think about anything happening to Colin.

He must've picked up on the tension cording inside her when he said that last part because he said, "Nothing's going to happen to me. I just have to consider all the worst-case scenarios."

"And if something happens to me instead?" she asked. "What about that?"

"There isn't a case in which I will allow that to happen. Period. Angelina needs her mother, and my family is committed to making sure she has you." His voice was steady and steel and reassuring even though she probably shouldn't let it be. There was so much determination that she couldn't help herself.

"She needs her dad, too," Melissa said, placing a kiss on Colin's lips. "And I need you. I tried to live my life without you, Colin. It didn't work. None of this works without you."

Surprisingly, a few tears sprang from her eyes.

He kissed one as it rolled down her cheek.

"Then I better be damn careful because I have no intention of letting you down."

Chapter Sixteen

"Stay low," Colin said to Melissa as he saw an occasional flash of light as a vehicle twisted and turned along the road leading to the camp. He'd already heard the Jeep's engine as it wound up the road. The horn honked twice. Then, nothing for two beats before a third beep sounded.

"They're here." Colin popped to his feet before offering a hand up to Melissa. She accepted the help and then he held on to one of her hands as they walked to the Jeep.

Colin let go long enough to embrace his brothers, Joshua and Austin. "Where's Tyler?"

Joshua must've seen the panic in Melissa's eyes because he said, "Angelina is doing great and she's safe on the ranch."

"Thank you," Melissa said.

"As for Tyler, he's hanging around at the camp entrance. Ryder stayed back to care for his pregnant wife and offer reinforcements at the ranch." Joshua held up his cell phone. "We'll be in constant contact."

"You guys already know Melissa," Colin said.

Austin leaned in for a hug even though his gaze

trained on Colin and Melissa's linked fingers. "Good to see you again."

He'd give them an update as soon as he figured out what the hell was going on between them.

Joshua echoed Austin's sentiment, also reaching in for a quick hug. He seemed less interested in the two holding hands. His law enforcement training would keep him focused on the situation at hand and Colin was grateful. "Angelina is a little sweetheart. You guys did good, and I want you both to know that she's being well cared for."

"I've never seen Janis, the housekeeper, happier now that we have so many kids on the ranch," Austin said. He smiled, even though Colin knew his brother's situation had been gnawing at him. His wife, Maria, had left him and their relationship status was up in the air. Austin wasn't talking about it. The subject was off-limits, which didn't signal good things. No one pressed for information. His brother knew that any one of them would be there for him in a heartbeat when he was ready to open up about it.

"You being here means a lot," Colin said to Austin, acknowledging his sacrifice.

"I just wish Mom and Dad could've met their grand-kids," Austin said, redirecting the conversation. He was good at avoiding talking about what was really on his mind.

"I was crushed to hear about your parents," Melissa said. "I had no idea anything had happened or I would've come."

"We appreciate the thought," Joshua said.

"Any closer to figuring out who was behind it?" she asked.

Colin had been so wrapped up in keeping her and the baby safe that he hadn't had time to check in with his brothers on the case.

"The investigation has been set back with Tommy in the hospital. His deputies are volunteering for shifts to look through Hollister McCabe's papers. He'd forced the Hattie family out of town for their land," Joshua said.

"Their ranch backs up to yours, doesn't it?" she asked. She didn't seem fazed by the fact that Hollister McCabe would be involved in something illegal. It would be no surprise to anyone who knew him, and his reputation extended far beyond Bluff.

"It does," Joshua said. "Tommy was on to something before he was shot. He'd called Dallas and said that he wanted to meet with us. I'd imagine all that's going to be on hold while he heals. His recovery is everyone's top priority."

Austin seemed to anticipate the next question. He held his hand up. "He's doing much better. Doc McConnell brought in a special surgeon to make sure they got all the bullet fragments out of his ribs. He has a long way to go to heal but he's talking and asking for food."

"That's a good sign," Colin said.

Melissa smiled. It didn't reach her eyes. He could see the worry in the lines of her forehead. "I wondered... I'm afraid... There's a possibility that *he* could be behind what happened to your parents." Guilt washed over her. She stared at a spot on the ground. "Early on, he was convinced that I was still in love with Colin and he was right. He might've done that to get to me. I didn't even know what had happened."

Tears free-fell.

"It's not your fault," Colin said, and both of his brothers were quick to agree.

"What if it is and they're dead because of me, because I wasn't convincing enough?" She just stood there, looking so bereft.

"He targeted you. He manipulated you. But he didn't break you," Colin said. "Remember that."

"If Richard killed our parents, that's on him, not you," Joshua said emphatically. "And we'll make sure justice is served for everything he's done to this family. Because when he took you away from us, he didn't just take a shot at my brother, he hurt all of us."

"I'm so sorry." Melissa threw her arms around Colin's neck.

"You did nothing wrong," Colin said, and he meant it. Anger welled inside him. He shot a look at Joshua, who nodded in response.

Rancic would be added to the suspect list once they returned to Bluff.

And if it turned out that man was responsible, there'd be more than hell to pay for his actions.

"I REMEMBER THIS PLACE," Joshua said to Colin as he studied the area from the center point, the fire pit.

"We were kids the last time we were here," Colin said. "Not too much has changed."

Colin hadn't been sure what kind of reaction Melissa would get from his brothers and was grateful they'd welcomed her with open arms. He had a lot of catching up to do with them. Hell, first he needed to figure out his and Melissa's relationship for himself. All he knew was that he wanted her in his life. The details of what that meant would have to come later.

"That's a good thing," Joshua said. "We don't have much sun left. I'll want to walk the perimeter before it gets dark."

"Someone followed us most of the way here. We let him believe we didn't know," Austin said. "Lost him as we got close by cutting through Denver."

Joshua had worked for Denver PD before returning to the ranch to take his rightful place. He would know the area well enough to easily lose someone and, more importantly, had the law enforcement contacts they would need to pull off an arrest.

"There were two in the car and they'll alert Richard. After talking it over with Joshua and doing some calculations, our best guess is that Richard will most likely be in the area sometime tonight. He'll have to drive if he wants to get anywhere near us and if he isn't stopped on the way here, which is a possibility, it'll take him a minute to figure out where we are. Took us nearly two hours to make it up the mountain," Austin added.

"Have you discussed the right time to bring in law enforcement?" Colin asked. He wasn't planning on taking any chances when it came to Melissa. If he could avoid a confrontation with Richard, that would be the best-case scenario. Although, there was a very big part of him that just wanted ten minutes alone with Rancic.

"Joshua's planning to make the call to law enforcement about a sighting at first light," Austin said. "He'll call his old supervising officer."

Melissa stiffened next to him.

"So, Richard is here by morning, possibly earlier," he recapped, taking her hand in his.

"But that means Richard could be here and gone before they set foot on camp soil," Melissa finally spoke, and her voice was shaky.

"We've accounted for that possibility," Austin said. "That's a risk we're going to have to take. We doubt there's been a leak in law enforcement but we can't ignore the chance, either. We just don't know at this point, and we can't risk Richard knowing that law enforcement will be involved until the last minute. It's the best way to protect you."

"What's your professional opinion about law enforcement being involved?" Colin asked Joshua.

"It's unlikely but not impossible." Joshua rubbed the scruff on his chin. "There's a better chance Rancic managed to pick up on communications by stealing Marshal Davis's laptop and phone."

"Which means it's safe to assume that when we reach out to law enforcement, he'll know," Colin said.

"I believe so," Joshua said. "We'll need to get moving. We don't have a lot of time to familiarize ourselves with the plan or practice."

Colin knew the implications of that from his military training. There was a reason so many former servicemen and women made careers in law enforcement when they were discharged. Colin was proud to serve his country and there was no other option in his mind for him to return to the ranch afterward. The only thing he loved as much as his country was the land he lived on and worked.

Joshua walked the perimeter as Colin caught Austin up-to-date.

"Did it all come back to you?" Colin asked Joshua when he returned.

"Amazing how little has changed," he said. "Saw

that you're set up with a rifle in the tree line between the outdoor pavilion and the swimming hole beneath. That's smart. With the way the road winds up, you'll have a great vantage point."

"True. My gut says he's not coming at us straight, though," Colin said. "I can still see the entrance and reposition as needed. But my money is on the fact that he'll come in from behind the mess hall or one of the sides, which would be the cabins."

"Agreed," Joshua said as the last of the sunlight disappeared.

"I set up camp for you guys in one corner of the mess hall. It's too easy a guess for you to be set up in one of the girls' cabins and Rancic doesn't strike me as stupid. He's a criminal, but not incompetent, and it would be dangerous to underestimate him."

"True," Joshua said as Austin nodded.

"I cleaned up one of the cabins anyway and made it seem like I didn't want him to check one on the boys' side by leaving tracks leading up to the door. Just enough to make it seem like there might actually be someone inside," Colin said.

"From the mess hall I can watch both," Joshua said.

"It's the biggest barrier for us visually and the easiest way for him to come in from the backside without being noticed. He'll most likely come that way and then splinter off before he gets to the building," Joshua said.

"That's what I would do," Colin agreed.

"The main variable is how many men he has working for him or will bring with him," Joshua said.

Austin nodded. "He has a brother who's gone missing. We can assume those two are working together."

He turned to Melissa. "How many others does he associate with on a regular basis?"

"Half a dozen," she supplied.

Colin could almost feel the thin sheen of ice coating her words when she spoke about Richard. Thinking of what she'd endured, of the life his child had been brought into even for a few months, caused heat to pour off him in waves.

"We came in contact with a pair yesterday morning," Colin said. "So we know of at least two more on the job."

"Or they could be included in the six you said Melissa mentioned to you. No way to know for sure. Either way, we'll prepare for a small army," Joshua said.

Melissa gasped.

Colin wanted to reassure her, tell her everything would be okay. Right now, their future was uncertain. And the situation was as unpredictable as a spring thunderstorm.

All he could do was wrap his arm around her waist and hold her.

MELISSA COULDN'T SLEEP. It came as no surprise. As the sun went down, the cold settled in again. She thought about the irony of spring, the clash of cold leftover from winter with the warmth from the promise of summer. She thought about how their interaction caused powerful storms—storms big enough to produce tornadoes that could devastate an entire town. Richard was cold—he'd tried to keep her in his icy grip. And Colin was the opposite.

The thought of those two systems crashing into each other, the fallout that would follow, took her breath away. The more Melissa had listened to plans to take down Richard, the more tension had tightened her shoulder blades. Her life with Richard had been like living in an arctic cave. Colin was the sun—the promise of warmth and sunshine and better days.

Both of those lives were about to clash.

The O'Briens had brought plenty of ammunition to the fight. So would Richard. She said a silent prayer that there'd be no bloodshed by morning, even though everything inside her said there would be.

She sucked in a deep breath.

"What is it?" Colin asked. They'd set up in the small gift shop behind the outdoor pavilion for a few hours of sleep. His warm body was flush with hers. Her head was on his chest, and she'd settled into the crook of his arm.

"Thinking about tomorrow," she said. Austin had joined Tyler in the mess hall for a few hours of sleep while Joshua took a shift keeping watch at the front entrance. "About trying to figure out a way we all get out of this alive. If anyone gets hurt…"

"It won't be your fault. Rancic didn't just target you. He targeted our family." Colin pressed a kiss to her forehead. "If you want to change your mind about being here, we can disappear. Take Angelina and get out of the country if you want. I've been thinking a lot about it. We only have to stay away long enough for law enforcement to catch Richard."

"And always be looking over my shoulder? Never knowing when he might show up or hurt our daughter?" she said. "We need to end this now while Angelina's safe at the ranch."

"I'd feel better about this whole scenario if you were

tucked away somewhere safe, too," he said, and there was so much honesty in his voice.

"There's no one who can protect me better than you," she said, and she meant it. No one would love her more or care more about her going home to take care of Angelina than Colin. His brothers came in a close second. "The ranch is the perfect place for her to be, and there's nowhere I'd rather be than here with you. We're going to take that monster down and not live in fear of shadows anymore." Her resolve grew with every word. No matter what else happened tomorrow, Angelina would be safe.

Colin's grip tightened around her. "I love you, Melissa. When this is all over, we need to sit down and figure out how that changes things. Right now, all I want is to have you right where you are."

Melissa tilted her head up and kissed him. He wasn't making any promises to her, and she wasn't sure if that was because he had no idea what to do with their relationship or he wasn't the kind of man who would promise something that he wasn't certain he could deliver. The latter goose bumped her arms. "Promise me you won't do anything crazy when you see him."

And by *crazy* she meant do anything that might get himself killed.

"I promise to keep you safe above all else," he said.

She was afraid of that.

But for now, tonight, she wanted to make love to him in these last few hours while he belonged to her.

And that's exactly what she did.

Chapter Seventeen

Colin had an hour of shut-eye before he forced himself to wake. He'd battled back and forth on leading Richard away from Melissa for a fight before he'd let himself nod off.

Now that he was awake and his mind was clear, he wanted to stay right where he was a few more minutes, holding her. There'd been too many nights in the past year that he'd wished for this very thing, to have her back with him where she belonged.

His mind churned through scenarios one more time. There was an obvious problem with trying to lead Rancic away from camp. If Rancic figured out what Colin was doing, all he had to do was circle back. With Colin away, his brothers would be down a man.

No one had a clue how many men Rancic would bring to the fight.

But if there was any chance that Colin could go at Rancic one-on-one, he wouldn't hesitate. One man against one man. A fair fight. But again, he had no idea how many people Richard planned to bring. Besides, the words *Rancic* and *fair fight* didn't even belong in the same sentence.

The possibility that Rancic would come alone was

next to nil, so it wasn't worth spending too much time considering. There was a slight possibility that he wouldn't come at all. He could send someone in his place.

But Rancic wanted revenge. He wanted Melissa. And he wanted her to pay.

He was on the run and this was the first real chance he'd had at finding her. He had to know that the longer he was in the US, the more risk he was taking. Based on his volatile temperament, Colin figured the man would take the bait. He'd come fast, figuring that he could get to them before they had time to fortify the area.

He was almost right.

They had a few tricks up their sleeves, which was why Colin needed to stick with the plan. Any other scenario carried unnecessary risk—risk he couldn't afford to take with his brothers or the woman he loved. Yeah, he loved her. He loved Melissa. He'd never stopped.

So, rather than risk leaving her vulnerable he would go along with the plan he and his brothers had developed last night. He would stay the course. The plan they'd come up with was the best they had to work with under the circumstances. Austin had set up in an adjacent cabin with his attention directed toward the decoy boy cabin. He was visible enough that Rancic might just believe he was there to protect Melissa. Colin's job was to set up at the rifle/sleeping bag location, and Tyler was situated under the outdoor pavilion. Again, his attention was set to the cabin.

Inside, they'd stuffed blankets on a lower bunk in the corner of the room to make it look like the shape of a woman. In reality, the only woman on the campus was in the souvenir shop tucked behind the counter sleeping.

If she could wake and this whole ordeal be over without a scratch on anyone he loved, Colin wouldn't complain.

Enough time had most likely passed for Rancic to have figured out where they were after being tipped off. According to their calculations, 3:00 a.m. was the absolute earliest he could make it to the camp.

Colin untangled his body from Melissa's, missing her warmth the second he peeled out of the sleeping bag they'd shared. He zipped it up, tucking the corners around her to keep her warm. At this elevation, it was cold this time of year at night.

His watch read two thirty in the morning. He'd gotten just enough sleep to energize himself. He fired off a few push-ups to get his blood pumping and then threw on his hunter green hoodie. He'd blend in better at night with the dark color. If there was still snow on the ground, it would be a different story. Snow was up the mountain at higher elevations and so he was safe.

He moved around the counter in order to block Melissa from the light on his phone. She needed sleep and, if he had his way, she'd sleep right through everything that was about to go down.

Colin texted Joshua to let him know he was awake and moving toward his post. Joshua's shift at the entrance should finish soon and he would take his place in the mess hall. Colin had volunteered but everyone had agreed that it would be best for him to stick close to Melissa for as long as possible. Besides, Rancic would assume that Melissa was with Colin. That knowledge was his secret weapon because he had every intention of leading the man away from her. Leaving the souvenir shop would be difficult, but he needed to take his post.

The souvenir shop was protected from three sides.

The likelihood that Rancic would pay it much attention was miniscule. As a precaution, he'd left Melissa a P2K, a lightweight semiautomatic pistol, ready to shoot if necessary. Even though she'd grown up in Texas, she didn't have a lot of experience with guns. She'd been around plenty but that was different than needing to use one and especially once adrenaline kicked in.

Colin may have only met his daughter forty-eight hours ago, but he missed her from a place so deep he hadn't known it existed before. How something so tiny could take up so much space in a man's heart was something that he would never figure out. Angelina had.

Colin settled on top of the sleeping bag, staying low in order to stave off the cold night air. The wind bit through his jacket and the temperature had dropped a good twenty degrees, hovering near freezing.

He could cover pretty much everything and everyone from his vantage point. The outdoor pavilion was slightly to his right and in front of him. The souvenir shop was behind that. Tyler had a clear view from his vantage point, as well. With Austin in the cabin to the right of the decoy, they had solid coverage.

The girls' cabins were on the other side of the fire pit. If it were Colin, he'd check those first. No way would he go to the boys' side where everyone was stationed. He'd give the girls' side a fifty-fifty chance of being empty. Even so, he'd investigate there first after surveying the entire area and seeing that they wanted him to check out the first cabin on the boys' side.

Colin hoped everything would go according to plan. He almost laughed out loud. What mission had ever been executed flawlessly? He couldn't remember a single one. And that's why he'd stay alert and minimize distractions. Focus and patience won battles. Take the battle, win the war.

Cold settled on top of him like a blanket. He had to periodically flex and release his fingers to keep them from going completely numb.

More than two hours had gone by when he saw movement near the mess hall. *Yep.* Just like he'd figured. Through his rifle's scope, he picked up two figures.

Colin looked left, reaching for his phone to send out the warning signal. Out of the corner of his eye, he caught the outline of a dark male figure launching toward him. He must've followed the creek.

Instead of bracing himself against the force coming at him, Colin grabbed onto the guy and used momentum to propel him. Shoulder first, the guy slammed into a nearby tree. Since the pine tree clustered with dozens of others, it was tall and skinny. The frame cracked in half with the blow.

Colin popped to his feet before the guy could rebalance from the impact.

With the rage of an angry bull, Colin dove into the man…into who he could now see was Richard. An animal-like growl tore from Colin's throat as he took a blow to the face. His head snapped back and he instantly knew that he was going to feel that later. He had several inches of height and a lot more muscle on Richard. For his size, the guy threw a decent punch. Colin would give him that, and that was all he'd give.

Both men tumbled to the ground. Colin hopped to his feet first and threw a punch, connecting with the side of Richard's head. He ducked—about a second too late—and rolled.

Colin followed and then his legs were swept out from underneath him as Richard spun around.

The ground was cold and hard. Colin's shoulder took the brunt of the fall, and that was also going to hurt later. Right now, Colin's adrenaline pumped and all he could think about was stopping Richard.

With a couple seconds of a head start, Richard was retreating down the hill by the time Colin got to his feet. There was no use trying to use his backup weapon. There were too many trees in the way to get off a clean shot. So, he started down after Richard.

There could be a trap set up, so Colin needed to stop Richard. *Now.*

Anger and rage fueled Colin's movements.

Pouring on the speed, Colin dove down the hill, aiming at Richard, who was running at a decent clip. He couldn't outrun Colin. Richard was about to find that out as Colin made contact just below the man's knees.

Richard fell backward and on top of Colin. The two, connected by momentum, rolled down the hill out of control.

First came a *ker-plunk* sound and then the shock of freezing water. Colin gasped a second before his head submerged. If that had happened a second sooner, he'd be in trouble. He needed to get his bearings and get the hell out of the water.

At this temperature, he estimated that he had roughly two minutes before his muscles would weaken and slow down since he wore no protective clothing. He could already feel the effects of the cold in his hands and fingers. They were going numb. It wouldn't be long before his arms and legs felt the impact, too.

He kicked until his head broke the surface. The

shoreline wasn't too far. He searched for signs of Rancic. Damn it, this would be too easy of an out for him. The man needed to pay for what he'd done.

With heavy arms, Colin swam until he could stand. He could barely feel his limbs by the time he pushed to standing. His arms were already numbing by the time he heaved himself up and out of the water.

His breath came out in bursts as he skimmed the top of the water for any sign of Richard. Disappointment settled in when he saw nothing. This area was dark and even though Colin's eyes had long ago adjusted, it was still difficult to see clearly. He'd left his cell phone at the campsite, which was a good fifty yards uphill. Shouting wouldn't do any good, but he did it anyway.

A shot was fired, echoing down the mountain and the blood in Colin's veins froze. The entire operation had exploded in a nanosecond and Colin could only pray everyone was okay above him. He had to trust that his brothers could handle it. He briefly thought about Melissa being up there alone in the gift shop. At least Rancic was in the water. There was no way Colin could leave the area until the man surfaced.

Colin's body began shaking. Wearing cold, wet clothes would cause his body to continue to decline, so he stripped off his shoes, followed by his jeans and his shirt. He fired off a few push-ups to warm his muscles as he kept his gaze focused on the surface of the water.

Not a minute had passed when Rancic's head surfaced. He'd managed to swim to the opposite bank and was pulling himself out of the water. That was at least thirty feet away. Colin popped up. He could take advantage of the fact that Richard's muscles would be cold. He was moving slowly and that gave Colin the advantage. He recalled Melissa flinching when he made a move toward her and the nightmare to give him an edge. Anger boiled through him when he added his daughter to the equation.

Rancic was on his knees, pushing off the ground by the time Colin reached him. Not sparing a second, Colin threw a punch.

Richard dropped down to the ground after it connected with his jaw. Another jab to his nose and blood squirted.

In the next second, Colin pinned Richard down. Something, a knife or sharp stick, sliced through Colin's right thigh. At least he still had feeling in his legs. He took it as a good sign and pushed on, biting back a curse as he took another swing at Rancic.

Colin wrestled the weapon out of the man's hand…a knife, and then tossed the blade into the water.

Cold was taking hold and Colin's body trembled.

"You think this is over. It's not," Rancic bit out. "You heard the shots. My family is taking care of that lying slut you love so much."

It took everything inside Colin not to grab hold of the man's neck and squeeze until there was no air left in his lungs. Death was too easy.

"You need to know before you spend the rest of your life in prison that Angelina is my daughter, not yours," Colin ground out through his anger. Since Richard was so big on family, he should know that Angelina was an O'Brien and would never be a Rancic.

Richard squirmed underneath Colin who had the guy trapped with his powerful thighs. "You should save your energy because you're not going anywhere except jail."

Based on his reaction, Colin had scored a direct hit.

"How can you be so sure?" Richard said, and there was a twitch in his voice that belied his words.

"Do the math. Melissa was already pregnant when you blackmailed her into marriage," Colin said, his anger rising at thinking about what she'd endured at the hands of this man. His fists clenched and released as he continued to give reasons as to why he shouldn't wring this guy's neck. A quick snap and Colin could erase Richard's existence. And that would feel incredible for a few seconds. But that would end Richard's misery at living out the rest of his life in jail before it even started. "It's the only reason she didn't leave you from the get-go. She wouldn't risk our child."

Richard made a move to knock Colin off him. Colin fisted his hand and belted Richard. His jaw snapped right and he spit blood.

Colin could hear footsteps thundering from behind and voices that he recognized as his brothers'. He listened for the sweet sound of Melissa's voice and tensed when he didn't hear it. He refused to give Rancic the satisfaction of seeing his fear.

"You're about to be arrested and face your crimes. Know this. If you or anyone you know ever messes with my family again from either side of the bars that you're about to spend a very long time getting to know, there won't be a place on earth that you can hide from me," Colin said through clenched teeth.

Richard sneered. "We'll see about that."

It took pretty much everything Colin had inside him at that moment not to put his hands around that man's neck and choke the life out of him for what he'd done to Melissa. He wasn't an impulsive guy. And being a good person meant doing the right thing and allowing justice to be served.

"Put your hands in the air where we can see them," an authoritative voice said from behind. Colin knew that tone would come from someone in law enforcement.

Colin complied, continuing to pin Richard while giving him the leeway he needed to put his own arms where officers could see them.

Richard's right hand fisted.

"I wouldn't try anything stupid if I were you," Colin said. "Or maybe not. How about you give them a reason to shoot. There's nothing I'd like to see more than you bleeding out right here."

Richard lifted his hands above his head where officers could see them.

"That's my brother." Joshua's voice was a welcomed relief. Colin's gaze snapped to his brother, who was pointing at Colin as another officer ran toward him.

Colin, arms high, eased off Richard as an officer rushed to them.

"Is she okay?" Colin asked.

"Yes," Joshua said, his gaze intent on Colin's right leg.

"Everyone else?" Colin asked. He was starting to get very cold.

"We're good," Joshua said. "The others are giving statements to law enforcement while Rancic's brother and buddies are being tucked into the backs of cruisers. It's over."

The officer forced Richard onto his stomach, facing the ground, and then jerked his arms up high behind him. Zip cuffs were on a few seconds later as the officer's knee jabbed into Richard's back. The officer seemed unfazed by Richard's threats of a lawsuit.

The officer held out a hand with a concerned expression. "Can you move?"

Colin followed the officer's line of sight to the blood streaming out of the top of his thigh.

"That's gonna leave a mark," Colin quipped as he heard the officer radio for medical treatment.

Joshua dropped to Colin's side a few seconds later, urging him to lie on his back.

And then Melissa was there, her beautiful face looking at him, her cheeks streaked with tears.

"It's cold," Colin said, and he could feel his teeth chatter.

"He needs something, blankets, coats, whatever you've got," she said, keeping her gaze on him. "I need you, Colin. Angelina needs you. You stay with us, okay."

A few seconds later warm blankets were being placed around him as Joshua worked on Colin's leg. A belt tightened around his upper thigh.

"I'm not going anywhere, sweetheart," Colin said to her. "No more tears. You're safe now."

"That should hold until we can get medical evacuation," Joshua said.

Colin looked over at Richard, whose face was covered in his own blood. Colin was pretty sure he'd busted the guy's nose.

"He can't hurt you anymore," he said as he shivered harder. His limbs were too heavy to move.

"Colin," she said as he was being lifted onto a stretcher.

The sound of her sweet voice was the last thing he heard before everything went black.

Chapter Eighteen

Melissa paced. She couldn't even look at Joshua, Tyler or Austin. All three of them wore the same expression that she felt inside...panic.

Colin had looked so white, except for his lips. They'd been blue. And he'd looked so weak.

She twisted her fingers together and took another walk around the Jeep.

Seeing Richard in the backseat of a cruiser after believing for so long that she'd never be free of him almost felt unreal. Justice would finally be served for all the families he'd hurt, for the law enforcement officer he'd shot, and for Tommy. Her heart still hurt for Marshal Davis's family and she wanted to do something for them. The least she could do was organize a scholarship fund for his children. His wife shouldn't have to worry about money after everything she'd been through. Melissa would reach out to her.

Richard was finally going to get exactly what he deserved, and she could only pray that prison wouldn't be kind to him.

An EMT walked toward her.

"Ma'am," he said. His nametag read PHILLIP.

"Yes." Her heart leapt to her throat.

"He's asking for you," Phillip said, motioning for her to follow him.

She glanced at his brothers as she hurried behind Phillip. It had to be a good sign that he was talking. She'd take what she could get.

Melissa had expected to feel differently as she watched the cruiser pull away with Richard in the back. She'd thought she'd feel lighter somehow. Except that she didn't. Not while Colin lay on a stretcher being worked on by two EMTs.

Her life had blown up before her eyes. She knew that Colin could never truly trust her again, but she loved him with all her heart and he had to be okay.

"You were so cold," she said, her chest squeezing at seeing him on that stretcher, wrapped in thick blankets.

"I'll be warmer if you'll slip under the covers with me," he said with that wry grin that was so charming. His gaze fixed on a spot behind her.

She turned in time to see Phillip standing there.

"Can you give us a few minutes of privacy?" Colin asked.

"Sure," Phillip said. "As long as you stay put."

"Where am I going to go?" Colin relented, sounding a little like a kid who'd just been told to sit in the corner.

"Okay, then." Phillip closed the doors.

"Come closer," Colin said to Melissa.

She scooted toward him on the bench, fighting back tears.

"I was serious about you joining me in here," he said, lifting the blanket. "Phillip said I'd warm up faster using body heat."

Before she could respond, he was tugging on her

arm. She made a move to join him, her gaze freezing on the white bandage covering his right thigh.

She gasped. "Colin."

"It's all right. Barely a scratch," he said.

"You've always been a bad liar, Colin," Melissa said. It was true. He'd been much better at telling the truth.

"It'll heal in a few days," he said nonchalantly.

Melissa eased onto the gurney. He pulled her close, her back against his strong chest. He shivered as he wrapped his arms around her.

"Are you sure this is a good idea?" she asked, not wanting to make his injuries worse.

"Phillip offered to climb in but I told him that I'd rather have you in here," he quipped. His easy charm had always been good at making her laugh when she shouldn't.

"I'm concerned about you, Colin."

"I know," he said against her neck before planting a kiss there.

A sensual shiver ran down her back and the mood shifted.

"I'm pretty sure Phillip wouldn't approve of you exerting too much energy right now," she said, melting against his body.

"Phillip doesn't know what's best for me." Colin's lips trailed down the sensitive spots along her neck.

"We need to be serious for a minute. I need to know that you're okay. I was so scared," she said.

"You're safe now," he said. "It's over."

The force of those words hit her like a physical punch. Richard was being hauled off in the back of a cruiser. He was going to go to jail for the rest of his life. The man who'd shot and killed Marshal Davis would never see the outside of prison gates. The man who had tortured her for a long year and stripped away everyone she loved couldn't hurt her anymore.

His top men, along with his brother, were being arrested at that exact moment, and Angelina would grow up away from the shadow of that horrible man.

Melissa couldn't stem her tears. She just lay there, Colin's arms around her, her strength. Her comfort.

Angelina would get to grow up knowing her real father.

She heard a noise outside the ambulance and gasped.

"It's okay. I'm here," Colin said, reassuring her.

But for how long?

Her life was a mess and even though he knew about Angelina and the two of them had shared many moments that gave her a spark of hope for a future, the bottom line was that he would never trust her again.

Richard had won, after all.

Nothing in her life made sense without Colin.

"I'll be right back." She slipped out of the covers and climbed out of the ambulance.

Colin shouted after her but she ignored him. He would be okay. His family was safe. Richard was going to jail.

Melissa could go home to her daughter and begin to build a new life. She needed to figure out her next steps for her father, and she needed to get a job to support her family. She could return to the town she loved and her daughter could finally claim her birthright. Angelina O'Brien. The name sounded right.

She glanced around. The O'Briens were busy packing up.

They were going home. Why did that make her feel so empty?

Melissa needed to get it together because there was a lot to think about.

She heard arguing coming from the ambulance and turned in time to see Phillip helping Colin out of the back.

"What's going on?" she asked.

"I was hoping you could convince him to let us give him a ride to the hospital," Phillip said, looking flustered.

"I'm fine," Colin said, hopping on his left leg.

Phillip had to hold on to him in order to keep him from falling.

"Once he makes up his mind, it's pretty difficult to convince him otherwise," Melissa said, grateful they were all standing there smiling.

"Then, I'm all done here," Phillip said. "Bandages need to be changed every day."

"Will do," Colin said before thanking Phillip and then shaking his hand.

"Are you sure this is a good idea?" she asked Colin.

"You took off so fast a minute ago," he said. "I didn't get a chance to tell you that Phillip was about to release me."

Phillip shot Colin a look, excused himself and then disappeared around the side of the ambulance.

"It's over. I have to try to pick up the pieces." She couldn't look up at him. The thought of going on to a life without him pierced her chest. He'd be in her life at least partially because of Angelina. That was something. She needed to change the subject before she lost it again. "I was just thinking about trying to kick-start a fund-raiser for Marshal Davis's family."

"I already made a call to have a scholarship set up for his kids," he said. "I'd like to make sure his widow is taken care of, as well."

"That was really sweet of you." She was grateful to have the O'Brien name involved. Colin could get the job done with one call. "I know that money can't bring back or replace a husband and father, but I'd like to do as much as possible to ease the burden on the family."

"Good. We can work together on it," he said.

"Colin, I know you and I know that your trust in me has been…broken." She kept her eyes focused on the ground so she wouldn't start crying. There'd been enough tears in the past year to last a lifetime.

Colin took a step toward her and then lifted her chin until their eyes met.

"I want you to look at me when I say this because it's important to me," he started.

She took in a deep breath.

"I love you, Melissa," he said. "That won't change."

That last word echoed in her mind. *Change*. Didn't that encompass so much of her life, of her?

"But you have?" she asked.

"I've always loved you. It's always been you," he said, and her heart pounded inside her chest. "But I respect you even more now for what you've suffered."

There was so much love and respect in his gaze.

"I couldn't be more proud of you," he said.

"I… I didn't think you'd understand," she said.

"There's a big part of me that still wishes you'd trusted me enough to tell me earlier, but you put our daughter first and I could never be angry with you for doing that," he said. "You're an amazing mother and I love you even more after seeing you with Angelina. I know that everything you did, all your actions, were meant to protect her. And in your heart you believed that you were protecting me and my family, too."

Melissa's heart flowered with hope for a future together as a family. "Will you ever trust me again?"

"Will you ever fully trust me?" he asked.

"Me?"

"I may have acted on impulse in the past and been immature as all hell sometimes, but that all stopped when I met you, Melissa." Colin wrapped his arms around her waist and she leaned into him. "You're the only person I want to be with other than a three-month-old big-eyed beauty who looks a lot like you."

"Can we start over?" she asked, hopeful for the future she never thought would be within reach.

"I don't want a new beginning," he said. "I love you now as much as I ever did, and I'd like to pick up where we left off, planning our wedding."

She tilted her head up and kissed him.

When she finally pulled back, he looked straight into her eyes and said, "You and that little girl are my family and I want to make it official so the three of us can be together for the rest of our lives."

"I do, too," was all she said, all she had to say, before he pulled her in tight and kissed her again.

"I love you, Colin O'Brien. I should've trusted you before but I do now. I'm trusting you with our child and with all my heart."

"Then there's only one more thing I need you to say." He took a knee, wincing in pain.

"Don't hurt yourself," she said, but he waved her off.

This time, it didn't feel like a fairy tale, like something unreal or out of reach. Colin was right there. And a lifetime with him was within her grasp.

Melissa touched his face as he asked the words again.

"Will you marry me?" he asked.

"Yes."

"Hey, you two," Austin called over to them.

"Whatever you have to say, it can wait. I'm about to kiss my future wife." Colin stood up—with great effort and some wincing—and took Melissa in his arms. He then gave her the kind of kiss that stole her breath.

All three of his brothers clapped.

"Well, when you two are done there's a jet sitting on a tarmac at Denver Airport waiting to take us home," Austin quipped.

"On the way, we need to call Carolina to thank her for bringing you to the Spring Fling," Colin said to her.

She beamed up at him.

Colin linked his and Melissa's fingers. "Are you ready to go home to our daughter?"

"Yes, I am. I want to go home."

* * * * *

Look for the next book in USA TODAY
Bestselling Author Barb Han's
CATTLEMEN CRIME CLUB *series,*
TEXAS SHOWDOWN,
available next month.

And don't miss the previous titles in the
CATTLEMEN CRIME CLUB *series:*

STOCKYARD SNATCHING
DELIVERING JUSTICE
ONE TOUGH TEXAN
TEXAS-SIZED TROUBLE

Available now from Mills & Boon Intrigue!

MILLS & BOON®

INTRIGUE
Romantic Suspense

A SEDUCTIVE COMBINATION OF DANGER AND DESIRE